RICK RIORDAN

MAGNUS CHASE
and the GODS of ASGARD

THE SWORD OF SUMMER

DISNEP • HYPERION
Los Angeles   New York

First Edition, October 2015
1 3 5 7 9 10 8 6 4 2

FAC-020093-15196

Printed in the United States of America

Rune art by Michelle Gengaro-Kokmen

Library of Congress Cataloging in Publication Control Number: 2015018467

ISBN 978-1-4231-6091-5

Reinforced binding

Visit www.DisneyBooks.com

To Cassandra Clare
Thanks for letting me share the excellent name Magnus

CONTENTS

MAGNUS CHASE

and the GODS of ASGARD

THE SWORD OF SUMMER

ONE

Good Morning!
You're Going to Die

YEAH, I KNOW. You guys are going to read about how I died in agony, and you're going be like, "Wow! That sounds cool, Magnus! Can I die in agony too?"

No. Just no.

Don't go jumping off any rooftops. Don't run into the highway or set yourself on fire. It doesn't work that way. You will not end up where I ended up.

Besides, you wouldn't want to deal with my situation. Unless you've got some crazy desire to see undead warriors hacking one another to pieces, swords flying up giants' noses, and dark elves in snappy outfits, you shouldn't even *think* about finding the wolf-headed doors.

My name is Magnus Chase. I'm sixteen years old. This is the story of how my life went downhill after I got myself killed.

My day started out normal enough. I was sleeping on the sidewalk under a bridge in the Public Garden when a guy kicked me awake and said, "They're after you."

By the way, I've been homeless for the past two years.

Some of you may think, *Aw, how sad.* Others may think, *Ha, ha, loser!* But if you saw me on the street, ninety-nine percent of you would walk right past like I'm invisible. You'd pray, *Don't let him ask me for money.* You'd wonder if I'm older than I look, because surely a teenager wouldn't be wrapped in a stinky old sleeping bag, stuck outside in the middle of a Boston winter. *Somebody should help that poor boy!* Then you'd keep walking. Whatever. I don't need your sympathy. I'm used to being laughed at. I'm definitely used to being ignored. Let's move on.

The bum who woke me was a guy called Blitz. As usual, he looked like he'd been running through a dirty hurricane. His wiry black hair was full of paper scraps and twigs. His face was the color of saddle leather, and was flecked with ice. His beard curled in all directions. Snow caked the bottom of his trench coat where it dragged around his feet—Blitz being about five feet five—and his eyes were so dilated, the irises were all pupil. His permanently alarmed expression made him look like he might start screaming any second.

I blinked the gunk out of my eyes. My mouth tasted like day-old hamburger. My sleeping bag was warm, and I really didn't want to get out of it.

"Who's after me?"

"Not sure." Blitz rubbed his nose, which had been broken so many times it zigzagged like a lightning bolt. "They're handing out flyers with your name and picture."

I cursed. Random police and park rangers I could deal with. Truant officers, community service volunteers, drunken college kids, addicts looking to roll somebody small and weak— all those would've been as easy to wake up to as pancakes and orange juice.

But when somebody knew my name and my face—that was

bad. That meant they were targeting me specifically. Maybe the folks at the shelter were mad at me for breaking their stereo. (Those Christmas carols had been driving me crazy.) Maybe a security camera caught that last bit of pickpocketing I did in the Theater District. (Hey, I needed money for pizza.) Or maybe, unlikely as it seemed, the police were still looking for me, wanting to ask questions about my mom's murder. . . .

I packed my stuff, which took about three seconds. The sleeping bag rolled up tight and fit in my backpack with my toothbrush and a change of socks and underwear. Except for the clothes on my back, that's all I owned. With the backpack over my shoulder and the hood of my jacket pulled low, I could blend in with pedestrian traffic pretty well. Boston was full of college kids. Some of them were even more scraggly and younger-looking than me.

I turned to Blitz. "Where'd you see these people with the flyers?"

"Beacon Street. They're coming this way. Middle-aged white guy and a teenage girl, probably his daughter."

I frowned. "That makes no sense. Who—"

"I don't know, kid, but I gotta go." Blitz squinted at the sunrise, which was turning the skyscraper windows orange. For reasons I'd never quite understood, Blitz hated the daylight. Maybe he was the world's shortest, stoutest homeless vampire. "You should go see Hearth. He's hanging out in Copley Square."

I tried not to feel irritated. The local street people jokingly called Hearth and Blitz my mom and dad because one or the other always seemed to be hovering around me.

"I appreciate it," I said. "I'll be fine."

Blitz chewed his thumbnail. "I dunno, kid. Not today. You gotta be extra careful."

"Why?"

He glanced over my shoulder. "They're coming."

I didn't see anybody. When I turned back, Blitz was gone. I hated it when he did that. Just— *Poof.* The guy was like a ninja. A homeless vampire ninja.

Now I had a choice: go to Copley Square and hang out with Hearth, or head toward Beacon Street and try to spot the people who were looking for me.

Blitz's description of them made me curious. A middle-aged white guy and a teenage girl searching for me at sunrise on a bitter-cold morning. Why? Who were they?

I crept along the edge of the pond. Almost nobody took the lower trail under the bridge. I could hug the side of the hill and spot anyone approaching on the higher path without them seeing me.

Snow coated the ground. The sky was eye-achingly blue. The bare tree branches looked like they'd been dipped in glass. The wind cut through my layers of clothes, but I didn't mind the cold. My mom used to joke that I was half polar bear.

Dammit, Magnus, I chided myself.

After two years, my memories of her were still a minefield. I stumbled over one, and instantly my composure was blown to bits.

I tried to focus.

The man and the girl were coming this way. The man's sandy hair grew over his collar—not like an intentional style, but like he couldn't be bothered to cut it. His baffled expression reminded me of a substitute teacher's: *I know I was hit by a spit wad, but I have no idea where it came from.* His dress shoes were totally wrong for a Boston winter. His socks were different shades of brown. His tie looked like it had been tied while he spun around in total darkness.

The girl was definitely his daughter. Her hair was just as thick and wavy, though lighter blond. She was dressed more sensibly in snow boots, jeans, and a parka, with an orange T-shirt peeking out at the neckline. Her expression was more determined, angry. She gripped a sheaf of flyers like they were essays she'd been graded on unfairly.

If she was looking for me, I did not want to be found. She was scary.

I didn't recognize her or her dad, but something tugged at the back of my skull . . . like a magnet trying to pull out a very old memory.

Father and daughter stopped where the path forked. They looked around as if just now realizing they were standing in the middle of a deserted park at no-thank-you o'clock in the dead of winter.

"Unbelievable," said the girl. "I want to strangle him."

Assuming she meant me, I hunkered down a little more.

Her dad sighed. "We should probably avoid killing him. He *is* your uncle."

"But *two years?*" the girl demanded. "Dad, how could he not tell us for *two years?*"

"I can't explain Randolph's actions. I never could, Annabeth."

I inhaled so sharply, I was afraid they would hear me. A scab was ripped off my brain, exposing raw memories from when I was six years old.

Annabeth. Which meant the sandy-haired man was . . . *Uncle Frederick?*

I flashed back to the last family Thanksgiving we'd shared: Annabeth and me hiding in the library at Uncle Randolph's town house, playing with dominoes while the adults yelled at each other downstairs.

You're lucky you live with your momma. Annabeth stacked another domino on her miniature building. It was amazingly good, with columns in front like a temple. *I'm going to run away.*

I had no doubt she meant it. I was in awe of her confidence.

Then Uncle Frederick appeared in the doorway. His fists were clenched. His grim expression was at odds with the smiling reindeer on his sweater. *Annabeth, we're leaving.*

Annabeth looked at me. Her gray eyes were a little too fierce for a first grader's. *Be safe, Magnus.*

With a flick of her finger, she knocked over her domino temple.

That was the last time I'd seen her.

Afterward, my mom had been adamant: *We're staying away from your uncles. Especially Randolph. I won't give him what he wants. Ever.*

She wouldn't explain what Randolph wanted, or what she and Frederick and Randolph had argued about.

You have to trust me, Magnus. Being around them . . . it's too dangerous.

I trusted my mom. Even after her death, I hadn't had any contact with my relatives.

Now, suddenly, they were looking for me.

Randolph lived in town, but as far as I knew, Frederick and Annabeth still lived in Virginia. Yet here they were, passing out flyers with my name and photo on them. Where had they even *gotten* a photo of me?

My head buzzed so badly, I missed some of their conversation.

"—to find Magnus," Uncle Frederick was saying. He checked his smartphone. "Randolph is at the city shelter in the South End. He says no luck. We should try the youth shelter across the park."

"How do we even know Magnus is alive?" Annabeth asked miserably. "Missing for *two years*? He could be frozen in a ditch somewhere!"

Part of me was tempted to jump out of my hiding place and shout, *TA-DA!*

Even though it had been ten years since I'd seen Annabeth, I didn't like seeing her distressed. But after so long on the streets, I'd learned the hard way: you never walk into a situation until you understand what's going on.

"Randolph is sure Magnus is alive," said Uncle Frederick. "He's somewhere in Boston. If his life is truly in danger . . ."

They set off toward Charles Street, their voices carried away by the wind.

I was shivering now, but it wasn't from the cold. I wanted to run after Frederick, tackle him, and demand to hear what was going on. How did Randolph know I was still in town? Why were they looking for me? How was my life in danger now more than on any other day?

But I didn't follow them.

I remembered the last thing my mom ever told me. I'd been reluctant to use the fire escape, reluctant to leave her, but she'd gripped my arms and made me look at her. *Magnus, run. Hide. Don't trust anyone. I'll find you. Whatever you do, don't go to Randolph for help.* Then, before I'd made it out the window, the door of our apartment had burst into splinters. Two pairs of glowing blue eyes had emerged from the darkness. . . .

I shook off the memory and watched Uncle Frederick and Annabeth walk away, veering east toward the Common.

Uncle Randolph . . . For some reason, he'd contacted Frederick and Annabeth. He'd gotten them to Boston. All this time, Frederick and Annabeth hadn't known that my mom was dead and I was missing. It seemed impossible, but if it were true, why would Randolph tell them about it now?

Without confronting him directly, I could think of only one way to get answers. His town house was in Back Bay, an easy walk from here. According to Frederick, Randolph wasn't home. He was somewhere in the South End, looking for me.

Since nothing started a day better than a little breaking and entering, I decided to pay his place a visit.

TWO

The Man with the Metal Bra

THE FAMILY MANSION SUCKED.

Oh, sure, *you* wouldn't think so. You'd see the massive six-story brownstone with gargoyles on the corners of the roof, stained glass transom windows, marble front steps, and all the other blah, blah, blah, rich-people-live-here details, and you'd wonder why I'm sleeping on the streets.

Two words: *Uncle Randolph.*

It was *his* house. As the oldest son, he'd inherited it from my grandparents, who died before I was born. I never knew much about the family soap opera, but there was a lot of bad blood between the three kids: Randolph, Frederick, and my mom. After the Great Thanksgiving Schism, we never visited the ancestral homestead again. Our apartment was, like, half a mile away, but Randolph might as well have lived on Mars.

My mom only mentioned him if we happened to be driving past the brownstone. Then she would point it out the way you might point out a dangerous cliff. *See? There it is. Avoid it.*

After I started living on the streets, I would sometimes walk by at night. I'd peer in the windows and see glowing display cases of antique swords and axes, creepy helmets with facemasks staring at me from the walls, statues silhouetted in the upstairs windows like petrified ghosts.

Several times I considered breaking in to poke around, but I'd never been tempted to knock on the door. *Please, Uncle Randolph, I know you hated my mother and haven't seen me in ten years; I know you care more about your rusty old collectibles than you do about your family; but may I live in your fine house and eat your leftover crusts of bread?*

No thanks. I'd rather be on the street, eating day-old falafel from the food court.

Still . . . I figured it would be simple enough to break in, look around, and see if I could find answers about what was going on. While I was there, maybe I could grab some stuff to pawn.

Sorry if that offends your sense of right and wrong.

Oh, wait. No, I'm not.

I don't steal from just anybody. I choose obnoxious jerks who have too much already. If you're driving a new BMW and you park it in a handicapped spot without a disabled placard, then yeah, I've got no problem jimmying your window and taking some change from your cup holder. If you're coming out of Barneys with your bag of silk handkerchiefs, so busy talking on your phone and pushing people out of your way that you're not paying attention, I am there for you, ready to pickpocket your wallet. If you can afford five thousand dollars to blow your nose, you can afford to buy me dinner.

I am judge, jury, and thief. And as far as obnoxious jerks went, I figured I couldn't do better than Uncle Randolph.

The house fronted Commonwealth Avenue. I headed around back to the poetically named Public Alley 429. Randolph's parking spot was empty. Stairs led down to the basement entrance. If there was a security system, I couldn't spot it. The door was a simple latch lock without even a dead-bolt. *Come on, Randolph. At least make it a challenge.*

Two minutes later I was inside.

In the kitchen, I helped myself to some sliced turkey, crackers, and milk from the carton. No falafel. Dammit. Now I was really in the mood for some, but I found a chocolate bar and stuffed it in my coat pocket for later. (Chocolate must be savored, not rushed.) Then I headed upstairs into a mau-soleum of mahogany furniture, oriental rugs, oil paintings, marble tiled floors, and crystal chandeliers. . . . It was just embarrassing. Who lives like this?

At age six, I couldn't appreciate how expensive all this stuff was, but my general impression of the mansion was the same: dark, oppressive, creepy. It was hard to imagine my mom growing up here. It was easy to understand why she'd become a fan of the great outdoors.

Our apartment over the Korean BBQ joint in Allston had been cozy enough, but Mom never liked being inside. She always said her real home was the Blue Hills. We used to go hiking and camping there in all kinds of weather—fresh air, no walls or ceilings, no company but the ducks, geese, and squirrels.

This brownstone, by comparison, felt like a prison. As I stood alone in the foyer, my skin crawled with invisible beetles.

I climbed to the second floor. The library smelled of lemon polish and leather, just like I remembered. Along one wall was a lit glass case full of Randolph's rusty Viking helmets and corroded ax blades. My mom once told me that Randolph taught history at Harvard before some big disgrace got him fired. She wouldn't go into details, but clearly the guy was still an artifact nut.

You're smarter than either of your uncles, Magnus, my mom once told me. *With your grades, you could easily get into Harvard.*

That had been back when she was still alive, I was still in school, and I might have had a future that extended past finding my next meal.

In one corner of Randolph's office sat a big slab of rock like a tombstone, the front chiseled and painted with elaborate red swirly designs. In the center was a crude drawing of a snarling beast—maybe a lion or a wolf.

I shuddered. Let's not think about *wolves.*

I approached Randolph's desk. I'd been hoping for a computer, or a notepad with helpful information—anything to explain why they were looking for me. Instead, spread across the desk were pieces of parchment as thin and yellow as onionskin. They looked like maps a school kid in medieval times had made for social studies: faint sketches of a coastline, various points labeled in an alphabet I didn't know. Sitting on top of them, like a paperweight, was a leather pouch.

My breath caught. I recognized that pouch. I untied the drawstring and grabbed one of the dominoes . . . except it wasn't a domino. My six-year-old self had assumed that's what Annabeth and I had been playing with. Over the years, the memory had reinforced itself. But instead of dots, these stones were painted with red symbols.

The one in my hand was shaped like a tree branch or a deformed *F*:

ᚠ

My heart pounded. I wasn't sure why. I wondered if coming here had been such a good idea. The walls felt like they were closing in. On the big rock in the corner, the drawing of the beast seemed to sneer at me, its red outline glistening like fresh blood.

I moved to the window. I thought it might help to look outside. Along the center of the avenue stretched the Commonwealth Mall—a ribbon of parkland covered in snow. The bare trees were strung with white Christmas lights. At the end of the block, inside an iron fence, the bronze statue of Leif Erikson stood on his pedestal, his hand cupped over his eyes. Leif gazed toward the Charlesgate overpass as if to say *Look, I discovered a highway!*

My mom and I used to joke about Leif. His armor was on the skimpy side: a short skirt and a breastplate that looked like a Viking bra.

I had no clue why that statue was in the middle of Boston, but I figured it couldn't be a coincidence that Uncle Randolph grew up to study Vikings. He'd lived here his whole life. He'd probably looked at Leif every day out the window. Maybe as a child Randolph had thought, *Someday, I want to study Vikings. Men who wear metal bras are cool!*

My eyes drifted to the base of the statue. Somebody was standing there . . . looking up at me.

You know how when you see somebody out of context and it takes you a second to recognize them? In Leif Erikson's shadow stood a tall pale man in a black leather jacket, black motorcycle pants, and pointy-toed boots. His short spiky hair was so blond it was almost white. His only dash of color was a striped red-and-white scarf wrapped around his neck and spilling off his shoulders like a melted candy cane.

If I didn't know him, I might've guessed he was cosplaying

some anime character. But I *did* know him. It was Hearth, my fellow homeless dude and surrogate "mom."

I was a little creeped out, a little offended. Had he seen me on the street and followed me? I didn't need some fairy godstalker looking after me.

I spread my hands: *What are you doing here?*

Hearth made a gesture like he was plucking something from his cupped hand and throwing it away. After two years of hanging around him, I was getting pretty good at reading sign language.

He was saying *GET OUT.*

He didn't look alarmed, but it was hard to tell with Hearth. He never showed much emotion. Whenever we hung out, he mostly just stared at me with those pale gray eyes like he was waiting for me to explode.

I lost valuable seconds trying to figure out what he meant, why he was here when he was supposed to be in Copley Square.

He gestured again: both hands pointing forward with two fingers, dipping up and down twice. *Hurry.*

"Why?" I said aloud.

Behind me, a deep voice said, "Hello, Magnus."

I nearly jumped out of my shoes. Standing in the library doorway was a barrel-chested man with a trim white beard and a skullcap of gray hair. He wore a beige cashmere overcoat over a dark wool suit. His gloved hands gripped the handle of a polished wooden cane with an iron tip. Last time I'd seen him his hair had been black, but I knew that voice.

"Randolph."

He inclined his head a millimeter. "What a pleasant

surprise. I'm glad you're here." He sounded neither surprised nor glad. "We don't have much time."

The food and milk started to churn in my stomach. "M-much time . . . before what?"

His brow furrowed. His nose wrinkled as if he detected a mildly unpleasant odor. "You're sixteen today, aren't you? They'll be coming to kill you."

THREE

Don't Accept Rides
from Strange Relatives

WELL, HAPPY BIRTHDAY TO ME!

Was it January 13? Honestly, I had no idea. Time flies when you're sleeping under bridges and eating from Dumpsters.

So I was officially sixteen. For my present, I got cornered by Uncle Freaky, who announced that I was marked for assassination.

"Who—" I started to ask. "You know what? Never mind. Nice seeing you, Randolph. I'll be going now."

Randolph remained in the doorway, blocking my exit. He pointed the iron tip of his cane at me. I swear I could feel it pushing against my sternum from across the room.

"Magnus, we need to talk. I don't want them to get to you. Not after what happened to your mother. . . ."

A punch in the face would've been less painful.

Memories from that night spun through my head like a sickening kaleidoscope: our apartment building shuddering, a scream from the floor below, my mother—who'd been tense and paranoid all day—dragging me toward the fire escape, telling me to run. The door splintered and burst. From the hallway, two beasts emerged, their pelts the color of dirty snow, their eyes glowing blue. My fingers slipped off the fire escape railing and I fell, landing in a pile of garbage bags in the alley. Moments later, the windows of our apartment exploded, belching fire.

My mom had told me to run. I did. She'd promised to find me. She never did. Later, on the news, I heard that her body had been recovered from the fire. The police were searching for me. They had questions: signs of arson; my record of disciplinary problems at school; neighbors' reports of shouting and a loud crash from our apartment just before the explosion; the fact that I'd run from the scene. None of the reports mentioned wolves with glowing eyes.

Ever since that night I'd been hiding, living under the radar, too busy surviving to grieve properly for my mom, wondering if I'd hallucinated those beasts . . . but I knew I hadn't.

Now, after all this time, Uncle Randolph wanted to help me.

I gripped the little domino stone so tightly, it cut into my palm. "You don't know what happened to my mom. You never cared about either of us."

Randolph lowered his cane. He leaned on it heavily and stared at the carpet. I could almost believe I'd hurt his feelings.

"I pleaded with your mother," he said. "I wanted her to bring you here—to live where I could protect you. She refused. After she died . . ." He shook his head. "Magnus, you have no idea how long I've looked for you, or how much danger you're in."

"I'm fine," I snapped, though my heart was thumping against my ribs. "I've been taking care of myself pretty well."

"Perhaps, but those days are over." The certainty in Randolph's voice gave me a chill. "You're sixteen now, the age of manhood. You escaped them once, the night your mother died. They won't let you escape again. This is our last chance. Let me help you, or you won't live through the day."

The low winter light shifted across the stained glass transom, washing Randolph's face in changing colors, chameleon-style.

I shouldn't have come here. Stupid, stupid, stupid. Over and over, my mom had given me one clear message: *Don't go to Randolph.* Yet here I was.

The longer I listened to him, the more terrified I got, and the more desperately I wanted to hear what he had to say.

"I don't need your help." I set the strange little domino on the desk. "I don't want—"

"I know about the wolves."

That stopped me.

"I know what you saw," he continued. "I know who sent the creatures. Regardless of what the police think, I know how your mother really died."

"How—"

"Magnus, there's so much I need to tell you about your parents, about your inheritance. . . . About your father."

An ice-cold wire threaded its way down my spine. "You knew my father?"

I didn't want to give Randolph any leverage. Living on the street had taught me how dangerous leverage could be. But he had me hooked. I *needed* to hear this information. Judging from the appraising gleam in his eyes, he knew it.

"Yes, Magnus. Your father's identity, your mother's murder, the reason she refused my help . . . it's all connected." He gestured toward his display of Viking goodies. "My whole life, I've been working toward one goal. I've been trying to solve a historical mystery. Until recently, I didn't see the whole picture. Now I do. It's all been leading to *this* day, your sixteenth birthday."

I backed up to the window, as far as I could get from Uncle Randolph. "Look, I don't understand ninety percent of what you're saying, but if you can tell me about my dad—"

The building rattled like a volley of cannons had gone off in the distance—a *rumble* so low I felt it in my teeth.

"They'll be here soon," Randolph warned. "We're running out of time."

"Who are *they?*"

Randolph limped forward, relying on his cane. His right knee didn't seem to work. "I'm asking a lot, Magnus. You have no reason to trust me. But you need to come with me *right now*. I know where your birthright is." He pointed to the old maps on the desk. "Together, we can retrieve what is yours. It's the only thing that might protect you."

I glanced over my shoulder, out the window. Down in the Commonwealth Mall, Hearth had disappeared. I should have done the same. Looking at Uncle Randolph, I tried to see any resemblance to my mother, anything that might inspire me to trust him. I found nothing. His imposing bulk, his intense dark eyes, his humorless face and stiff manner . . . he was the exact opposite of my mom.

"My car is out back," he said.

"M-maybe we should wait for Annabeth and Uncle Frederick."

Randolph grimaced. "They don't believe me. They *never* believed me. Out of desperation, as a last resort, I brought them to Boston to help me look for you, but now that you're here—"

The building shook again. This time the *boom* felt closer and stronger. I wanted to believe it was from construction nearby, or a military ceremony, or anything easily explainable. But my gut told me otherwise. The noise sounded like the fall of a gargantuan foot—like the noise that had shaken our apartment two years ago.

"Please, Magnus." Randolph's voice quavered. "I lost my *own* family to those monsters. I lost my wife, my daughters."

"You—you had a family? My mom never said anything—"

"No, she wouldn't have. But your mother . . . Natalie was my only sister. I loved her. I hated to lose her. I can't lose you, too. Come with me. Your father left something for you to find—something that will change the worlds."

Too many questions crowded my brain. I didn't like the crazy light in Randolph's eyes. I didn't like the way he said *worlds*, plural. And I didn't believe he'd been trying to find me since my mom died. I had my antenna up constantly. If Randolph had been asking about me by name, one of my street friends would've tipped me off, like Blitz had done this morning with Annabeth and Frederick.

Something had changed—something that made Randolph decide I was worth looking for.

"What if I just run?" I asked. "Will you try to stop me?"

"If you run, they'll find you. They'll kill you."

My throat felt like it was full of cotton balls. I didn't trust Randolph. Unfortunately, I believed he was in earnest about people trying to kill me. His voice had the ring of truth.

"Well, then," I said, "let's go for a ride."

FOUR

Seriously, the Dude
Cannot Drive

YOU'VE HEARD ABOUT bad Boston drivers? That's my Uncle Randolph.

The dude gunned his BMW 528i (of course it *had* to be a BMW) and shot down Commonwealth Avenue, ignoring the lights, honking at other cars, weaving randomly from lane to lane.

"You missed a pedestrian," I said. "You want to go back and hit her?"

Randolph was too distracted to answer. He kept glancing at the sky as if looking for storm clouds. He gunned the BMW through the intersection at Exeter.

"So," I said, "where are we going?"

"The bridge."

That explained everything. There were, like, twenty bridges in the Boston area.

I ran my hand along the heated leather seat. It had been maybe six months since I'd ridden in a car. The last time it had been a social worker's Toyota. Before that, a police cruiser. Both times I'd used a fake name. Both times I'd escaped, but over the past two years I'd come to equate cars with holding cells. I wasn't sure my luck had changed any today.

I waited for Randolph to answer any of the nagging little

questions I had, like, oh: Who's my dad? Who murdered my mom? How did you lose your wife and kids? Are you presently hallucinating? Did you really have to wear that clove-scented cologne?

But he was too busy causing traffic havoc.

Finally, just to make small talk, I asked, "So who's trying to kill me?"

He turned right on Arlington. We skirted the Public Garden, past the equestrian statue of George Washington, the rows of gaslight lampposts and snow-covered hedges. I was tempted to bail out of the car, run back to the swan pond, and hide in my sleeping bag.

"Magnus," said Randolph, "I've made my life's work studying the Norse exploration of North America."

"Wow, thanks," I said. "That really answered my question."

Suddenly, Randolph *did* remind me of my mom. He gave me the same exasperated scowl, the same look over the top of his glasses, like *Please, kid, cut the sarcasm*. The similarity made my chest ache.

"Fine," I said. "I'll humor you. Norse exploration. You mean the Vikings."

Randolph winced. "Well . . . *Viking* means *raider*. It's more of a job description. Not all Norse people were Vikings. But, yes, those guys."

"The statue of Leif Erikson . . . Does that mean the Vikings—er, the Norse—discovered Boston? I thought the Pilgrims did that."

"I could give you a three-hour lecture on that topic alone."

"Please don't."

"Suffice it to say, the Norse explored North America and even built settlements around the year 1000, almost five hundred years before Christopher Columbus. Scholars agree on that."

"That's a relief. I hate it when scholars disagree."

"But no one is sure how far south the Norse sailed. Did they make it to what is now the United States? That statue of Leif Erikson . . . that was the pet project of a wishful thinker in the 1800s, a man named Eben Horsford. He was convinced that Boston was the lost Norse settlement of Norumbega, their farthest point of exploration. He had an instinct, a gut feeling, but no real proof. Most historians wrote him off as a crackpot."

He looked at me meaningfully.

"Let me guess . . . you don't think he's a crackpot." I resisted the urge to say *Takes one to believe one.*

"Those maps on my desk," Randolph said. "*They* are the proof. My colleagues call them forgeries, but they're not. I staked my reputation on it!"

And that's why you got fired from Harvard, I thought.

"The Norse explorers did make it this far," he continued. "They were searching for something . . . and they found it here. One of their ships sank nearby. For years I thought the shipwreck was in Massachusetts Bay. I sacrificed everything to find it. I bought my own boat, took my wife, my children on expeditions. The last time . . ." His voice broke. "The storm came out of nowhere, the fires . . ."

He didn't seem anxious to share more, but I got the general idea: he'd lost his family at sea. He really *had* staked everything on his crazy theory about Vikings in Boston.

I felt bad for the guy, sure. I also didn't want to be his next casualty.

We stopped at the corner of Boylston and Charles.

"Maybe I'll just get out here." I tried the handle. The door was locked from the driver's side.

"Magnus, listen. It's no accident you were born in Boston. Your father wanted you to find what he lost two thousand years ago."

My feet got jumpy. "Did you just say . . . two thousand years?"

"Give or take."

I considered screaming and pounding on the window. Would anybody help me? If I could get out of the car, maybe I could find Uncle Frederick and Annabeth, assuming they were any less insane than Randolph.

We turned onto Charles Street, heading north between the Public Garden and the Common. Randolph could've been taking me anywhere—Cambridge, the North End, or some out-of-the-way body dump.

I tried to keep calm. "Two thousand years . . . that's a longer lifespan than your average dad."

Randolph's face reminded me of the Man in the Moon from old black-and-white cartoons: pale and rotund, pitted and scarred, with a secretive smile that wasn't very friendly. "Magnus, what do you know about Norse mythology?"

This just gets better and better, I thought.

"Uh, not much. My mom had a picture book she used to read me when I was little. And weren't there a couple of movies about Thor?"

Randolph shook his head in disgust. "Those movies . . .

ridiculously inaccurate. The real gods of Asgard—Thor, Loki, Odin, and the rest—are much more powerful, much more terrifying than anything Hollywood could concoct."

"But . . . they're myths. They're not real."

Randolph gave me a sort of a pitying look. "Myths are simply stories about truths we've forgotten."

"So, look, I just remembered I have an appointment down the street—"

"A millennium ago, Norse explorers came to this land." Randolph drove us past the Cheers bar on Beacon Street, where bundled-up tourists were taking photos of themselves in front of the sign. I spotted a crumpled flyer skittering across the sidewalk: it had the word MISSING and an old picture of me. One of the tourists stepped on it.

"The captain of these explorers," Randolph continued, "was a son of the god Skirnir."

"A son of a god. Really, anywhere around here is good. I can walk."

"This man carried a very special item," Randolph said, "something that once belonged to your father. When the Norse ship went down in a storm, that item was lost. But you— you have the ability to find it."

I tried the door again. Still locked.

The really bad part? The more Randolph talked, the less I could convince myself that he was nuts. His story seeped into my mind—storms, wolves, gods, Asgard. The words clicked into place like pieces of a puzzle I'd never had the courage to finish. I was starting to believe him, and that scared the baked beans out of me.

Randolph whipped around the access road for Storrow

Drive. He parked at a meter on Cambridge Street. To the north, past the elevated tracks of the Mass General T station, rose the stone towers of the Longfellow Bridge.

"That's where we're going?" I asked.

Randolph fished for quarters in his cup holder. "All these years, it was so much closer than I realized. I just needed *you!*"

"I'm definitely feeling the love."

"You are sixteen today." Randolph's eyes danced with excitement. "It's the perfect day for you to reclaim your birthright. But it's also what your enemies have been waiting for. We have to find it first."

"But—"

"Trust me a little while longer, Magnus. Once we have the weapon—"

"Weapon? Now my birthright is a *weapon?*"

"Once you have it in your possession, you'll be much safer. I can explain everything to you. I can help you train for what's to come."

He opened his car door. Before he could get out, I grabbed his wrist.

I usually avoid touching people. Physical contact creeps me out. But I needed his full attention.

"Give me one answer," I said. "One *clear* answer, without the rambling and the history lectures. You said you knew my dad. Who is he?"

Randolph placed his hand over mine, which made me squirm. His palm was too rough and calloused for a history professor's. "On my life, Magnus, I swear this is the truth: your father is a Norse god. Now, hurry. We're in a twenty-minute parking spot."

FIVE

I've Always Wanted to Destroy a Bridge

"YOU CAN'T DROP a bombshell like that and walk away!" I yelled as Randolph walked away.

Despite his cane and his stiff leg, the guy could really move. He was like an Olympic gold medalist in hobbling. He forged ahead, climbing the sidewalk of the Longfellow Bridge as I jogged after him, the wind screaming in my ears.

The morning commuters were coming in from Cambridge. A single line of cars was backed up the length of the span, barely moving. You'd think my uncle and I would be the only ones dumb enough to walk across the bridge in subzero weather, but this being Boston, half a dozen runners were chugging along, looking like emaciated seals in their Lycra bodysuits. A mom with two kids bundled in a stroller was walking on the opposite sidewalk. Her kids looked about as happy as I felt.

My uncle was still fifteen feet ahead of me.

"Randolph!" I called. "I'm talking to you!"

"The drift of the river," he muttered. "The landfill on the banks . . . allowing for a thousand years of shifting tidal patterns—"

"Yo!" I caught the sleeve of his cashmere coat. "Rewind to the part about a Norse god being my pappy."

Randolph scanned our surroundings. We'd stopped at

one of the bridge's main towers—a cone of granite rising fifty feet above us. People said the towers looked like giant salt and pepper shakers, but I'd always thought they looked like Daleks from *Doctor Who*. (So I'm a nerd. Sue me. And, yes, even homeless kids watch TV sometimes—in shelter rec rooms, on public library computers. . . . We have our ways.)

A hundred feet below us, the Charles River glistened steel gray, its surface mottled with patches of snow and ice like the skin of a massive python.

Randolph leaned so far over the railing it made me jittery.

"The irony," he muttered. "Here, of all places . . ."

"So, anyway," I said, "about my father . . ."

Randolph gripped my shoulder. "Look down there, Magnus. What do you see?"

Cautiously I glanced over the side. "Water."

"No, the carved ornamentation, just below us."

I looked again. About halfway down the side of the pier, a shelf of granite jutted over the water like a theater seating box with a pointy tip. "It looks like a nose."

"No, it's . . . Well, from this angle, it *does* sort of look like a nose. But it's the prow of a Viking longship. See? The other pier has one too. The poet Longfellow, for whom the bridge was named—he was fascinated by the Norse. Wrote poems about their gods. Like Eben Horsford, Longfellow believed the Vikings had explored Boston. Hence the designs on the bridge."

"You should give tours," I said. "All the rabid Longfellow fans would pay big bucks."

"Don't you see?" Randolph still had his hand on my shoulder, which wasn't making me any less anxious. "So many people over the centuries have known. They've *felt* it instinctively, even if they had no proof. This area wasn't just *visited* by the Vikings. It was *sacred* to them! Right below us—somewhere near these decorative longships—is the wreck of an *actual* longship, holding a cargo of incalculable value."

"I still see water. And I still want to hear about Dad."

"Magnus, the Norse explorers came here searching for the axis of the worlds, the very trunk of the tree. They found it—"

A low *boom* echoed across the river. The bridge shook. About a mile away, amid the thicket of chimneys and steeples of Back Bay, a column of oily black smoke mushroomed skyward.

I steadied myself against the railing. "Um, wasn't that close to your house?"

Randolph's expression hardened. His stubbly beard glistened silver in the sunlight.

"We're out of time. Magnus, extend your hand over the water. The sword is down there. Call it. Focus on it as if it's the most important thing in the world—the thing you want the most."

"A sword? I—look, Randolph, I can tell you're having a hard day, but—"

"DO IT."

The sternness in his voice made me flinch. Randolph *had* to be insane, talking about gods and swords and ancient shipwrecks. Yet the column of smoke over Back Bay was very real. Sirens wailed in the distance. On the bridge, drivers stuck their heads out their windows to gawk, holding up smartphones and taking pictures.

And as much as I wanted to deny it, Randolph's words

resonated with me. For the first time, I felt like my body was humming at the right frequency, like I'd finally been tuned to match the crappy soundtrack of my life.

I stretched my hand out over the river.

Nothing happened.

Of course nothing happened, I chided myself. *What were you expecting?*

The bridge shook more violently. Down the sidewalk, a jogger stumbled. From behind me came the *crunch* of one car rear-ending another. Horns blared.

Above the rooftops of Back Bay, a second column of smoke billowed. Ash and orange cinders sprayed upward as if the explosion were volcanic, spewing from the ground.

"That—that was a lot closer," I noted. "It's like something is zeroing in on us."

I really hoped Randolph would say *Nah, of course not. Don't be silly!*

He seemed to get older before my eyes. His wrinkles darkened. His shoulders slumped. He leaned heavily on his cane. "Please, not again," he muttered to himself. "Not like last time."

"*Last* time?" Then I remembered what he'd said about losing his wife and daughters—a storm out of nowhere, fires.

Randolph locked eyes with me. "Try again, Magnus. Please."

I thrust my hand toward the river. I imagined I was reaching for my mom, trying to pull her from the past—trying to save her from the wolves and the burning apartment. I reached for answers that might explain why I'd lost her, why my whole life since then had been nothing but a downhill spiral of *suck.*

Directly below me, the surface of the water began to steam.

Ice melted. Snow evaporated, leaving a hole in the shape of a hand—*my* hand, twenty times larger.

I didn't know what I was doing. I'd had the same feeling when my mom first taught me to ride a bike. *Don't think about what you're doing, Magnus. Don't hesitate, or you'll fall. Just keep going.*

I swept my hand back and forth. A hundred feet below, the steaming hand mirrored my movements, clearing the surface of the Charles. Suddenly I stopped. A pinpoint of warmth hit the center of my palm as if I'd intercepted a beam of sunlight.

Something was down there . . . a heat source buried deep in the frigid mud of the river bottom. I closed my fingers and pulled.

A dome of water swelled and ruptured like a dry-ice bubble. An object resembling a lead pipe shot upward and landed in my hand.

It looked nothing like a sword. I held it by one end, but there was no hilt. If it had ever had a point or a sharp edge, it didn't now. The thing was about the right size for a blade, but it was so pitted and corroded, so encrusted with barnacles and glistening with mud and slime, I couldn't even be sure it was metal. In short, it was the saddest, flimsiest, most disgusting piece of scrap I'd ever magically pulled from a river.

"At last!" Randolph lifted his eyes to the heavens. I got the feeling that, if not for his bum knee, he might've knelt on the pavement and offered a prayer to the nonexistent Norse gods.

"Yeah." I hefted my new prize. "I feel safer already."

"You can renew it!" Randolph said. "Just try!"

I turned the blade. I was surprised that it hadn't already disintegrated in my hand.

"I dunno, Randolph. This thing looks *way* past renewing. I'm not even sure it can be recycled."

If I sound unimpressed or ungrateful, don't get me wrong. The way I'd pulled the sword out of the river was so cool it freaked me out. I'd always wanted a superpower. I just hadn't expected mine to entail retrieving garbage from river bottoms. The community service volunteers were going to love me.

"Concentrate, Magnus!" Randolph said. "Quickly, before—"

Fifty feet away, the center of the bridge erupted in flames. The shock wave pushed me against the rail. The right side of my face felt sunburned. Pedestrians screamed. Cars swerved and crashed into one another.

For some stupid reason, I ran toward the explosion. It was like I couldn't help myself. Randolph shuffled after me, calling my name, but his voice seemed far away, unimportant.

Fire danced across the roofs of cars. Windows shattered from the heat, spraying the street with glass gravel. Drivers scrambled out of their vehicles and fled.

It looked like a meteor had hit the bridge. A ten-foot-diameter circle of asphalt was charred and steaming. In the center of the impact zone stood a human-size figure: a dark man in a dark suit.

When I say dark, I mean his skin was the purest, most beautiful shade of black I'd ever seen. Squid ink at midnight would not have been so black. His clothes were the same: a well-tailored jacket and slacks, a crisp dress shirt and tie—all cut from the fabric of a neutron star. His face was inhumanly handsome, chiseled obsidian. His long hair was combed back in an immaculate oil slick. His pupils glowed like tiny rings of lava.

I thought, If Satan were real, he would look like this guy.

Then I thought, No, Satan would be a schlub next to this guy. This guy is like Satan's fashion consultant.

Those red eyes locked on to me.

"Magnus Chase." His voice was deep and resonant, his accent vaguely German or Scandinavian. "You have brought me a gift."

An abandoned Toyota Corolla stood between us. Satan's fashion consultant walked straight through it, melting a path down the middle of the chassis like a blowtorch through wax.

The sizzling halves of the Corolla collapsed behind him, the wheels melted to puddles.

"I will make you a gift as well." The dark man extended his hand. Smoke curled off his sleeve and ebony fingers. "Give me the sword and I will spare your life."

SIX

Make Way for Ducklings, or They Will Smack You Upside the Head

I'D SEEN SOME WEIRD STUFF IN MY LIFE.

I once watched a crowd of people wearing nothing but Speedos and Santa hats jog down Boylston in the middle of winter. I met a guy who could play the harmonica with his nose, a drum set with his feet, a guitar with his hands, and a xylophone with his butt all at the same time. I knew a woman who'd adopted a grocery cart and named it Clarence. Then there was the dude who claimed to be from Alpha Centauri and had philosophical conversations with Canada geese.

So a well-dressed Satanic male model who could melt cars . . . why not? My brain just kind of expanded to accommodate the weirdness.

The dark man waited, his hand outstretched. The air around him rippled with heat.

About a hundred feet down the span, a Red Line commuter train ground to a halt. The conductor gawked at the chaos in front of her. Two joggers tried to pull a guy from a half-crushed Prius. The lady with the double stroller was unfastening her screaming kids, the stroller's wheels having melted into ovals. Standing next to her, instead of helping, one idiot held up his smartphone and tried to film the destruction.

His hand was shaking so badly I doubted he was getting a very good picture.

Now at my shoulder, Randolph said, "The sword, Magnus. Use it!"

I got the uncomfortable impression my big burly uncle was hiding behind me.

The dark man chuckled. "Professor Chase . . . I admire your persistence. I thought our last encounter would've broken your spirit. But here you are, ready to sacrifice another family member!"

"Be quiet, Surt!" Randolph's voice was shrill. "Magnus has the sword! Go back to the fires from whence you came."

Surt didn't seem intimidated, though personally I found the word *whence* very intimidating.

Fire Dude studied me like I was as barnacle-encrusted as the sword. "Give it here, boy, or I will show you the power of Muspell. I will incinerate this bridge and everyone on it."

Surt raised his arms. Flames slithered between his fingers. At his feet, the pavement bubbled. More windshields shattered. The train tracks groaned. The Red Line conductor yelled frantically into her walkie-talkie. The pedestrian with the smartphone fainted. The mom collapsed over the stroller, her kids still crying inside. Randolph grunted and staggered backward.

Surt's heat didn't make me pass out. It just made me angry. I didn't know who this fiery jack-hole was, but I knew a bully when I met one. First rule of the streets: Never let a bully take your stuff.

I pointed my once-might-have-been-a-sword at Surt. "Cool

down, man. I have a corroded piece of metal and I'm not afraid to use it."

Surt sneered. "Just like your father, you are no fighter."

I clenched my teeth. *Okay,* I thought, *time to ruin this guy's outfit.*

But before I could take action, something whizzed past my ear and smacked Surt in the forehead.

Had it been a *real* arrow, Surt would've been in trouble. Fortunately for him, it was a plastic toy projectile with a pink heart for a point—a Valentine's Day novelty, I guessed. It hit Surt between the eyes with a cheerful *squeak*, fell to his feet, and promptly melted.

Surt blinked. He looked as confused as I was.

Behind me a familiar voice shouted, "Run, kid!"

Charging up the bridge came my buddies Blitz and Hearth. Well . . . I say *charging.* That implies it was impressive. It really wasn't. For some reason, Blitz had donned a broad-brimmed hat and sunglasses along with his black trench coat, so he looked like a grungy, very short Italian priest. In his gloved hands he wielded a fearsome wooden dowel with a bright yellow traffic sign that read: MAKE WAY FOR DUCKLINGS.

Hearth's red-striped scarf trailed behind him like limp wings. He nocked another arrow in his pink plastic Cupid's bow and fired at Surt.

Bless their demented little hearts, I understood where they'd gotten the ridiculous weapons: the toy store on Charles Street. I panhandled in front of that place sometimes, and they had that stuff in their window display. Somehow, Blitz and Hearth must've followed me here. In their rush, they'd done a smash-and-grab of the nearest deadly objects. Being crazed homeless guys, they hadn't chosen very well.

Dumb and pointless? You bet. But it warmed my heart that they wanted to look out for me.

"We'll cover you!" Blitz charged by me. "Run!"

Surt hadn't been expecting an attack by lightly armed bums. He stood there while Blitz smacked him across the head with the MAKE WAY FOR DUCKLINGS sign. Hearth's next squeaky arrow misfired and hit me in the butt.

"Hey!" I complained.

Being deaf, Hearth couldn't hear me. He ran past me and into battle, thwacking Surt in the chest with his plastic bow.

Uncle Randolph grabbed my arm. He was wheezing badly. "Magnus, we have to go. NOW!"

Maybe I should have run, but I stood there frozen, watching my only two friends attack the dark lord of fire with cheap plastic toys.

Finally Surt tired of the game. He backhanded Hearth and sent him flying across the pavement. He kicked Blitz in the chest so hard the little guy stumbled backward and landed on his butt right in front of me.

"Enough." Surt extended his arm. From his open palm, fire spiraled and elongated until he was holding a curved sword made entirely of white flame. "I am annoyed now. You will all die."

"Gods' galoshes!" Blitz stammered. "That's not just any fire giant. That's the Black One!"

As opposed to the Yellow One? I wanted to ask, but the sight of the flaming sword kind of stifled my will to joke.

Around Surt, flames began to swirl. The firestorm spiraled outward, melting cars to slag heaps, liquefying the pavement, popping rivets from the bridge like champagne corks.

I'd only *thought* it was warm before. Now Surt was really turning up the temperature.

Hearth slumped against the railing about thirty feet away. The unconscious pedestrians and trapped motorists wouldn't last long either. Even if the flames didn't touch them, they'd die from asphyxiation or heat stroke. But for some reason, the heat still didn't bother me.

Randolph stumbled, hanging off my arm with his full weight. "I—I . . . hum, umm . . ."

"Blitz," I said, "get my uncle out of here. Drag him if you have to."

Blitz's sunglasses were steaming. The brim of his hat was beginning to smolder. "Kid, you can't fight that guy. That's Surt, the Black One himself!"

"You said that already."

"But Hearth and me—we're supposed to protect *you!*"

I wanted to snap *And you're doing a great job with the* MAKE WAY FOR DUCKLINGS *sign!* But what could I expect from a couple of homeless dudes? They weren't exactly commandos. They were just my friends. There was no way I'd let them die defending me. As for Uncle Randolph . . . I hardly knew the guy. I didn't much like him. But he was family. He'd said he couldn't stand to lose another family member. Yeah, well neither could I. This time I wasn't going to run away.

"Go," I told Blitz. "I'll get Hearth."

Somehow Blitz managed to hold up my uncle. Together they stumbled off.

Surt laughed. "The sword will be mine, boy. You cannot change fate. I will reduce your world to cinders!"

I turned to face him. "You're starting to aggravate me. I have to kill you now."

I walked into the wall of flames.

SEVEN

You Look Great
Without a Nose, Really

WOW, MAGNUS, you're probably thinking. *That was . . . stupid!*

Thanks. I have my moments.

Normally I don't go stepping into walls of flame. But I had a feeling it wouldn't hurt me. I know that sounds weird, but so far I hadn't passed out. The heat didn't feel so bad, even though the pavement was turning to sludge at my feet.

Extreme temperatures have never bothered me. I don't know why. Some people are double-jointed. Some people can wiggle their ears. I can sleep outside in the winter without freezing to death or hold matches under my hand without getting burned. I'd won some bets that way in the homeless shelters, but I'd never thought of my tolerance as something special . . . *magical.* I'd definitely never tested its limits.

I walked through the curtain of fire and smacked Surt in the head with my rusty sword. Because, you know, I always try to keep my promises.

The blade didn't seem to hurt him, but the swirling flames died. Surt stared at me for a millisecond, completely shocked. Then he punched me in the gut.

I'd been punched before, just not by a fiery heavyweight whose ring name was the Black One.

I folded like a deck chair. My vision blurred and tripled. When I regained my focus, I was on my knees, staring at a puddle of regurgitated milk, turkey, and crackers steaming on the asphalt.

Surt could have taken my head off with his fiery sword, but I guess he didn't feel I was worth it. He paced in front of me, making *tsk-tsk* sounds.

"Feeble," he said. "A soft little boy. Give me the blade of your own free will, Vanir-spawn. I promise you a quick death."

Vanir-spawn?

I knew a lot of good insults, but I'd never heard that one.

The corroded sword was still in my hand. I felt my pulse against the metal as if the sword itself had developed a heartbeat. Resonating up the blade, all the way to my ears, was a faint hum like a car engine turning over.

You can renew it, Randolph had told me.

I could almost believe the old weapon was stirring, waking up. Not fast enough, though. Surt kicked me in the ribs and sent me sprawling.

I lay flat on my back, staring at the smoke in the winter sky. Surt must have kicked me hard enough to trigger a near-death hallucination. A hundred feet up, I saw a girl in armor on a horse made of mist, circling like a vulture over the battle. She held a spear made of pure light. Her chain mail shone like silvered glass. She wore a conical steel helmet over a green head wrap, sort of like a medieval knight. Her face was beautiful but stern. Our eyes met for a fraction of a second.

If you're real, I thought, *help.*

She dissolved into smoke.

"The sword," Surt demanded, his obsidian face looming over me. "It's worth more to me freely surrendered, but if I must, I will pry it from your dead fingers."

In the distance, sirens wailed. I wondered why emergency crews hadn't shown up already. Then I remembered the other two giant explosions in Boston. Had Surt caused them, too? Or brought along some fiery friends?

At the edge of the bridge, Hearth staggered to his feet. A few unconscious pedestrians had started to stir. I couldn't see Randolph and Blitz anywhere. Hopefully they were out of danger by now.

If I could keep Burning Man occupied, maybe the rest of the bystanders would have time to clear out too.

Somehow I managed to stand.

I looked at the sword and . . . yeah, I was definitely hallucinating.

Instead of a corroded piece of junk, I held an actual weapon. The leather-wrapped grip felt warm and comfortable in my hand. The pommel, a simple polished steel oval, helped counterweight the thirty-inch blade, which was double-edged and rounded at the tip, more for hacking than for stabbing. Down the center of the blade, a wide groove was emblazoned with Viking runes—the same kind I'd seen in Randolph's office. They shimmered in a lighter shade of silver, as if they'd been inlaid while the blade was forged.

The sword was definitely humming now, almost like a human voice trying to find the right pitch.

Surt stepped back. His lava-red eyes flickered nervously. "You don't know what you have there, boy. You won't live long enough to find out."

He swung his scimitar.

I'd had no experience with swords, unless you count watching *The Princess Bride* twenty-six times as a kid. Surt would've cut me in half—but my weapon had other ideas.

Ever held a spinning top on the tip of your finger? You can feel it moving under its own power, tilting in all directions. The sword was like that. It swung itself, blocking Surt's fiery blade. Then it spun in an arc, dragging my arm along with it, and hacked into Surt's right leg.

The Black One screamed. The wound in his thigh smoldered, setting his pants on fire. His blood sizzled and glowed like the flow from a volcano. His fiery blade dissipated.

Before he could recover, my sword leaped upward and slashed his face. With a howl, Surt stumbled back, cupping his hands over his nose.

To my left, someone screamed—the mother with the two kids.

Hearth was trying to help her extract her toddlers from the stroller, which was now smoking and about to combust.

"Hearth!" I yelled, before remembering that was no good.

With Surt still distracted, I limped over to Hearth and pointed down the bridge. "Go! Get the kids out of here!"

He could read lips just fine, but he didn't like my message. He shook his head adamantly, hoisting one of the toddlers into his arms.

The mom was cradling the other kid.

"Leave now," I told her. "My friend will help you."

The mom didn't hesitate. Hearth gave me one last look: *This is not a good idea.* Then he followed her, the little kid bouncing up and down in his arms crying, "Ah! Ah! Ah!"

Other innocent people were still stuck on the bridge: drivers trapped in their cars, pedestrians wandering around in a daze, their clothes steaming and their skin lobster red. Emergency sirens were closer now, but I didn't see how the police or paramedics could help if Surt was still storming around being all fiery and stuff.

"Boy!" The Black One sounded like he was gargling with syrup.

He took his hands from his face, and I saw why. My self-guided sword had taken off his nose. Molten blood streamed down his cheeks, splattering on the pavement in sizzling droplets. His pants had burned off, leaving him in a pair of flame-patterned red boxers. Between that and the newly sawed-off snout, he looked like a diabolical version of Porky Pig.

"I have tolerated you long enough," he gargled.

"I was just thinking the same thing about you." I raised the sword. "You want this? Come and get it."

In retrospect, that was a pretty stupid thing to say.

Above me, I caught a glimpse of the weird gray apparition—a girl on a horse, circling like a vulture, watching.

Instead of charging, Surt bent down and scooped asphalt from the road with his bare hands. He molded it into a red-hot sphere of steaming gunk and pitched it toward me like a fastball.

Another game I'm not good at: baseball. I swung the sword, hoping to knock away the projectile. I missed. The asphalt cannonball plowed into my gut and embedded itself—burning, searing, destroying.

I couldn't breathe. The pain was so intense I felt every cell in my body explode in a chain reaction.

Despite that, a strange sort of calm fell over me: I was dying. I wasn't coming back from this. Part of me thought, *All right. Make it count.*

My vision dimmed. The sword hummed and tugged at my hand, but I could barely feel my arms.

Surt studied me, a smile on his ruined face.

He wants the sword, I told myself. *He can't have it. If I'm going out, he's going with me.*

Weakly, I raised my free hand. I flipped him a gesture that he wouldn't need to know sign language to understand.

He roared and charged.

Just as he reached me, my sword leaped up and ran him through. I used the last of my strength to grapple him as his momentum carried us both over the railing.

"No!" He fought to free himself, bursting into flames, kicking and gouging, but I held on as we plummeted toward the Charles River, my sword still embedded in his stomach, my own organs burning away from the molten tar in my gut. The sky flashed in and out of view. I caught a glimpse of the smoky apparition—the girl on the horse diving toward me at a full gallop, her hand outstretched.

FLOOM! I hit the water.

Then I died. The end.

EIGHT

Mind the Gap, and Also the Hairy Guy with the Ax

BACK IN SCHOOL, I loved ending stories that way.

It's the perfect conclusion, isn't it? *Billy went to school. He had a good day. Then he died. The end.*

It doesn't leave you hanging. It wraps everything up nice and neat.

Except in my case, it didn't.

Maybe you're thinking, *Oh, Magnus, you didn't* really *die. Otherwise you couldn't be narrating this story. You just came close. Then you were miraculously rescued, blah, blah, blah.*

Nope. I actually died. One hundred percent: guts impaled, vital organs burned, head smacked into a frozen river from forty feet up, every bone in my body broken, lungs filled with ice water.

The medical term for that is *dead.*

Gee, Magnus, what did it feel like?

It hurt. A lot. Thanks for asking.

I started to dream, which was weird—not only because I was dead, but because I never dream. People have tried to argue with me about that. They say everybody dreams and I just don't remember mine. But I'm telling you, I always slept like the dead. Until I *was* dead. Then I dreamed like a normal person.

I was hiking with my mom in the Blue Hills. I was maybe ten years old. It was a warm summer day, with a cool breeze through the pines. We stopped at Houghton's Pond to skip stones across the water. I managed three skips. My mom managed four. She always won. Neither of us cared. She would laugh and hug me and that was enough for me.

It's hard to describe her. To really understand Natalie Chase, you had to meet her. She used to joke that her spirit animal was Tinker Bell from *Peter Pan*. If you can imagine Tinker Bell at age thirty-something, minus the wings, wearing flannel, denim, and Doc Martens, you've got a pretty good picture of my mom. She was a petite lady with delicate features, short blond pixie hair, and leaf-green eyes that sparkled with humor. Whenever she read me stories, I used to gaze at the spray of freckles across her nose and try to count them.

She radiated joy. That's the only way I can put it. She loved life. Her enthusiasm was infectious. She was the kindest, most easygoing person I ever knew . . . until the weeks leading up to her death.

In the dream, that was still years in the future. We stood together at the pond. She took a deep breath, inhaling the scent of warm pine needles.

"This is where I met your father," she told me. "On a summer day just like this."

The comment surprised me. She rarely talked about my dad. I'd never met him, never even seen pictures of him. That might sound strange, but my mom didn't make a big deal out of their relationship, so neither did I.

She was clear that my dad hadn't abandoned us. He'd just moved on. She wasn't bitter. She had fond memories of their brief time together. After it ended, she found out she was pregnant with me, and she was elated. Ever since, it had been just the two of us. We didn't need anyone else.

"You met him at the pond?" I asked. "Was he good at skipping stones?"

She laughed. "Oh, yeah. He *destroyed* me at stone skipping. That first day . . . it was perfect. Well, except for one thing." She pulled me close and kissed my forehead. "I didn't have *you* yet, pumpkin."

Okay, yes. My mom called me *pumpkin.* Go ahead and laugh. As I got older, it embarrassed me, but that was while she was still alive. Now I'd give anything to hear her call me pumpkin again.

"What was my dad like?" I asked. It felt strange to say *my dad.* How can somebody be *yours* if you never met him? "What happened to him?"

My mom spread her arms to the sunlight. "That's why I bring you here, Magnus. Can't you feel it? He's all around us."

I didn't know what she meant. Usually she didn't talk in metaphors. My mom was about as literal and down-to-earth as you could get.

She ruffled my hair. "Come on, I'll race you to the beach."

My dream shifted. I found myself standing in Uncle Randolph's library. In front of me, lounging sideways across the desk, was a man I'd never seen before. He was walking his fingers across the collection of old maps.

"Death was an interesting choice, Magnus."

The man grinned. His clothes looked fresh from the store: blinding white sneakers, crisp new jeans, and a Red Sox home jersey. His feathery hair was a mix of red, brown, and yellow, tousled in a fashionable *I-just-got-out-of-bed-and-I-look-this-good* sort of way. His face was shockingly handsome. He could've done ads for aftershave in men's magazines, but his scars ruined the perfection. Burn tissue splashed across the bridge of his nose and his cheekbones, like impact lines on the moon's surface. His lips were marred by a row of welts all the way around his mouth—maybe piercing holes that had closed over. But why would anyone have that many mouth piercings?

I wasn't sure what to say to the scarred hallucination, but since my mom's words were still lingering in my head, I asked, "Are you my father?"

The hallucination raised his eyebrows. He threw back his head and laughed.

"Oh, I *like* you! We'll have fun. No, Magnus Chase, I'm not your father, but I'm definitely on your side." He traced his finger under the Red Sox logo on his jersey. "You'll meet *my* son soon enough. Until then, a little advice: Don't trust appearances. Don't trust your comrades' motives. Oh, and"—he lunged forward and grabbed my wrist—"tell the All-Father I said hello."

I tried to break free. His grip was like steel. The dream changed. Suddenly I was flying through cold gray fog.

"Stop struggling!" said a female voice.

Holding my wrist was the girl I'd seen circling the bridge. She charged through the air on her nebulous horse, pulling me along at her side like I was a sack of laundry. Her blazing spear was strapped across her back. Her chain mail armor glinted in the gray light.

She tightened her grip. "Do you *want* to fall into the Gap?"

I got a feeling she wasn't talking about the clothing store.

Looking below me, I saw nothing—just endless gray. I decided I did not want to fall into it.

I tried to speak. I couldn't. I shook my head weakly.

"Then stop struggling," she ordered.

Beneath her helmet, a few wisps of dark hair had escaped her green headscarf. Her eyes were the color of redwood bark.

"Don't make me regret this," she said.

My consciousness faded.

I awoke gasping, every muscle in my body tingling with alarm.

I sat up and grabbed my gut, expecting to find a burning hole where my intestines used to be. No smoldering asphalt was embedded there. I felt no pain. The strange sword was gone. My clothes looked perfectly fine—not wet or burned or torn.

In fact, my clothes looked *too* fine. The same stuff I'd been wearing for weeks—my only pair of jeans, my layers of shirts, my jacket—didn't smell. They'd seemingly been washed, dried, and put back on me while I was unconscious, which was an unsettling idea. They even had a warm lemony scent that reminded me of the good old days when my mom did my laundry. My shoes were like new, as shiny as when I dug them out of the Dumpster behind Marathon Sports.

Even weirder: *I* was clean. My hands weren't caked with grime. My skin felt freshly scrubbed. I ran my fingers through my hair and found no tangles, no twigs, no pieces of litter.

Slowly I got to my feet. There wasn't a scratch on me. I bounced on my heels. I felt like I could run a mile. I breathed in the smell of chimney fires and an approaching snowstorm. I almost laughed with relief. Somehow I'd survived!

Except . . . that wasn't possible.

Where was I?

Gradually my senses expanded. I was standing in the entry courtyard of an opulent town house, the kind you might see on Beacon Hill—eight stories of imposing white limestone and gray marble jutting into the winter sky. The double front doors were dark heavy wood bound with iron. In the center of each was a life-size wolf's-head doorknocker.

Wolves . . . that alone was enough to make me hate the place.

I turned to look for a street exit. There wasn't one, just a fifteen-foot-tall white limestone wall surrounding the courtyard. How could you not have a front gate?

I couldn't see much over the wall, but I was obviously still in Boston. I recognized some of the surrounding buildings. In the distance rose the towers of Downtown Crossing. I was probably on Beacon Street, just across from the Common. But how had I gotten here?

In one corner of the courtyard stood a tall birch tree with pure white bark. I thought about climbing it to get over the wall, but the lowest branches were out of reach. Then I realized the tree was in full leaf, which shouldn't have been possible in the winter. Not only that: its leaves glittered gold as if someone had painted them with twenty-four-karat gilt.

Next to the tree, a bronze plaque was affixed to the wall. I hadn't really noticed it earlier, since half the buildings in Boston had historic markers, but now I looked closer. The inscriptions were in two languages. One was the Norse alphabet I'd seen earlier. The other was English:

WELCOME TO THE GROVE OF GLASIR.

NO SOLICITING. NO LOITERING.

HOTEL DELIVERIES: PLEASE USE THE NIFLHEIM ENTRANCE.

Okay . . . I'd exceeded my daily quota of bizarre. I had to get out of here. I had to get over that wall, find out what had happened to Blitz and Hearth—and maybe Uncle Randolph if I was feeling generous—then possibly hitchhike to Guatemala. I was *done* with this town.

Then the double doors swung inward with a groan. Blinding golden light spilled out.

A burly man appeared on the stoop. He wore a doorman's uniform: top hat, white gloves, and a dark green jacket with tails and the interlocking letters HV embroidered on the lapel, but there was no way this guy was an actual doorman. His warty face was smeared with ashes. His beard hadn't been trimmed in decades. His eyes were bloodshot and murderous, and a double-bladed ax hung at his side. His name tag read: HUNDING, SAXONY, VALUED TEAM MEMBER SINCE 749 C.E.

"S-s-sorry," I stammered. "I must . . . um, wrong house."

The man scowled. He shuffled closer and sniffed me. He smelled like turpentine and burning meat. "Wrong house? I don't think so. You're checking in."

"Uh . . . what?"

"You're dead, aren't you?" the man said. "Follow me. I'll show you to registration."

NINE

You Totally Want the Minibar Key

WOULD IT SURPRISE you to learn that the place was bigger on the inside?

The foyer alone could've been the world's largest hunting lodge—a space twice as big as the mansion appeared on the outside. An acre of hardwood floor was covered with exotic animal skins: zebra, lion, and a forty-foot-long reptile that I wouldn't want to have met when it was alive. Against the right wall, a fire crackled in a bedroom-size hearth. In front of it, a few high-school-age guys in fluffy green bathrobes lounged on overstuffed leather couches, laughing and drinking from silver goblets. Over the mantel hung the stuffed head of a wolf.

Oh, joy, I thought with a shudder. *More wolves.*

Columns made from rough-hewn tree trunks held up the ceiling, which was lined with spears for rafters. Polished shields gleamed on the walls. Light seemed to radiate from everywhere—a warm golden glow that hurt my eyes like a summer afternoon after a dark theater.

In the middle of the foyer, a freestanding display board announced:

TODAY'S ACTIVITIES

SINGLE COMBAT TO THE DEATH!—OSLO ROOM, 10 A.M.

GROUP COMBAT TO THE DEATH!—STOCKHOLM ROOM, 11 A.M.

BUFFET LUNCH TO THE DEATH!—DINING HALL, 12 P.M.

FULL ARMY COMBAT TO THE DEATH!—MAIN COURTYARD, 1 P.M.

BIKRAM YOGA TO THE DEATH!—COPENHAGEN ROOM,

BRING YOUR OWN MAT, 4 P.M.

The doorman Hunding said something, but my head was ringing so badly I missed it.

"Sorry," I said, "what?"

"Luggage," he repeated. "Do you have any?"

"Um . . ." I reached for my shoulder strap. My backpack had apparently not been resurrected with me. "No."

Hunding grunted. "No one brings luggage anymore. Don't they put *anything* on your funeral pyre?"

"My what?"

"Never mind." He scowled toward the far corner of the room, where an overturned boat's keel served as the reception desk. "Guess there's no putting it off. Come on."

The man behind the keel apparently used the same barber as Hunding. His beard was so big it had its own zip code. His hair looked like a buzzard that had exploded on a windshield. He was dressed in a forest green pinstriped suit. His name tag read: HELGI, MANAGER, EAST GOTHLAND, VALUED TEAM MEMBER SINCE 749 C.E.

"Welcome!" Helgi glanced up from his computer screen. "Checking in?"

"Uh—"

"You realize check-in time is three P.M.," he said. "If you die earlier in the day, I can't guarantee your room will be ready."

"I can just go back to being alive," I offered.

"No, no." He tapped on his keyboard. "Ah, here we are." He grinned, revealing exactly three teeth. "We've upgraded you to a suite."

Next to me, Hunding muttered under his breath, "Everyone is upgraded to a suite. All we *have* are suites."

"Hunding . . ." warned the manager.

"Sorry, sir."

"You don't want me to use the stick."

Hunding winced. "No, sir."

I looked back and forth between them, checking their name tags.

"You guys started working here the same year," I noted. "749 . . . what is *C.E.*?"

"Common Era," said the manager. "What you might call A.D."

"Then why don't you just say A.D.?"

"Because Anno Domini, *in the Year of Our Lord,* is fine for Christians, but Thor gets a little upset. He still holds a grudge that Jesus never showed up for that duel he challenged him to."

"Say what now?"

"It's not important," Helgi said. "How many keys would you like? Is one sufficient?"

"I still don't get where I am. If you guys have been here since 749, that's over a thousand years."

"Don't remind me," Hunding grumbled.

"But that's impossible. And . . . and you said I'm dead? I don't feel dead. I feel fine."

"Sir," Helgi said, "all this will be explained tonight at dinner. That's when new guests are formally welcomed."

"Valhalla." The word surfaced from the depths of my

brain—a half-remembered story my mom had read me when I was little. "The *HV* on your lapel. The *V* stands for *Valhalla*?"

Helgi's eyes made it clear I was straining his patience. "Yes, sir. The Hotel Valhalla. Congratulations. You've been chosen to join the hosts of Odin. I look forward to hearing about your brave exploits at dinner."

My legs buckled. I leaned on the desk for support. I'd been trying to convince myself this was all a mistake—some elaborate theme hotel where I'd been mistaken for a guest. Now I wasn't so sure.

"Dead," I mumbled. "You mean I'm actually . . . I'm actually—"

"Here is your room key." Helgi handed me a stone engraved with a single Viking rune, like the stones in Uncle Randolph's library. "Would you like the minibar key?"

"Uh—"

"He wants the minibar key," Hunding answered for me. "Kid, you want the minibar key. It's going to be a long stay."

My mouth tasted like copper. "How long?"

"Forever," Helgi said, "or at least until Ragnarok. Hunding will now show you to your room. Enjoy your afterlife. Next!"

TEN

My Room Does Not Suck

I WASN'T PAYING the closest attention as Hunding guided me through the hotel. I felt as if I'd been spun around fifty times then released into the middle of a circus and told to have fun.

Each hall we walked through seemed bigger than the one before. Most of the hotel guests looked like they were in high school, though some looked slightly older. Guys and girls sat together in small groups, lounging in front of fireplaces, chatting in many different languages, eating snacks or playing board games like chess and Scrabble and something that involved real daggers and a blowtorch. Peeking into side lounges, I spotted pool tables, pinball machines, an old-fashioned video arcade, and something that looked like an iron maiden from a torture chamber.

Staff members in dark green shirts moved among the guests, bringing platters of food and pitchers of drink. As far as I could tell, all the servers were buff female warriors with shields on their backs and swords or axes on their belts, which is not something you see a lot in the service industry.

One heavily armed waitress passed me with a steaming plate of egg rolls. My stomach rumbled.

"How can I be hungry if I'm dead?" I asked Hunding. "*None* of these people look dead."

Hunding shrugged. "Well, there's dead and then there's dead. Think of Valhalla more like . . . an upgrade. You're one of the *einherjar* now."

He pronounced the word like *in-HAIR-yar*.

"Einherjar," I repeated. "Just rolls right off the tongue."

"Yeah. Singular: *einherji*." He said it like *in-HAIR-yee*. "We're the chosen of Odin, soldiers in his eternal army. The word *einherjar* is usually translated as *lone warriors*, but that doesn't really capture the meaning. It's more like . . . the *once warriors*—the warriors who fought bravely in the last life and will fight bravely again on the Day of Doom. Duck."

"The Day of Doom Duck?"

"No, duck!"

Hunding pushed me down as a spear flew past. It impaled a guy sitting on the nearest sofa, killing him instantly. Drinks, dice, and Monopoly money flew everywhere. The people he'd been playing with rose to their feet, looking mildly annoyed, and glared in the direction the spear had come from.

"I saw that, John Red Hand!" Hunding yelled. "The lounge is a *No Impaling* area!"

From the billiard room, somebody laughed and called back in . . . Swedish? He didn't sound very remorseful.

"Anyway." Hunding resumed walking as if nothing had happened. "The elevators are right over here."

"Wait," I said. "That guy was just murdered with a spear. Aren't you going to *do* anything?"

"Oh, the wolves will clean up."

My pulse went into double time. "Wolves?"

Sure enough, while the other Monopoly players were sorting their pieces, a pair of gray wolves bounded into the lounge, grabbed the dead man by his legs, and dragged him away, the spear still sticking out of his chest. The trail of blood evaporated instantly. The perforated sofa mended itself.

I cowered behind the nearest potted plant. I don't care how that sounds. My fear simply took control. These wolves didn't have glowing blue eyes like the animals that had attacked my apartment, but still I wished I'd ended up in an afterlife where the mascot was a gerbil.

"Aren't there any rules against killing?" I asked in a small voice.

Hunding raised a bushy eyebrow. "That was just a bit of fun, boy. The victim will be fine by dinner." He pulled me out of my hiding place. "Come on."

Before I could ask more about the "bit of fun," we reached an elevator. Its cage door was made out of spears. Overlapping gold shields lined the walls. The control panel had so many buttons, it stretched from floor to ceiling. The highest number was 540. Hunding pressed 19.

"How can this place have five hundred and forty floors?" I said. "It would be the tallest building in the world."

"If it only existed in one world, yes. But it connects with all the Nine Worlds. You just came through the Midgard entrance. Most mortals do."

"Midgard . . ." I vaguely remembered something about the Vikings believing in nine different worlds. Randolph had used the term *worlds* too. But it had been a long time since my mom read me those Norse bedtime stories. "You mean, like, the world of humans."

"Aye." Hunding took a breath and recited, *"Five hundred and forty floors has Valhalla; five hundred and forty doors leading out into the Nine Worlds."* He grinned. "You never know when or where we'll have to march off to war."

"How often has that happened?"

"Well, never. But still . . . it could happen at any time. I, for one, can't wait! Finally, Helgi will have to stop punishing me."

"The manager? What's he punishing you for?"

Hunding's expression soured. "Long story. He and I—"

The elevator's spear-cage door rolled open.

"Forget it." Hunding clapped me on the back. "You'll like floor nineteen. Good hallmates!"

I'd always thought of hotel corridors as dark, depressing, and claustrophobic. Floor nineteen? Not so much. The vaulted ceiling was twenty feet tall, lined with—you guessed it—more spears for rafters. Valhalla had apparently gotten a good deal at the Spear Wholesale Warehouse. Torches burned in iron sconces, but they didn't seem to make any smoke. They just cast warm orange light across the wall displays of swords, shields, and tapestries. The hall was so wide you could've played a regulation soccer game, no problem. The bloodred carpet had tree branch designs that moved as if swaying in the wind.

Set about fifty feet apart, each guest room door was rough-hewn oak bound in iron. I didn't see any doorknobs or locks. In the center of each door, a plate-size iron circle was inscribed with a name surrounded by a ring of Viking runes.

The first read HALFBORN GUNDERSON. Behind that door I heard shouting and metal clanging like a sword fight was in progress.

The next read MALLORY KEEN. Behind that door, silence.

Then: THOMAS JEFFERSON, JR. The popping of gunfire came from inside, though it sounded more like a video game than the actual thing. (Yes, I've heard both.)

The fourth door was simply marked X. In front, a room-service cart sat in the hallway with the severed head of a pig on a silver platter. The pig's ears and nose looked slightly nibbled.

Now, I'm not a food critic. Being homeless, I could never afford to be. But I draw the line at pig heads.

We'd almost reached the T at the end of the hall when a large black bird shot around the corner and zipped past me, almost clipping my ear. I watched the bird disappear down the hall—a raven, with a notepad and a pen in its talons.

"What was that?" I asked.

"A raven," Hunding said, which I found very helpful.

Finally we stopped at a door inscribed MAGNUS CHASE.

Seeing my name written in iron, inscribed with runes, I started to tremble. My last hope that this might be a mistake, birthday prank, or cosmic mix-up finally evaporated. The hotel was expecting me. They'd spelled my name right and everything.

For the record, Magnus means *great*. My mom named me that because our family was descended from Swedish kings or something a billion years ago. Also, she said I was the greatest thing that ever happened to her. I know. One, two, three: *Awwwwww.* It was an annoying name to have. People tended to spell it Mangus, rhymes with Angus. I always corrected them: *No, it's Magnus, rhymes with swag-ness.* At which point they would stare at me blankly.

Anyway, there was my name on the door. Once I went

through, I would be checked in. According to the manager, I'd have a new home until doomsday.

"Go ahead." Hunding pointed at the runestone key in my hand. The symbol looked sort of like an infinity sign or a sideways hourglass:

ᛞ

"It's *dagaz*," Hunding said. "Nothing to be afraid of. It symbolizes new beginnings, transformations. It also opens your door. Only you have access."

I swallowed. "What if, for instance, the staff wants to get in?"

"Oh, we use the staff key." Hunding patted the ax on his belt. I couldn't tell if he was kidding.

I held up the runestone. I didn't want to try it, but I also didn't want to stay in the hallway until I got impaled by a random spear or injured by a raven hit-and-run. Instinctively, I touched the stone to the matching dagaz mark on the door. The ring of runes glowed green. The door swung open.

I stepped inside, and my jaw hit the floor.

The suite was nicer than any place I'd ever lived, nicer than any place I'd ever visited, including Uncle Randolph's mansion.

In a trance, I moved to the middle of the suite, where a central atrium was open to the sky. My shoes sank into the thick green grass. Four large oak trees ringed the garden like pillars. The lower branches spread into the room across the ceiling, interweaving with the rafters. The taller branches grew up through the opening of the atrium, making a lacy canopy. Sunlight warmed my face. A pleasant breeze wafted through the room, bringing the smell of jasmine.

"How?" I stared at Hunding. "Hundreds of floors are above us, but that's open sky. And it's the middle of winter. How can it feel sunny and warm?"

Hunding shrugged. "I don't know—magic. But this is *your* afterlife, boy. You've earned some perks, eh?"

Had I? I didn't feel particularly perk-worthy.

I turned in a slow circle. The suite was shaped like a cross, with four sections radiating from the central atrium. Each wing was as large as my old apartment. One was the entry hall where we'd come in. The next was a bedroom with a king-size bed. Despite its size, the room was spare and simple: a beige comforter and fluffy-looking pillows on the bed, beige walls with no artwork or mirrors or other decoration. Heavy brown curtains could be drawn to close off the space.

I remembered when I was a kid, how my mom used to make my room as no-frills as possible. I'd always found it hard to sleep indoors unless I had total darkness and nothing to distract me. Looking at this bedroom, I felt like somebody had reached into my mind and pulled out exactly what I needed to be comfortable.

The wing to the left was a dressing area/bathroom tiled in black and beige, my favorite colors. The perks included a sauna, a hot tub, a walk-in closet, a walk-in shower, and a walk-in toilet. (Just kidding on that last one, but it *was* a fancy throne, suitable for the honored dead.)

The suite's fourth wing was a full kitchen and living room. At one end of the living room, a big leather couch faced a plasma-screen TV with about six different game systems stacked in the media cabinet. On the other side, two recliners sat in front of a crackling fireplace and a wall of books.

Yes, I like to read. I'm weird that way. Even after dropping out of school, I spent a lot of time in the Boston Public Library, learning random stuff just to pass the time in a warm, safe place. For two years I had missed my old book collection; I never seriously thought I would have one again.

I walked over to check out the titles on the shelves. Then I noticed the picture framed in silver on the fireplace mantel.

Something like a bubble of helium made its way up my esophagus. "No way . . ."

I picked up the photo. It showed me, at age eight, and my mom at the summit of Mount Washington in New Hampshire. That had been one of the best trips of my life. We'd asked a park ranger to take the photo. In the shot, I was grinning (which I don't do much anymore), showing off my missing two front teeth. My mom knelt behind me with her arms wrapped around my chest, her green eyes crinkling at the corners, her freckles dark from the sun, her blond hair swept sideways by the wind.

"This is impossible," I murmured. "There was only one copy of this picture. It burned in the fire . . ." I turned to Hunding, who was wiping his eyes. "You okay?"

He cleared his throat. "Fine! Of course I'm fine. The hotel likes to provide you with keepsakes, reminders of your old life. Photographs . . ." Under his beard, his mouth might have been quivering. "Back when I died, they didn't have photographs. It's just . . . you're lucky."

No one had called me *lucky* in a very long time. The idea shook me out of my daze. I'd been without my mom for two years. I'd been dead, or *upgraded*, for only a few hours. This bellhop from Saxony had been here since 749 C.E. I wondered how he had died, and what family he'd left behind. Twelve hundred years later, he was still getting teary-eyed about them, which seemed like a cruel way to spend an afterlife.

Hunding straightened and wiped his nose. "Enough of that! If you have any questions, call the front desk. I look forward to hearing about your brave exploits tonight at dinner."

"My . . . brave exploits?"

"Now, don't be modest. You wouldn't have been chosen unless you did something heroic."

"But—"

"Been a pleasure serving you, sir, and welcome to the Hotel Valhalla."

He held out his palm. It took me a second to realize he wanted a tip.

"Oh, um . . ." I dug into my jacket pockets, not expecting to find anything. Miraculously, the chocolate bar I'd swiped from Uncle Randolph's house was still there, undamaged from its trip through the Great Beyond. I gave it to Hunding. "Sorry, that's all I have."

His eyes turned the size of drink coasters. "Gods of Asgard! Thank you, kid!" He sniffed the chocolate and held it up like a holy chalice. "Wow! Okay, you need anything, you let me know. Your Valkyrie will come get you right before dinner. Wow!"

"My Valkyrie? Wait. I don't have a Valkyrie."

Hunding laughed, his eyes still fixed on the chocolate bar. "Yeah, if I had *your* Valkyrie, I'd say the same thing. She's caused her share of trouble."

"What do mean?"

"See you tonight, kid!" Hunding headed for the door. "I got things to eat—I mean *do*. Try not to kill yourself before dinner!"

ELEVEN

Pleased to Meet You. I Will Now Crush Your Windpipe

I COLLAPSED ON THE GRASS.

Gazing up through the tree branches at the blue sky, I had trouble breathing. I hadn't had an asthma attack in years, but I remembered all the nights my mom had held me while I wheezed, feeling like an invisible belt was tightening around my chest. Maybe you're wondering why my mom would take me camping and climbing mountains if I had asthma, but being outside always helped.

Lying in the middle of the atrium, I breathed in the fresh air and hoped my lungs would settle down.

Unfortunately, I was pretty sure this wasn't an asthma attack. This was a complete nervous breakdown. What shook me wasn't just the fact that I was dead, stuck in a bizarre Viking afterlife where people ordered pig heads from the room service menu and impaled each other in the lobby.

The way my life had gone so far, I could accept that. Of *course* I'd end up in Valhalla on my sixteenth birthday. Just my luck.

What really hit me: for the first time since my mom died, I was in a comfortable place, alone and safe (as far as I could tell at the moment). Shelters didn't count. Soup kitchens and rooftops and sleeping bags under bridges didn't count. I'd always slept with one eye open. I could never relax. Now, I was free to think.

And thinking wasn't a good thing.

I'd never had the luxury of grieving properly for my mom. I'd never had time to sit and feel sorry for myself. In a way, that had been as helpful to me as the survival skills my mom had taught me—how to navigate, how to camp, how to make a fire.

All those trips to the parks, the mountains, the lakes. As long as her old beat-up Subaru was working, we'd spend every weekend out of town, exploring the wilderness.

What are we running from? I asked her one Friday, a few months before she died. I was annoyed. I wanted to crash at home for once. I didn't understand her frantic rush to pack and leave.

She'd smiled, but she seemed more preoccupied than usual. *We have to make the most of our time, Magnus.*

Had my mom been deliberately preparing me to survive on my own? Almost as if she'd known what would happen to her . . . but that wasn't possible. Then again, having a Norse god for a dad wasn't possible either.

My breathing still rattled, but I got up and paced around my new room. In the photo on the mantel, eight-year-old Magnus grinned at me with his tangled hair and his missing teeth. That kid was so clueless, so unappreciative of what he had.

I scanned the bookshelves: my favorite fantasy and horror authors from when I was younger—Stephen King, Darren Shan, Neal Shusterman, Michael Grant, Joe Hill; my favorite graphic novel series—Scott Pilgrim, Sandman, Watchmen, Saga; plus a lot of books I'd been meaning to read at the library. (Pro homeless tip: public libraries are safe havens. They have bathrooms. They hardly ever kick out kids who are reading as long as you don't smell too bad or cause a scene.)

I pulled down the illustrated children's book of Norse myths my mom read to me when I was little. Inside were simplistic pictures of happy smiling Viking gods, rainbows, flowers, and pretty girls with blond hair. And sentences like *The gods dwelt in a wonderful and beautiful realm!* There was nothing about the Black One Surt who burned baby carriages and threw molten asphalt, nothing about wolves that murdered people's mothers and made apartments explode. That made me angry.

On the coffee table was a leather-bound notebook titled GUEST SERVICES. I flipped through it. The room service menu went on for ten pages. The TV channel list was almost as long, and the hotel map was so convoluted, divided into so many subsections, I couldn't make sense of it. There were no clearly marked emergency doors labeled: EXIT HERE TO RETURN TO YOUR OLD LIFE!

I threw the guest services book into the fireplace.

As it burned, a new copy appeared on the coffee table. Stupid magical hotel wouldn't even allow me to properly vandalize things.

In a rage, I flipped the sofa. I didn't expect it to go far, but it cartwheeled across the room and smashed into the far wall.

I stared at the trail of dislodged cushions, the upside-down sofa, the cracked plaster and leather skid marks on the wall. How had I done that?

The sofa didn't magically right itself. It stayed where I'd thrown it. The anger drained out of me. I'd probably just made extra work for some poor staff member like Hunding. That didn't seem fair.

I paced some more, thinking about the dark fiery guy on the bridge and why he'd wanted the sword. I hoped Surt had died with me—more *permanently* than I had—but I wasn't optimistic. As long as Blitz and Hearth had gotten away safely. (Oh, yeah. Randolph, too, I guess.)

And the sword itself . . . where was it? Back on the river bottom? Valhalla could resurrect me with a chocolate bar in my pocket, but not a sword in my hand. That was messed up.

In the old stories, Valhalla was for heroes who died in battle. I remembered that much. I definitely didn't feel like a hero. I'd gotten my butt kicked and my guts cannonballed. By stabbing Surt and toppling off the bridge, I'd simply failed in the most productive way possible. A brave death? Not so much.

I froze.

An idea struck me with the force of a sledgehammer.

My mom . . . If anyone had died bravely, *she* had. To protect me from—

Just then someone knocked on my door.

It swung opened and a girl stepped inside . . . the same girl who had circled over the battle on the bridge then pulled me through the gray void.

She had ditched her helmet, chain mail, and glowing spear. Her green headscarf was now around her neck, letting her long brown hair spill freely over her shoulders. Her white dress was embroidered with Viking runes around the collar and cuffs. From her golden belt hung a set of old-fashioned keys and a single-bladed ax. She looked like the maid of honor at someone's Mortal Kombat wedding.

She glanced at the overturned sofa. "Did the furniture offend you?"

"You're real," I noted.

She patted her own arms. "Yes, it appears I am."

"My mother," I said.

"No," she said, "I'm not your mother."

"I mean, is she here in Valhalla?"

The girl's mouth formed a silent *Oh*. She gazed over my shoulder as if considering her answer. "I'm sorry. Natalie Chase is not among the Chosen."

"But *she* was the brave one. She sacrificed herself for me."

"I believe you." The girl examined her key ring. "But I would know if she were here. We Valkyries are not allowed to choose everyone who dies bravely. There are . . . many factors, many different afterlives."

"Then where is she? I want to be there. I'm no hero!"

She surged toward me, pushing me against the wall as easily as I'd flipped the sofa. She pressed her forearm against my throat.

"Don't say that," the girl hissed. "DO—NOT—SAY—THAT! Especially not tonight at dinner."

Her breath smelled like spearmint. Her eyes were somehow dark and bright at the same time. They reminded me of a fossil my mom used to have—a cross section of a nautilus-like sea animal called an ammonite. It seemed to glow from within, as if it had absorbed millions of years of memories while lying under the earth. The girl's eyes had that same sort of luster.

"You don't understand," I croaked. "I have to—"

She pushed harder against my windpipe. "What do you think I don't understand? Grieving for your mother? Being judged unfairly? Being somewhere you don't want to be, forced to deal with people you'd rather not deal with?"

I didn't know how to respond to that, especially since I couldn't breathe.

She stepped away. As I choked and gagged, she paced the foyer, glaring at nothing in particular. Her ax and keys swung on her belt.

I rubbed my bruised neck.

Stupid, Magnus, I told myself. *New place: learn the rules.*

I couldn't start whining and making demands. I had to set aside the question of my mother. If she were anywhere, I'd figure that out later. Right now, being in this hotel was no different than walking into an unfamiliar youth shelter, alley encampment, or church basement soup kitchen. Every place had rules. I had to learn the power structure, the pecking order, the no-nos that would get me stabbed or rolled. I had to survive . . . even if I was already dead.

"Sorry," I said. My throat felt like I'd swallowed a live rodent with lots of claws. "But why do you care if I'm a hero or not?"

She smacked her forehead. "Wow, okay. Maybe because I *brought* you here? Maybe because my career is on the line? One more slipup and—" She caught herself. "Never mind. When you're introduced, go along with what I say. Keep your mouth shut, nod your head, and try to look brave. Don't make me regret bringing you here."

"All right. But for the record, I didn't ask for your help."

"Odin's Eye! You were *dying*! Your other options were Helheim or Ginnungagap or . . ." She shuddered. "Let's just say there are worse places to spend your afterlife in than Valhalla.

I saw what you did on the bridge. Whether you recognize it or not, you acted bravely. You sacrificed yourself to save a lot of people."

Her words sounded like a compliment. Her tone sounded like she was calling me an idiot.

She marched over and poked me in the chest. "You have potential, Magnus Chase. *Don't* prove me wrong or—"

From the wall speakers, a horn blast sounded so loudly it rattled the picture on the mantel.

"What's that?" I asked. "An air raid?"

"Dinner." The girl straightened. She took a deep breath and extended her hand. "Let's start again. Hi, I'm Samirah al-Abbas."

I blinked. "Don't take this the wrong way, but that doesn't sound like a very Viking-ish name."

She smiled tightly. "You can call me Sam. Everyone does. I'll be your Valkyrie this evening. Pleased to meet you properly."

She shook my hand, her grip so tight my finger bones popped. "I will now escort you to dinner." She forced a smile. "If you embarrass me, I'll be the first to kill you."

TWELVE

At Least I'm Not on Goat-Chasing Duty

IN THE HALLWAY, my neighbors were starting to emerge. Thomas Jefferson, Jr. looked about my age. He had short curly hair, a lanky frame, and a rifle slung over one shoulder. His blue woolen coat had brass buttons and chevrons on the sleeve—a U.S. Army Civil War uniform, I guessed. He nodded and smiled. "How you doing?"

"Um, dead, apparently," I said.

He laughed. "Yeah. You'll get used to it. Call me T.J."

"Magnus," I said.

"Come on." Sam pulled me along.

We passed a girl who must've been Mallory Keen. She had frizzy red hair, green eyes, and a serrated knife, which she was shaking in the face of a six-foot-seven guy outside the door marked x.

"Again with the pig's head?" Mallory Keen spoke in a faint Irish brogue. "X, do you think I want to see a severed pig's head every time I step out my front door?"

"I could not eat anymore," X rumbled. "The pig head does not fit in my refrigerator."

Personally, I would not have antagonized the guy. He was built like a bomb containment chamber. If you happened to have a live grenade, I was pretty sure you could safely dispose of it simply by asking X to swallow it. His skin was the color of a shark's belly, rippling with muscles and stippled with warts. There were so many welts on his face it was hard to tell which one was his nose.

We walked past, X and Mallory too busy arguing to pay us any attention.

When we were out of earshot, I asked Sam, "What's the deal with the big gray dude?"

Sam put her finger to her lips. "X is a half-troll. He's a little sensitive about that."

"A half-troll. That's an actual thing?"

"Of course," she said. "And he deserves to be here as much as you."

"Hey, no doubt. Just asking."

The defensiveness in her voice made me wonder what the story was.

As we passed the door for HALFBORN GUNDERSON, an ax blade split the wood from the inside. Muffled laughter came from the room.

Sam ushered me onto the elevator. She pushed away several other einherjar who were trying to get on. "Next car, guys."

The spear-cage door slid shut. Sam inserted one of her keys into an override slot on the panel. She pressed a red rune and the elevator descended. "I'll take you into the dining hall before the main doors open. That way you can get the lay of the land."

"Uh . . . sure. Thanks."

Nordic easy listening music started playing from the ceiling.

Congratulations, Magnus! I thought. *Welcome to warrior paradise, where you can listen to Frank Sinatra in Norwegian FOREVER!*

I tried to think of something to say, preferably something that would not make Sam crush my windpipe.

"So . . . everybody on floor nineteen looks about my age," I noted. "Or—our age. Does Valhalla only take teenagers?"

Samirah shook her head. "The einherjar are grouped by the age they were when they died. You're in the youngest tier, which goes up to about age nineteen. Most of the time, you won't even see the other two tiers—adults and seniors. It's better that way. The adults . . . well, they don't take teens seriously, even if the teens have been here hundreds of years longer."

"Typical," I said.

"As for the senior warriors, they don't always mix well. Imagine a really violent retirement home."

"Sounds like some shelters I've been in."

"Shelters?"

"Forget it. So you're a Valkyrie. You chose all the people in the hotel?"

"Yes," she said. "I personally chose everyone in this hotel."

"Ha, ha. You know what I meant. Your . . . sisterhood or whatever."

"That's right. Valkyries are responsible for choosing the einherjar. Each warrior here died a valiant death. Each had a belief in honor, or some connection to the Norse gods that made him or her eligible for Valhalla."

I thought about what Uncle Randolph had told me, how the sword had been a birthright from my father. "A connection . . . like being the child of a god?"

I was afraid Sam might laugh at me, but she nodded gravely. "Many einherjar are demigods. Many are regular mortals. You're chosen for Valhalla because of your courage and honor, not your heritage. At least, that's how it's supposed to be. . . ."

I couldn't decide if her tone was wistful or resentful.

"And you?" I asked. "How did you become a Valkyrie? Did you die a noble death?"

She laughed. "Not yet. I'm still among the living."

"How does that work exactly?"

"Well, I live a double life. Tonight, I'll escort you to dinner. Then I have to rush home and finish my calculus homework."

"You're not joking, are you?"

"I never joke about calculus homework."

The elevator doors opened. We stepped into a room the size of a concert arena.

My mouth dropped. "Holy—"

"Welcome," Samirah said, "to the Feast Hall of the Slain."

Tiers of long tables like stadium seating curved downward from the nosebleed section. In the center of the room, instead of a basketball court, a tree rose taller than the Statue of Liberty. Its lowest branches were maybe a hundred feet up. Its canopy spread over the entire hall, scraping against the domed ceiling and sprouting through a massive opening at the top. Above, stars glittered in the night sky.

My first question probably wasn't the most important. "Why is there a goat in the tree?"

In fact, a lot of animals skittered among the branches. I couldn't tell what most of them were, but wobbling along the lowest branch was a very fat shaggy goat. Its swollen udders rained milk like leaky showerheads. Below, on the dining-hall floor, a team of four stocky warriors carried a big golden bucket on poles set across their shoulders. They shuffled back and forth, trying to stay under the goat so they could catch the streams of milk. Judging by how soaked the warriors were, they missed a lot.

"The goat is Heidrun," Sam told me. "Her milk is brewed to make the mead of Valhalla. It's good stuff. You'll see."

"And the guys chasing her around?"

"Yeah, that's a thankless job. Behave yourself, or you might get assigned to vat duty."

"Uh . . . couldn't they just, I don't know, bring the goat down here?"

"She's a free-range goat. Her mead tastes better that way."

"Of course it does," I said. "And . . . all the other animals? I see squirrels and possums and—"

"Sugar gliders and sloths," Sam offered. "Those are cute."

"Okay. But you guys eat dinner here? That can't be hygienic with all the animal droppings."

"The animals in the Tree of Laeradr are well-behaved."

"The Tree of . . . Lay-rah-dur. You named your tree."

"Most important things have names." She frowned at me. "Who are you again?"

"Very funny."

"Some of the animals are immortal and have particular jobs. I can't spot him right now, but somewhere up there is a stag named Eikthrymir. We call him Ike for short. You see that waterfall?"

It was hard to miss. From somewhere high in the tree, water ran down grooves in the bark and formed one powerful torrent that cascaded off a branch in a roaring white curtain. It crashed into a pond the size of an Olympic pool between two of the tree's roots.

"The stag's horns spray water nonstop," Sam said. "It flows down the branches into that lake. From there, it goes underground and feeds every river in every world."

"So . . . *all* water is stag-horn runoff? I'm pretty sure that's not what they taught me in earth science."

"It's not all from Ike's horns. There's also snowmelt, rainwater, pollutants, and trace amounts of fluoride and jotun spit."

"Jotun?"

"You know, giants."

She didn't appear to be kidding, though it was hard to be sure. Her face was full of tense humor—her eyes darting and alert, her lips pressed together like she was either suppressing a laugh or expecting an attack. I could imagine her doing stand-up comedy, though maybe not with the ax at her side. Her features also seemed strangely familiar—the line of her nose, the curve of her jaw, the subtle streaks of red and copper in her dark hair.

"Have we met before?" I asked. "I mean . . . before you chose my soul for Valhalla?"

"I doubt it," she said.

"But you're mortal? You live in Boston?"

"Dorchester. I'm a sophomore at King Academy. I live with my grandparents and spend most of my time finding excuses to cover for my Valkyrie activities. Tonight, Jid and Bibi think I'm tutoring a group of elementary students in math. Any other questions?"

Her eyes sent the opposite message: *Enough with the personal stuff.*

I wondered why she lived with her grandparents. Then I remembered what she'd said earlier, about understanding what it was like to grieve for a mother.

"No more questions," I decided. "My head would explode."

"That would be messy," Sam said. "Let's get your seat before—"

Around the perimeter of the room, a hundred doors burst open. The armies of Valhalla swarmed in.

"Dinner is served," Sam said.

THIRTEEN

Phil the Potato
Meets His Doom

WE WERE SWEPT UP in a tidal wave of hungry warriors. Einherjar poured in from every direction, pushing, joking, and laughing as they headed for their seats.

"Hold on," Sam told me.

She grabbed my wrist and we flew into the air Peter Pan–style.

I yelped. "A little warning?"

"I *said* hold on."

We skimmed above the heads of the warriors. Nobody paid us much attention except for one guy I accidentally kicked in the face. Other Valkyries were also zipping around—some escorting warriors, some carrying platters of food and pitchers of drink.

We headed toward what was obviously the head table—where the home team would've sat if this were a Celtics game. A dozen grim-looking dudes were taking their seats in front of golden plates and jewel-encrusted goblets. In the place of honor stood an empty wooden throne with a high back, where two ravens perched, grooming their feathers.

Sam landed us at the table to the left. Twelve other people were just getting seated—two girls and four guys in regular street clothes; six Valkyries dressed more or less like Sam.

"Other newcomers?" I asked.

Sam nodded, her eyebrows furrowed. "Seven in one night is a lot."

"Is that good or bad?"

"More heroes dying means more bad things are stirring in the world. Which means . . ." She pursed her lips. "Never mind. Let's get seated."

Before we could, a tall Valkyrie stepped in our path. "Samirah al-Abbas, what have you brought us tonight—another half-troll? Perhaps a spy from your father?"

The girl looked about eighteen. She was big enough to play power forward, with snow-blond hair in braids down either shoulder. Over her green dress she wore a bandolier of ball-peen hammers, which struck me as an odd choice of weapon. Maybe Valhalla had a lot of loose nails. Around her neck hung a golden amulet shaped like a hammer. Her eyes were as pale blue and cold as a winter sky.

"Gunilla"—Sam's voice tightened—"this is Magnus Chase."

I held out my hand. "Gorilla? Pleased to meet you."

The girl's nostrils flared. "It is *Gunilla*, captain of the Valkyries. And you, newcomer—"

The foghorn I'd heard earlier echoed through the hall. This time I could see the source. Near the base of the tree, two guys held a black-and-white animal horn the size of a canoe while a third guy blew into it.

Thousands of warriors took their seats. Gorilla gave me one last stink-eye, then spun on her heel and marched off to the head table.

"Be careful," Sam warned me. "Gunilla is powerful."

"Also kind of a butt."

The corner of Sam's mouth twitched. "That, too."

She looked shaken, her knuckles white on the haft of her ax. I wondered what Gunilla had meant by *a spy from your father*, but since my windpipe was still sore from the last time I made Sam angry, I decided not to ask.

I sat at the end of the table next to Sam, so I didn't get to talk to the other newbies. Meanwhile, hundreds of Valkyries flew around the room, distributing food and drink. Whenever a Valkyrie's pitcher was empty, she would swoop over the golden vat now bubbling over a large fire, fill her pitcher with yummy goat's milk mead, and continue serving. The main course came from a roasting pit at the other end of the room. Rotating on a hundred-foot-long spit was the carcass of an animal. I wasn't sure what it had been when it was alive, but it was easily the size of a blue whale.

A Valkyrie flew past, depositing a platter of food and a goblet in front of me. I couldn't tell what the slices of meat were, but they smelled great, drizzled in gravy with potatoes on the side and thick slices of bread with butter. It had been a while since I'd had a hot meal, but I still hesitated.

"What kind of animal am I eating?"

Sam wiped her mouth with the back of her hand. "It's named Saehrimnir."

"Okay, first of all, who names their dinner? I don't want to know my dinner's name. This potato—is this potato named Steve?"

She rolled her eyes. "No, stupid. That's Phil. The *bread* is Steve."

I stared at her.

"Kidding," she said. "Saehrimnir is the magical beast of

Valhalla. Every day they kill it and cook it for dinner. Every morning it's resurrected alive and well."

"That must suck for the animal. But is it like a cow or a pig or—"

"It's whatever you want it to be. My portion is beef. Different sections of the animal are chicken or pork. I don't do pork, but some of the guys here love it."

"What if I'm a vegetarian? What if I want falafel?"

Sam became very still. "Was that some sort of joke?"

"Why would it be a joke? I like falafel."

Her shoulders relaxed. "Well, if you want falafel, just ask for the left flank. That part is tofu and bean curd. They can spice it to taste like just about anything."

"You have a magic animal whose left flank is made of tofu."

"This is Valhalla, paradise for warriors in the service of Odin. Your food will taste perfect, whatever you choose."

My stomach was getting impatient, so I dug in. The barbecue had just the right mix of spicy and sweet. The bread was like a warm cloud with a buttery crust. Even Phil the potato tasted great.

Not being a huge fan of free-range goat milk, I was reluctant to try the mead, but the stuff in my goblet looked more like sparkling cider.

I took a sip. Sweet, but not too sweet. Cold and smooth, with undercurrents I couldn't quite identify. Was that blackberry? Or honey? Or vanilla? I drained my glass.

Suddenly, my senses were on fire. It wasn't like alcohol (and, yes, I've tried alcohol, thrown up, tried alcohol again, thrown up). The mead didn't make me giddy, dopey, or nauseous. It was more like iced espresso without the bitter taste. It woke me up, filling me with a warm sense of confidence, but with no edginess or racing heartbeat.

"This stuff is good," I admitted.

A Valkyrie swooped in, refilled my cup, and flew away.

I glanced at Sam, who was brushing bread crumbs off of her scarf. "Do you ever do serving duty?"

"Yeah, sure. We take turns. It's an honor to serve the einherjar." She didn't even sound sarcastic.

"How many Valkyries are there?"

"Several thousand?"

"How many einherjar?"

Sam puffed her cheeks. "Tens of thousands? Like I said, this is just the first dinner. There are two other shifts for the older warriors. Valhalla has five hundred and forty doors. Each one is supposed to accommodate eight hundred warriors exiting for battle at once. That would mean four hundred and thirty-two thousand einherjar."

"That's a lot of tofu."

She shrugged. "Personally, I think the number is exaggerated, but only Odin knows for sure. We'll need a big army when Ragnarok rolls around."

"Ragnarok," I said.

"Doomsday," Sam said. "When the Nine Worlds are destroyed in a great conflagration and the armies of gods and giants meet in battle for the last time."

"Oh. *That* Ragnarok."

I scanned the sea of teenaged fighters. I remembered my first day of public high school in Allston, a few months before my mom died and my life turned to Dumpster sludge. The school had had around two thousand kids. Between classes, the halls were sheer chaos. The cafeteria was like a piranha tank. But it was nothing compared to Valhalla.

I pointed toward the head table. "What about the fancy dudes? Most of them look older."

"I wouldn't call them *fancy dudes*," Sam said. "Those are the thanes, the lords of Valhalla. Each one was personally invited by Odin to sit at his table."

"So the empty throne—"

"Is for Odin. Yes. He . . . well, it's been a while since he's shown up for dinner, but his ravens watch everything and report back to him."

Those ravens made me nervous with their beady black eyes. I got the feeling they were taking a particular interest in me.

Sam pointed to the right of the throne. "There's Erik Bloodax. And that's Erik the Red."

"A lot of Eriks."

"There's Leif Erikson."

"Whoa . . . but he's not wearing a metal bra."

"I'm going to ignore that comment. Over there is Snorri. Then our charming friend Gunilla. Then Lord Nelson and Davy Crockett."

"Davy . . . wait, *seriously?*"

"At the end is Helgi the hotel manager. You probably met him."

Helgi seemed to be having a good time, laughing with Davy Crockett and chugging mead. Behind his chair, the bellhop Hunding stood, looking miserable, carefully peeling grapes and handing them to Helgi one at a time.

"What's the deal with the manager and Hunding?"

Sam made a sour face. "Ancestral feud when they were alive. When they died, both made it to Valhalla, but Odin honored Helgi more. He put Helgi in charge of the hotel. Helgi's first order was that his enemy Hunding would be his servant and do his menial tasks for all time."

"That doesn't seem like much of a paradise for Hunding."

Sam hesitated. In a quieter voice, she said, "Even in Valhalla, there's a pecking order. You don't want to be at the bottom. Remember, when the ceremony begins—"

At the high table, the thanes began banging their cups on the table in unison. All around the hall, the einherjar joined in until the Hall of the Slain thundered with a metal heartbeat.

Helgi stood and raised his goblet. The noise died down.

"Warriors!" The manager's voice filled the hall. He looked so regal it was hard to believe he was the same guy who a few hours ago had offered me a suite upgrade and a minibar key. "Seven new fallen have joined us today! That would be reason enough to celebrate, but we also have a special treat for you. Thanks to Valkyrie Captain Gunilla, today, for the first time, we will not just *hear* about our newcomers' worthy deeds, we will be able to *see* them!"

Next to me, Sam made a choking sound. "No," she muttered. "No, no, no . . ."

"Let the presentation of the dead commence!" Helgi bellowed.

Ten thousand warriors turned and looked expectantly in my direction.

FOURTEEN

Four Million Channels
and There's Still Nothing On
Except Valkyrie Vision

HOORAY FOR GOING LAST.

I was relieved when the presentations started with einherjar at the other end of the table . . . until I saw what the *other*
newbies had done to get into Valhalla.

Helgi called, "Lars Alhstrom!"

A heavyset blond guy rose with his Valkyrie. Lars was so
nervous he knocked over his goblet, splashing magic mead all
over his crotch. A wave of laughter rippled through the hall.

Helgi smiled. "As many of you know, Captain Gunilla has
been phasing in new equipment over the past few months.
She's been fitting her Valkyries' armor with cameras to keep
everyone accountable—and hopefully to keep *us* entertained!"

The warriors cheered and banged their mugs, drowning
out the sound of Sam cursing next to me.

Helgi raised his goblet. "I present to you, Valkyrie Vision!"

Around the tree trunk, a ring of giant holographic screens
flickered to life, floating in midair. The video was choppy,
apparently taken from a camera on the shoulder of a Valkyrie.
We were high in the air, circling over the scene of a sinking ferry
in a gray sea. Half the lifeboats dangled sideways from their
cables. Passengers jumped overboard, some without life vests.
The Valkyrie swooped in closer. The video's focus sharpened.

Lars Ahlstrom scrambled along the tilting deck, a fire extinguisher in his hands. The door to the inside lounge was blocked by a large metal container. Lars struggled to move it, but it was too heavy. Inside the lounge, a dozen people were trapped, banging desperately on the windows.

Lars shouted something to them in . . . Swedish? Norwegian? The meaning was clear: *GET BACK!*

As soon they did, Lars smashed the extinguisher against the window. On the third try, it shattered. Despite the cold, Lars stripped off his coat and laid it across the broken glass.

He stayed at the window until the last passengers were safely out. They ran for the lifeboats. Lars picked up the fire extinguisher again and started to follow, but the ship lurched violently. His head slammed into the wall and he slid down, unconscious.

His body began to glow. The Valkyrie's arm appeared in the frame, reaching out. A shimmering golden apparition rose from Lars's body—his soul, I guessed. Golden Lars took the Valkyrie's hand, and the video screens went dark.

All around the feast hall, warriors cheered.

At the head table, the thanes debated among themselves. I was close enough to hear some of it. One guy—Lord Nelson?— questioned whether a fire extinguisher could count as a weapon.

I leaned toward Sam. "Why does that matter?"

She tore her bread into smaller and smaller pieces. "To get into Valhalla, a warrior must die in battle with a weapon in his or her hand. That's the only way."

"So," I whispered, "anyone could get into Valhalla if they just grabbed a sword and died?"

She snorted. "Of course not. We can't have kids taking up weapons and dying on purpose. There's nothing heroic about suicide. The sacrifice, the bravery has to be unplanned—a genuine heroic response to a crisis. It has to come from the heart, without any thought of reward."

"So . . . what if the thanes decide that a newbie shouldn't have been picked? Does he go back to being alive?" I tried not to sound too hopeful.

Sam wouldn't meet my eyes. "Once you're an einherji, there's no going back. You might get the worst work assignments. You might have a hard time earning respect. But you stay in Valhalla. If the thanes rule the death unworthy. . . well, the Valkyrie takes the punishment for that."

"Oh." Suddenly I understood why all the Valkyries at our table looked a little tense.

The thanes took a vote among themselves. They agreed unanimously that the fire extinguisher could count as a weapon and Lars's death could be seen as in combat.

"What greater enemy is there than the sea?" said Helgi. "We find Lars Ahlstrom worthy of Valhalla!"

More applause. Lars almost fainted. His Valkyrie held him up while smiling and waving at the crowd.

When the noise died down, Helgi continued. "Lars Ahlstrom, do you know your parentage?"

"I—" The newcomer's voice cracked. "I never knew my father."

Helgi nodded. "That is not uncommon. We will seek wisdom from the runes, unless the All-Father wishes to intercede."

Everyone turned toward the unoccupied throne. The

ravens ruffled their feathers and squawked. The throne remained empty.

Helgi didn't look surprised, but his shoulders slumped with disappointment. He motioned toward the fire pit. From a cluster of servers and cooks, a lady in a green hooded robe shuffled forward. Her face was hidden in the shadows of her cowl, but judging from her stooped posture and her gnarled hands, she must have been ancient.

I murmured to Sam, "Who's the Wicked Witch?"

"A *vala*. A seer. She can cast spells, read the future, and . . . other stuff."

The vala approached our table. She stopped in front of Lars Alhstrom and pulled a leather pouch from the folds of her robe. She plucked out a handful of runestones like the ones in Uncle Randolph's study.

"And the runes?" I whispered to Sam. "What are they for?"

"They're the old Viking alphabet," she said, "but each letter also symbolizes something powerful—a god, a type of magic, a force of nature. They're like the genetic code of the universe. The vala can read the stones to see your fate. The greatest sorcerers, like Odin, don't even need to use the stones. They can manipulate reality simply by speaking the name of a rune."

I made a mental note to avoid Odin. I didn't need my reality manipulated any further.

In front of our table, the vala muttered something under her breath. She cast the stones at her feet. They landed on the dirt floor—some faceup, some facedown. One rune in particular seemed to catch everyone's attention. The holographic screens projected its image to everyone in the hall.

ᚦ

The mark meant nothing to me, but hundreds of warriors shouted with approval.

"Thor!" they cried. Then they started to chant, "THOR, THOR, THOR!"

Sam grunted. "As if we need another child of Thor."

"Why? What's wrong with them?"

"Nothing. They're great. Gunilla over there . . . she's a daughter of Thor."

"Oh."

The Valkyrie captain was smiling, which was even scarier than her scowl.

As the chanting subsided, the vala raised her withered arms. "Lars, son of Thor, rejoice! The runes say you shall fight well at Ragnarok. And tomorrow, in your first combat, you shall prove your valor and be decapitated!"

The audience cheered and laughed. Lars suddenly looked very pale. That just made the warriors laugh harder, as if decapitation were a hazing ritual no worse than a wedgie. The vala gathered her runes and retreated while Lars's Valkyrie helped him back into his seat.

The ceremony continued. Next up was a newcomer named Dede. She'd saved a bunch of kids at her village school when a warlord's soldiers had tried to kidnap them. She'd flirted with one of the soldiers, tricked him into letting her hold his assault rifle, then turned it on the warlord's men. She was killed, but her selfless act gave the other kids time to get away. The video was pretty violent. The Vikings loved it. Dede got a standing ovation.

The vala read the runes. She confirmed that Dede's parents were regular mortals, but nobody seemed to mind that. According to Dede's fortune, she would fight valiantly at Ragnarok. Over the next week she would lose her arms several times in combat. Within a hundred years she would rise to the thanes' table.

"Oooooo!" the crowd murmured appreciatively.

The other four newcomers were equally impressive. They'd all saved people. They'd sacrificed their lives bravely. Two were mortals. One was a son of Odin, which caused a minor commotion.

Sam leaned toward me. "Like I said, Odin has not been seen in quite a while. We welcome any sign that he still moves among mortals."

The last newcomer was a daughter of Heimdall. I wasn't sure who that was, but the Vikings seemed impressed.

My head was swimming from too much information. My senses were on fire from too much mead. I didn't even realize we'd reached the end of the table until Helgi called my name.

"Magnus Chase!" he bellowed. "Rise and impress us with your courage!"

FIFTEEN

My Blooper Video Goes Viral

MY COURAGE IMPRESSED NO ONE.

I squirmed in my seat as the video played. The einherjar watched the screens in shocked silence. Then the mumbling and grumbling began, punctuated by bursts of incredulous laughter.

Valkyrie Vision showed only portions of what had happened. I saw myself on the bridge, facing Surt as he summoned a fiery tornado. The camera zoomed in on me threatening him with my corroded piece of metal. Then Hearth and Blitz appeared. Blitz hit the Black One with his MAKE WAY FOR DUCKLINGS sign. Hearth's squeaky toy arrow hit me in the butt. Surt punched me. Surt kicked me in the ribs. I puked and squirmed in agony.

The video fast-forwarded to me backing up against the bridge railing. Surt threw his fiery asphalt cannonball. I swung my sword and missed. In the feast hall, thousands of warriors grunted "Ooooo!" as the chunk of pavement hit me in the gut. Surt charged, and we both went over the side, grappling as we fell.

Just before we hit the water, the video froze and zoomed in. The sword was now sticking out of Surt's gut, but my hands weren't on the grip. They were wrapped around Surt's big neck.

An uncomfortable murmur spread through the room.

"No," I said. "No, that's not how— Someone edited that. It's like a blooper reel."

Sam's face had turned to stone. At the thanes' table, Captain Gunilla smirked. *Her cameras,* I realized, *her editing.*

For some reason, Gunilla wanted to disgrace Sam by making me look like an idiot . . . which, granted, wasn't a difficult task.

Helgi set down his goblet. "Samirah al-Abbas . . . explain."

Sam touched the edge of her scarf. I had a feeling she wanted to pull it over her head and hope the room disappeared. I couldn't blame her.

"Magnus Chase died bravely," she said. "He stood alone against Surt."

More uneasy murmuring.

One of the thanes stood. "You say that was Surt. A fire jotun, certainly, but if you are suggesting it was the Lord of Muspellheim himself—"

"I know what I saw, Erik Bloodax. This one"—Sam gestured at me like I was a prize specimen—"saved many lives on that bridge. The video does not show the whole story. Magnus Chase acted like a hero. He deserves to be among the fallen."

Another thane rose. "He didn't actually die with the sword in his hand."

"Lord Ottar"—Sam's voice sounded strained—"the thanes have looked past such a technicality before. Whether or not Magnus gripped the sword at the moment of death, he died bravely in combat. That is the spirit of Odin's law."

Lord Ottar sniffed. "Thank you, Samirah al-Abbas, daughter of Loki, for teaching us the spirit of Odin's law."

The tension level in the hall went up about thirty notches. Sam's hand drifted toward her ax. I doubted anyone but me could see how her fingers twitched.

Loki . . . I knew *that* name—Norse mythology's big villain, born of giants. He was the archenemy of the gods. If Sam was his daughter, why was she here? How had she become a Valkyrie?

I happened to meet Gunilla's eyes. The captain was obviously loving this drama. She could barely suppress a smile. If she was Thor's kid, that explained why she hated Sam. In the old stories, Thor and Loki were always trying to melt each other's faces.

The thanes debated among themselves.

Finally, Helgi the manager spoke. "Samirah, we're not seeing any heroism in this boy's death. We see a dwarf and an elf with toy weapons—"

"A dwarf and an elf?" I asked, but Helgi ignored me.

"—we see a fire jotun who fell off a bridge and took the boy with him. That's an unusual situation, a son of Muspell crossing into Midgard, but it has happened before."

"Shoot," muttered a thane with bushy sideburns. "Y'all should've seen the big ol' fire jotun Santa Anna had with him at the Alamo. I tell you—"

"Yes, thank you, Lord Crockett." Helgi cleared his throat. "As I was saying, we see very little evidence that Magnus Chase was a worthy choice for Valhalla."

"My lords"—Sam spoke slowly and carefully, like she was addressing children—"the video is not accurate."

Helgi laughed. "Are you suggesting we shouldn't trust our own eyes?"

"I'm suggesting that you hear the story from my point of view. It has always been our tradition to *tell* of the hero's deeds."

Gunilla stood. "Pardon me, my lords, but Samirah is correct. Perhaps we should let the daughter of Loki speak."

The crowd booed and hissed. Some called, "No! No!"

Helgi gestured for silence. "Gunilla, you do your sisterhood credit by defending a fellow Valkyrie, but Loki has always been a master of smooth, honeyed words. Personally, I would rather trust what I see than have it *spun* for me in some clever explanation."

Warriors applauded.

Gunilla shrugged like, *Oh, well, I tried!* and sank back into her chair.

"Magnus Chase!" Helgi called. "Do you know your parentage?"

I counted to five. My first inclination was to yell, *No, but your dad was apparently a jackass!*

"I don't know my father," I admitted. "But, look, about that video—"

"Perhaps you have potential we do not recognize," Helgi said. "Perhaps you are a son of Odin or Thor or some other noble war god, and your presence brings us honor. We will seek wisdom from the runes, unless the All-Father would intercede?"

He glanced at the throne, which remained empty. The ravens studied me with dark hungry eyes.

"Very well," Helgi said. "Bring forth the vala and—"

Between the roots of the tree, where the waterfall hit the dark lake, a massive bubble erupted. *BLOOP!* On the surface of the water stood three women shrouded in white.

Except for the crackle of cooking fire and the sound of the waterfall, the hall was silent. Thousands of warriors watched, frozen in amazement, as the three white women glided across the floor, heading toward me.

"Sam?" I whispered. "Sam, what's going on?"

Her hand fell from her ax.

"The Norns," she said. "The Norns themselves have come to read your fate."

SIXTEEN

Norns. Why Did It Have to Be Norns?

I REALLY WISHED someone had warned me I was going to die. Like, *Hey, you're diving off a bridge tomorrow and becoming an undead Viking, so go read up on Valhalla.*

I felt seriously unprepared.

I remembered hearing about Norns, the ladies who controlled mortal destinies, but I didn't know their names or their motivation or the proper etiquette for meeting them. Was I supposed to bow? Offer them gifts? Run away screaming?

Next to me, Sam muttered, "This is bad. The Norns only show up in extreme cases."

I didn't want to be an extreme case. I wanted to be an easy case: *Hey, good job. You're a hero. Have a cookie.*

Or even better: *Oops. This was all a mistake. You can go back to your regularly scheduled life.*

Not that my regularly scheduled life was so great, but it beat getting judged unworthy by twelve bearded guys named Erik.

As the Norns got closer, I realized how big they were—at least nine feet tall each. Under their hoods, their faces were beautiful but unnerving—blank white, even their eyes. Trailing behind them came a sheet of fog like a bridal train. They stopped twenty feet in front of my table and turned up their palms. Their skin was like sculpted snow.

Magnus Chase. I couldn't tell which Norn had spoken. The soft disembodied voice resonated through the hall, seeping into my head, turning my skull into an icebox. *Harbinger of the Wolf.*

The crowd stirred uneasily. I'd seen the word *harbinger* somewhere before, maybe in a fantasy novel, but I couldn't remember what it meant. I didn't like the sound of it. I liked the sound of *wolf* even less.

I'd just about decided that running away screaming was my smartest option. Then, in the hands of the middle Norn, fog collected, solidifying into half a dozen runestones. She threw them into the air. They floated above her, each rune expanding into a luminous white symbol as big as a poster board.

I couldn't read runes, but I recognized the one in the center. It was the same symbol I'd picked from the pouch in Uncle Randolph's office:

Fehu, announced the cold voice. *The rune of Frey.*

Thousands of warriors shifted in their seats, clanking restlessly in their armor.

Frey . . . Who was Frey? My mind felt coated with frost. My thoughts were sluggish.

The Norns spoke together, three ghostly voices chanting in unison, shaking leaves from the giant tree:

> *Wrongly chosen, wrongly slain,*
> *A hero Valhalla cannot contain.*
> *Nine days hence the sun must go east,*
> *Ere Sword of Summer unbinds the beast.*

The glowing runes dissolved. The three Norns bowed to me. They melted into the fog and disappeared.

I glanced at Sam. "How often does that happen?"

She looked like she'd been smacked between the eyes with one of Gunilla's hammers. "No. Choosing you *couldn't* have been a mistake. I was told . . . I was promised—"

"Someone *told* you to pick me up?"

Instead of answering, she murmured under her breath—as if running calculations for a rocket that had gone off course.

At the thanes' table, the lords conferred. All around the hall, thousands of einherjar studied me. My stomach folded itself into various origami shapes.

Finally, Helgi faced me. "Magnus Chase, son of Frey, your destiny is troubling. The lords of Valhalla must think on this further. For the time being, you shall be welcomed as a comrade. You are one of the einherjar now. That cannot be reversed, even if it was a mistake."

He scowled at Sam. "Samirah al-Abbas, the Norns themselves have pronounced your judgment in error. Do you have any defense?"

Sam's eyes widened as if she'd just realized something. "The son of Frey . . ." She looked around the room desperately. "Einherjar, don't you see? This is the son of Frey! Surt himself was on that bridge! That means the sword . . ." She turned to the thanes' table. "Gunilla, you *must* see what that means. We have to find that sword! A quest, immediately—"

Helgi banged his fist on the table. "Enough! Samirah, you stand in judgment for a grave mistake. It is not your place to tell us what to do. It is *definitely* not your place to order a quest!"

"I did not make a mistake," Sam said. "I did as I was ordered! I—"

"Ordered?" Helgi narrowed his eyes. "Ordered by whom?"

Sam's mouth shut. She seemed to deflate.

Helgi nodded grimly. "I see. Captain Gunilla, before I announce the thanes' judgment on this Valkyrie, do you wish to speak?"

Gunilla stirred. The gleam in her eyes was gone. She looked like someone who'd gotten in line for the merry-go-round and unexpectedly found herself trapped on a roller coaster.

"I—" She shook her head. "No, my lord. I—I have nothing to add."

"Very well," said Helgi. "Samirah al-Abbas, for your poor judgment with this einherji Magnus Chase, and for your past mistakes, the thanes rule that you be expelled from the sisterhood of Valkyries. You are hereby stripped of your powers and privileges. Return to Midgard in disgrace!"

Sam grabbed my arm. "Magnus, listen to me. You have to find the sword. You have to stop them—"

Like a camera flash: a burst of light and Sam was gone. Her half-eaten meal and the bread crumbs around her seat were the only signs she'd ever existed.

"So concludes our feast," Helgi announced. "I will see you all tomorrow on the field of battle! Sleep well, and dream of glorious death!"

SEVENTEEN

I Did Not Ask for Biceps

I DIDN'T SLEEP MUCH. I definitely didn't dream of glorious death. Been there, done that, got the afterlife.

While I was at dinner, my sofa had been put back and repaired. I sat on it and thumbed through my old children's book of Norse mythology, but it didn't have much about Frey. One tiny picture showed a blond guy in a tunic frolicking in the woods, a blond lady at his side, a couple of cats playing at their feet.

Frey was the god of spring and summer! read the caption. *He was the god of wealth, abundance, and fertility. His twin sister, Freya, the goddess of love, was very pretty! She had cats!*

I tossed the book aside. Great. My dad was a D-list god who frolicked in the woods. He was probably eliminated early last season on *Dancing with the Asgardians.*

Did it crush me to learn this? Not really. You might not believe it, but my dad's identity had never been a big deal to me. It wasn't like I ever felt incomplete—like if only I knew my dad, my life would make sense. I knew who I was. I was Natalie Chase's son. As for life making sense . . . I'd seen too much weirdness to expect that.

Still, I had a lot of items on my *I-don't-get-it* list. At the very top: How could a homeless kid have a dad who was the god of abundance and wealth? Talk about a cruel joke.

Also, why would I get targeted by a big bad dude like Surt? If he was the lord of Muspellheim, High King Roasty Toasty, shouldn't he pick on more interesting heroes, like the children of Thor? At least their dad had a movie franchise. Frey didn't even have his own cats. He had to borrow his sister's.

And the Sword of Summer . . . assuming that was the blade I had pulled from the Charles River, how had it ended up there? Why was it so important? Uncle Randolph had been searching for it for years. Sam's last words to me were about finding the sword again. If it had belonged to my dad, and my dad was an immortal god, why had he allowed his weapon to sit at the bottom of a river for a thousand years?

I stared at the empty fireplace. The Norns' words kept playing in my head, though I wanted to forget them.

Harbinger of the Wolf. I remembered what a harbinger was now: something that signaled the arrival of a powerful force, like a doorman announcing the president, or a red sky before a hurricane. I did not want to be the harbinger of the wolf. I'd seen enough wolves to last me an eternal lifetime. I wanted to be the harbinger of ice cream, or falafel.

Wrongly chosen, wrongly slain.

A little late to announce that now. I was a freaking ein-herji. My name was on the door. I had a key to the minibar.

A hero Valhalla cannot contain.

I liked this line better. Maybe it meant I could bust out of here. Or I guessed it could mean that the thanes would vaporize me in a burst of light or feed me to their magical goat.

Nine days hence the sun must go east,
Ere Sword of Summer unbinds the beast.

Those lines bothered me the most. Last I checked, the sun moved east to west. And who was the beast? I was betting a wolf, because it's always a stinking wolf. If the sword was supposed to let loose a wolf, the sword should've stayed lost.

Some memory nagged at me . . . a bound wolf. I stared at the children's book of mythology, half tempted to pick it up again. But I was already unsettled enough.

Magnus, listen to me, Sam had said. *You have to find the sword. You have to stop them.*

I felt bad about Samirah al-Abbas. I was still miffed at her for bringing me here, especially if it had been a mistake, but I didn't want to see her kicked out of the Valkyries because some doctored video made me look like a doofus. (Okay, *more* of a doofus than usual.)

I decided I should sleep. I didn't feel tired, but if I stayed awake thinking any longer, my brain would overheat.

I tried the bed. Too soft. I ended up in the atrium, sprawled on the grass, gazing at the stars through the tree branches.

At some point, I must have fallen asleep.

A sharp sound startled me awake—a branch cracking. Someone cursed.

Above me, the sky was turning gray in the predawn light. A few leaves helicoptered through the air. Branches bobbed as if something heavy had just scrambled through them.

I lay still, listening, watching. Nothing. Had I imagined that voice?

Over in the foyer, a piece of paper slid under my doorway.

I sat up groggily.

Maybe the management was giving me the bill and letting me check out. I staggered toward the door.

My hand trembled as I picked up the paper, but it wasn't a bill. It was a handwritten note in really nice cursive:

> *Hi, neighbor.*
> *Join us in lounge 19 for breakfast. Down the hall*
> *to the left. Bring your weapons and armor.*
> *T.J.*

T.J. . . . Thomas Jefferson, Jr., the guy across the hall.

After the fiasco last night, I didn't know why he'd want to invite me to breakfast. I also didn't understand why I needed weapons and armor. Maybe Viking bagels fought back.

I was tempted to barricade my door and hide in my room. Perhaps everyone would leave me alone. Maybe once all the warriors were busy with their Bikram yoga to the death, I could sneak out and find an exit to Boston.

On the other hand, I wanted answers. I couldn't shake the idea that if this was a place for the brave dead, my mom might be here somewhere. Or someone might know which afterlife she *had* gone to. At least this guy T.J. seemed friendly. I could hang with him for a while and see what he could tell me.

I trudged to the bathroom.

I was afraid the toilet would be some Viking death machine with ax blades and a flush-operated crossbow, but it worked like a normal one. It definitely wasn't any scarier than the public restrooms in the Common.

The medicine cabinet was stocked with all my usual toiletries . . . or at least the toiletries I *used* to like when I had a home.

And the shower . . . I tried to remember the last time I'd had a leisurely hot shower. Sure, I'd arrived in Valhalla feeling magically dry-cleaned, but after a bad night's sleep in the atrium, I was ready for a good old-fashioned scrub down.

I peeled off my layers of shirts and almost screamed.

What was wrong with my chest? Why did my arms look that way? What were those weird bulgy areas?

Usually I avoided looking at my reflection. I wasn't somebody I wanted to see on a regular basis. But now I faced the mirror.

My hair was the same, a bit less grimy and tangled, but still hanging to my jawline in a curtain of dirty blond, parted in the middle.

You look like Kurt Cobain, my mom used to tease me. *I loved Kurt Cobain, except for the fact that he died.*

Well, guess what, Mom? I thought. *I have that in common with him too now!*

My eyes were gray—more like my cousin Annabeth's than my mom's. They had a haunted, scary emptiness to them, but that was normal. The look had served me well on the streets.

My upper body, however, I hardly recognized. Ever since my bad asthma days when I was little, I'd always been on the scrawny side. Even with all the hiking and camping, I'd had a concave chest, sticking-out ribs, and skin so pale you could trace the road map of blue veins.

Now . . . those strange new bulgy areas looked suspiciously like muscles.

Don't get me wrong. It wasn't as dramatic as turning into Captain America. I was still lean and pale, but my arms had definition. My chest didn't look like it would collapse in the next strong wind. My skin was smoother, less translucent. All the rashes and nicks and bites that came from living on the street had disappeared. Even the scar on my left palm, where I'd cut myself on a hunting knife at age ten, had vanished.

I remembered how strong I'd felt when I first arrived at Valhalla, how I'd tossed my sofa across the room last night. I hadn't really stopped to think about it.

What had Hunding called Valhalla . . . *an upgrade?*

I made a fist.

I'm not sure what came over me. I guess when I realized that even my body wasn't my own, the anger, fear, and uncertainty of the last twenty-four hours reached critical mass. I'd been plucked out of my life. I'd been threatened, humiliated, and forcibly upgraded. I hadn't asked for a suite. I hadn't asked for biceps.

I hit the wall. Literally.

My fist went straight through the tile, the drywall, and a two-by-four stud. I pulled out my hand. I wriggled my fingers. Nothing felt broken.

I regarded the fist-shaped hole I'd made above the towel bar. "Yep," I grumbled. "Housekeeping loves me."

The shower helped calm me down. Afterward, wrapped in a fluffy HV-embroidered bathrobe, I padded to the closet to search for clothes. Inside were three sets of blue jeans, three green T-shirts (all marked PROPERTY OF HOTEL VALHALLA), underwear, socks, a pair of good running shoes, and a sheathed sword. Leaning against the ironing board was a circular green shield with the golden rune of Frey painted in the middle.

Okay, then. I guess I knew what I was wearing today.

I spent ten minutes trying to figure out how to position the sword's sheath on my belt. I was left-handed. Did that mean the sword went on the right? Were left-handed swords different from right-handed ones?

I attempted to draw the blade and just about ripped my pants off. Oh, yeah, I was going to be a hit on the battlefield.

I practiced swinging the sword. I wondered if it would start humming and guiding my hand, the way the sword on the bridge had done when I faced Surt. But no. This blade seemed to be a regular piece of non-humming metal with no cruise-control feature. I managed to sheathe it without losing any fingers. I slung the shield across my back, the way the warriors at dinner last night had been wearing theirs. The strap dug into my neck and made me want to gag.

I looked in the mirror again.

"You, sir," I muttered, "look like a huge dork."

My reflection did not argue.

I went out to find breakfast and kill it with my sword.

EIGHTEEN

I Do Mighty Combat with Eggs

"THERE HE IS." T.J. rose and grabbed my hand. "Sit. Join us. You made quite a first impression last night!"

He was dressed the same as yesterday: a blue wool army jacket over a green hotel T-shirt, jeans, and leather boots.

With him sat the half-troll X, the redhead Mallory Keen, and a guy I guessed was Halfborn Gunderson, who looked like Robinson Crusoe on steroids. His shirt was a patchwork of animal pelts. His hide pants were in tatters. Even by Viking standards his beard was wild, decorated with most of a cheese omelet.

My four hallmates made room for me at the table, which felt pretty good.

Compared to the main feast hall, lounge nineteen was downright intimate. Scattered around the room were a dozen tables, most unoccupied. In one corner, a fireplace crackled in front of a beat-up sofa. Along the other wall, a buffet table was laden with every kind of breakfast food imaginable (and a few kinds I had *never* imagined).

T.J. and company had parked themselves in front of a big picture window overlooking a vast field of ice and swirling snow. It made no sense, considering that it was summer in my atrium right down the hall, but I'd already learned that the hotel's geography was wack.

"That's Niflheim," T.J. explained, "the realm of ice. The view changes daily, cycling through the Nine Worlds."

"The Nine Worlds . . ." I stared at my scrambled eggs, wondering which solar system they'd come from. "I keep hearing about nine worlds. Hard to believe."

Mallory Keen blew powdered sugar off her doughnut. "Believe it, newbie. I've visited six of them so far."

"Five here." Halfborn grinned, showing me the rest of his cheese omelet. "'Course, Midgard hardly counts. That's the human world. Been to Alfheim, Nidavellir, Jotunheim—"

"Disney World," X said.

Mallory sighed. With her red hair, green eyes, and powdered sugar around her mouth, she reminded me of a reverse-color-scheme Joker. "For the last time, you numbskull, Disney World is not one of the nine."

"Why is it called a world, then?" X nodded smugly, the argument won, and went back to his meal, sucking meat from the shell of a large crustacean.

T.J. pushed his empty plate away. "Magnus, I don't know if it helps, but the Nine Worlds aren't really separate planets. They're more like . . . different dimensions, different layers of reality, all connected by the World Tree."

"Thanks," I said. "That's much more confusing."

He laughed. "Yeah, I guess it is."

"The World Tree is the tree in the feast hall?"

"Nah," Mallory said. "The World Tree is *much* bigger. You'll see, sooner or later."

That sounded ominous. I tried to concentrate on my food, but it was difficult with X right next to me demolishing a slimy mutant crab.

I pointed at T.J.'s jacket. "That's a Civil War uniform?"

"Private in the Fifty-Fourth Massachusetts, my friend. I'm a Boston boy, same as you. I just got here a little earlier."

I did the calculations. "You died in battle a hundred and fifty years ago?"

T.J. beamed. "The assault on Fort Wagner, South Carolina. My dad was Tyr, god of courage, law, and trial by combat. My mom was a runaway slave."

I tried to fit that into my new worldview: a teenager from the 1860s, the son of a former slave and a Norse god, who was now having breakfast with me in an extra-dimensional hotel.

X belched, which put things in perspective.

"Gods of Asgard!" Mallory complained. "That smell!"

"Sorry," X grunted.

"Is your name really X?" I asked.

"No. My real name is—" The half-troll said something that started with *K*s and went on for about thirty seconds.

Halfborn wiped his hands on his pelt shirt. "You see? Nobody can pronounce that. We call him X."

"X," agreed X.

"He's another one of Sam al-Abbas's acquisitions," T.J. said. "X stumbled across a dogfight . . . one of those illegal ones in, where, Chicago?"

"Chee-cah-go," affirmed X.

"He saw what was going on and went nuts. Started smashing up the place, walloping the bettors, freeing the animals."

"Dogs should fight for themselves," X said. "Not for greedy

humans. They should be wild and free. They should not be kept in cages."

I didn't want to argue with the big guy, but I wasn't sure I liked the idea of wild dogs fighting for themselves. That sounded a lot like wolves—an animal I refused to harbinge.

"Anyway," T.J. said, "it turned into a full-scale battle: X against a bunch of gangsters with automatic weapons. They finally killed him, but X took down a lot of scumbags and freed a lot of dogs. That was what . . . a month ago?"

X grunted and continued sucking his shellfish.

T.J. spread his hands. "Samirah judged him worthy and brought him here. She got some flak for that decision."

Mallory snorted. "That's putting it mildly. A troll in Valhalla. Who could possibly object?"

"Half-troll," X corrected. "That is my *better* half, Mallory Keen."

"She didn't mean anything, X," T.J. said. "It's just that prejudice dies hard. When I got here in 1863, I wasn't exactly welcomed with open arms, either."

Mallory rolled her eyes. "Then you won them over with your dazzling personality. I swear, you lot are giving floor nineteen a bad name. And now we have Magnus."

Halfborn leaned toward me. "Don't mind Mallory. She's a sweetheart, once you get past the fact that she's a horrible person."

"Shut up, Halfborn."

The big guy chuckled. "She's just grumpy because she died trying to disarm a car bomb with her face."

Mallory's ears turned as red as hummingbird juice. "I didn't—it wasn't— Argh!"

"Magnus, don't worry about that mess last night," continued Halfborn. "Folks will forget about it in a few decades. Believe me, I've seen it all. I died during the Viking invasion of East Anglia, fought under the banner of Ivar the Boneless. I took twenty arrows in the chest protecting my thane!"

"Ouch," I said.

Halfborn shrugged. "I've been here for . . . oh, going on twelve hundred years now."

I stared at him. Despite his bulk and his beard, Halfborn looked maybe eighteen, tops. "How do you stand it without going crazy? And why do they call you Halfborn?"

His smile faded. "Second question first . . . when I was born, I was so big, strong, and ugly that my mother said I looked like I'd been half born, half carved from rock. The name stuck."

"And you're still ugly," Mallory muttered.

"As for how to avoid going crazy here . . . Some do lose it, Magnus. Waiting for Ragnarok is hard. The trick is to keep busy. There's plenty to do here. Me, I've learned a dozen languages, including English. I earned a doctorate in Germanic literature, and I learned to knit."

T.J. nodded. "That's why I invited you to breakfast, Magnus."

"To learn knitting?"

"To keep active! Spending too much time alone in your room can be dangerous. If you isolate yourself, you start to fade. Some of the old-timers . . ." He cleared his throat. "It doesn't matter. You're here! Just keep showing up every morning until Doomsday, and you'll be fine."

I stared out the window at the swirling snow. I thought about Sam's warning to find the sword, the Norns chanting that something bad would happen in nine days. "You said you've visited the other worlds. That means you can leave the hotel."

The group exchanged uneasy glances.

"Yes," Halfborn said. "But our main job is to wait for Ragnarok. Train, train, train."

"I rode the train at Disney World," said X.

Maybe he meant it as a jest. The half-troll seemed to have two facial expressions: wet cement and dry cement.

"Occasionally," said T.J., "einherjar are sent into the Nine Worlds on missions."

"Tracking down monsters," Mallory offered. "Killing giants who cross into Midgard. Stopping witches and wights. And of course, dealing with rogues—"

"Wights? Rogues?" I asked.

"Point is," said Halfborn, "we only leave Valhalla under orders from Odin or the thanes."

"But, hypothetically," I said, "I could go back to earth, Midgard, whatever—"

"Hypothetically, yes," T.J. said. "Look, I know that business with the Norns must be driving you bonkers, but we don't know what the prophecy means. Give the thanes some time to decide what to do. You can't rush off and do something stupid."

"Gods forbid," said Mallory. "We *never* do anything stupid. Like that late-night pizza run to Santarpio's. That never happened."

"Shut up, woman," Halfborn growled.

"*Woman?*" Mallory reached for the knife at her belt. "Watch your words, you overgrown Swedish hamster."

"Hold on," I said. "You guys know how to sneak out of—"

T.J. coughed loudly. "Sorry, I didn't hear that. I'm sure you weren't asking about anything against the rules. Magnus, first of all: if you returned to Midgard so soon, how would you explain it to those who knew you? Everyone thinks you're dead. Usually, *if* we go back, we wait until everyone we knew is dead. It's easier all the way around. Besides, it takes a while, sometimes years, for your einherji strength to develop fully."

I tried to imagine waiting here for years. I didn't have many friends or relatives to go back to. Still, I didn't want to be stuck here—learning new languages, knitting sweaters—for ages. After seeing my cousin Annabeth, I kind of wanted to reconnect with her before she died. And if Samirah was right about my mom not being in Valhalla . . . I wanted to find her, wherever she was.

"But it's possible to leave without permission," I persisted. "Maybe not forever, just for a while."

T.J. shifted uncomfortably. "Valhalla has doors into every world. The hotel is designed that way. Most exits are guarded, but . . . well, there are a lot of ways to Boston, since Boston is the center of Midgard."

I glanced around the table. Nobody was laughing. "It is?"

"Sure," T.J. said. "It's right at the trunk of the World Tree, the easiest spot from which to access the other worlds. Why do you think Boston is called the Hub of the Universe?"

"Wishful thinking?"

"No. Mortals have always known there was something about that location, even if they couldn't put their finger on what it was. The Vikings searched for the center of the world for years. They knew the entrance to Asgard was in the west. That's one reason they kept exploring into North America. When they met the Native Americans—"

"We called them the skraelings," Halfborn said. "Vicious fighters. I liked them."

"—the natives had all sorts of stories about how strong the spirit world was in this area. Later, when the Puritans settled, well . . . John Winthrop's vision of a shining 'City on a Hill'? That wasn't just a metaphor. He had a vision of Asgard, a glimpse into the other worlds. And the Salem witch trials? Hysteria caused by magic seeping into Midgard. Edgar Allan Poe was born in Boston. It's no accident his most famous poem was about a raven, one of Odin's sacred animals."

"Enough." Mallory gave me a disgusted look. "T.J. will take forever when answering a yes/no question. The answer is yes, Magnus. It is possible to leave, with or without permission."

X cracked a crab claw. "You would not be immortal."

"Yeah," T.J. said. "That's the second big problem. In Valhalla, you can't die—not permanently. You'll just keep getting resurrected. It's part of the training."

I remembered the guy who had gotten impaled in the lobby and dragged off by wolves. Hunding had said he would be fine again by dinner.

"But outside of Valhalla?"

"Out in the Nine Worlds," T.J. said, "you're still an einherji. You're faster and stronger and tougher than any regular mortal. But if you die out there, you stay dead. Your soul might go to Helheim. Or you might simply dissolve into the primordial void—Ginnungagap. Hard to know. It's not worth the risk."

"Unless . . ." Halfborn picked some egg out of his beard. "Unless he really *did* find the sword of Frey, and the legends are true—"

"It's Magnus's first day," T.J. said. "Let's not go into that. He's already freaked out enough."

"Freak me out more," I said. "What legends exactly?"

In the hallway, a horn blasted. At the other tables, einher-jar started to get up and clear their plates.

Halfborn rubbed his hands eagerly. "Talking will have to wait. It's battle time!"

"Battle time," X agreed.

T.J. grimaced. "Magnus, we should probably warn you about the first day initiation. Don't be discouraged if—"

"Oh, shush," said Mallory. "Don't spoil the surprise!" She gave me a powdered sugar smile. "I can't wait to see the new boy get dismembered!"

NINETEEN

Do Not Call Me Beantown. Like, *Ever*

I TOLD MY NEW FRIENDS I was allergic to dismemberment. They just laughed and herded me toward the combat arena. This is why I don't like making new friends.

The battlefield was so huge I couldn't process what I was seeing.

Back in the good old days when I was a street kid, I used to sleep on rooftops in the summertime. I could see the entire cityscape of Boston from Fenway Park to Bunker Hill. Valhalla's battlefield was bigger than that. It offered maybe three square miles of interesting places to die, all contained within the hotel like an interior courtyard.

On all four sides rose the walls of the building—cliffs of white marble and gold-railed balconies, some hung with banners, some decorated with shields, some fitted with catapults. The upper floors seemed to dissolve in the hazy glow of the sky, as blank white as a fluorescent light.

In the center of the field loomed a few craggy hills. Clumps of forest marbled the landscape. The outer rim was mostly rolling pastures, with a river as wide as the Charles snaking through. Several villages dotted the riverbank, maybe for those who preferred their warfare urban.

From hundreds of doors in the walls around the field,

battalions of warriors were streaming in, their weapons and armor glinting in the harsh light. Some einherjar wore full plate mail like medieval knights. Others wore chain mail shirts, breeches, and combat boots. A few sported camo fatigues and AK-47s. One guy wore nothing but a Speedo. He'd painted himself blue and was armed only with a baseball bat. Across his chest were the words COME AT ME, BRO.

"I feel underdressed," I said.

X cracked his knuckles. "Armor does not make victory. Neither do weapons."

Easy for him to say. He was larger than some sovereign nations.

Halfborn Gunderson was also taking the minimalist approach. He'd stripped down to nothing but his leggings, though he did sport a pair of vicious-looking double-bladed axes. Standing next to anyone else, Halfborn would've looked massive. Next to X, he looked like a toddler . . . with a beard, abs, and axes.

T.J. fastened his bayonet to his rifle. "Magnus, if you want more than the basic equipment, you'll have to capture it or trade for it. The hotel armories take red gold, or they work on a barter system."

"Is that how you got your rifle?"

"Nah, this is the weapon I died with. I hardly ever fire it. Bullets don't have much effect on einherjar. Those guys out there with the assault rifles? That's all flash and noise. They're the least dangerous people on the field. But this bayonet? It's bone steel, a gift from my father. Bone steel works just fine."

"Bone steel."

"Yeah. You'll learn."

My sword hand was already sweating. My shield felt much too flimsy. "So which groups are we fighting against?"

Halfborn clapped me on the back. "All of them! Vikings fight in small groups, my friend. We are your shield brothers."

"And shield sister," Mallory said. "Though some of us are shield idiots."

Halfborn ignored her. "Stick with us, Magnus, and . . . well, you won't do fine. You'll get killed quickly. But stick with us anyway. We'll wade into battle and slaughter as many as possible!"

"That's your plan?"

Halfborn tilted his head. "Why would I have a plan?"

"Oh, sometimes we do," said T.J. "Wednesdays are siege warfare. That's more complicated. Thursdays they bring out the dragons."

Mallory drew her sword and serrated dagger. "Today is free-for-all combat. I love Tuesdays."

From a thousand different balconies, horns blasted. The einherjar charged into battle.

Until that morning, I'd never understood the term *blood-bath*. Within a few minutes, we were literally slipping in the stuff.

We'd just stepped onto the field when an ax flew out of nowhere and stuck in my shield, the blade going right through the wood above my arm.

Mallory yelled and threw her knife, which sank into the ax thrower's chest. He fell to his knees, laughing. "Good one!" Then he collapsed, dead.

Halfborn waded through enemies, his axes whirling, chopping off heads and limbs until he looked like he'd been playing paintball with only red paint. It was disgusting. And horrifying. And the most disturbing part? The einherjar treated it like a game. They killed with glee. They died as if someone had just taken down their avatar in *Call of Duty*. I'd never liked that game.

"Ah, that sucks," one guy muttered as he studied the four arrows in his chest.

Another yelled, "I'll get you tomorrow, Trixie!" before falling sideways, a spear stuck through his gut.

T.J. sang "The Battle Hymn of the Republic" while he stabbed and parried with his bayonet.

X smashed through one group after another. A dozen arrows now stuck out of his back like porcupine quills, but they didn't seem to bother him. Every time his fist connected, an einherji turned two-dimensional.

As for me, I shuffled along in abject terror, my shield raised, my sword dragging. I'd been told that death here wasn't permanent, but I had a hard time believing it. A bunch of warriors with sharp pointy objects were trying to kill me. I didn't want to be killed.

I managed to parry a sword strike. I deflected a spear with my shield. I had a clear opening to stab one girl whose guard was down, but I just couldn't make myself do it.

That was a mistake. Her ax bit into my thigh. Pain flared all the way up to my neck.

Mallory cut the girl down. "Come on, Chase, keep moving! You'll get used to the pain after a while."

"Great." I grimaced. "Something to look forward to."

T.J. jabbed his bayonet through the faceplate of a medieval

knight. "Let's take that hill!" He pointed to a nearby ridge at the edge of the woods.

"Why?" I yelled.

"Because it's a hill!"

"He loves taking hills," Mallory grumbled. "It's a Civil War thing."

We waded through the battle, heading for the high ground. My thigh still hurt, but the bleeding had stopped. Was that normal?

T.J. raised his rifle. He yelled, "Charge!" just as a javelin ran him through from behind.

"T.J.!" I yelled.

He caught my eye, managed a weak smile, then face-planted in the mud.

"For Frigg's sake!" Mallory cursed. "Come on, newbie."

She grabbed my arm and pulled me along. More javelins sailed over my head.

"You guys do this every *day*?" I demanded.

"No. Like we told you—Thursdays are dragons."

"But—"

"Hey, Beantown, the whole point is to get used to the horrors of battle. You think this is bad? Wait until we actually have to fight at Ragnarok."

"Why am *I* Beantown? T.J.'s from Boston. Why isn't *he* Beantown?"

"Because T.J. is slightly less annoying."

We reached the edge of the woods. X and Halfborn guarded our backs, slowing down the pursuing horde. And the enemies *were* a horde now. All the scattered groups within sight had stopped fighting one another and were after us. Some pointed at me. Some called my name, and not in a friendly way.

"Yeah, they've spotted you." Mallory sighed. "When I said I wanted to see you eviscerated, I didn't mean I wanted to be standing *next* to you. Oh, well."

I almost asked why everyone was after me. But I got it. I was a newbie. Of *course* the other einherjar would gang up on me and the other newcomers. Lars Ahlstrom was probably already decapited. Dede might be running around with her arms cut off. The veteran einherjar would make this as painful and terrifying for us as possible to see how we handled ourselves. That made me angry.

We climbed the hill, weaving from tree to tree for cover. Halfborn threw himself into a group of twenty guys who were following us. He destroyed them all. He came up laughing, an insane light in his eyes. He was bleeding from a dozen wounds. A dagger stuck out of his chest, right over his heart.

"How is he not dead yet?" I asked.

"He's a berserker." Mallory glanced back, her expression a mix of disdain and exasperation and something else . . . admiration? "That idiot will keep fighting until he is literally hacked to pieces."

Something clicked in my head. Mallory *liked* Halfborn. You don't call somebody an idiot that many times unless you're really into them. Under different circumstances, I might have teased her, but while she was distracted there was a wet *thwack*. An arrow sprouted from her neck.

She scowled at me as if to say, *Totally your fault.*

She collapsed. I knelt at her side, putting my hand on her neck. I could feel the life seeping out of her. I could sense the severed artery, the fading heartbeat, all the damage that had to be mended. My fingers seemed to grow warmer. If I had a little more time—

"Look out!" shouted X.

I raised my shield. A sword clanged against it. I pushed back, knocking the attacker downhill. My arms ached. My head was throbbing, but somehow I got to my feet.

Halfborn was forty yards away, surrounded by a mob of warriors all jabbing him with spears, shooting him full of arrows. Somehow he kept fighting, but even *he* wouldn't be able to stand much longer.

X ripped a guy's AK-47 out of his hands and smacked him over the head with it.

"Go, Magnus Beantown," said the half-troll. "Take the crest for floor nineteen!"

"My nickname will not be Beantown," I muttered. "I refuse."

I stumbled uphill until I reached the summit. I put my back against a big oak tree while X smashed and backhanded and head-butted Vikings into oblivion.

An arrow hit my shoulder, pinning me to the tree. The pain almost made me black out, but I snapped the shaft and pulled myself free. The bleeding stopped instantly. I felt the wound closing as if somebody had filled it with hot wax.

A shadow passed over me—something large and dark hurtling from the sky. It took me a millisecond to realize it was a boulder, probably shot from a balcony catapult. It took me another millisecond to realize where it would land.

Too late. Before I could shout a warning to X, the half-troll and a dozen other einherjar disappeared under a twenty-ton chunk of limestone, the side of which was painted: WITH LOVE FROM FLOOR 63.

A hundred warriors stared at the rock. Leaves and broken twigs fluttered around them. Then the einherjar all turned toward me.

Another arrow hit me in the chest. I screamed, more in rage than in pain, and pulled it out.

"Wow," one of the Vikings commented. "He's a fast healer."

"Try a spear," someone suggested. "Try *two* spears."

They spoke as if I wasn't worth addressing—as if I were a cornered animal they could experiment with.

Twenty or thirty einherjar raised their weapons. The anger inside me exploded. I shouted, expelling energy like the shockwave from a bomb. Bowstrings snapped. Swords fell out of their owners' hands. Spears and guns and axes went flying into the trees.

As quickly as it started, the surge of power shut off. All around me, a hundred einherjar had been stripped of their weapons.

The blue-painted guy stood in the front row, his baseball bat at his feet. He stared at me in shock. "What just happened?"

The warrior next to him had an eye patch and red leather armor decorated with silver curlicues. Cautiously, he crouched and retrieved his fallen ax.

"Alf seidr," said Eye Patch. "Nicely done, son of Frey. I haven't seen a trick like that in centuries. But bone steel is better."

My eyes crossed as his ax blade spun toward my face. Then everything went dark.

TWENTY

Come to the Dark Side.
We Have Pop-Tarts

A FAMILIAR VOICE SAID, "Dead again, eh?"

I opened my eyes. I was standing in a pavilion ringed with gray stone columns. Outside was nothing but empty sky. The air was thin. Cold wind whipped across the marble floor, stirring the fire in the central hearth, making the flames gutter in the braziers on either side of the tall dais. Three steps led up to a double throne—a loveseat of white wood carved with intricate shapes of animals, birds, and tree branches. The seat itself was lined with ermine. Sprawling across it, eating Pop-Tarts from a silver wrapper, was the man in the Red Sox jersey.

"Welcome to Hlidskjalf." He grinned, his scarred lips like the sides of a zipper. "The High Seat of Odin."

"You're not Odin," I said, using process of elimination. "You're Loki."

Sox Man chuckled. "Nothing escapes your keen intellect."

"First, what are we doing here? Second, why is Odin's throne named Lid Scalp?"

"*Hlidskjalf.* Put an *h* at the beginning and an *f* at the end. On that first letter you have to sound like you're hawking spit."

"On further reflection, I don't care."

"You should. This is where it all started. That's the answer to your second question—why we're here." He patted the seat next to him. "Join me. Have a Pop-Tart."

"Uh, no thanks."

"Your loss." He broke off the edge of a pastry and tossed it into his mouth. "This purple icing . . . I don't know what flavor it's supposed to be, but it is *insanely* good."

My pulse throbbed in my neck, which was strange since I was dreaming, and probably also dead.

Loki's eyes unnerved me. They had that same intense glow as Sam's, but Sam kept the flames under control. Loki's gaze flitted restlessly like the fire in the hearth, pushed by the wind, looking for anything it could set ablaze.

"Frey once sat here." He stroked the ermine fur. "Do you know the story?"

"No, but . . . isn't it illegal for anyone to sit there except Odin?"

"Oh, yes. Well, Odin and Frigg, the king and queen. They can sit here and see anywhere in the Nine Worlds. They merely have to concentrate and they will find whatever they are look-ing for. But if anyone else sits here . . ." He made *tsk-tsk* sounds. "The throne's magic can be a terrible curse. *I* certainly would never risk it if this weren't an illusion. But your father did. It was his one moment of rebellion." Loki took another bite of purple Pop-Tart. "I always admired him for that."

"And?"

"And instead of seeing what he was looking for, he saw what he most desired. It ruined his life. It's the reason he lost his sword. He—" Loki winced. "Excuse me."

He turned his head, his features contorting like he was about to sneeze. Then he let loose a scream of agony. When he faced me again, wisps of steam rose from the scar tissue across the bridge of his nose.

"Sorry," he said. "Every so often the poison splashes in my eyes."

"The poison." I remembered a fragment of a myth. "You killed somebody. The gods captured you and tied you up. There was something about poison. Where are you now, really?"

He gave me that twisted grin. "Right where I always am. The gods had me, ah, properly restrained. But that's not important. I can still send out splinters of my essence from time to time—like I'm doing now, to speak with my favorite friends!"

"Just because you're wearing a Sox jersey does not mean we're friends."

"I'm hurt!" His eyes sparkled. "My daughter Samirah saw something in you. We could help each other."

"You ordered her to take me to Valhalla?"

"Oh, no. That wasn't my idea. You, Magnus Chase, are of interest to many different parties. Some of them are not as charming or helpful as I."

"How about being charming and helpful to your daughter? She got kicked out of the Valkyries for choosing me."

His smile faded. "That's the gods for you. They banished me, too, and how many times did I save their hides? Don't worry about Samirah. She is strong. She'll be fine. I'm more worried about *you*."

Cold wind blew through the pavilion, so strong it pushed me a few inches across the polished stone floor.

Loki crumpled his Pop-Tart wrapper. "You'll be waking up soon. Before you go, some advice."

"I don't suppose I can refuse."

"The Sword of Summer," Loki said. "When your father sat on this throne, what he saw doomed him. He gave his sword away. It passed to his servant and messenger, Skirnir."

For a moment I was back on the Longfellow Bridge, the sword humming in my hand as if trying to speak.

"Uncle Randolph mentioned Skirnir," I said. "His descendant was in that shipwreck."

Loki pantomimed wild applause. "And there the sword lay for a thousand years, waiting for someone to reclaim it—someone who had the right to wield the blade."

"Me."

"Ah, but you aren't the only one who can use the sword. We know what will happen at Ragnarok. The Norns have told us our fates. Frey . . . poor Frey, because of the choices he made, will die at the hands of Surt. The lord of the fire giants will cut him down with his own lost sword."

A spike of pain hit me between the eyes, right about where the einherji's ax had killed me. "That's why Surt wants the sword. So he'll be ready for Ragnarok."

"Not only that. He'll use the sword to set in motion a chain of events to hasten Doomsday. In eight days, unless you stop him, he will cut loose my son, the Wolf."

"Your son . . . ?" My arms were evaporating. My eyesight grew hazy. Too many questions crowded into my head. "Wait . . . aren't you destined to fight against the gods at Ragnarok too?"

"Yes, but that was the *gods'* choice, not mine. The thing about fate, Magnus: even if we can't change the big picture, our choices can alter the details. *That's* how we rebel against destiny, how we make our mark. What will you choose to do?"

His image flickered. For a moment I saw him spread-eagle on a slab of stone, his wrists and ankles tied with slimy ropes, his body writhing in pain. Then I saw him in a hospital bed, a female doctor leaning over him, her hand resting gently on his forehead. She looked like an older version of Sam—curls of dark hair escaping from a scarlet headscarf, her mouth set tight with concern.

Loki appeared on the throne again, brushing Pop-Tart crumbs from his Red Sox jersey. "I won't tell you what to do, Magnus. That's the difference between me and the other gods. I'll only ask you this question: when you get a chance to sit on Odin's throne—and that day is coming—will you search for your heart's desire, knowing it may doom you as it doomed your father? Think on that, son of Frey. Perhaps we'll speak again, if you survive the next eight days."

My dream changed. Loki vanished. The braziers burst, showering hot coals across the dais, and the High Seat of Odin erupted in flames. The clouds turned into rolling banks of volcanic ash. Above the burning throne, two glowing red eyes appeared in the smoke.

YOU. The voice of Surt washed over me like a flamethrower. *YOU HAVE ONLY DELAYED ME. YOU HAVE EARNED A MORE PAINFUL, MORE PERMANENT DEATH.*

I tried to speak. The heat sucked the oxygen from my lungs. My lips cracked and blistered.

Surt laughed. *THE WOLF THINKS YOU MAY STILL BE USEFUL. I DO NOT. WHEN WE MEET AGAIN, YOU WILL BURN, SON OF FREY. YOU AND YOUR FRIENDS WILL BE MY TINDER. YOU WILL START THE FIRE THAT BURNS THE NINE WORLDS.*

The smoke thickened. I couldn't breathe, couldn't see.

My eyes flew open. I bolted upright, gasping for air. I was in bed in my hotel room. Surt was gone. I touched my face, but it wasn't burned. No ax was embedded there. All my battlefield wounds had vanished.

Still, my whole body was buzzing with alarm. I felt like I'd fallen asleep on active train tracks and the Acela Express had just roared past.

The dream was already erasing itself. I struggled to hold on to the specifics: the throne of Odin; Loki and Pop-Tarts; *my son, the Wolf*; Surt promising to burn the Nine Worlds. Trying to make sense of it was even more painful than getting an ax in my face.

Someone knocked on my door.

Thinking it might be one of my hallmates, I leaped out of bed and ran to answer. I threw open the door, found myself face-to-face with the Valkyrie Gunilla, and only then realized I was wearing nothing but underwear.

Her face turned magenta. Her jaw muscles knotted. "Oh."

"Captain Gorilla," I said. "What an honor."

She recovered quickly, glaring at me like she was trying to activate her freeze-ray vision. "Magnus Chase. I, um—you resurrected with incredible speed."

From her tone, I guessed that she hadn't expected to find me here. But then why had she knocked?

"I wasn't timing my resurrection," I said. "Was it fast?"

"Very." She glanced past me, maybe looking for something. "We have a few hours before dinner. Perhaps I could give you a tour of the hotel, since your own Valkyrie has been dismissed."

"You mean since you *got* her dismissed."

Gunilla turned up her palms. "I don't control the Norns. They decide all our fates."

"That's convenient." I remembered what Loki had said: *Our choices can alter the details.* That's *how we rebel against destiny.* "What about me? Have you—I mean *the Norns*—decided my fate?"

Gunilla scowled. Her posture was stiff and uneasy. Something was bothering her—maybe even scaring her.

"The thanes are discussing your situation now." She unhooked the key ring from her belt. "Take a tour with me. We can talk. If I understand you better, I may be able to speak to the thanes on your behalf. Unless, of course, you want to take your chances without my help. You might get lucky. The thanes might sentence you to bellhop duty for a few centuries. Or washing dishes in the kitchen."

The last thing I wanted was quality time with Gunilla. On the other hand, a tour of the hotel might show me some important features—like the exits. Also, after the dream I'd just had, I didn't want to be alone.

Besides, I could imagine how many dirty dishes would need washing after three rounds of dinner in the feast hall.

"I'll take the tour," I said. "But I should probably put some clothes on first."

TWENTY-ONE

Gunilla Gets Blowtorched and It's Not Funny. Okay, It's a Little Bit Funny

THE MAIN THING I discovered: Valhalla needed GPS. Even Gunilla got turned around in the endless corridors, banquet halls, gardens, and lounges.

At one point we were riding in a service elevator when Gunilla said, "Here's the food court."

The doors opened and a wall of flames engulfed us both.

My heart leaped into my throat. I thought Surt had found me. Gunilla screamed and staggered backward. I smashed random buttons until the doors shut. Then I did my best to put out the burning hem of Gunilla's dress.

"You okay?" My pulse was still racing. Gunilla's arms were covered with patches of steaming red skin.

"My skin will heal," Gunilla said. "My pride may not. That— that was Muspellheim, not the food court."

I wondered if Surt had engineered our little detour somehow, or if elevator doors in Valhalla often opened into the world of fire. I wasn't sure which possibility was more disturbing.

The tightness in Gunilla's voice told me how much pain she was in. I remembered standing over Mallory Keen when she fell in battle—the way I'd been able to sense the damage and how it could be mended if I'd had more time.

I knelt next to the Valkyrie. "May I?"

"What are you—"

I touched her forearm.

My fingers began to steam, drawing the heat from her skin. The redness faded. Her burns disappeared. Even the singed tip of her nose healed.

Gunilla stared at me as if I'd sprouted horns. "How did you . . . ? You weren't burned, either. How?"

"I don't know." My head spun with exhaustion. "Good luck? Healthy living?"

I tried to stand and promptly collapsed.

"Whoa, son of Frey." Gunilla grabbed my arm.

The elevator doors opened again. This time we really were at a food court. The smells of lemon chicken and pizza wafted in.

"Let's keep walking," Gunilla said. "Clear your head."

We got some strange looks as we stumbled through the dining area, me leaning against the Valkyrie captain for support, Gunilla's dress still smoking and tattered.

We turned into a corridor lined with conference rooms. Inside one, a guy in studded leather armor was giving a PowerPoint presentation to a dozen warriors, explaining the weaknesses of mountain trolls.

A few doors down, Valkyries in glittering party hats socialized over cake and ice cream. The birthday candle was shaped like the number 500.

"I think I'm okay now," I told Gunilla. "Thanks."

I wobbled a few steps on my own but managed to stay upright.

"Your healing abilities are remarkable," Gunilla said. "Frey is the god of abundance and fertility, growth and vitality—I guess that explains it. Still, I've never seen an einherji who can heal himself so quickly, much less heal others."

"Your guess is as good as mine," I said. "Normally I have trouble just opening Band-Aids."

"And your immunity to fire?"

I concentrated on the carpet designs, keeping one foot in front of the other. I could walk now, but healing Gunilla's burns had left me feeling like I'd just had a bad case of pneumonia.

"I don't think it's fire immunity," I said. "I've burned myself before. I just . . . I have a high tolerance for extreme temperatures. Cold. Heat. The same thing happened on the Longfellow Bridge when I walked into the flames . . ." My voice faltered. I remembered that Gunilla had edited that video and made me look like a fool. "But you know all about that."

Gunilla didn't seem to notice the sarcasm. She absently stroked one of the hammers in her bandolier as if it were a kitten. "Perhaps. . . . In the beginning of creation, only two worlds existed: Muspellheim and Niflheim, fire and ice. Life rose between those extremes. Frey is the god of moderate climes and the growing season. He represents the middle ground. Perhaps that's why you can resist heat and cold." She shook her head. "I don't know, Magnus Chase. It has been a long time since I met a child of Frey."

"Why? Are we not allowed in Valhalla?"

"Oh, we have some children of Frey from the old days. The kings of Sweden were his descendants, for instance. But we haven't seen a new one in Valhalla for centuries. Frey is Vanir, for one thing."

"Is that bad? Surt called me *Vanir-spawn*."

"That wasn't Surt."

I thought about my dream: those glowing eyes in the smoke. "It *was* Surt."

Gunilla looked like she wanted to argue, but she let it drop. "Whatever the case, the gods are divided into two tribes. The Aesir are mostly gods of war: Odin, Thor, Tyr, and the rest. The Vanir are more like the gods of nature: Frey, Freya, their father, Njord. That's an oversimplification, but anyway—long ago, the two tribes had a war. They almost destroyed the Nine Worlds. They finally settled their differences. They intermarried. They joined forces against the giants. But still they're different clans. Some Vanir have palaces in Asgard, the seat of the Aesir gods, but the Vanir also have their own world, Vanaheim. When a child of the Vanir dies bravely, they don't usually go to Valhalla. More often they go to the Vanir afterlife, overseen by the goddess Freya."

It took me a minute to digest all that. Clans of gods. Wars. Whatever. But that last part, *the Vanir afterlife* . . . "You're telling me there's another place like Valhalla, except for Vanir children, and I'm not there? What if that's where my mom went? What if I was supposed to—"

Gunilla took my arm. Her blue eyes were intense with anger. "That's right, Magnus. Think about what Samirah al-Abbas has done. I'm not saying *all* children of the Vanir go to Folkvanger—"

"You put them in a Volkswagen?"

"*Folkvanger.* It's the name of Freya's hall for the slain."

"Oh."

"My point is, you could have gone there. It would've been more likely. Half the honored dead go to Odin. Half go to

Freya. That was part of the agreement that ended the gods' war eons ago. So why did Samirah bring you here? *Wrongly chosen, wrongly slain.* She's the daughter of Loki, the father of evil. She cannot be trusted."

I wasn't sure how to answer. I hadn't known Samirah all that long, but she seemed pretty nice. Of course, so did her dad, Loki. . . .

"You may not believe this," Gunilla said, "but I'm giving you the benefit of the doubt. I think you may be innocent of Samirah's plans."

"What plans?"

She laughed bitterly. "To hasten Doomsday, of course. To bring the war before we are ready. That's what Loki wants."

I was tempted to protest that Loki had told me otherwise. He seemed more interested in *stopping* Surt from getting my dad's sword. . . . But I decided it wouldn't be wise to tell Gunilla I'd been having chats with the father of evil.

"If you hate Sam so much," I said, "why did you let her be a Valkyrie in the first place?"

"That wasn't my choice. I oversee the Valkyries, but Odin picks them. Samirah al-Abbas was the last Valkyrie he chose, two years ago, under what were . . . unusual circumstances. The All-Father has not appeared in Valhalla since."

"You think Sam killed him?"

I meant it as a joke, but Gunilla actually seemed to consider it. "I think Samirah should never have been chosen as a Valkyrie. I think she's working for her father as a spy and a saboteur. Getting her kicked out of Valhalla was the best thing I ever did."

"Wow."

"Magnus, you don't know her. There was another child of Loki here once. He—he wasn't what he seemed. He—" She stopped herself, looking like someone had just stepped on her heart. "Never mind. I swore to myself I wouldn't be fooled again. I intend to delay Ragnarok for as long as possible."

The edge of fear had crept back into her voice. She didn't sound much like the daughter of a war god.

"Why delay?" I asked. "Isn't Ragnarok what you're all training for? It's like your big graduation party."

"You don't understand," she said. "Come. There's something I need to show you. We will go through the gift shop."

When she said *gift shop*, I imagined a glorified closet selling cheap Valhalla souvenirs. Instead, it was a five-level department store combined with a convention center trade show. We passed through a supermarket, a clothing boutique with the latest in Viking fashions, and an IKEA outlet (naturally).

Most of the showroom floor was a maze of stalls, kiosks, and workshops. Bearded guys in leather aprons stood outside their forges offering free samples of arrowheads. There were specialized merchants for shields, spears, crossbows, helmets, and drinking cups (lots and lots of drinking cups). Several of the larger booths had full-size boats for sale.

I patted the hull of a sixty-foot warship. "I don't think this would fit in my bathtub."

"We have several lakes and rivers in Valhalla," Gunilla said. "There's also the Whitewater Rafting Experience on floor twelve. All einherjar should know how to fight at sea as well as on land."

I pointed to a riding ring where a dozen horses were teth-
ered. "And those? You can ride a horse through the hallways?"

"Of course," said Gunilla. "We're pet-friendly. But notice,
Magnus—the lack of weapons. The scarcity of armor."

"You're kidding, right? This place has *thousands* of weapons for sale."

"Not enough," Gunilla said. "Not for Ragnarok."

She led me down the Nordic Knickknacks aisle to a big
iron door marked: AUTHORIZED PERSONNEL ONLY.

She slipped one of her keys into the lock. "I don't show this
to many people. It's too disturbing."

"Not another wall of fire, is it?"

"Worse."

Behind the door was a set of stairs. Then another set of
stairs. Then another set of stairs. By the time we reached the
top, I'd lost count of how many flights. My upgraded einherji
legs felt like overcooked linguine.

At last we stepped out onto a narrow balcony.

"This," Gunilla said, "is my favorite view."

I couldn't answer. I was too busy trying not to die from
vertigo.

The balcony ringed the opening in the roof above the Hall
of the Slain. The tree Laeradr's topmost branches stretched
upward, making a green dome the size of Spaceship Earth at
Epcot Center. Inside, far below, hotel staff scurried around the
tables like termites, getting things ready for dinner.

From the outer edge of the balcony, the roofline of Valhalla
sloped away—a thatch-work of gold shields blazing red in the
evening sun. I felt like I was standing on the surface of a metal
planet.

"Why don't you show this to people?" I asked. "It's . . . well, intimidating, but it's also beautiful."

"Over here." Gunilla pulled me to a spot where I could gaze down between two sections of roof.

My eyeballs felt like they were going to implode. I flashed back to a presentation my sixth grade science teacher once gave about the size of the universe. He explained how vast the earth was, then described how that was nothing compared to the solar system, which in turn was nothing compared to the galaxy, et cetera, et cetera, until I felt as significant as a speck on the underarm of a flea.

Stretching out around Valhalla, gleaming to the horizon, was a city of palaces, each as big and impressive as the hotel.

"Asgard," Gunilla said. "The realm of the gods."

I saw roofs made entirely of silver ingots, hammered bronze doors big enough to fly a B-1 bomber through, sturdy stone towers that pierced the clouds. Streets were paved in gold. Each garden was as vast as Boston Harbor. And circling the edge of the city were white ramparts that made the Great Wall of China look like a baby fence.

At the very edge of my vision, the city's widest avenue ran through a gateway in the walls. On the far side, the pavement dissolved into multicolored light—a roadway of prismatic fire.

"The Bifrost," Gunilla said. "The rainbow bridge leading from Asgard to Midgard."

I'd heard about the Bifrost Bridge. In my children's myth book, it was a seven-color pastel arc with happy bunny rabbits dancing around the base. *This* bridge had no happy bunnies. It was terrifying. It was a rainbow in the way a nuclear explosion was a mushroom.

"Only the gods may cross over," Gunilla said. "Anyone else would burn the moment they set foot on it."

"But . . . we're *in* Asgard?"

"Of course. Valhalla is one of Odin's halls. That's why, within the hotel, the einherjar are immortal."

"So you can go down there and see the gods, sell Girl Scout cookies door-to-door or whatever?"

Gunilla curled her lip. "Even gazing upon Asgard, you have no sense of reverence."

"Not really, no."

"Without the express permission of Odin, we aren't allowed to visit the city of the gods, at least not until the day of Ragnarok, when we will defend the gates."

"But you can fly."

"It's forbidden to go there. If I tried, I would fall from the sky. You're missing the point, Magnus. Look at the city again. What do you notice?"

I scanned the neighborhood, trying to see past all the silver and gold and the scary huge architecture. In one window, rich drapes hung in tatters. Along the streets, fire braziers stood empty and cold. The statues in one garden were completely overgrown with thorn bushes. The streets were deserted. No fires burned in any of the windows.

"Where is everybody?" I asked.

"Exactly. I would not be selling many Girl Scout cookies."

"You mean the gods are *gone?*"

Gunilla turned toward me, her string of hammers glinting orange in the sunset. "Some may be slumbering. Some are roaming the Nine Worlds. Some still appear from time to time. The fact is, we don't know what's going on. I've been in

Valhalla five hundred years, and I have never seen the gods so quiet, so inactive. The last two years . . ."

She plucked a leaf from a low-hanging branch of Laeradr. "Two years ago, something changed. The Valkyries and thanes all felt it. The barriers between the Nine Worlds began to weaken. Frost giants and fire giants raided Midgard more frequently. Monsters from Helheim broke into the worlds of the living. The gods grew distant and silent. This was around the time when Samirah became a Valkyrie—the last time we saw Odin. It was also when your mother died."

A raven circled overhead. Two more joined it. I thought about my mom—how she used to joke that birds of prey were stalking us when we went hiking. *They think we're dead. Quick, start dancing!*

At the moment I wasn't tempted to dance. I wanted to borrow Gunilla's hammers and knock the birds out of the sky.

"You think there's a connection between those things?" I asked.

"All I know . . . we are poorly prepared for Ragnarok. Then *you* arrive. The Norns issue dire warnings, calling you the Harbinger of the Wolf. That's not good, Magnus. Samirah al-Abbas may have been watching you for years, waiting for the right moment to insert you into Valhalla."

"*Insert* me?"

"Those two friends of yours on the bridge, the ones who had been monitoring you since you became homeless, perhaps they were working with her."

"You mean Blitz and Hearth? They're homeless guys."

"Are they? Don't you find it strange they looked after you so carefully?"

I wanted to tell her to go to Helheim, but Blitz and Hearth *had* always seemed a little . . . unusual. Then again, when you live on the streets, the definition of normal gets a little fuzzy.

Gunilla took my arm. "Magnus, I didn't believe it at first, but if that *was* Surt on the bridge, if you *did* find the Sword of Summer . . . then you're being used by the forces of evil. If Samirah al-Abbas wants you to retrieve the sword, then that's exactly what you *cannot* do. Stay in Valhalla. Let the thanes deal with this prophecy. Swear you'll do this, and I will speak to the thanes on your behalf. I'll convince them that you can be trusted."

"Do I detect an *or else?*"

"Only this: by tomorrow morning, the thanes will announce their decision regarding your fate. If we *cannot* trust you, then we will have to take precautions. We must know whose side you're on."

I looked down at the empty golden streets. I thought about Sam al-Abbas dragging me through the cold void, putting her career on the line because she thought I was brave. *You have potential, Magnus Chase. Don't prove me wrong.* Then she'd been vaporized in the feast hall thanks to Gunilla's edited blooper reel.

I pulled my arm away. "You said Frey is about the middle ground between fire and ice. Maybe this isn't about choosing sides. Maybe I don't want to pick an extreme."

Gunilla's expression rolled shut like a storm window. "I can be a powerful enemy, Magnus Chase. I will warn you one time: if you follow the plans of Loki, if you seek to hasten Ragnarok, I will destroy you."

I tried to meet her eyes, and to ignore my lungs flopping around in my chest. "I'll keep that in mind."

Below us, the dinner horn echoed through the feast hall.

"The tour is over," Gunilla announced. "From this point on, Magnus Chase, I will guide you no more."

She leaped over the side of the balcony and flew down through the branches, leaving me to find my own way back. Without GPS.

TWENTY-TWO

My Friends
Fall Out of a Tree

FORTUNATELY, a friendly berserker found me wandering through the spa on the hundred and twelfth floor. He'd just gotten the gentleman's pedicure ("Just Because You Kill People Doesn't Mean Your Feet Should!") and was happy to lead me back to the elevators.

By the time I reached the feast hall, dinner was under way. I navigated toward X—who was hard to miss even in the huge crowd—and joined my hallmates from floor nineteen.

We traded stories about the morning's battle.

"I hear you used alf seidr!" Halfborn said. "Impressive!"

I'd almost forgotten about the energy blast that had knocked everybody's weapons away. "Yeah, uh . . . what exactly is *alf seidr?*"

"Elf magic," Mallory said. "Sneaky Vanir-style witchcraft unfit for a true warrior." She punched me in the arm. "I like you better already."

I tried for a smile, though I wasn't sure how I'd managed to wield elf magic. As far as I knew, I was not an elf. I thought about the way I resisted extreme temperatures, and the way I'd healed Gunilla in the elevator . . . was that alf seidr too? Maybe it came from being a son of Frey, though I didn't understand how the powers were related.

T.J. complimented me on taking the crest of the hill. X complimented me on staying alive longer than five minutes.

It was good to feel like part of the group, but I didn't pay much attention to their conversation. My head was still buzzing from the tour with Gunilla, and the dream of Loki at the throne of Odin.

At the head table, Gunilla occasionally murmured something to Helgi, and the manager would scowl in my direction. I kept waiting for him to call me up and put me on grape-peeling duty with Hunding, but I guess he was contemplating some better punishment.

Tomorrow morning, Gunilla had warned, *we will have to take precautions.*

At the end of dinner, a couple of newbies were welcomed to Valhalla. Their videos were suitably heroic. No Norns showed up. No Valkyries got banished in disgrace. No butts were shot with squeaky arrows.

As the crowds filed out of the feast hall, T.J. clapped me on the shoulder. "Get some rest. Another glorious death tomorrow!"

"Yippee," I said.

Back in my room, I couldn't sleep. I spent hours pacing around like a zoo animal. I didn't want to wait for the thanes' judgment in the morning. I'd seen how wisely they judged when they exiled Sam.

But what choice did I have? Sneak around the hotel randomly opening doors, hoping to find one that led back to Boston? Even if I succeeded, there was no guarantee I'd be allowed to go back to my luxurious life as a homeless kid. Gunilla or Surt or some other Norse nasty might track me down again.

We must know whose side you are on, Gunilla had said.

I was on *my* side. I didn't want to get wrapped up in some Viking Doomsday, but something told me it was too late. My mom had died two years ago, around the same time a bunch of other bad stuff was breaking loose in the Nine Worlds. With my luck, there was a connection. If I wanted justice for my mother—if I wanted to find out what had happened to her—I couldn't go back to hiding under a bridge.

I also couldn't keep hanging out in Valhalla, taking Swedish lessons and watching PowerPoint presentations on killing trolls.

At about five in the morning, I finally gave up on sleeping. I went to the restroom to wash my face. Clean towels hung on the rod. The hole in the wall had been repaired. I wondered if it had been done by magic or if some poor schmuck had had to fix it as a punishment from the thanes. Maybe tomorrow I'd be the one plastering drywall.

I walked to the atrium and stared at the stars through the trees. I wondered what sky I was looking at—what world, what constellations.

The branches rustled. Something dark and man-shaped toppled out of the tree. He landed at my feet with a nasty crunch.

"OW!" he wailed. "Stupid gravity!"

My old buddy Blitz lay on his back, moaning and cradling his left arm.

A second person dropped lightly to the grass—Hearth, dressed in his usual black leather clothes and candy-striped scarf. He signed: *Hi.*

I stared at them. "What are you—how did you—?" I started to grin. I'd never been happier to see anyone.

"Arm!" Blitz yelped. "Broken!"

"Right." I knelt, trying to focus. "I might be able to heal this."

"*Might?*"

"Wait . . . did you get a makeover?"

"You're asking about my *wardrobe?*"

"Well, yeah." I'd never seen Blitz look so nice.

His chaotic hair had been washed and combed back. His beard was trimmed. His Cro-Magnon unibrow had been plucked and waxed. Only his zigzag nose had not been cosmetically corrected.

As for the clothes, he'd apparently robbed several high-end boutiques on Newbury Street. His boots were alligator leather. His black wool suit was tailored to fit his stocky five-feet-five frame and looked lovely with his dark skin tone. Under the jacket, he was rocking a charcoal paisley vest with a gold watch chain, a turquoise dress shirt, and a bolo tie. He looked like a very short, well-groomed African American cowboy hit man.

Hearth clapped to get my attention. He signed: *Arm. Fix?*

"Right. Sorry." I placed my hand gently on Blitz's forearm. I could feel the fracture under the skin. I willed it to mend. *Click.* Blitz yelped as the bone moved back into place.

"Try it now," I said.

Blitz moved the arm. His expression changed from pain to surprise. "That actually worked!"

Hearth looked even more shocked. He signed, *Magic? How?*

"I've been wondering that myself," I said. "Guys, don't take this the wrong way, because I'm really glad to see you. But why are you falling out of my trees?"

"Kid," Blitz said, "for the past twenty-four hours we've been climbing all over the World Tree looking for you. We thought we found you last night, but—"

"I think you might have," I said. "Just before dawn I heard somebody moving in the branches."

Blitz turned to Hearth. "I *told* you that was the right room!"

Hearth rolled his eyes and signed too fast for me to read.

"Oh, please," Blitz said. "Your idea, my idea—it doesn't matter. The point is, we're here, and Magnus is alive! Well . . . technically he's dead. But he's alive. Which means the boss might not kill us!"

"The boss?" I asked.

Blitz developed a tic in his eye. "Yeah. We have a confession to make."

"You're not really homeless," I said. "Last night, one of the thanes saw you guys on video and—"

Video? Hearth signed.

"Yeah. Valkyrie Vision. Anyway, this thane called you a dwarf and an elf. I'm guessing"—I pointed at Blitz—"you're the dwarf?"

"Typical," Blitz grumbled. "Assume I'm the dwarf because I'm short."

"So you're not the dwarf?"

He sighed. "No. I'm the dwarf."

"And you . . ." I looked at Hearth, but I couldn't even make myself say it. I'd hung out with this guy for two years. He'd taught me curses in sign language. We'd eaten burritos out of trash cans together. What kind of elf does that?

E-L-F. Hearth signed the individual letters. *Sometimes spelled A-L-F.*

"But . . . you guys don't look that different from humans."

"Actually," Blitz said, "humans don't look that different from dwarves and elves."

"I can't believe I'm having this conversation, but you're not *that* short. Like, for a dwarf. You could pass for a regular short human."

"Which I've been doing," Blitz said, "for two years now. Dwarves come in different sizes, just like humans. I happen to be a *svartalf*."

"A fart elf?"

"Gah! Clean your ears, kid. A *svartalf*. It means *dark elf*. I'm from *Svartalfheim*."

"Um, I thought you just said you're a dwarf."

"Dark elves aren't actually elves, kid. It's . . . what do you call it? A misnomer. We're a subset of dwarves."

"Well, that certainly clears things up."

Hearth developed a faint smile, which for him was the equivalent of rolling on the floor laughing. He signed, *fart elf.*

Blitz pointedly ignored him. "Svartalfs tend to be taller than your average Nidavellir dwarves. Plus we're devilishly handsome. But that's not important right now. Hearthstone and I are here to help you."

"Hearthstone?"

Hearth nodded. *My full name. He is B-L-I-T-Z-E-N.*

"Kid, we don't have much time. We've been watching you for the last two years, trying to keep you safe."

"For your boss."

"That's right."

"And who is your boss?"

"That's . . . classified. But he's one of the good guys. He's the head of our organization, dedicated to delaying Ragnarok as long as possible. And you, my friend, have been his most important project."

"So, just taking a wild guess here . . . you're not working for Loki?"

Blitzen looked outraged. Hearth signed one of those curses he'd taught me.

"That was uncalled for, kid." Blitzen sounded genuinely hurt. "I dressed up like a homeless person every day for two years for you. I let my personal hygiene go to Helheim. You know how long I had to stay in the bubble bath every morning to get the *smell* out?"

"Sorry. So . . . were you working with Samirah, the Valkyrie?"

Another curse sign from Hearthstone. *The one who took you? No. She made things hard for us.*

Actually the literal signs were more like: *HER. TOOK. YOU. MADE. DIFFICULT. US.* But I'd gotten fairly good at interpreting.

"You weren't supposed to die, kid," said Blitzen. "Our job was to protect you. But now . . . well, you're an einherji. Maybe we can still make this work. We've got to get you out of here. We have to find that sword."

"Let's go, then," I said.

"Now, don't argue," Blitzen said. "I know you're in warriors' paradise and it's all very new and exciting—"

"Blitz, I said sure."

The dwarf blinked. "But I had this whole speech prepared."

"No need. I trust you."

The strange thing? I was telling the truth.

Maybe Blitzen and Hearthstone were professional stalkers who'd been keeping an eye on me for a top-secret anti-Ragnarok organization. Maybe their idea of protecting me involved attacking the lord of the fire giants with cheap plastic toys. Maybe they weren't even the same species as me.

But they'd stuck by me while I was homeless. They were my best friends. Yes . . . that's how messed up my life was.

"Well, then." Blitzen brushed the grass from his paisley vest. "We'll just climb back into the World Tree before—"

From somewhere above, an explosive *yap!* reverberated through the room. It sounded like a rabid six-thousand-pound Boston terrier choking on a mammoth bone.

Hearthstone's eyes widened. The sound was so loud he'd probably felt the vibrations through his shoes.

"Gods almighty!" Blitzen grabbed my arm. Together with Hearthstone, he pulled me away from the atrium. "Kid, please tell me you know another way out of this hotel. Because we *aren't* using the tree."

Another *yap* shook the room. Broken branches tumbled to the floor.

"Wh-what's up there?" I asked, my knees shaking. I thought about the Norns' prophecy, naming me a harbinger of evil. "Is it—the Wolf?"

"Oh, much worse," Blitzen said. "It's the Squirrel."

TWENTY-THREE

I Recycle Myself

WHEN SOMEONE SAYS, *It's the Squirrel*, you don't ask questions. You run. The barking alone was enough to scare the mead out of me.

I grabbed my hotel-issued sword on the way out. Since I was wearing green silk Valhalla pajamas, I doubted I would need it. If I had to fight anyone, they would die laughing before I ever drew the blade.

We burst into the hallway to find T.J. and Mallory already standing there, bleary-eyed and hastily dressed.

"What was that sound?" Mallory scowled at me. "Why do you have a dwarf and an elf in your room?"

"SQUIRREL!" Blitzen yelled, slamming my door shut.

Hearth said the same thing in sign language—a gesture that looked disturbingly like a set of mandibles rending flesh.

T.J. looked like he'd been slapped across the face. "Magnus, what have you done?"

"I need to leave the hotel. *Now.* Please don't stop us."

Mallory cursed in what was maybe Gaelic. Our little hallway group was a veritable United Nations of Cussing.

"We won't stop you," she said. "This is going to get us laundry duty for a decade, but we'll help you."

I stared at her. "Why? You've known me less than a day."

"Long enough to know you're an idiot," she grumbled.

"What she's trying to say," T.J. offered, "is that hallmates always protect each other. We'll cover your escape."

The door of my room shook. Cracks spiderwebbed from the nameplate. A decorative spear fell off the wall of the corridor.

"X!" T.J. called. "Help!"

The half-troll's door exploded off its hinges. X lumbered into the hallway as if he'd been standing just inside, waiting for the call. "Yes?"

T.J. pointed. "Magnus's door. Squirrel."

"Okay."

X marched over and shoved his back against my door. It shuddered again, but X held firm. Enraged barking echoed from inside.

Halfborn Gunderson stumbled out of his room wearing nothing but smiley-face boxers, double-bladed axes in his hands.

"What's going on?" He glowered at Blitz and Hearth. "Should I kill the dwarf and the elf?"

"No!" Blitzen yelped. "Don't kill the dwarf and the elf!"

"They're with me," I said. "We're leaving."

"Squirrel," T.J. explained.

Halfborn's shaggy eyebrows achieved orbit. "Squirrel as in *squirrel* squirrel?"

"*Squirrel* squirrel," Mallory agreed. "And I'm surrounded by moron morons."

A raven soared down the hall. It landed on the nearest light fixture and squawked at me accusingly.

"Well, that's great," Mallory said. "The ravens have sensed your friends' intrusion. That means the Valkyries won't be far behind."

From the direction of the elevator banks, half a dozen howls pierced the air.

"And those would be Odin's wolves," Halfborn said. "Very friendly unless you're trespassing or leaving the hotel without permission, in which case they'll tear you apart."

An unmanly sob started to build in my throat. I could accept being killed by a squirrel, or an army of Valkyries, or even another ax in my face, but not wolves. My legs threatened to give out beneath me.

"Blitz and Hearth"—my voice trembled—"is there any alarm you guys *failed* to set off?"

Not fair, Hearth signed. *We avoided the tree mines.*

"*Tree* mines?" I wasn't sure I'd understood him correctly.

Halfborn Gunderson hefted his ax. "I'll slow down the wolves. Good luck, Magnus!"

He charged down the hall screaming, "DEATH!" while the smiley faces rippled on his boxer shorts.

Mallory's face turned red—with embarrassment or delight, I couldn't tell. "I'll stay with X in case the squirrel breaks through," she said. "T.J., you take them to recycling."

"Yeah."

"*Recycling?*" Blitz asked.

Mallory drew her sword. "Magnus, I can't say it's been a pleasure. You're a true pain in the *nári*. Now get out of here."

The door of my room shuddered again. Plaster rained from the ceiling.

"The squirrel is strong," X grunted. "Hurry."

T.J. fixed his bayonet. "Let's go."

He led us down the corridor, his blue Union jacket over his pj's. I got a feeling he probably slept in that jacket. Behind us, wolves howled and Halfborn Gunderson bellowed in Old Norse.

As we ran, a few einherjar opened their doors to see what was going on. When they spotted T.J. with his bayonet, they ducked back inside.

Left, right, right, left—I lost track of the turns. Another raven shot past, cawing angrily. I tried to swat it.

"Don't," T.J. warned. "They're sacred to Odin."

We were just passing a T in the hallway when a voice shouted, "MAGNUS!"

I made the mistake of looking.

To our left, fifty feet away, Gunilla stood in full armor, a hammer in either hand. "Take another step," she snarled, "and I will destroy you."

T.J. glanced at me. "You three keep going. Next right, there's a chute marked 'recycling.' Jump in."

"But—"

"No time." T.J. grinned. "Go kill some rebs for me—or monsters—or whatever."

He pointed his rifle at the Valkyrie, shouted, "Fifty-Fourth Massachusetts!" and charged.

Hearth grabbed my arm and pulled me along. Blitz found the recycling chute and yanked it open. "GO, GO!"

Hearthstone dove in headfirst.

"You next, kid," said the dwarf.

I hesitated. The smell coming out of the chute reminded me of my Dumpster-diving days. Suddenly the comforts of the Hotel Valhalla didn't seem so bad.

Then more wolves howled, closer this time, and I recycled myself.

TWENTY-FOUR

You Had One Job

TURNS OUT VALHALLA had been sending its recycling to home plate at Fenway, which could explain any problems the Red Sox were having with their offensive lineup.

Hearthstone was just getting to his feet when I landed on top of him and knocked him flat. Before I could extricate myself, Blitzen plowed into my chest. I pushed him off and rolled away just in case anyone else decided to drop out of the sky.

I struggled to my feet. "Why are we in Fenway Park?"

"Don't ask me." Blitzen sighed dismally. His nice wool suit looked like it had passed through the digestive tract of a snail. "The doors in and out of Valhalla are notoriously wonky. At least we're in Midgard."

Rows of red bleachers stood empty and silent, uncomfortably similar to the Feast Hall of the Slain before the einherjar marched in. The field was covered in a patchwork of frozen tarps that crunched under my feet.

It must have been around six in the morning. The eastern sky was just starting to turn gray. My breath steamed in the air.

"What were we running from?" I asked. "What kind of mutant squirrel—"

"Ratatosk," Blitz said. "The bane of the World Tree. Anyone

who dares climb Yggdrasil's branches sooner or later has to deal with that monster. Count yourself lucky we escaped."

Hearthstone pointed toward the dawn. He signed: *Sun. Bad for Blitzen.*

Blitz squinted. "You're right. After that business on the bridge, I can't stand any more direct exposure."

"What do you mean?" I looked more closely at his face. "Are you turning gray?"

Blitzen looked away, but there was no doubt. His cheeks had lightened to the color of wet clay. "Kid, you may have noticed I never hung around with you much during the day?"

"I . . . yeah. It was like Hearth took the day shift. You took the night shift."

"Exactly. Dwarves are subterranean creatures. Sunlight is deadly to us. Mind you, not as deadly as it is to *trolls*. I can stand a little bit, but if I'm out for too long I start to . . . uh, petrify."

I remembered the fight on Longfellow Bridge, how Blitzen had been wearing a broad-brimmed hat, coat, gloves, and sunglasses—a strange fashion statement, especially with the MAKE WAY FOR DUCKLINGS sign. "If you cover up, will you be okay?"

"It helps. Thick clothing, sunscreen, et cetera. But at the moment"—he gestured to his clothes—"I'm not prepared. I dropped my supply pack somewhere in the World Tree."

Hearthstone signed: *After bridge, his legs turned to stone. No walking until night.*

A lump formed in my throat. Blitz and Hearth's attempt to protect me on the Longfellow Bridge had been pretty ridiculous, but they'd *tried*. Just by being out in the daytime, Blitzen had risked his life.

As many questions as I had, as messed up as my life (death?) was at the moment, knowing that Blitzen was in danger again for my sake readjusted my priorities.

"Let's get you someplace dark," I said.

The easiest option was the Green Monster—the famous home-run-blocking four-story wall along the left outfield. I'd been behind it once before on a school trip—first grade, maybe? I remembered there were service doors under the scoreboard.

I found one unlocked, and we slipped inside.

There wasn't much to see—just metal scaffolding, stacks of green number cards hanging on the wall, and the stadium's concrete ribs tattooed with a hundred years of graffiti. The space had one important requirement, though: it was dark.

Blitzen sat on a pile of mats and pulled off his boots. Acorns spilled out. His socks were gray paisley, matching his vest.

The socks amazed me as much as anything I'd encountered in Valhalla. "Blitz, what's with the outfit? You look so . . . spiffy."

He puffed up his chest. "Thank you, Magnus. It hasn't been easy dressing like a bum the last two years. No offense, of course."

"Of course."

"This is how I usually dress. I take my appearance very seriously. I'll admit I'm a bit of a clotheshorse."

Hearth made a sound between a sneeze and a snort. He signed: *A bit?*

"Oh, be quiet," Blitz grumbled. "Who bought you that scarf, eh?" He turned to me for support. "I told Hearth he needed a splash of color. The black clothes. The platinum blond hair. The red-striped scarf makes a bold statement, don't you think?"

"Uh . . . sure," I said. "As long as *I* don't have to wear it. Or the paisley socks."

"Don't be silly. Patterned fabric would look terrible on you." Blitz frowned at his boot. "What were we talking about again?"

"How about why you've been watching me for the last two years?"

Hearth signed: *Told you. The boss.*

"Not Loki," I said. "Odin, then?"

Blitz laughed. "No. The Capo is even smarter than Odin. He likes to work behind the scenes, stay anonymous. He assigned us to watch you and, uh"—he cleared his throat—"keep you alive."

"Ah."

"Yeah." Blitzen shook the acorns out of his other boot. "We had one job. We failed. 'Keep him alive,' said the Capo. 'Watch him. Protect him if needed, but don't interfere with his choices. He's important to the plan.'"

"The plan."

"The Capo knows stuff. The future, for instance. He does his best to nudge events in the right direction, keep the Nine Worlds from spiraling into chaos and exploding."

"That sounds like a good plan."

"He told us you were the son of Frey. He didn't go into details, but he was very insistent: you were important, had to be protected. When you died . . . well, I'm just glad we found you in Valhalla. Maybe all isn't lost. Now we've got to report to the Capo and get new orders."

Hearthstone signed: *And hope he doesn't kill us.*

"That, too." Blitzen didn't sound optimistic. "The thing is, Magnus, until we talk to the boss, I can't really go into many details."

"Even though I'm important to the plan."

That's why *we can't,* Hearth signed.

"What about what happened after I fell off the bridge? Can you tell me that?"

Blitz picked a leaf out of his beard. "Well, Surt disappeared into the water with you."

"It *was* Surt."

"Oh, yeah. And I gotta say, nice job with that. A mortal taking down the lord of the fire giants? Even if you died doing it, that was impressive."

"So . . . I killed him?"

No such luck, Hearth signed.

"Yeah," Blitz agreed. "But fire giants don't do well in icy water. I imagine the impact shocked him right back to Muspellheim. And cutting off his nose . . . that was brilliant. It'll take him a while to regain enough strength to travel between worlds."

A few days, Hearth guessed.

"Maybe longer," Blitz said.

I looked back and forth between them, two nonhumans discussing the mechanics of traveling between worlds the way somebody else might debate how long it would take to fix a carburetor.

"You guys got away okay, obviously," I said. "What about Randolph?"

Hearthstone wrinkled his nose. *Your uncle. Annoying, but fine.*

"Kid, you saved lives," Blitzen said. "There were a lot of injuries, a lot of damage, but no mortals died—um, except you. The last time Surt visited Midgard, it didn't go so well."

Great Chicago Fire, Hearth signed.

"Yeah," said Blitz. "Anyway, the Boston explosions made national news. The humans are still investigating. They're speculating the damage was caused by meteor strikes."

I remember thinking that myself at first. And later wondering whether Surt had been responsible for them all. "But dozens of people saw Surt on the bridge! At least one guy caught him on video."

Blitz shrugged. "You'd be amazed what mortals *don't* see. Not just humans. Dwarves and elves are just as bad. Besides, giants are experts at glamour."

"*Glamour.* I'm guessing you don't mean fashion."

"No. Giants are *horrible* at fashion. I mean glamour like illusions. Giants are magic by nature. They can manipulate your senses without even trying. One time a giant made Hearthstone think I was a warthog, and Hearth almost killed me."

No more about the warthog! Hearthstone pleaded.

"So, anyway," Blitz said, "you fell in the river and died. The emergency services retrieved your body, but—"

"My body . . ."

Hearthstone pulled a newspaper clipping from his jacket pocket and handed it to me.

I read my own obituary. There was my class picture from fifth grade—my hair in my eyes, my uncomfortable *why-am-I-here* smile, my ratty DROPKICK MURPHYS T-shirt. The obituary didn't say much. Nothing about my two-year disappearance, my homelessness, my mom's death. Just: *Untimely demise. Survived by two uncles and a cousin. Private service to be held.*

"But my body is here," I said, touching my chest. "I *have* a body."

"A new and improved body," Blitz agreed, squeezing my biceps in admiration. "They retrieved your *old* body. Hearth and I did our own search of the river. There was no sign of Surt. Worse . . . there was no sign of the sword. If it's not at the bottom of the river again—"

"Could Randolph have found it?" I asked.

Hearthstone shook his head. *We watched him. Doesn't have it.*

"Then Surt has the sword," I guessed.

Blitz shuddered. "Let's not assume that. There's still a chance it's with your old body."

"Why would it be?"

Blitz pointed to Hearth. "Ask him. He's the expert at magic."

Hard to explain in signs, Hearth gestured. *A magic sword stays with you. You claimed it.*

"But . . . I didn't."

You summoned it, Hearth signed. *Held it first, before Surt. Hope that means Surt didn't get it. Don't know why the sword didn't go to Valhalla.*

"I wasn't holding the sword when I hit the river," I said. "It slipped out of my hand."

"Ah." Blitz nodded. "That might be why. Still, the sword would traditionally go into your grave, or get burned on your pyre. So there's a decent chance it will materialize next to your dead body. We need to look in your coffin."

My skin crawled. "You want me to go to my own funeral?"

Hearth signed: *No. We go before.*

"According to your obituary notice," Blitz said, "your body is at the funeral home today for viewing hours. The service isn't until tonight. If you go now, you should have the place to yourself. The building isn't open yet, and you won't exactly have mourners lining up outside."

"Thanks a lot."

Blitzen tugged on his boots. "I'll go talk to the boss. On the way, I'll pop by Svartalfheim and pick up some proper anti-sunlight supplies."

"You'll pop by the world of the dark elves?"

"Yeah. It's not as hard as it sounds. I've had a lot of practice, and Boston is at the center of Yggdrasil. Slipping between worlds is easy here. One time Hearth and I stepped off a curb in Kendall Square and fell into Niflheim by accident."

That was cold, Hearth signed.

"While I'm gone," Blitz said, "Hearthstone will take you to the funeral home. I'll meet you . . . where?"

Arlington–nearest T stop, Hearth signed.

"Good." Blitzen stood. "Get that sword, kid . . . and be careful. Outside Valhalla, you can die like anybody else. The last thing we need to explain to the boss is *two* Magnus Chase corpses."

TWENTY-FIVE

My Funeral Director
Dresses Me Funny

ONE GOOD THING about being homeless: I knew where to find free clothes. Hearth and I raided a charity drop box on Charlesgate so I wouldn't have to walk around town in my pj's. Soon I was resplendent in stonewashed jeans, a hunting jacket, and a T-shirt peppered with holes. I looked more like Kurt Cobain than ever, except I doubt Cobain ever wore a shirt that read: WIGGLES ROCK & ROLL PRESCHOOL TOUR! The really disturbing thing was that they made shirts like that in my size.

I held up my hotel-issued sword. "Hearth, what about this? I doubt the cops will like me walking around with a three-foot blade."

Glamour, Hearth signed. *Attach it to your belt.*

As soon as I did, the weapon shrank and melted into a simple loop of chain, which was only slightly less fashionable than the Wiggles T-shirt.

"Great," I said. "Now my humiliation is complete."

Still a sword, Hearth signed. *Mortals are not good at seeing magical things. Between Ice and Fire is Mist, G-i-n-n-u-n-g-a-g-a-p. Obscures appearances. Hard to explain in signs.*

"Okay." I remembered what Gunilla had told me about the worlds forming between ice and fire, and how Frey represented the temperate zone between. Apparently, though, Frey's children didn't inherit an innate understanding of what the heck that meant.

I read my obituary again for the address of the funeral home. "Let's go pay our respects to me."

It was a long, cold walk. The temperature didn't bother me, but Hearth shivered in his leather jacket. His lips were cracked and peeling. His nose was runny. From all the fantasy books and movies I had devoured in middle school, I'd gotten an impression of elves as noble creatures of unearthly beauty. Hearthstone looked more like an anemic college kid who hadn't eaten in a few weeks.

Still . . . I began to notice non-human details about him. His pupils were strangely reflective, like a cat's. Under his translucent skin, his veins were more green than blue. And despite his disheveled appearance, he didn't reek like a normal homeless person—body odor, alcohol, stale grease. He smelled more like pine needles and woodsmoke. How had I not realized that before?

I wanted to ask him about elves, but walking and talking in sign language don't mix. Nor could Hearth read lips very well on the move. I kind of liked that, actually. You couldn't multitask while talking to him. The dialogue required one hundred percent focus. If all conversations were like that, I imagined people wouldn't say so much stupid garbage.

We were passing Copley Square when he pulled me into the doorway of an office building.

Gómez, he signed. *Wait.*

Gómez was a beat cop who knew us by sight. He didn't

know my real name, but if he'd seen a recent picture of me on the news, I would have a hard time explaining why I wasn't dead. Also, Gómez wasn't the friendliest guy.

I tapped Hearth's shoulder for attention. "What's it like . . . where you're from?"

Hearth's expression turned guarded. *Alfheim not so different. Only brighter. No night.*

"No night . . . like *ever?*"

No night. The first time I saw a sunset . . .

He hesitated, then splayed both hands in front of his chest like he was having a heart attack: the sign for *scared.*

I tried to imagine living in a world where it was always daytime, then watching the sun disappear in a wash of blood-colored light on the horizon.

"That would be freaky," I decided. "But don't elves have stuff *humans* would be scared of? Like . . . alf seidr?"

A light kindled in Hearth's eyes. *How do you know that term?*

"Uh . . . yesterday on the battlefield, somebody said I did it." I told him about the blast that had knocked everyone's weapons away. "And when I healed Blitz's arm, or walked into that wall of flames on the Longfellow Bridge . . . I wondered if it was all the same kind of magic."

Hearth seemed to take longer than usual to process my words.

Not sure. His gestures were smaller, more careful. *Alf seidr can be many things—usually peaceful magic. Healing. Growing. Stopping violence. It cannot be learned. Not like rune magic. You have alf seidr in your blood, or you do not. You are son of Frey. Maybe have some of his abilities.*

"Frey is an elf?"

Hearth shook his head. *Frey is the lord of Alfheim, our patron god. Vanir are close to elves. Vanir were the source of all alf seidr.*

"Past tense? Don't elves still talk to trees and speak with birds and stuff?"

Hearth grunted with irritation. He peeked around the corner to check on our neighborhood policeman.

Alfheim not like that, he signed. *Not for centuries. Almost no one is born with alf seidr. No one practices magic. Most elves think Midgard is a myth. Humans live in castles and wear plate mail and tights.*

"Maybe a thousand years ago."

Hearth nodded. *Back then, our worlds interacted more. Now, both worlds have changed. Elves spend most of their time staring at screens, watching funny pixie videos when they are supposed to be working.*

I wasn't sure I'd interpreted his signs correctly—*pixie videos?*—but Alfheim sounded depressingly like Midgard.

"So you don't know any more about magic than I do," I said.

I don't know what it looked like in the old days. But I am trying to learn. I have given up everything to try.

"What do you mean?"

He glanced around the corner again. *Gómez is gone. Come on.*

I wasn't sure if he'd missed my question or he'd just chosen to ignore it.

The funeral home was near Washington and Charles, tucked in a row of Bay Village town houses that seemed lost among the newer concrete and glass skyscrapers. A sign on the awning read: TWINING & SONS MEMORIAL SERVICES.

A display by the door listed upcoming viewings. The top

one read: MAGNUS CHASE. The date was today, starting at ten A.M. The door was locked. The lights were off.

"Early for my own funeral," I said. "Typical."

My hands were shaking. The idea of seeing my dead self was more unnerving than actually dying. "So do we break in?"

I'll try something, Hearth signed.

From his coat, he pulled a leather pouch. The contents clattered with a familiar sound.

"Runestones," I guessed. "You know how to use them?"

He shrugged like, *We're about to find out.* He took one stone and tapped it against the door handle. The lock clicked. The door swung open.

"Nice," I said. "Would that work on any door?"

Hearth put away the pouch. I couldn't quite read his expression—a mixture of sadness and wariness.

I'm learning, he signed. *Only tried that once before, when I met Blitz.*

"How did you two—"

Hearth cut me off with a wave. *Blitz saved my life. Long story. You go inside. I will stand guard here. Dead human bodies . . .* He shuddered and shook his head.

So much for my elfish backup.

Inside, the funeral home smelled of moldering bouquets. The threadbare red carpet and dark wood paneling made the whole place feel like one giant coffin. I crept down the hallway and peeked into the first room.

It was a set up like a chapel: three stained glass windows on the back wall, rows of folding chairs facing an open coffin on a dais. I hated this already. I'd been raised nonreligious. I'd always considered myself an atheist.

So, of course, my punishment was to find out I was the son of a Norse deity, go to a Viking afterlife, and have an open-coffin memorial in a cheesy uni-faith chapel. If there was an Almighty God up there, a head honcho of the universe, He was totally laughing at me right now.

At the entrance of the room was a poster-size portrait of me, wreathed in black crepe paper. They'd chosen the same goofy fifth grade picture from my elementary school yearbook. Next to it, on a small table, was a guest book.

I was tempted to pick up the pen and write the first entry: *Thanks for coming to my funeral!–Magnus.*

Who would be here, anyway? Uncle Randolph? Maybe Frederick and Annabeth, if they were still in town. My old classmates from two years ago? Yeah, right. If the funeral home offered snacks, some of my homeless buddies might show up, but the only ones I really cared about were Blitzen and Hearthstone.

I realized I was procrastinating. I wasn't sure how long I'd been standing in the chapel doorway. I forced myself down the aisle.

When I saw my own face in the coffin, I nearly threw up.

Not because I'm *that* ugly, but because . . . well, you know how weird it is to hear your own voice on a recording? And how irritating it can be to see yourself in a photo if you don't think you look good? Okay, imagine seeing your actual body lying right in front of you. It was so real, and yet so *not* me.

My hair was shellacked to the sides of my head. My face was caked with makeup, probably to cover cuts and bruises. My mouth was fixed in a weird little smile that I never would've made in real life. I was dressed in a cheap-looking blue suit with a blue tie. I hated blue. My hands were clasped over my stomach, hiding the place where I'd been impaled by a molten piece of asphalt.

"No, no, no." I gripped the sides of the coffin.

The *wrongness* of it made me feel like my guts were burning all over again.

I'd always had an image of what would happen to my body after death. This wasn't it. My mom and I had a pact—which sounds creepy, but it really wasn't. She made me promise that when she died, I'd have her cremated. I'd scatter her ashes in the woods of the Blue Hills. If I died first, she promised she would do the same for me. Neither of us liked the idea of being embalmed, turned into some chemically stabilized exhibition, then buried in a box. We wanted to be in the sunshine and the fresh air and just kind of dissolve.

I hadn't been able to keep my promise to my mother. Now I was getting exactly the kind of funeral I didn't want.

My eyes watered. "I'm sorry, Mom."

I wanted to push over the coffin. I wanted to torch this place. But I had a job to do. *The sword.*

If it was in the coffin, it wasn't in plain sight. I held my breath and slipped my hand along the inside lining like I was searching for loose change. Nothing.

Thinking the sword might be hidden by a glamour, I stretched my arm over the coffin, trying to sense the blade's presence like I'd done on the Longfellow Bridge. No heat. No humming.

The only other option was to check under the body.

I looked down at Magnus 1.0. "Sorry, man."

I tried to tell myself the corpse was an inanimate object like a scarecrow. Not a real person. Certainly not me.

I rolled him to one side. He was heavier than I would've thought.

Nothing underneath but safety pins holding the coat in place. A label on the white lining read, 50% SATIN, 50% POLYES-TER, PRODUCT OF TAIWAN.

I lowered the body back into place. Dead Magnus's hair was all messed up now. The left side bloomed like a bird-of-paradise flower. My hands had come unclasped so I appeared to be giving everybody the finger.

"Much better," I decided. "At least that looks like me."

Behind me, a broken voice said, "Magnus?"

I almost jumped out of my Wiggles shirt.

Standing in the doorway was my cousin Annabeth.

TWENTY-SIX

Hey, I Know You're Dead, But Call Me Maybe

EVEN IF I HADN'T seen her in the park two days before, I would've recognized her up close. Her wavy blond hair hadn't changed since childhood. Her gray eyes had the same determined look—like she'd chosen a target in the distance and was going to march over and destroy it. She was better dressed than me—orange North Face ski jacket, black jeans, lace-up winter boots—but if people saw us together they would've mistaken us for brother and sister.

She stared at me, then at the coffin. Slowly her expression changed from shock to cold calculation.

"I knew it," she said. "I *knew* you weren't dead."

She tackled me in a hug. As I may have mentioned, I'm not a big fan of physical contact, but after all I'd been through, a hug from Annabeth was enough to make me crumble.

"Yeah . . . um . . ." My voice turned ragged. I extracted myself as gently as I could and blinked tears out of my eyes. "It's really good to see you."

She wrinkled her nose at the corpse. "Are you going to make me ask? I thought you were dead, you butt."

I couldn't help smiling. It had been ten years since she'd called me a butt. We were overdue. "Hard to explain."

"I guessed that much. The body is fake? You're trying to convince everyone you died?"

"Uh . . . not exactly. It's best if people think I'm dead, though. Because . . ." *Because I am dead,* I thought. *Because I went to Valhalla, and now I'm back with a dwarf and an elf!* How could I say that?

I glanced at the chapel doorway. "Wait . . . Did you pass an el—a guy on the way in? My friend was supposed to be keeping watch."

"No. Nobody was out there. The front door was unlocked."

My equilibrium tilted. "I should check—"

"Whoa. Not until I get some answers."

"I— Honestly, I don't know where to start. I'm in kind of a dangerous situation. I don't want to get you involved."

"Too late." She crossed her arms. "And I know a lot about dangerous situations."

Somehow, I believed her. Here I was, a reborn superwarrior from Valhalla, and Annabeth still intimidated me. The way she held herself, her steely confidence—I could tell she'd overcome some hard stuff, the same way I could tell which guys in the shelters were the most dangerous. I couldn't just blow her off. But I also didn't want to drag her into my mess.

"Randolph almost got killed on that bridge," I said. "I don't want anything to happen to you."

She laughed without humor. "Randolph—I swear, I'm going to shove that cane of his . . . Never mind. He wouldn't explain why he took you to the bridge. He kept talking about how you were in danger because of your birthday. He said he was trying to help. Something about our family history—"

"He told me about my father."

Annabeth's eyes darkened. "You never knew your dad."

"Yeah. But apparently . . ." I shook my head. "Look, it would sound crazy. Just . . . there's a connection between what happened on the bridge and what happened to my mom two years ago, and—and who my father is."

Annabeth's expression transformed. She looked as if she'd opened a window expecting to see a swimming pool and instead found the Pacific Ocean.

"Magnus . . . oh, gods."

Gods, I noted. *Plural.*

She paced in front of my coffin, her hands tented like she was praying. "I should've known. Randolph kept rambling about how our family was special, how we attracted attention. But I had no idea you . . ." She froze, then grabbed my shoulders. "I'm so sorry I didn't know sooner. I could've helped you."

"Um, I'm not sure—"

"My dad's flying back to California tonight after the funeral," she continued. "I was going to catch the train for New York, but school can wait. I *get* it now. I can help you. I know a place where you'll be safe."

I pulled away.

I wasn't sure what Annabeth knew, or what she thought she knew. Maybe she'd gotten mixed up with the Nine Worlds somehow. Maybe she was talking about something totally different. But every nerve in my body tingled with warning when I thought about telling her the truth.

I appreciated her offer of help. I could tell it was genuine. Still . . . those words: *I know a place where you'll be safe.* Nothing activated the flight instincts of a homeless kid faster than hearing that.

I was trying to figure out how to explain that when Hearthstone stumbled into the chapel doorway. His left eye was swollen shut. He gesticulated so frantically I could barely read the signs: *HURRY. DANGER.*

Annabeth turned, following my gaze. "Who—"

"That's my friend," I said. "I really have to go. Listen, Annabeth . . ." I took her hands. "I have to do this by myself. It's like . . . like a personal—"

"Quest?"

"I was going to say pain in the—yeah, *quest* works. If you really want to help me, please, just pretend you didn't see me. Later, after I'm done, I'll find you. I'll explain everything, I promise. Right now, I have to go."

She took a shaky breath. "Magnus, I probably *could* help. But . . ." She reached into her coat pocket and pulled out a folded piece of paper. "Recently I learned the hard way that sometimes I have to step back and let other people do their own quests, even people I care about. At least take this."

I unfolded the paper. It was one of the MISSING flyers she and Uncle Frederick had been handing out.

"The second number is my phone. Call me. Let me know when you're okay, or if you change your mind and—"

"I'll call." I kissed her cheek. "You're the best."

She sighed. "You're still a butt."

"I know. Thanks. Bye."

I ran to Hearthstone, who was bouncing up and down with impatience. "What happened?" I demanded. "Where were you?"

He was already running. I followed him out of the funeral home, north on Arlington. Even pouring on the speed with my upgraded einherji legs, I could barely keep up. Elves, I discovered, could run fast when they wanted to.

We reached the stairs to the T stop just as Blitzen was coming up. I recognized the wide-brimmed hat and coat from the Longfellow Bridge. He'd added larger sunglasses, a ski mask, leather gloves, and a scarf. In one hand he carried a black canvas bag. I guessed he was going for that *Invisible-Man-Goes-Bowling* look.

"Whoa, whoa, whoa!" Blitz grabbed Hearth to keep him from tumbling into traffic. "What happened to your eye? Did you guys find the sword?"

"No sword," I gasped. "Hearth's eye—I don't know—something about danger."

Hearth clapped for our attention.

Knocked out, he signed. *Girl jumped from second story of funeral home. Landed on me. I woke up in alley.*

"A girl in the funeral home?" I scowled. "You don't mean Annabeth? She's my cousin."

He shook his head. *Not her. Other girl. She was—* His hands froze when he noticed Blitz's bag.

Hearth stepped back, shaking his head in disbelief. *You brought him?* He spelled it out: H-I-M, so I knew I hadn't misunderstood.

Blitz hefted the bag. His face was impossible to read, swaddled in anti-sunlight protection, but his voice was heavy. "Yeah. Capo's orders. First things first. Magnus, your cousin was at the funeral home?"

"It's okay." I resisted the urge to ask why there was a *him* in the bowling bag. "Annabeth won't say anything."

"But . . . *another* girl was there?"

"I didn't see her. I guess she heard me coming in and went upstairs."

The dwarf turned to Hearth. "At which point, she jumped from the second-floor window, knocked *you* out, and got away?"

Hearth nodded. *She had to be looking for the sword.*

"You think she found it?" Blitz asked.

Hearth shook his head.

"How can you be sure?" I asked.

Because she's right there.

Hearth pointed across Boylston. A quarter mile down Arlington Street, walking at a fast clip, was a girl in a brown peacoat and a green headscarf. I recognized that scarf.

Hearth's swollen eye had been compliments of Samirah al-Abbas, my ex-Valkyrie.

TWENTY-SEVEN

Let's Play Frisbee
with Bladed Weapons!

AT THE NORTH END of the park, Sam crossed Beacon Street, heading for the footbridge over Storrow Drive.

"Where's she going?" I asked.

"The river, obviously," Blitz said. "She checked out your body at the funeral home—"

"Can we please not phrase it that way?"

"She didn't find the sword. Now she's checking the river."

Sam climbed the spiral ramp of the footbridge. She glanced back in our direction and we had to hide behind a pile of dirty snow. During the summer tourist season, it would've been easier to follow her without attracting attention. Now, the sidewalks were mostly empty.

Blitzen adjusted his dark glasses. "I don't like it. *Best* case scenario, the Valkyries sent her, but—"

"No," I said. "She was kicked out of the Valkyries."

I told them the story as we crouched behind our snowbank.

Hearth looked aghast. His swollen eye had turned the color of Kermit the Frog. *Daughter of Loki?* he signed. *She's working for her dad.*

"I don't know," I said. "I can't quite believe that."

Because she saved you?

I wasn't sure. Maybe I didn't want to believe she was playing for Team Evil. Maybe Loki's words had wormed their way into my head: *I'm definitely on your side!*

I pointed at Hearth's eye and signed *P* for *Permission?* I touched his eyelid. A spark of warmth passed through my fingertip. The bruising faded.

Blitz chuckled. "You're getting good at that, Magnus."

Hearthstone grabbed my hand. He studied my fingertips as if looking for residual magic.

"Whatever." I pulled my hand away, a little embarrassed. The last thing I wanted to be was Magnus Chase, Viking Paramedic. "We're losing Sam. Let's go."

Sam headed downstream on the Esplanade jogging trail. We crossed the footbridge. Beneath us, cars edged along bumper to bumper, honking incessantly. Judging from all the construction vehicles and flashing lights on the Longfellow Bridge, the traffic was probably my fault. My battle with Surt had completely closed the span.

We lost sight of Sam as we took the spiral ramp to the Esplanade. We walked past the playground. I figured we would spot her somewhere down the path, but she had disappeared.

"Well, that's just great," I said.

Blitz limped into the shadow of the closed concession stand. He looked like he was having trouble carrying his bowling bag.

"You okay?" I asked.

"Legs are just slightly petrified. Nothing to worry about."

"That sounds like something to worry about."

Hearth paced. *Wish I had a bow. I could have shot her.*

Blitzen shook his head. "Stick to magic, my friend."

Hearth's gestures were sharp with irritation. *Can't read your lips. The beard is bad enough. The ski mask–impossible.*

Blitz set down the bowling bag, then signed while he spoke. "Hearth is very good with runes. He knows more rune magic than any living mortal."

"Mortal like human?" I asked.

Blitz snorted. "Kid, humans aren't the only mortal species. I meant humans, dwarves, *or* elves. You can't count giants— they're weird. Or the gods, obviously. Or the soothsayers who live in Valhalla. I never understood *what* they were. But among the three mortal species, Hearthstone is the best magician! Well, he's also the *only* magician, as far as I know. He's the first person in centuries to dedicate his life to magic."

I'm blushing, Hearthstone signed, clearly not blushing.

"My point is, you've got real talent," Blitz told him. "But still you want to be an archer!"

Elves were great archers! Hearth protested.

"A thousand years ago!" Blitzen chopped his hand twice between his opposite thumb and forefinger, the sign for *annoyed.* "Hearth is a romantic. He longs for the old days. He's the sort of elf who goes to Renaissance festivals."

Hearth grunted. *I went* one *time.*

"Guys," I said, "we have to find Sam."

No point, Hearth signed. *She'll search the river. Let her waste her time. We already looked.*

"What if we missed the sword?" Blitz asked. "What if she's got another way to find it?"

"It's not in the river," I said.

Blitz and Hearth both stared at me.

"You sure about that?" Blitz asked.

"I . . . Yeah. Don't ask me how, but now that I'm closer to the water . . ." I stared out over the Charles, its rippling gray lines etched with ice. "I feel the same as when I stood over my coffin. There's a kind of hollowness—like when you rattle a can and you can tell there's nothing inside. I just know—the sword isn't anywhere close."

"Rattling a can . . ." Blitzen mused. "Okay. I don't suppose you could direct us toward the cans we *should* be rattling?"

"That would be good," said Samirah al-Abbas.

She charged from behind the concession building and kicked me in the chest, propelling me backward into a tree. My lungs imploded like paper sacks. By the time I could see straight again, Blitzen was slumped against the wall. Hearth's bag of runestones had scattered across the pavement, and Sam was swinging her ax at him.

"Stop it!" I meant to yell, but it came out as more of a wheeze.

Hearth dodged the ax and tried to tackle her. Sam judo-flipped him over her knee. Hearth landed flat on his back.

Blitzen tried to get up. His hat was tilted sideways. His glasses had been knocked off, and the skin around his eyes was turning gray in the daylight.

Sam turned to ax-smack him. Anger roared through me. I reached for the chain on my belt. Instantly, it was a sword again. I pulled the blade and sent it spinning like a Frisbee. It clanged against Sam's ax, knocking the weapon from her hand, almost taking off her face in the process.

She stared at me in disbelief. "What the Helheim?"

"You started it!"

Hearth grabbed her ankle. Sam kicked him away.

"And stop kicking my elf!" I said.

Sam pushed back her headscarf, letting her dark hair sweep her shoulders. She crouched in a wrestler's stance, ready to take us all on. "So help me, Magnus, if I had my full powers, I would rip your soul from your body for all the trouble you've caused me."

"That's nice," I said. "Or you could tell us what you're doing here. Maybe we could help each other."

Blitzen snatched up his sunglasses. "Help *her*? Why would we help *her*? She knocked out Hearth at the funeral home! My eyes feel like chunks of quartz!"

"Well, maybe if you hadn't been stalking me," Sam said.

"Bah!" Blitzen readjusted his hat. "Nobody was stalking you, Valkyrie! We're looking for the same thing—the sword!"

Still lying on the ground, Hearth signed, *Somebody please kill her.*

"What's he doing?" Sam demanded. "Is he making rude elf gestures at me?"

"It's ASL," I said. "American Sign Language."

"*Alf* Sign Language," Blitz corrected.

"Anyway"—I raised my palms—"can we call a truce and talk? We can always go back to killing each other later."

Sam paced, muttering under her breath. She retrieved her ax and my sword.

Nice job, Magnus, I told myself. *Now she has all the weapons.*

She tossed the sword back to me. "I should never have chosen you for Valhalla."

Blitzen snorted. "On that, at least, we agree. If you hadn't interfered on the bridge—"

"*Interfered?*" Sam demanded. "Magnus was already dead

when I chose him! You and the elf weren't doing him any good with your plastic sign and your squeaky arrows!"

Blitz stood straight, which didn't make him much taller. "I'll have you know my friend is a great rune caster."

"Really?" Samirah asked. "I didn't see him using magic on the bridge against Surt."

Hearthstone looked offended. *Would have. Got sidetracked.*

"Exactly," Blitz said. "And as for me, I have *many* skills, Valkyrie."

"For instance?"

"For instance, I could fix your disgraceful outfit. *No one* wears a brown peacoat with a green headscarf."

"A dwarf in sunglasses and a ski mask is giving me fashion advice."

"I have daylight issues!"

"Guys," I said, "stop, please. Thank you."

I helped Hearthstone to his feet. He scowled at Sam and began collecting his runestones.

"Okay," I said. "Sam, why are you looking for the sword?"

"Because it's my only chance! Because—" Her voice cracked. All the rage seemed to ebb out of her. "Because I honored your stupid bravery. I rewarded you with Valhalla. And it cost me *everything*. If I can find the sword, *maybe* the thanes will reinstate me. I can convince them that . . . that I'm not—"

"The daughter of Loki?" Blitzen asked, but his voice had lost some of its edge.

Sam lowered her ax. "I can't do anything about that. But I'm *not* working for my father. I'm loyal to Odin."

Hearthstone glanced at me skeptically, like, *Are you buying this?*

"I trust her," I said.

Blitz grunted. "Is this another rattle-the-can instinct?"

"Maybe," I said. "Look, we all want to find this sword, right? We want to keep it away from Surt."

"Assuming Surt doesn't already have it," Sam said. "Assuming we can figure out what's going on. Assuming the Norns' prophecy for you isn't as bad as it sounds—"

"One way to find out." Blitz held up the bowling ball bag.

Sam stepped away. "What's in there?"

Hearth made a claw and tapped it twice on his shoulder— the sign for *boss.*

"Answers," Blitz said, "whether we want them or not. Let's confer with the Capo."

TWENTY-EIGHT

Talk to the Face, 'Cause That's Pretty Much All He's Got

BLITZ LED US down the Esplanade, where a pier extended into an icy lagoon. At the base of the dock, a candy-striped pole listed sideways.

"This is where they do gondola rides in the summer," I said. "I don't think you're going to find one now."

"We just need water." Blitz sat on the dock and unzipped the bowling bag.

"Oh, gods." Sam peered inside. "Is that human hair?"

"Hair, yes," Blitz said. "Human, no."

"You mean . . ." She pressed her hand to her stomach. "You're not serious. You work for *him?* You brought *him* here?"

"He insisted." Blitz pushed down the sides of the bag, revealing . . . yep, a severed head. The most messed-up thing about that? After two days in Valhalla, I wasn't even surprised.

The beheaded man's face was shriveled like a month-old apple. Tufts of rust-colored hair clung to his scalp. His closed eyes were sunken and dark. His bearded jaw protruded bull-dog style, revealing a crooked row of bottom teeth.

Blitz unceremoniously shoved the head in the water, bag and all.

"Dude," I said, "the state river authority isn't going to like that."

The head bobbed on the surface of the lagoon. The water around it bubbled and swirled. The man's face inflated, his wrinkles softening, his skin turning pink. He opened his eyes.

Sam and Hearth both knelt. Sam elbowed me to take a knee.

"Lord Mimir," Sam said. "You honor us."

The head opened his mouth and spewed water. More came out of his nostrils, his ears, his tear ducts. He reminded me of a catfish dragged from the bottom of a lake.

"Man, I hate—" The head coughed more water. His eyes turned from chalk white to blue. "I hate traveling in that bag."

Blitzen bowed. "Sorry, Capo. It was that or the fish tank. And the fish tank breaks easily."

The head gurgled. He scanned the faces on the dock until he found me. "Son of Frey, I've come a long way to speak with you. Hope you appreciate it."

"You're the mysterious classified boss," I said. "Hearth and Blitz have been watching me for two years . . . because they got orders from a severed head?"

"Show some respect, boyo." Mimir's voice reminded me of the longshoremen down at the Union Hall—their lungs half nicotine, half seawater.

Hearth frowned at me. *Told you C-A-P-O. Capo means head. Why surprised?*

"I am Mimir," said the head. "Once I was mighty among the Aesir. Then came the war with the Vanir. Now I got my own operation."

His face was so ugly it was hard to tell whether he was giving me an ugly look.

"Did Frey cut off your head?" I asked. "Is that why you're mad at me?"

Mimir huffed. "I'm not mad. You'll know when I'm mad."

I wondered what that meant. Maybe he would gurgle more threateningly.

"Your dad was part of the reason I lost my head, though," said Mimir. "See, as part of the truce to end the war, the two godly tribes exchanged hostages. Your father, Frey, and *his* father, Njord, came to live in Asgard. The god Honir and I—we were sent to live in Vanaheim."

"I'm guessing that didn't go well."

More water spouted from Mimir's ears. "Your father made me look bad! He was this great general among the Vanir—all golden and shiny and handsome. He and Njord got all kinds of respect in Asgard. As for me and Honir—the Vanir weren't so impressed."

"No kidding."

"Well, Honir was never very, how you say, charismatic. The Vanir would ask his opinions on important business. He'd mumble, 'Yeah, whatever. It's all good.' Me, I tried to pull my weight. I told the Vanir they should be getting into casinos."

"Casinos."

"Yeah, busloads of retirees coming to Vanaheim. Easy money. And the Vanir had all these dragons. I told them, race-tracks. In the sky. With dragons. They'd make a killing."

I looked at Blitz and Hearth. They seemed resigned, like they'd heard this story many times before.

"So anyway," said Mimir, "the Vanir didn't like my worthy counsel. They felt cheated in the hostage swap. As a protest, they cut off my head and sent it to Odin."

"Shocking. When they could've had casinos."

Sam coughed loudly. "Of course, great Mimir, both Aesir and Vanir honor you now. Magnus didn't mean to insult you. He is not so stupid."

She glared at me like, *You are so stupid.*

Around Mimir's head, the water bubbled faster. It trickled from his pores and streamed from his eyes. "Forget about it, son of Frey. I don't hold a grudge. Besides, when Odin received my severed head, he didn't take revenge. See, the All-Father was smart. He knew the Vanir and Aesir had to unite against our common enemy, the Triads."

"Uh . . ." Blitz adjusted his hat. "I think you mean the giants, boss."

"Right. Those guys. So Odin carried me to a hidden cave in Jotunheim where this magical spring feeds the roots of Yggdrasil. He placed my head in the well. The water brought me back to life, and I soaked in all the knowledge of the World Tree. My wisdom increased a thousandfold."

"But . . . you're still a severed head."

Mimir made a sideways nod. "It's not so bad. I operate across the Nine Worlds—loans, protection, pachinko machines—"

"Pachinko."

"Pachinko is huge. Plus I'm always working to delay Ragnarok. Ragnarok would be bad for business."

"Right." I decided to sit down, because it seemed like this could take a while. Once I did it, Sam and Hearth followed my example. Chickens.

"Also," Mimir said, "Odin visits me for advice from time to time. I'm his consigliere. I guard the well of knowledge.

Sometimes I let travelers drink from its waters, though that kind of intel never comes without a price."

The word *price* settled over the dock like a heavy blanket. Blitzen sat so still I was afraid he'd turned to stone. Hearthstone studied the grain of the planks. I began to understand how my friends had gotten involved with Mimir. They'd drunk from his waters (gross), and paid the price by watching me for the past two years. I wondered if what they'd learned had been worth it.

"So, Great and Well-Connected Mimir," I said, "what do you want with me?"

Mimir spit out a minnow. "I don't have to tell you, boyo. You already know."

I wanted to disagree, but the longer I listened to Mimir, the more I felt like I was breathing pure oxygen. I don't know why. The Capo wasn't exactly inspiring. Yet being around him, my mind seemed to function better, weaving together bits and pieces of weirdness I'd experienced over the last few days into one strangely cohesive picture.

An illustration from my old children's book of Norse myths came back to me—a tale so terrifying, even in its watered-down kiddie version, that I had buried it in my memory for years.

"The Wolf," I said. "Surt wants to free Fenris Wolf."

I was hoping somebody would contradict me. Hearth lowered his head. Sam closed her eyes like she was praying.

"Fenris," said Blitzen. "There's a name I was hoping never to hear again."

Mimir kept crying ice water. His lips curled in a faint smile. "There you go, son of Frey. Now tell me: What do you know about Fenris Wolf?"

I buttoned my hunting jacket. The wind off the river seemed cold even to me. "Correct me if I'm wrong. I'd *love* to be wrong. Ages ago, Loki had an affair with a giantess. They had three monstrous kids."

"I was *not* one of them," Sam muttered. "I've heard all the jokes."

Hearthstone winced, like he'd been wondering about that.

"One," I said, "was a huge snake."

"Jormungand," Sam said. "The World Serpent, which Odin threw into the sea."

"The second was Hel," I continued. "She became, like, the goddess of the dishonorable dead."

"And the third," Blitzen said, "was Fenris Wolf."

His tone was bitter, full of pain.

"Blitz," I said, "you sound like you know him."

"Every dwarf knows of Fenris. That was the first time the Aesir came to us for help. Fenris grew so savage he would've devoured the gods. They tried to tie him up, but he broke every chain."

"I remember," I said. "Finally the dwarves made a rope strong enough to hold him."

"Ever since," Blitzen said, "the children of Fenris have been enemies of the dwarves." He looked up, his dark shades reflecting my face. "You're not the only one who's lost family to wolves, kid."

I had a strange urge to hug him. Suddenly I didn't feel so bad about all the time he'd spent watching me. We were brothers in something more than homelessness. Still . . . I resisted the impulse. Whenever I'm tempted to hug a dwarf, that's usually a sign I need to move along.

"On Ragnarok," I said, "the Day of Doom, one of the first things that's supposed to happen is Fenris gets freed."

Sam nodded. "The old stories don't say how that happens—"

"But one way," Blitz said, "would be to cut him loose. The rope Gleipnir is unbreakable, but . . ."

Frey's sword, Hearth signed, *is the sharpest blade in the Nine Worlds.*

"Surt wants to free the Wolf with my father's sword." I looked at Mimir. "How are we doing so far?"

"Not bad," the head burbled. "Which brings us to your task."

"Stop Surt," I said. "Find the sword before he does . . . assuming he hasn't got it already."

"He doesn't," Mimir said. "Believe me, an event like that would make the Nine Worlds tremble. I'd taste fear in the waters of Yggdrasil."

"Yuck," I said.

"You have no idea," said Mimir. "But you must hurry."

"The Norns' prophecy. Nine days hence, blah, blah, blah."

Water bubbled out of Mimir's ears. "I'm pretty sure they didn't say *blah, blah, blah.* However, you're correct. The island where the gods imprisoned Fenris is only accessible on the first full moon of each year. That's now seven days hence."

"Who makes up these rules?" I asked.

"*I* made up that rule," Mimir said. "So shut up. Find the sword. Reach the island before Surt does."

Sam raised her hand. "Um, Lord Mimir, I understand finding the sword. But why take it to the island? Isn't that where Surt *wants* the sword?"

"See, Miss al-Abbas . . . this is why I'm the boss and you're not. Yeah, bringing the sword to the island is dangerous. Yeah, Surt could use it to free the Wolf. But Surt is gonna find a way to free Fenris with or without it. I did mention I can see the future, right? The only person who might be able to stop Surt is Magnus Chase—assuming he can find the sword and learn to wield it properly."

I'd shut up for almost a whole minute, so I figured I could raise my hand. "Lord Mister Bubbles—"

"Mimir."

"If this sword is such a big deal, why did everybody let it sit on the bottom of the Charles River for a thousand years?"

Mimir sighed foam. "My regular minions never ask so many questions."

Blitz coughed. "Actually, we do, boss. You just ignore us."

"To answer your question, Magnus Chase, the sword can only be found by a descendant of Frey upon reaching the age of maturity. Others have tried, failed, and died. Right now, you're the only living descendant of Frey."

"The only one . . . in the world?"

"In the *Nine* Worlds. Frey doesn't get out much anymore. Your mother—she must've been really something to attract his attention. Anyway, a lot of people in the Nine Worlds—gods, giants, bookies, you name it—have been waiting for you to turn sixteen. Some wanted you killed so you couldn't find the sword. Some wanted you to succeed."

Hot pins pressed against the base of my neck. The idea of a bunch of gods peering through their Asgardian telescopes, watching me grow up, creeped me out. My mom must have known all along. She'd done her best to keep me safe, to teach me survival skills. The night the wolves attacked our apartment, she'd given her life to save me.

I met the Capo's watery eyes. "And you?" I asked. "What do you want?"

"You're a risky bet, Magnus. A lot of possible fates intersect in your life. You could deal the forces of evil a great setback and delay Ragnarok for generations. Or, if you fail, you could hasten the Day of Doom."

I tried to swallow. "Hasten it, like, by how much?"

"How does next week work for you?"

"Oh."

"I decided to take the bet," Mimir said. "After the children of Fenris killed your mother, I sent Blitz and Hearth to guard you. You probably don't realize how many times they've saved your life."

Hearth held up seven fingers.

I shuddered, but mostly from the mention of Fenris's two children, the wolves with blue eyes. . . .

"To succeed," said Mimir, "you're gonna need this team. Hearthstone here—he's dedicated his life to rune magic. Without him, you'll fail. You'll also need an able dwarf like Blitzen who understands dwarven crafting. You might need to strengthen the Wolf's bindings, or even replace them."

Blitz shifted. "Uh, boss . . . my crafting skills are, well, you know—"

"Don't give me that," said Mimir. "No dwarf has a stouter heart. No dwarf has traveled farther in the Nine Worlds or has more of a desire to keep Fenris chained. Also, you're in my service. You'll do what I say."

"Ah." Blitzen nodded. "When you put it that way . . ."

"What about me, Lord Mimir?" asked Sam. "What's my part in your plan?"

Mimir frowned. Around his beard, the water bubbled a darker shade of green. "You weren't part of the plan at all. There's a cloud around your fate, Miss al-Abbas. Taking Magnus to Valhalla—I didn't see that coming. It wasn't supposed to happen."

Sam looked away, her lips pressed tight with anger.

"Sam's got a part to play," I said. "I'm sure of it."

"Do not patronize me, Magnus. I chose you because—" She stopped herself. "It was supposed to happen."

I remembered what she'd said in the feast hall: *I was told . . . I was promised.* By whom? I decided not to ask that in front of the Capo.

Mimir studied her. "I hope you're right, Miss al-Abbas. When Magnus first took the sword from the river, he couldn't control it very well. Maybe now that he's an einherji, he'll have the strength, in which case you've saved the day. Or maybe you've completely messed up his destiny."

"We're going to succeed," I insisted. "Just two questions: Where is the sword, and where is the island?"

Mimir nodded, which made him look like an oversize fishing bobber. "Well, that's the trick, isn't it? To find that kinda information, I'd have to tear the veils between the worlds, grease a lot of palms, see into the realms of the other gods."

"Couldn't we just drink your magic well water?"

"You could," he agreed. "But it would cost you. Are you and Samirah al-Abbas ready to be bound to my service?"

Hearth's face froze in apprehension. From the tension in

Blitz's shoulders, I guessed he was trying very hard not to leap to his feet and scream, *Don't do it!*

"You couldn't make an exception?" I asked the Capo. "Seeing as how you *want* this job done?"

"No can do, boyo. I'm not being greedy. It's just, well, you get what you pay for. Something comes cheap, it ain't worth much. That's true for knowledge especially. You can pay for a shortcut, get the information right now, or you'll have to find it on your own, the hard way."

Sam crossed her arms. "Apologies, Lord Mimir. I may be kicked out of the Valkyries, but I still consider myself bound to Odin's service. I can't take on another master. Magnus can make his own choice, but—"

"We'll figure it out on our own," I agreed.

Mimir made a low sloshing sound. He looked almost impressed. "Interesting choice. Good luck, then. If you succeed, you'll have a house account at all my pachinko parlors. If you fail . . . I'll see you next week for Doomsday."

The god's head swirled and disappeared into the icy water of the lagoon.

"He flushed himself," I said.

Hearth looked even paler than usual. *What now?*

My stomach rumbled. I hadn't eaten anything since last night, and apparently my system had gotten spoiled after a couple of all-you-can-eat Viking buffets.

"Now," I said, "I'm thinking lunch."

TWENTY-NINE

We Are Falafel-Jacked
by an Eagle

WE DIDN'T TALK MUCH as we headed back through the park. The air smelled of incoming snow. The wind picked up and howled like wolves, or maybe I just had wolves on the brain.

Blitz limped along, zigzagging from shadow to shadow as best he could. Hearth's brightly striped scarf didn't match his grim expression. I wanted to ask him more about rune magic now that I knew he was the best (and only) mortal practitioner. Maybe there was a rune that could make wolves explode, preferably from a safe distance. But Hearth kept his hands shoved in his pockets—the sign language equivalent of *I don't want to talk.*

We were passing my old sleeping spot under the footbridge when Sam grumbled, "Mimir. I should've known he was involved."

I glanced over. "A few minutes ago, you were all, *Lord Mimir, you honor us; we're not worthy.*"

"Of *course* I showed respect when he was right in front of me! He's one of the oldest gods. But he's unpredictable. It's never been clear whose side he's on."

Blitzen jumped to the shade of a willow tree, alarming several ducks. "The Capo is on the side of everybody in the world who doesn't want to die. Isn't that enough?"

Sam laughed. "I suppose you two work for him of your own free will? You didn't drink from his well and pay the price?"

Neither Blitz nor Hearth responded.

"That's what I thought," Sam said. "I'm not part of Mimir's plan because I would never blindly go along with it and drink his magical knowledge Kool-Aid."

"It doesn't taste like Kool-Aid," Blitz objected. "It's more like root beer with a hint of clove."

Sam turned to me. "I'm telling you, this doesn't add up. Finding the Sword of Summer—I get that. But taking it to the very place where Surt wants to use it? Unwise."

"Yeah, but if *I* have the sword—"

"Magnus, the sword is *destined* to fall into Surt's hands sooner or later. At Ragnarok, your father will die because he gave his sword away. Surt will kill him with it. That's what most of the stories say, anyway."

I got claustrophobic just thinking about it. How could anybody, even a god, avoid going crazy if he knew centuries in advance exactly how he was going to die?

"Why does Surt hate Frey so much?" I asked. "Couldn't he pick on a big strong war god?"

Blitzen frowned. "Kid, Surt wants death and destruction. He wants fire to run rampant across the Nine Worlds. A war god can't stop that. Frey can. He's the god of the growing season—the god of health and new life. He keeps the extremes in check, both fire and ice. There's nothing Surt hates worse than being restrained. Frey is his natural enemy."

And by extension, I thought, *Surt hates* me.

"If Frey knew what his fate would be," I said, "why did he give up his blade in the first place?"

Blitz grunted. "Love. Why else?"

"Love?"

"Ugh," Sam said. "I *hate* that story. Where are you taking us for lunch, Magnus?"

Part of me wanted to hear the story. Part of me remembered my conversation with Loki: *Will you search for your heart's desire, knowing it may doom you as it doomed your father?*

A lot of Norse stories seemed to have the same message: Knowing things wasn't always worth the price. Unfortunately for me, I'd always been the curious type.

"It's . . . uh, just up ahead," I said. "Come on."

The food court at the Transportation Building wasn't Valhalla, but if you were homeless in Boston, it was pretty close. The indoor atrium was warm, open to the public, and never crowded. It was only halfheartedly patrolled by private security. As long as you had a drink cup or a plate of half-eaten food, you could sit at the tables for a long time before anybody made you move.

On the way in, Blitzen and Hearthstone started toward the garbage cans to check for lunch leavings, but I stopped them.

"Guys, no," I said. "We're eating actual meals today. My treat."

Hearth raised an eyebrow. He signed, *You have money?*

"He's got that friend here," Blitzen recalled. "The falafel guy."

Sam froze in her tracks. "What?"

She looked around as if just realizing where we were.

"It's cool," I promised. "I know a guy at Fadlan's Falafel. You'll thank me for it. Stuff is amazing—"

"No—I—oh, gods—" She hastily put her scarf over her hair. "Maybe I'll wait outside—I can't—"

"Nonsense." Blitz hooked his arm through hers. "They might serve more food if we've got a pretty woman with us!"

Sam clearly wanted to bolt, but she allowed Hearth and Blitz to steer her into the food court. I guess I should've paid more attention to how uncomfortable she was acting, but once you put me within a hundred feet of Fadlan's Falafel, I get tunnel vision.

Over the past two years, I'd struck up a friendship with the manager, Abdel. I think he saw me as his community service project. The shop always had surplus food—slightly out-of-date pita bread, day-old shawarma, kibbeh that had been sitting under the heat lamps a little too long. Abdel couldn't legally sell the stuff, but it still tasted perfectly fine. Instead of throwing it out, Abdel gave it to me. Whenever I came around, I could count on a falafel flatbread sandwich or something just as tasty. In return, I made sure the other homeless folks in the atrium stayed polite and cleaned up after themselves so Abdel's paying customers weren't scared away.

In Boston, you couldn't walk a block without stumbling into some icon of liberty—the Freedom Trail, the Old North Church, the Bunker Hill Monument, whatever—but to me, liberty tasted like Fadlan's Falafel. That stuff had kept me alive and independent ever since my mom died.

I didn't want to overwhelm Abdel with too many people, so I sent Blitz and Hearth to grab a table while I escorted Sam to get the food. The whole way, she dragged her feet, turning aside, fiddling with her headscarf as if she wanted to disappear inside it.

"What's the matter with you?" I asked.

"Maybe he's not there," she muttered. "Maybe you can say I'm your tutor."

I didn't know what she was talking about. I bellied up to the counter while Sam hung back, doing her best to hide behind a potted ficus tree.

"Is Abdel here?" I asked the guy at the register.

He started to say something, but then Abdel's son Amir came out from the back, grinning and wiping his hands on his apron. "Jimmy, how's it going?"

I relaxed. If Abdel wasn't around, Amir was the next best thing. He was eighteen or nineteen, trim and good-looking, with slick dark hair, an Arabic tattoo on his biceps, and a smile so brilliant, it could've sold truckloads of teeth whitener. Like everybody at Fadlan's Falafel, he knew me as "Jimmy."

"Yeah, I'm good," I said. "How's your pop?"

"He's at the Somerville location today. Can I get you some food?"

"Man, you're the best."

Amir laughed. "No biggie." He glanced over my shoulder and did a double take. "And there's Samirah! What are you doing here?"

She shuffled forward. "Hi, Amir. I am . . . tutoring Ma—Jimmy. I am tutoring Jimmy."

"Oh, yeah?" Amir leaned on the counter, which made his arm muscles flex. The dude worked full-time at his dad's various shops, yet he somehow managed to avoid getting even a speck of grease on his white T-shirt. "Don't you have school?"

"Um, yes, but I get credit for tutoring off campus. Jimmy and . . . his classmates." She pointed toward Blitz and Hearth, who were having a rapid-fire argument in sign language, tracing circles in the air. "Geometry," Samirah said. "They're hopeless with geometry."

"Hopeless," I agreed. "But food helps us study."

Amir's eyes crinkled. "I've got you covered. Glad to see you're okay, Jimmy. That bridge accident the other day—the paper had this picture of a kid who died? Looked a lot like you. Different name, but we were worried."

I'd been so focused on falafel that I'd forgotten to think about them making that connection. "Ah, yeah, I saw that. I'm good. Just studying geometry. With my tutor."

"Okay!" Amir smiled at Sam. The awkwardness was so thick you could've cut it with a broadsword. "Well, Samirah, say hi to Jid and Bibi for me. You guys go ahead and sit. I'll bring out some food in a sec."

Sam muttered something that might have been *Thanks a lot* or *Kill me now.* Then we joined Blitz and Hearth at the table.

"What was that about?" I asked her. "How do you know Amir?"

She pulled her scarf a little lower over her forehead. "Don't sit too close to me. Try to look like we're talking about geometry."

"Triangles," I said. "Quadrilaterals. Also, why are you embarrassed? Amir is awesome. If you know the Fadlan family, you're like a rock star to me."

"He's my cousin," she blurted. "Second cousin, twice removed. Or something."

I looked at Hearth. He was scowling at the floor. Blitz had taken off his ski mask and glasses, I guess because the interior light didn't bother him as much, and was now sullenly spinning a plastic fork on the table. Apparently I'd missed a good argument between him and Hearth.

"Okay," I said. "But why so nervous?"

"Can you drop it?" she said.

I raised my hands. "Fine. Let's all start over. Hi, everybody. I'm Magnus, and I'm an einherji. If we're not going to study geometry, could we talk about how we're going to find the Sword of Summer?"

Nobody answered.

A pigeon waddled past, pecking at crumbs.

I glanced back at the falafel shop. For some reason, Amir had rolled down the steel curtain. I'd never seen him close the shop during lunch hour. I wondered if Sam had somehow offended him and he'd cut off my falafel allowance.

If so, I was going to go berserker.

"What happened to our food?" I wondered.

At my feet, a small voice croaked, "I can help with both those questions."

I looked down. My week had been so wack I didn't even flinch when I realized who had spoken.

"Guys," I said, "this pigeon wants to help."

The pigeon fluttered onto our table. Hearth nearly fell out of his chair. Blitz snatched up a fork.

"Service here can be a little slow," said the pigeon. "But I can speed up your order. I can also tell you where to find the sword."

Sam reached for her ax. "That's not a pigeon."

The bird regarded her with a beady orange eye. "Maybe not. But if you kill me, you'll never get your lunch. You'll also never find the sword or see your intended again."

Samirah's eyes looked like they were going to shoot across the atrium.

"What is he talking about?" I said. "Intended *what?*"

The bird cooed. "If you ever want Fadlan's Falafel to open again—"

"Okay, that's a declaration of war." I considered grabbing for the bird, but even with my einherji reflexes, I doubted I could catch it. "What did you do? What's happened to Amir?"

"Nothing yet!" said the pigeon. "I'll bring you your lunch. All I want is first pick of the food."

"Uh-huh," I said. "And assuming I believe you, what would you want in exchange for information about the sword?"

"A favor. It's negotiable. Now, does that falafel shop stay closed forever, or do we have a deal?"

Blitzen shook his head. "Don't do it, Magnus."

Hearth signed, *Pigeons cannot be trusted.*

Sam met my eyes. Her expression was pleading—almost frantic. Either she liked falafel even more than I did, or she was worried about something else.

"Fine," I said. "Bring us our lunch."

Immediately the shop's steel curtain rolled up. The cashier stood like a statue, the phone to his ear. Then he unfroze, glanced over his shoulder, and shouted an order to the cook as if nothing had happened. The pigeon took off and sped toward the shop, disappearing behind the counter. The cashier didn't seem to notice.

A moment later, a much larger bird shot out of the kitchen—a bald eagle with a tray in his claws. He landed in the middle of our table.

"You're an eagle now?" I asked.

"Yeah," he said in the same croaky voice. "I like to mix it up. Here's your food."

It was everything I could've asked for: steaming squares of spiced ground beef kibbeh; a stack of lamb kebabs with mint yogurt dip; four fresh slabs of pita bread filled with deep-fried nuggets of chickpea goodness, drizzled in tahini sauce and garnished with pickle wedges.

"Oh, Helheim yes." I reached for the tray, but the eagle pecked at my hand.

"Now, now," he chided. "I get first pick."

Ever seen an eagle eat falafel?

That horrifying image now haunts my nightmares.

Faster than I could blink, the eagle struck, vacuuming up everything but a single wedge of pickle.

"Hey!" I yelled.

Sam rose, hefting her ax. "He's a giant. He's got to be!"

"We had a deal." The eagle belched. "Now about the sword—"

I let loose a guttural roar—the cry of a man who has been deprived of his rightful kibbeh. I drew my sword and smacked the eagle with the flat of the blade.

It wasn't the most rational move, but I was hungry. I was angry. I hated being taken advantage of, and I didn't particularly like bald eagles.

The blade hit the bird's back and stuck there like superglue. I tried to pull it away, but it wouldn't move. My hands were grafted to the sword grip.

"Okay, then," the eagle squawked, "we can play it that way."

He took off through the food court at sixty miles an hour, dragging me along behind him.

THIRTY

An Apple a Day
Will Get You Killed

ADD TO MY LIST of Least Favorite Activities: eagle surfing.

The stupid bird shouldn't have been able to take off with a more-or-less-full-grown Magnus in tow. Yet he did.

Behind me, Blitz and Sam yelled helpful stuff like "Hey! Stop!" as the eagle dragged me through tables, chairs, and potted plants, then blasted through the double glass doors and soared over Charles Street.

A guy having lunch in the tenth-floor condo across the street spewed Cheetos when I shot past. I left a nice footprint on his window.

"Let me go!" I yelled at the eagle.

The bird cackled as he pulled me along a rooftop. "You sure about that? Heads up!"

I twisted, barely avoiding a face-first encounter with an industrial AC unit. I plowed through a brick chimney, using my chest as a battering ram. Then the eagle plummeted down the other side of the building.

"So!" the eagle said. "You ready to negotiate that favor?"

"With a mutant pigeon who steals falafel?" I yelled. "No thanks!"

"Suit yourself." The eagle veered, slamming me into a fire

escape. I felt my ribs crack, like vials of acid breaking inside my chest. My empty stomach tried unsuccessfully to hurl.

We climbed above one of the churches on Boylston and circled the steeple. I had an addled thought about Paul Revere and the whole *One if by land, two if by sea* thing.

And if you see a dude being dragged by a giant eagle, uh, I don't even know how many lights that is.

I tried to heal my ribs through willpower, but I couldn't concentrate. The pain was too intense. I kept running into walls and kicking out windows.

"All I want," the eagle said, "is a favor for a favor. I'll tell you how to get the sword, but you have to get me something while you're at it. Nothing much. Just an apple. One apple."

"What's the catch?"

"The catch is that if you don't agree . . . oh, look! Pigeon spikes!"

Ahead of us, the edge of a hotel roof bristled with steel like a miniature line of World War I barbed wire. The spikes were there to discourage roosting birds, but they'd also do a great job shredding my soft underbelly.

Fear got the best of me. I don't like pointy objects. My gut was still sensitive from my recent death by molten asphalt.

"Fine!" I yelled. "No spikes!"

"Say: *By my troth, I agree to your terms.*"

"I don't even know what that means!"

"Say it!"

"By my troth, I agree to your terms! Yes, apples! No, spikes!"

The eagle climbed, narrowly clearing the roof. The tips

of my shoes twanged against the barbs. We circled Copley Square and landed on the roof of the Boston Public Library.

The sword came free of the eagle's back. My hands unglued themselves, which was great, except that I now had nothing to hold on to. The red curved clay tiles were almost impossible to stand on. The roof slanted precariously. Eighty feet below me stretched a wide expanse of pavement-flavored death.

I crouched to avoid falling. Carefully, I sheathed my sword, which melted back into a length of chain.

"Ow," I said.

My ribs ached. My arms had been pulled half out of their sockets. My chest felt like it had been permanently tattooed with a brick wall design.

To my left, the eagle perched on a lightning-rod spire, lording over the decorative bronze griffins around the base.

I'd never thought of eagles as having expressions, but this one definitely looked smug.

"I'm glad you saw reason!" he said. "Though, honestly, I enjoyed our little flight through the city. It's good to speak with you alone."

"I'm blushing," I grumbled. "Oh, no, wait. That's the blood all over my face."

"Here's the information you need," the eagle continued. "When your sword fell in the river, the current carried it downstream. It was claimed by the goddess Ran. Lots of valuable things end up in her net."

"Ran?"

The eagle clicked his beak. "Sea goddess. Has a net. Try to keep up."

"Where do I find her? And please don't say 'the sea.'"

"She could be anywhere, so you'll have to get her attention. The way to do that: I know this guy, Harald. He's got a boat at the Fish Pier, does deep-sea excursions. Tell him Big Boy sent you."

"Big Boy."

"One of my many names. Harald will know what you mean. Convince him to take you fishing in Massachusetts Bay. If you cause enough of a ruckus out there, you'll attract Ran's attention. Then you can negotiate. Ask her for the sword and one of Idun's apples."

"Eden."

"Are you just going to repeat every name I give you? It's I-D-U-N. She distributes the apples of immortality that keep the gods young and spry. Ran is sure to have one lying around, because seriously, once you see her, you'll be able to tell she's not good about remembering to eat her apples. When you have the apple, bring it back here. Give it to me, and I'll release you from your vow."

"Two questions. Are you insane?"

"No."

"Second question: How is fishing in the bay going to create a ruckus that attracts a sea goddess?"

"That depends on what you fish for. Tell Harald you need the special bait. He'll understand. If he protests, tell him Big Boy insists."

"I have no idea what that means," I confessed. "Assuming I meet Ran, how am I supposed to bargain with her?"

"That's three questions. Also, that's your problem."

"Last question."

"This is four now."

"What's to keep me from getting the sword and not bringing you an apple?"

"Well, you swore by your troth," said the eagle. "Your troth is your word, your faith, your honor, your soul. It's a binding oath, especially for an einherji. Unless you want to spontaneously combust and find yourself trapped forever in the icy darkness of Helheim . . ."

I chewed my lip. "I guess I'll keep my promise."

"Excellent!" The eagle flapped his wings. "Here come your friends, which is my cue to leave. I'll see you when you have my fresh produce!"

The eagle soared away and disappeared behind the glass walls of the Hancock Tower, leaving me to find my own way off the roof.

Down in Copley Square, Blitzen, Hearthstone, and Sam were just running onto the frozen lawn. Sam saw me first. She stopped in her tracks and pointed.

I waved.

I couldn't see her expression, but she spread her arms like, *What the heck are you doing up there?*

With some difficulty, I got to my feet. Thanks to my ValhallaCare health plan, my injuries were already starting to mend, but I still felt sore and stiff. I picked my way to the edge of the roof and peered over. Magnus 1.0 never would've considered it, but now I plotted a series of ten-foot jumps—to that window ledge, that flagpole, the top of that light fixture, then the front steps—and I thought, *Yeah, no problem.*

In a matter of seconds, I'd safely reached the ground. My friends met me at the sidewalk.

"What was *that* about?" Blitzen demanded. "Was he a giant?"

"Dunno," I said. "His name is Big Boy, and he likes apples."

I told them the story.

Hearthstone smacked his forehead. He signed: *You swore by your troth?*

"Well, it was either that or get shredded by pigeon spikes, so yeah."

Sam stared at the sky, maybe hoping to see an eagle she could hit with her ax. "This will end badly. Deals with giants always do."

"At least Magnus found out where the sword is," Blitzen said. "Besides, Ran's a goddess. She'll be on our side, right?"

Sam snorted. "I guess you haven't heard the stories about her that *I* have. But at this point, we don't have much choice. Let's find Harald."

THIRTY-ONE

Go Smelly or Go Home

I'D NEVER BEEN SCARED of boats until I saw Harald's.

Painted on the prow was HARALD'S DEEP-SEA EXCURSIONS AND DEATH WISHES, which seemed like a lot of verbiage for a twenty-foot-long dinghy. The deck was a mess of ropes, buckets, and tackle boxes. Nets and buoys festooned the sides like Christmas decorations. The hull had once been green but had faded to the color of well-chewed spearmint gum.

Nearby on the dock sat Harald himself, in splattered yellow coveralls and a T-shirt so grungy, my donation box Wiggles shirt would've been an upgrade. He was a sumo-size guy with arms as thick as the rotating meat spits back at Fadlan's Falafel. (Yes, I was still thinking about food.)

The weirdest thing about him was his hair. His shaggy locks, his beard, even his fuzzy forearms glistened whitish blue, as if he'd been caught outside overnight and glazed with frost.

As we approached, he looked up from the rope he was coiling. "Well, now. A dwarf, an elf, and two humans walk onto my pier . . . Sounds like the beginning of a joke."

"I hope not," I said. "We want to rent your boat for a fishing expedition. We'll need the special bait."

Harald snorted. "You four on one of *my* expeditions? I don't think so."

"Big Boy sent us."

Harald furrowed his brow, causing light snow to fall across his cheeks. "Big Boy, eh? What does he want with the likes of you?"

Sam stepped forward. "None of your concern." From her coat pocket she pulled a large coin and tossed it to Harald. "One red gold now; five more when we finish. Will you rent us the boat or not?"

I leaned toward her. "What is red gold?"

"The currency of Asgard and Valhalla," she said. "Widely accepted in the other realms."

Harald sniffed the coin. Its gold surface glowed so warmly it seemed to be on fire. "You have giantish blood, girl? I can see it in your eyes."

"That's also none of your concern."

"Humph. The payment is sufficient, but my boat is small. Two passengers maximum. I'll take you and the human boy, but the dwarf and the elf—forget it."

Blitzen cracked his knuckles inside his leather gloves. "Look here, Frosty—"

"HUR! Never call a frost giant *Frosty*. We hate that. Besides, you look half petrified already, dwarf. I don't need another anchor. As for elves, they are creatures of air and light. They're useless aboard a ship. Two passengers only. That's the deal. Take it or leave it."

I glanced at my friends. "Guys, sidebar please."

I led them down the dock, out of earshot from Harald. "That dude is a frost giant?"

Hearthstone signed: *Icy hair. Ugly. Big. Yes.*

"But . . . I mean, he's large, but he's not *giant*."

Sam's expression made me suspect she was not the most patient geometry tutor. "Magnus, giants aren't necessarily enormous. Some are. Some can *grow* to enormous size if they feel like it. But they're even more varied than humans. Many look like regular people. Some can change shape into eagles or pigeons or almost anything."

"But what's a frost giant doing on the docks in Boston? Can we trust him?"

"First answer," Blitzen said, "frost giants are all over the place, especially in the north of Midgard. As for trusting him— absolutely not. He might take you two straight to Jotunheim and throw you in a dungeon, or he might use you for bait. You have to insist that Hearth and I go with you."

Hearth tapped Blitz's shoulder.

Giant is right, he signed. *I told you—too much daylight. You are turning to stone. Too stubborn to admit.*

"Nah, I'm fine."

Hearth looked around the dock. He spotted a metal pail, picked it up, and slammed it over Blitz's head. Blitz didn't react, but the pail crumpled into the shape of his skull.

"Okay," Blitz admitted, "maybe I'm petrifying a little, but—"

"Get out of the light for a while," I told him. "We'll be fine. Hearth, can you find him a nice underground lair or something?"

Hearth nodded. *We will try to find out more about Fenris and his chains. Meet you tonight. Back at library?*

"Sounds good," I said. "Sam, let's go fishing."

We returned to Harald, who was fashioning his rope into a lovely noose.

"Okay," I told him, "two passengers. We need to fish as far

out in Massachusetts Bay as possible, and we need the special bait."

Harald gave me a twisted grin. His teeth might have been cut from the same fuzzy brown cord he was coiling. "By all means, little human." He pointed to a sliding door on the side of the warehouse. "Pick your own bait . . . if you can carry it."

When Sam and I opened the door, I almost passed out from the stench.

Sam gagged. "Odin's Eye, I've smelled less fragrant battle-fields."

Inside the storage room, hanging from meat hooks, was an impressive collection of rotting carcasses. The smallest was a five-foot-long shrimp. The largest was a severed bull's head the size of a Fiat.

I covered my nose with my jacket sleeve. That didn't help. I felt like somebody had filled a grenade with rotten egg, rusty metal, and raw onion, then tossed it into my sinus cavity.

"It hurts to breathe," I said. "Which of these tasty morsels do you think is the special bait?"

Sam pointed at the bull's head. "Go big or go home?"

"She said to the homeless kid." I forced myself to study the bull's head—its curved black horns, its lolling pink tongue like a hairy air mattress, its white steaming fur, and the glistening slime craters of its nostrils. "How is it possible that a bull grew that large?"

"It's probably from Jotunheim," Sam said. "Their cattle get pretty big."

"You don't say. Any idea what we're supposed to be fishing for?"

"There are lots of sea monsters in the deep. As long as it's not . . ." A shadow crossed her face. "Never mind. Probably just a sea monster."

"Just a sea monster," I said. "That's a relief."

I was tempted to take the jumbo shrimp and get out of there, but I had a feeling we'd need bigger bait if we were going to cause a ruckus that would attract a sea goddess.

"The bull's head it is," I decided.

Sam hefted her ax. "I'm not sure it'll even fit on Harald's boat, but—"

She threw her ax at the meat hook chain, which broke with a snap. The bull's head crashed to the floor like a large, disgusting piñata. The ax flew back to Sam's hand.

Together we gripped the meat hook and dragged the bull's head out of the storage locker. Even with help, I shouldn't have been able to move it, but my einherji strength was up to the task.

Die painfully. Go to Valhalla. Gain the ability to drag rancid, colossal severed heads across a dock. Hooray.

When we got to the boat, I yanked the chain with all my strength. The bull's head toppled off the pier and smashed onto the deck. The S.S. *Harald* almost capsized, but somehow it stayed afloat. The bull's head took up the back half of the ship. Its tongue hung over the stern. Its left eye rolled up in its head so it looked seasick.

Harald rose from his bait bucket. If he was at all surprised or annoyed that I'd dropped a five-hundred-pound cow head on his boat, he didn't show it.

"An ambitious choice of bait." Harald gazed across the harbor. The sky was darkening. Light sleet needled the surface of the water. "Let's get going, then. Lovely afternoon to fish."

THIRTY-TWO

My Years of Playing Bassmasters 2000 Really Pay Off

IT WAS A TERRIBLE AFTERNOON TO FISH.

The sea heaved and so did I, right over the side several times. The cold didn't bother me, but the sleet stung my face. The rocking of the deck made my legs feel like Slinkys. Harald the frost giant stood at the wheel, singing in a guttural language I assumed was Jotunese.

Sam didn't seem to mind the rough seas. She leaned against the bow rail and stared into the gray, her scarf rippling around her neck like gills.

"What's with the scarf anyway?" I asked. "Sometimes you cover your head. Sometimes you don't."

She laid her fingers protectively over the green silk. "It's a hijab. I wear it when I want to, or when I think I need to. Like when I take my grandmother to mosque on Friday, or—"

"Or when you see Amir?"

She muttered under her breath. "I almost thought you were going to let that go."

"The pigeon said Amir is your intended. Like . . . *engaged*? What are you, like, sixteen?"

"Magnus—"

"I'm just saying, if this is one of those forced arranged

marriages, that's messed up. You're a Valkyrie. You should be able to—"

"Magnus, shut it. Please."

The boat hit a swell, spraying us with saltwater buckshot.

Samirah gripped the rail. "My grandparents are old-fashioned. They were raised in Baghdad, but fled to the U.S. when Saddam Hussein was in power."

"And . . . ?"

"They've known the Fadlans since forever. They're good people. Distant kin. Successful, kind—"

"I know. Abdel is awesome. Amir seems cool. But a forced marriage if you don't love the guy—"

"Ugh! You don't get it. I've been in love with Amir since I was twelve."

The boat groaned as it dipped between the waves. Harald kept singing his Jotunese version of "Ninety-Nine Bottles of Beer."

"Oh," I said.

"Not that it's any of your business," Samirah said.

"Yeah. No."

"But sometimes when a family tries to find a good match, they actually *care* what the girl thinks."

"Okay."

"I didn't realize until I was older . . . After my mom died, my grandparents took me in but, well, my mom wasn't married when she had me. That's still a big deal for my grandparents' generation."

"Yeah." I decided not to add: *Plus the fact that your dad was Loki, the father of evil.*

Sam seemed to read my thoughts. "She was a doctor, my mom. She found Loki in the emergency room. He was . . . I don't know . . . he'd used up too much of his power trying to appear in Midgard in physical form. He got trapped somehow, divided between worlds. His manifestation in Boston was in agony, weak and helpless."

"She cured him?"

Sam brushed a droplet of seawater from her wrist. "In a way. She was kind to him. She stayed by his side. Loki can be very charming when he wants to be."

"I know." I blinked. "I mean . . . from the stories. You've met him in person?"

She shot me a dark look. "I don't approve of my father. He may be charismatic, but he's also a liar, a thief, a murderer. He's visited me several times. I refused to talk to him, which drives him nuts. He likes to be noticed. He's not exactly low-key."

"I get it," I said. "Loki. Low-key."

She rolled her eyes. "Anyway, my mom mostly raised me by herself. She was headstrong, unconventional. When she died . . . Well, in the local community, I was damaged goods, a bastard child. My grandparents were lucky, *very* lucky, to get the Fadlans' blessing for me to marry Amir. I won't really bring anything to the marriage. I'm not rich or respectable or—"

"Come on," I said. "You're smart. You're tough. You're an honest-to-Frigg Valkyrie. And I can't believe I'm finding reasons to support your arranged marriage. . . ."

Her dark hair whipped around her, collecting flecks of ice.

"The Valkyrie thing is a problem," she said. "My family . . . well, we're a little different. We have a long, long history with the Norse gods."

"How?"

She waved away the question like, *Too much to explain.*

"Still," she said, "if anyone found out about my other life . . . I don't think Mr. Fadlan would be okay with his eldest son marrying a girl who moonlights as a soul collector for pagan gods."

"Ah. When you put it that way . . ."

"I cover for my absences as best I can."

"Math tutoring."

"And some simple Valkyrie glamours. But a good Muslim girl is not supposed to hang out on her own with strange guys."

"Strange guys. Thanks."

I had a sudden image of Sam sitting in English class when her phone started to buzz. The screen flashed: ODIN CALLING. She dashed to the restroom, changed into her Super Valkyrie costume, and flew out the nearest window.

"When you got kicked out of Valhalla . . . uh, I mean, I'm sorry about that. But didn't you think, *Hey, maybe this is a good thing. I can have a normal life now?*"

"No. That's the problem. I want *both.* I want to marry Amir when the time comes. But also, all my life, I've wanted to fly."

"Flying like *airplanes* or flying like *zooming around on a magic horse?*"

"Both. When I was six, I started drawing pictures of airplanes. I wanted to be a pilot. How many Arab American female pilots do you know?"

"You would be the first," I admitted.

"I *like* that idea. Ask me any question about airplanes. I can answer it."

"So when you became a Valkyrie—"

"It was a total rush. A dream come true, being able to take off at a moment's notice. Besides, I felt like I was doing some good. I could find honorable, brave people who died protecting others, and I could bring them to Valhalla. You don't know how much I miss that."

I could hear the pain in her voice. *Honorable brave people . . .* She was including me in that group. After all the trouble she'd gotten into for my sake, I wanted to tell her that it would be all right. We would figure out a way so she could have both her lives.

But I couldn't even promise we'd live through this boat trip.

From the wheelhouse, Harald bellowed, "Mortals, you should bait your hooks! We're getting close to good fishing!"

Sam shook her head. "No. Go farther out!"

Harald scowled. "Not safe! Any farther—"

"You want your gold or not?"

Harald muttered something that was probably inappropriate in Jotunese. He gunned the motor.

I looked at Sam. "How do you know we need to go farther?"

"I can sense it," she said. "One of the advantages of my father's blood, I guess. I can usually tell where the biggest monsters are lurking."

"Joy and happiness."

I peered into the gloom. I thought about Ginnungagap, the primordial mist between ice and fire. We seemed to be sailing right into it. Any moment the sea might dissolve and we'd fall into oblivion. I hoped I was wrong. Sam's grandparents would probably be ticked off if she didn't get home in time for dinner.

The boat shuddered. The sea darkened.

"There," Sam said. "Did you feel it? We've passed from Midgard into Jotunheim waters."

I pointed off the port bow. A few hundred yards away, a granite spire jutted out of the fog. "But that's Graves Light. We're not too far from the harbor."

Sam grabbed one of the giant's fishing poles, which looked more appropriate for heavyweight pole-vaulting. "The worlds overlap, Magnus, especially near Boston. Go get the bait."

Harald slowed the engines when he saw me coming aft.

"Too dangerous to fish here," he warned. "Besides, I doubt you'll be able to cast that bait."

"Shut up, Harald." I grabbed the chain and dragged the bull's head forward, almost knocking the captain overboard with one of its horns.

When I got back to Sam, we examined the meat hook, which was embedded pretty well in the bull's skull.

"That should work for a fishing hook," Sam decided. "Let's get this chain tied on."

We spent a few minutes attaching the chain to the fishing line—a thin braided steel cable that made the reel weigh about three hundred pounds.

Together, Sam and I rolled the bull's head off the front of the boat. It sank slowly into the icy froth, the bull's dead eye staring at me as it submerged, like, *Not cool, man!*

Harald lumbered over carrying a large chair. He sunk its four feet into anchor holes on the deck. Then he lashed the seat in place with steel cables.

"If I were you, human," he said, "I'd buckle up."

With its leather harnesses, the seat looked a little too

much like an electric chair to me, but Sam held the fishing pole while I strapped myself in.

"So why am *I* in the chair?" I asked.

"Your promise," she reminded me. "You swore by your troth."

"Troth sucks." From the giant's supply kit, I pulled some leather gloves that were only four sizes too big and put them on.

Sam handed me the pole, and then found gloves for herself.

I had a disjointed memory from when I was ten years old, watching *Jaws* with my mom because she insisted. She warned me it was superscary, but the whole time I was either bored at the slow pace or laughing at the schlocky-looking rubber shark.

"Please let me catch a rubber shark," I muttered now.

Harald cut the engines. Suddenly it was freakishly quiet. The wind died. The sleet against the deck sounded like sand hitting glass. The waves calmed as if the sea was holding its breath.

Sam stood at the rail, feeding out cable as the bull's head sank into the depths. Finally the line went slack.

"Did we hit bottom?" I asked.

Sam bit her lip. "I don't know. I think—"

The line sprang taut with a sound like a hammer on a saw blade. Sam let go to avoid being catapulted into space. The pole was nearly ripped out of my hands, taking my fingers with it, but somehow I held on.

The chair groaned. The leather straps dug into my collarbones. The entire boat leaned forward into the waves with timbers creaking and rivets popping.

"Ymir's Blood!" Harald yelled. "We're breaking apart!"

"Give it more line!" Sam grabbed a bucket. She poured water on the cable, which steamed as it raced off the prow.

I gritted my teeth. My arm muscles felt like warm bread dough. Just when I was sure I couldn't hold on any longer, the pulling stopped. The line hummed with tension, laser-dotting on the gray water about a hundred yards starboard.

"What's going on?" I asked. "Is it resting?"

Harald cursed. "I don't like this. Sea monsters don't act this way. Even the biggest catches—"

"Reel it in," Sam said. "Now!"

I turned the handle. It was like arm-wrestling the Terminator. The rod bent. The cable creaked. Sam pulled the line, keeping it clear of the rail, but even with her help I could barely make any progress.

My shoulders went numb. My lower back spasmed. Despite the cold, I was soaked with sweat and shivering with exhaustion. I felt like I was reeling in a sunken battleship.

From time to time, Sam yelled encouraging things like, "No, you idiot! Pull!"

Finally, in front of the boat, the sea darkened in a fifty-foot-diameter oval. The waves sloshed and boiled.

Up in the wheelhouse, Harald must have had a better view of whatever was coming to the surface. He screamed in a very ungiantish voice, "Cut the line!"

"No," Sam said. "It's too late for that."

Harald snatched up a knife. He threw it at the cable, but Sam deflected the blade with her ax.

"Back off, giant!" she yelled.

"But you can't bring that thing up!" Harald wailed. "It's the—"

"Yes, I know!"

The rod began slipping from my hands. "Help!"

Sam lunged and grabbed the fishing pole. She wedged herself next to me in the chair to assist, but I was too tired and terrified to feel embarrassed.

"We may all die," she muttered, "but this will *definitely* get Ran's attention."

"Why?" I asked. "What is that thing?"

Our catch broke the surface and opened its eyes.

"Meet my older brother," Sam said, "the World Serpent."

THIRTY-THREE

Sam's Brother Wakes Up Kinda Cranky

WHEN I SAY the serpent opened his eyes, I mean he switched on green spotlights the size of trampolines. His irises glowed so intensely I was pretty sure everything I saw for the rest of my life would be tinted the color of lime Jell-O.

The good news: the rest of my life didn't look like it was going to be very long.

The monster's ridged forehead and tapered snout made him look more like an eel than a snake. His hide glistened in a camouflage patchwork of green, brown, and yellow. (Here I am calmly describing him. At the time the only thought in my mind was: YIKES! HUGE SNAKE!)

He opened his mouth and hissed—the stench of rancid bull's head and poison so strong my clothes smoked. He may not have used mouthwash, but obviously the World Serpent cared about flossing. His teeth gleamed in rows of perfect white triangles. His pink maw was big enough to swallow Harald's boat and a dozen of Harald's closest friends' boats.

My meat hook was embedded in the back of his mouth, right where the hangy-down uvula thing would be in a human mouth. The serpent didn't seem too happy about that.

He shook back and forth, raking the steel line across his teeth. My fishing pole whipped sideways. The boat seesawed port to starboard, planks cracking and popping, but somehow we stayed afloat. My line didn't break.

"Sam?" I said in a small voice. "Why hasn't he killed us yet?"

She pressed so close to me I could feel her shivering. "I think he's studying us, maybe even trying to talk to us."

"What is he saying?"

Sam gulped. "My guess? *How dare you?*"

The serpent hissed, spitting globs of poison that sizzled against the deck.

Behind us, Harald whimpered, "Drop the pole, you fools! You'll get us all killed!"

I tried to meet the serpent's gaze. "Hey, Mr. Jormungand. Can I call you Mr. J? Look, sorry to bother you. Nothing personal. We're just using you to get somebody's attention."

Mr. J didn't like that. His head surged out of the water, towering above us, then crashed down again off the bow, triggering a forty-foot-tall ring of waves.

Sam and I were definitely sitting in the splash zone. I ate salt water for lunch. My lungs discovered they could not in fact breathe the stuff. My eyes got a thorough power washing. But, incredibly, the boat didn't capsize. When the rocking and sloshing subsided, I found myself still alive, still holding the fishing pole with my line still attached to the World Serpent's mouth. The monster stared at me like, *Why are you not dead?*

Out of the corner of my eye, I saw the tsunami crash against the Graves, washing all the way up to the base of the lighthouse. I wondered if I'd just flooded Boston.

I remembered why Jormungand was called the World Serpent. Supposedly his body was so long it wrapped around the earth, stretching across the sea floor like a monstrous telecommunication cable. Most of the time he kept his tail in his mouth—Hey, I used a pacifier until I was almost two, so I can't judge—but apparently he'd decided our bull's-head bait was worth the switch.

The point being: if the World Serpent was shaking, the whole world might be shaking with him.

"So," I said to nobody in particular, "what now?"

"Magnus," Sam said in a strangled tone, "try not to panic. But look off the starboard side."

I couldn't imagine what would be more panic-inducing than Mr. J until I saw the woman in the whirlpool.

Compared to the serpent, she was tiny—only about ten feet tall. From the waist up, she wore a blouse of silver chain mail encrusted with barnacles. She might have once been beautiful, but her pearlescent skin was withered, her seaweed-green eyes were milky with cataracts, and her rippling blond hair was shot through with gray like blight in a wheat field.

From the waist down, things got weird. Spinning around her like a dancer's skirt, a waterspout swirled within a silver fishing net a hundred yards in diameter. Trapped in its weave was a kaleidoscope of ice floe, dead fish, plastic garbage bags, car tires, grocery carts, and other assorted flotsam. As the woman floated toward us, the edge of her net *thwapped* against our hull and scraped against the World Serpent's neck.

She spoke in a deep baritone. "Who dares interrupt my scavenging?"

Harald the frost giant screamed. He was a champion screamer. He scrambled to the bow and threw a bunch of gold coins over the side. Then he turned to Sam. "Quick, girl, your payment to me! Give it to Ran!"

Sam frowned, but she tossed another five coins overboard.

Instead of sinking, the red gold swirled into Ran's net and joined the floating merry-go-round of debris.

"O, Great Ran!" Harald wailed. "Please don't kill me! Here, take my anchor! Take these humans! You can even have my lunch box!"

"Silence!" The goddess shooed away the frost giant, who did his best to cower, grovel, and retreat all at the same time.

"I'll just be belowdecks," he sobbed. "Praying."

Ran regarded me as if deciding whether I was large enough to filet. "Release Jormungand, mortal! The last thing I need today is a world-flooding event."

The World Serpent hissed in agreement.

Ran turned on him. "And you shut up, you overgrown moray. All your writhing is stirring up the silt. I can't see a thing down there. How many times have I told you not to bite at any old rancid bull's head? Rancid bulls' heads are not native to these waters!"

The World Serpent snarled petulantly, tugging at the steel cable in his mouth.

"O, Great Ran," I said, "I am Magnus Chase. This is Sam al-Abbas. We've come to bargain with you. Also, just wondering . . . why can't you cut the fishing line yourself?"

Ran let loose a torrent of Norse curses that literally steamed in the air. Now that she was closer, I could see stranger things swirling in her net—ghostly bearded faces, gasping and terrified as they tried reach the surface; hands clawing at the ropes.

"Worthless einherji," said the goddess, "you know full well what you have done."

"I do?" I asked.

"You are Vanir-spawn! A child of Njord?" Ran sniffed the air. "No, your scent is fainter. Perhaps a grandchild."

Sam's eyes widened. "Right! Magnus, you're the son of Frey, son of Njord—god of ships, sailors, and fishermen. That's why our boat didn't capsize. That's why you were able to catch the serpent!" She looked at Ran. "Um, which, of course, we already knew."

Ran snarled. "Once brought to the surface, the World Serpent is not simply bound by your fishing line. He is connected to you by fate! *You* must now decide, and quickly, whether to cut him loose and return him to his slumber, or let him awaken fully and destroy your world!"

In the back of my neck, something snapped like a rusty spring—probably the last bit of my courage. I looked at the World Serpent. For the first time, I noticed that his glowing green peepers were covered by a thin translucent membrane— a second set of eyelids.

"You mean he's only partially awake?"

"If he were fully awake," said the goddess, "your entire Eastern Seaboard would already be underwater."

"Ah." I had to resist the urge the throw away the fishing pole, undo my safety harness, and run around the deck screaming like a little Harald.

"I will release him," I said. "But first, great Ran, you have to promise to negotiate with us in good faith. We want to barter."

"Barter with you?" Ran's skirts swirled faster. Ice and plastic crackled. Shopping carts plowed into one another. "By rights, Magnus Chase, you should *belong* to me! You died of drowning. Drowned souls are *my* property."

"Actually," Sam said, "he died in combat, so he belongs to Odin."

"Technicalities!" Ran snapped.

The faces in Ran's net gaped and gasped, pleading for help. Sam had told me, *There are worse places to spend your after-life in than Valhalla.* Imagining myself tangled in that silvery web, I was suddenly grateful to my Valkyrie.

"Well, okay then," I said. "I guess I can just let Mr. J wake up fully. I didn't have any plans for tonight."

"No!" Ran hissed. "Do you have any idea how hard it is to scavenge along the seafloor when Jormungand gets agitated? Let him go!"

"And you promise to negotiate in good faith?" I asked.

"Yes. Fine. I am in no mood for Ragnarok today."

"Say, 'By my troth—'"

"I am a goddess! I know better than to swear by my troth!"

I glanced at Sam, who shrugged. She handed me her ax, and I cut the fishing line.

Jormungand sank beneath the waves, glaring at me through a bubbling green cloud of poison as he descended, as if to say, *NEXT TIME, LITTLE MORTAL.*

Ran's swirling skirts slowed to the speed of a tropical storm. "Very well, einherji. I promised to barter in good faith. What do you want?"

"The Sword of Summer," I said. "I had it with me when I hit the Charles River."

Ran's eyes glistened. "Oh, yes. I could give you the sword. But in exchange, I would want something valuable. I'm thinking . . . your soul."

My Sword Almost Ends Up on eBay

"I'M THINKING NOT," I REPLIED.

Ran made a rumbling sound like a whale with heartburn. "You—the grandson of that meddler, Njord—come here asking to barter, disturbing the World Serpent, interrupting my scavenging, and you won't even agree to a reasonable offer? The Sword of Summer is the greatest artifact to come into my nets in ages. Your soul is a small price to pay in exchange!"

"Lady Ran." Sam took back her ax and slipped down from the fishing chair. "Magnus has already been claimed by Odin. He is einherji. That cannot be changed."

"Besides," I said, "you don't want my soul. It's really small. I don't use it much. I doubt it even works anymore."

The goddess's watery skirts swirled. Trapped souls clawed for the surface. Plastic garbage bags popped like Bubble Wrap. The smell of dead fish almost made me nostalgic for the bull's head.

"What do you offer me, then?" Ran demanded. "What could possibly be worth that sword?"

Good question, I thought.

I stared into the goddess's nets and an idea began to form.

"You said you were scavenging," I recalled. "What for?"

The goddess's expression softened. Her eyes shone a greedier shade of green. "Many things. Coins. Souls. Lost valuables of every description. Just before you woke the serpent, I had my eye on a Chevy Malibu radial hubcap that was worth forty dollars *easy*. Just sitting there at the bottom of the harbor. But now"—she threw up her hands—"gone."

"You collect stuff." I corrected myself: "I mean . . . wonderful treasures."

Sam squinted at me, clearly wondering if I'd lost my mind, but I was starting to understand what made Ran tick—what she cared about most.

The goddess stretched her fingers toward the horizon. "Have you heard of the Pacific garbage patch?"

"*I* have, Lady Ran," Sam said. "It's a floating collection of rubbish the size of Texas. It sounds terrible."

"It is amazing," said the goddess. "The first time I saw it, I was overwhelmed! It put my own collection to shame. For centuries, all shipwrecks of the northern seas have been mine to claim. Anything lost in the depths comes to me. But when I saw the wonders of the garbage patch, I realized how puny my efforts had been. Ever since, I've spent all my time scavenging the seafloor, looking for additions to my net. I would not have found your sword if I hadn't been so quick!"

I nodded with sympathy. Now I could fit this Norse goddess into the Magnus Chase worldview. Ran was a bag lady. I could work with a bag lady.

I peered overboard at the floating junk. A silver teaspoon balanced on an island of Styrofoam. A bicycle wheel spun past, shredding the ghostly head of a lost soul.

"Lady Ran," I said, "your husband, Aegir, is the lord of the sea, right? You share a golden palace with him at the bottom of the ocean?"

The goddess scowled. "What is your point?"

"Well . . . what does your husband think of your collection?"

"Aegir." Ran spat. "The great stirrer of sea storms! These days the only thing he wants to do is brew his mead. He's *always* been a brewer, but lately it's ridiculous. He spends all his time at the hops shop, or going on brewery tours with his buddies. And don't get me started on the flannel shirt, rolled-up skinny jeans, glasses, and the way he trims his beard. He's always talking about microbrews. He has a cauldron a mile wide! How can he *microbrew*?"

"Right," I said. "That must be annoying. He doesn't appreciate how important your treasures are."

"He has his lifestyle," Ran said. "I have mine!"

Sam looked bewildered, but all of this made total sense to me. I knew a bag lady in Charlestown whose husband had left her a six-million-dollar mansion on Beacon Hill, but sitting at home alone had made her feel suffocated, lonely, and unhappy. So instead she lived out on the streets, pushing her shopping cart, collecting plastic lawn ornaments and aluminum cans. *That* made her feel complete.

Ran frowned. "What were we talking about again?"

"The Sword of Summer," I said. "And what I could offer you in return."

"Yes!"

"What I'm offering," I said, "is to let you keep your collection."

Frost spread down the ropes of the net. Ran's tone turned dangerous. "Are you threatening to take my stuff?"

"Oh, no. I would never do that. I understand how valuable—"

"Because this whirling plastic sunflower ornament right here? They don't make these anymore! It's easily worth ten dollars."

"Right. But if you don't give me the Sword of Summer, Surt and his fire giants will come looking for it. And *they* won't show you such respect."

Ran scoffed. "The sons of Muspell cannot touch me. My realm is deadly to them."

"But Surt has many allies," Sam said, picking up on the idea. "They would annoy you, harass you, take your . . . treasures. They'll do anything to retrieve that sword. Once they have it, they'll start Ragnarok. Then there will be no more scavenging. The oceans will boil. Your collection will be destroyed."

"No!" shrieked the goddess.

"Yes," I said. "But if you give us the sword, Surt won't have any reason to bother you. We'll keep it safe."

Ran scowled at her nets, studying the patterns of glittering trash. "And how, son of Frey, will the sword be safer with you than with me? You cannot return it to your father. Frey gave up his rights to use the weapon when he gifted it to Skirnir."

For the millionth time, I wanted to find my frolicking summer-god dad and smack him. Why had he given away his weapon in the first place? For love? Weren't gods supposed to be smarter than that? Then again, Ran collected hubcaps, and Aegir was into microbrewing.

"I'll wield it myself," I said. "Or I'll take it back to Valhalla for safekeeping."

"In other words, you don't know." The goddess arched her kelpy eyebrows at Sam. "And you, daughter of Loki, why are you siding with the gods of Asgard? Your father is no friend of theirs—not anymore."

"I'm not my father," Sam said. "I'm a—I was a Valkyrie."

"Ah, yes. The girl who dreamed of flying. But the thanes of Valhalla expelled you. Why do you still try to earn their favor? You don't need them to fly. You know very well that with your father's blood—"

"Give us the sword, Lady Ran." Sam's voice hardened. "It's the only way to delay Ragnarok."

The goddess smiled sourly. "You even sound like Loki. He was such a persuasive speaker—one moment flattering, the next moment threatening. Once, he actually convinced me to lend him my net! That led to all sorts of trouble. Loki figured out the secrets of net weaving. The gods learned how, then the humans. Pretty soon *everyone* had nets. My trademark item! I won't be so easily convinced again. I'll keep the sword and take my chances with Surt."

I unstrapped myself from the fishing chair. I moved to the tip of the bow and locked eyes with the goddess. I didn't normally shake down bag ladies, but I had to make Ran take me seriously. I lifted the chain from my belt. The silver links glinted in the fading light.

"This chain is also a sword," I said. "An authentic blade from Valhalla. How many of those do you have in your net?"

Ran started to reach for the chain, then caught herself.

"Yes . . . I can see the sword through the glamour. But why would I trade—"

"A new sword for an old one," I offered. "This blade is shinier, only used once in combat. You could get twenty bucks for it, no problem. The Sword of Summer, however, has no resale value."

"Mmm, true, but—"

"The other option," I said, "is I *take* the Sword of Summer. It belongs to me."

Ran growled. Her fingernails stretched into jagged points like shark's teeth. "You dare threaten me, mortal?"

"Just telling the truth," I said, trying to stay calm. "I can sense the sword within your nets." (Total lie.) "I pulled it from the depths once before. I can do it again. The sword is the sharpest weapon in the Nine Worlds. Do you really want it cutting through your net, spilling all your stuff and freeing all those trapped souls? If they got away, do you think they'd fight *for* you or against you?"

Her gaze wavered. "You would not dare."

"Trade me a sword for a sword," I said. "And throw in one of Idun's apples for our trouble."

Ran hissed. "You said nothing about an apple!"

"That's an easy request," I said. "I know you've got an extra apple of immortality swirling around in there somewhere. Then we'll go in peace. We'll stop Ragnarok and let you go back to your scavenging. Otherwise"—I shrugged—"you'll find out what the son of Frey can do with his father's sword."

I was pretty sure the goddess would laugh in my face, capsize the boat, and add our drowned souls to her collection. But I stared her down like I had nothing to lose.

After a count of twenty—long enough for a bead of sweat to trickle down my neck and freeze at my collar—Ran snarled, "Very well."

She flicked her hand. The Sword of Summer came flying out of the water and landed in my grip. Immediately it began to hum, agitating every molecule in my body.

I tossed my chain overboard. "Now the apple."

A piece of fruit shot out from the net. It would've beaned Sam between the eyes if not for her fast reflexes. The apple didn't look like much—just a shriveled Golden Delicious—but Sam held it gingerly, as if it were radioactive. She slipped it into her coat pocket.

"Go now, as you promised," Ran said. "But I tell you this, son of Frey: your high-handed bargaining will cost you dearly. You have made an enemy of Ran. My husband, Aegir, lord of the waves, will also hear about this, if I can ever get him out of the hops shop. For your sake, I hope you're not planning any more sea voyages. Next time, your kinship with Njord will not save you. Cross my waters again and I will personally drag your soul to the bottom."

"Well," I said, "that's something to look forward to."

Ran spun. Her form blurred into a misty funnel cloud, her nets wrapping around her like twirled spaghetti. She sank into the depths and was gone.

Sam shuddered. "That was interesting."

Behind us, a ladder creaked. Harald's head popped up from below.

"Interesting?" he demanded. "Did you say it was *interesting*?"

He climbed out, glowering at us, his fists balled, his icy blue beard dripping. "World Serpent fishing—that's one thing.

But antagonizing Ran? I never would have taken you aboard if I had known, no matter what Big Boy said! I have to make a living on the ocean! I should throw you overboard—"

"I'll double your price," Sam said. "Ten red gold. Just get us back to dock."

Harald blinked. "Okay." He headed for the wheelhouse.

I studied the Sword of Summer. Now that I had it, I wasn't sure what to do with it. The steel glowed with its own light, silvery runes burning along the flat of the blade. The sword radiated warmth, heating the air around me, melting the frost on the railings, filling me with the same sense of quiet power I felt when I healed someone. It wasn't so much like holding a weapon . . . more like holding open a door to a different time, walking with my mom in the Blue Hills, feeling the sunlight on my face.

Sam reached over. Still wearing her oversize leather gloves, she brushed a tear from my cheek.

I hadn't realized I was crying.

"Sorry," I said, my voice hoarse.

Sam studied me with concern. "Could you really have summoned the sword from Ran?"

"I don't know."

"In that case, you're insane. But I'm impressed."

I lowered the blade. It kept humming as if trying to tell me something.

"What did Ran mean?" I asked. "She said you didn't need to be a Valkyrie to fly. Something about your father's blood?"

Sam's expression closed up faster than Ran's nets. "It's not important."

"You sure about that?"

She hung her ax on her belt. She looked everywhere but my eyes. "As sure as you could summon that sword."

The outboard engines rumbled. The ship began to turn.

"I'll be at the wheel with Harald," Sam said, apparently anxious to put some distance between us. "I'll make sure he takes us to Boston and not Jotunheim."

THIRTY-FIVE

Thou Shalt Not Poop
on the Head of Art

AFTER GIVING ME the slightly shriveled apple of immortality, Sam left me at the docks. Not that she wanted to, she said, but her grandparents were going to murder her, and she didn't want to be any later for that. We made plans to meet the next morning at the Public Garden.

I made my way toward Copley Square. I felt a little self-conscious walking the streets with a glowing broadsword, so I had a conversation with my weapon. (Because that wasn't crazy at all.)

"Could you do a glamour and turn into something smaller?" I asked it. "Preferably not a chain, since it's no longer the 1990s?"

The sword didn't reply (duh), but I imagined it was humming at a more interrogative pitch, like, *Such as what?*

"I dunno. Something pocket-size and innocuous. A pen, maybe?"

The sword pulsed, almost like it was laughing. I imagined it saying, *A pen sword. That is the stupidest thing I've ever heard.*

"You have a better idea?" I asked it.

The sword shrank in my hand, melting into a runestone on a gold chain. The small white stone was emblazoned with a black symbol:

ᚠ

"The rune of Frey," I said. "I'm not really a jewelry guy, but okay."

I fastened the chain around my neck. I discovered the stone was attached magnetically to its bail, so I could easily pull it off the chain. As soon as I did, the stone grew into a sword. If I wanted it back in pendant form, all I had to do was picture that. The sword shrank into a stone, and I could reattach it to the necklace.

"Cool," I admitted.

Perhaps the sword really *had* heard my request. Perhaps I'd somehow created the glamour by myself. Or maybe I was hallucinating and wearing a huge sword around my neck.

I doubted anyone would look twice at my new medallion. They'd see the ᚠ and assume it stood for ᚠailure.

By the time I reached Copley Square it was fully dark out. No sign of Blitz or Hearthstone, which made me apprehensive. The library had closed for the night. I wondered if Big Boy expected me to meet him on the roof, but I wasn't about to climb the walls of the library.

It had been a long day. Einherji superwarrior strength or not, I was exhausted and shaking from hunger. If Big Boy wanted the apple, he would have to come get it. Otherwise I'd eat it myself.

I sat on the front steps of the library, the stone swaying under me like I was still on Harald's ship. To either side of me, a bronze lady statue reclined on a marble throne. I remembered that one symbolized Art and the other Science, but to me they both looked ready for Recess. They leaned on their armrests, metal shawls covering their heads, glancing in my direction like, *Tough week, huh?*

This was the first time I'd been alone and not in imminent danger since . . . the funeral home? Did it count as being alone if you were staring at your own dead body?

My memorial service had probably happened by now. I imagined my coffin being lowered into an icy grave; Uncle Randolph leaning on his cane, frowning resentfully; Uncle Frederick looking baffled and distressed in his mismatched clothes; and Annabeth . . . I couldn't imagine what she was feeling.

She'd rushed to Boston to find me. She'd learned I was dead. Then she learned I *wasn't* dead, but she still had to attend my funeral and not tell anyone she'd seen me.

I believed she would keep her promise, but our meeting had unsettled me. Some of the things she'd said: *I can help you. I know a place where you'll be safe.*

I pulled the battered flyer from my coat pocket. MISSING! MAGNUS CHASE, 16 YEARS OLD. PLEASE CALL. I studied Annabeth's phone number, committing it to memory. I owed her an explanation, but not yet. I'd already gotten Hearthstone knocked unconscious, Blitzen half petrified, and Sam kicked out of the Valkyries. I couldn't risk dragging anyone else into my problems.

According to the Norns, Fenris Wolf would be unleashed seven days from now unless I stopped it from happening. Ragnarok would begin. Surt would consume the Nine Worlds in fire. I would never find my mom or get justice for her murder.

Despite all that, every time I thought about facing a wolf— facing *the* Wolf, Fenris himself—I wanted to curl up in my old sleeping bag, stick my fingers in my ears, and hum, *La, la, la, it's not happening.*

A shadow swooped over my head. Big Boy the eagle landed on the bronze statue to my left and promptly decorated her head with eagle droppings.

"Dude," I said, "you just pooped on Art."

"Did I?" Big Boy lifted his tail feathers. "Ah, well. I imagine she's used to it. I see you survived your fishing expedition!"

"Surprised?" I asked.

"Yes, actually. Do you have my apple?"

I pulled it from my pocket and tossed it over. Big Boy caught it in his left claw and began to eat. "Ah, that's the stuff!"

I'd seen some strange things recently, but an eagle eating an apple atop the poopy head of Art was definitely in the top twenty.

"So will you tell me who you are, now?" I asked.

Big Boy burped. "I suppose you've earned it. I'll confess: I'm not really an eagle."

"I'm shocked. Shocked, I tell you."

He snapped off another chunk of apple. "Also, I doubt you'll make many friends among the gods when they learn you've assisted me."

"Wonderful," I said. "I'm already on Ran and Aegir's naughty list."

"Oh, those two aren't properly *gods*. They are neither Aesir nor Vanir. I think they're more giantish, though of course the line between giant and god has always been blurred. Our clans have intermarried so many times over the years."

"*Our clans.* Meaning . . ."

The eagle grew. Shadows folded around him, adding to his

size like a snowball gathering mass. His shape resolved into a huge old man lounging in the lap of Art. He wore iron-shod boots, leather britches, and a tunic of eagle feathers that was probably not in compliance with the Endangered Species Act. His hair was gray, his face weathered with age. On one forearm he wore a gold bracer encrusted with bloodstones—the sort of armband worn by the thanes in Valhalla.

"You're a lord?" I asked.

"A king, in fact." Big Boy took another bite of apple. Immediately his hair darkened and some of his wrinkles faded. "Utgard-Loki at your service!"

I curled my fingers around my sword pendant. "Loki as in *Loki* Loki?"

The giant king made a sour face. "You have no idea how many times I get that question. *Are you the 'famous' Loki?*" He put *famous* in air quotes. "Ugh! I was named Loki before *he* ever came along. It's a popular name among giants! At any rate—no, Magnus Chase, I am not related to the *famous* Loki. I am Utgard-Loki, meaning Loki of the Outlands, king of the mountain giants. I've been watching you for years."

"I get that a lot."

"Well, you're much more interesting than those dense children of Thor who usually challenge me. You'll make a wonderful enemy!"

Pressure built in my ear canals. "We're enemies now?"

"Oh, there's no need to draw your sword just yet. Nice pendant, though. Someday we'll find ourselves on opposite sides. That can't be helped. But for the present, I'm happy to observe. I hope you'll learn to use the sword without getting yourself killed. That would be amusing. Surt, the old bag of smoke, deserves to be humiliated."

"Well, I'm always happy to amuse you."

The giant popped the rest of the apple in his mouth and swallowed it whole. He now looked about twenty-five, with coal-black hair, his handsome angular face free of wrinkles.

"Speaking of Surt," he said, "the fire lord will never let you keep that sword. You have . . . probably until morning before he realizes that you've found it."

My hand dropped from my pendant. My arms felt like wet sandbags. "I impaled Surt, cut off his nose, and dropped him in an icy river. That didn't even slow him down?"

"Oh, it did! Right now he's nothing but a seething noseless ball of fire, raging down in Muspellheim. He'll have to conserve all his power to manifest again on the day of the full moon."

"When he tries to free the Wolf." Maybe I shouldn't have been chatting about that with a self-declared enemy, but something told me Utgard-Loki already knew.

The giant nodded. "Surt is more anxious than anyone for Ragnarok to start. He knows he'll get to consume the Nine Worlds in flames, and that's what he's been waiting for since the dawn of time. Me, I like the way things are! I'm having fun. But fire giants . . . ah, there's no reasoning with them. It's all burn, burn, burn. Anyway, the good news is that Surt won't be able to kill you personally until the full moon. He's much too weak. The bad news: he has lots of minions."

"I hate minions."

"Surt's not the only one after you. Your former comrades

from Valhalla have been searching. They're not pleased that you left without permission."

I thought about Captain Gunilla and her bandolier of hammers. I imagined one spinning toward my face. "Well, that's just perfect."

"If I were you, Magnus, I'd get out of Midgard by dawn. That should throw your pursuers off your trail, at least temporarily."

"Leave the earth. Simple as that."

"I knew you were a quick learner." Utgard-Loki slid off the statue's lap. Standing up, he was easily twelve feet tall. "We'll meet again, Magnus Chase. Someday you'll need a favor only Utgard-Loki can grant. But for now . . . your friends would like a word. Farewell!"

Shadows funneled around him. Utgard-Loki was gone. In his place stood Blitzen and Hearthstone.

Hearth leaped away from me like a startled cat.

Blitzen dropped his duffel bag. "Heimdall's Horn, kid! Where did you come from?"

"Where did I— I've been here for almost an hour. I was talking to a giant."

Hearth crept toward me. He poked me in the chest to see if I was real.

We have been here for hours, he signed. *Waiting for you. We talked to giant. You just appeared.*

A sick feeling rose in my chest. "Maybe we should compare notes."

I told them what had happened since we parted ways: Harald's boat; Mr. J and Bag Lady Ran (which would make an awesome name for a rapper duo); and my conversation with Utgard-Loki.

"Ah. Not good." Blitzen stroked his beard. He'd dispensed with the anti-sun gear and was now wearing an eggplant-purple three-piece suit with a mauve dress shirt and a green carnation in the lapel. "The giant told us some of the same things, but . . . the giant did not tell us his own name."

Hearth signed, *Surprise,* opening his pinched fingers on either side of his eyes, which in this context I took to mean *YIKES!*

Utgard-Loki. He spelled out the name. *Most powerful sorcerer of Jotunheim. Can make any illusion.*

"We were lucky," Blitz said. "Utgard-Loki could've tricked us into seeing or doing *anything.* He could've made us walk off a roof, accidentally kill each other, or even eat steak tartar. In fact"—Blitz narrowed his eyes—"we could still be in an illusion. Any of us might be giants."

Blitzen punched Hearthstone in the arm.

OUCH! Hearth signed. He stepped on the dwarf's toes.

"Or maybe not," Blitzen decided. "Still, this is very bad. Magnus, you've given an apple of immortality to a giant king."

"And . . . what does that mean, exactly?"

Blitz fiddled with his carnation. "To be honest, I'm not sure. I've never understood how those apples work. I imagine it will make Utgard-Loki stronger as well as younger. And make no mistake, when Ragnarok comes, he won't be on our side."

Hearthstone signed: *Wish I'd known it was Utgard-Loki. I could have asked about magic.*

"Hmph," Blitz said. "You know plenty. Besides, you can't

trust a giant to give you straight answers. Right now, you two need sleep. Elves can't stay awake very long without sunlight. And Magnus looks like he's going to fall over."

Blitz was right. I was starting to see double Blitzens and double Hearthstones, and I didn't think it had anything to do with illusions.

We made camp in the library doorway, just like old times except with better supplies. Blitz pulled three down sleeping bags out of his duffel, along with a fresh change of clothes for me and some sandwiches, which I ate too fast to taste. Hearth collapsed in his bag and immediately began snoring.

"Rest," Blitz told me. "I'll keep watch. Tomorrow, we visit my kin."

"The dwarf world?" My thoughts were getting fuzzy. "Your home?"

"My home." Blitzen sounded uneasy. "Some of the research Hearth and I did today—it's looking like we'll need more information about the rope that bound Fenris. We can only get that in Nidavellir." He focused on the chain around my neck. "Can I see it? The sword?"

I pulled off the pendant and set the sword between us, its light making Blitz's face glitter like a vein of copper in the dark.

"Breathtaking," he murmured. "Bone steel . . . or something even more exotic."

"Bone steel . . . T.J. in Valhalla mentioned that."

Blitz didn't touch the blade, but he passed his hand over it reverently. "To make steel, iron is smelted with carbon. Most swordsmiths use coal, but you can also use bones—the bones of enemies, or monsters, or ancestors."

"Oh . . ." I stared at the blade, wondering if my great-great-grandparents might be in there somewhere.

"Forged correctly," Blitz said, "bone steel can cut down supernatural creatures, even giants and gods. Of course, you have to quench the blade in blood to harden it, preferably the blood of whatever type of creature you want the sword to be most lethal against."

The sandwiches weren't sitting so well in my stomach. "This blade was made like that?"

"I don't know," Blitz admitted. "The sword of Frey is Vanir work, which is a mystery to me. It might be closer to Hearth's elf magic."

My spirits sank. I'd had this idea that dwarves were good with weapon crafting. In the back of my mind, I'd been hoping Blitzen could tell me something about the blade's secrets.

I glanced at Hearth, still snoring peacefully. "You said Hearth knew a lot of magic. I'm not criticizing. I've just never seen him cast any . . . well, except maybe opening one door. What else can he do?"

Blitz set his hand protectively next to Hearth's feet. "Magic drains him. He's careful about using it. Also his family . . ."

He took a deep breath. "Modern elves don't approve of magic. His parents shamed Hearthstone pretty badly. It still makes him self-conscious about casting magic in front of others. Hearthstone wasn't the son his parents wanted, between the magic and the, you know . . ." Blitz tapped his own earlobes.

I felt like saying something rude about Hearthstone's parents in sign language. "It's not his fault he's deaf."

"Elves." Blitz shrugged. "They have a low tolerance for

anything that isn't perfect—music, art, appearances. Their own children."

I wanted to protest how messed up that was. Then I thought about humans, and I decided we weren't much better.

"Get some sleep, kid," Blitz urged. "Big day tomorrow. To keep Fenris Wolf bound, we're going to need help from a certain dwarf . . . and that help isn't going to come cheap. We'll need you at full strength when we jump to Nidavellir."

"Jump . . ." I said. "What do you mean *jump?*"

He gave me a worried look, as if I might be getting another funeral very soon. "In the morning, you're going to try climbing the World Tree."

THIRTY-SIX

Duck!

CALL ME CRAZY.

I was expecting the World Tree to be a tree. Not a row of bronze ducks.

"Behold!" Blitzen said. "The nexus of the universe!"

Hearthstone knelt reverently.

I glanced at Sam, who had joined us after a daring escape from first period physics. She wasn't laughing.

"So . . ." I said, "I'm just going to point out that this is the *Make Way for Ducklings* statue."

"Do you think it's a coincidence?" Blitzen demanded. "Nine Worlds? Nine ducks? The symbolism screams *portal*! This spot is the crux of creation, the center of the tree, the easiest place to jump from one duck—I mean one world—to another."

"If you say so." I'd passed these bronze ducks a thousand times. I'd never considered them much of a nexus. I hadn't read the children's book they were based on, but I gathered it was about a mama duck and her babies crossing a street in Boston, so they put a sculpture of it in the Public Garden.

In the summer, little kids would sit on Mrs. Mallard and get their pictures taken. At Christmas, the ducks got little Santa hats. At the moment they were naked and alone, buried up to their necks in fresh snowfall.

Hearthstone passed his hands over the statues like he was testing a stovetop for heat.

He glanced at Blitz and shook his head.

"As I feared," Blitz said. "Hearth and I have been traveling too much. We won't be able to activate the ducks. Magnus, we'll need you."

I waited for an explanation, but Blitz just studied the sculptures. He was testing out a new hat this morning—a pith helmet with dark netting that draped to his shoulders. According to Blitz, the net fabric was his own design. It blocked ninety-eight percent of the sunlight, allowing us to see his face while not covering up his fashionable outfit. It made him look like a beekeeper in mourning.

"Okay, I'll bite," I said. "How do I activate ducks?"

Sam scanned our surroundings. She didn't look like she'd slept much. Her eyes were puffy. Her hands were raw and blistered from our fishing expedition. She'd changed into a black wool trench coat, but otherwise she was dressed the same as yesterday: green hijab, ax, shield, jeans, winter boots—all the accoutrements of a fashionable ex-Valkyrie.

"However you do it," she said, "do it quickly. I don't like how close we are to the gates of Valhalla."

"But I don't know how," I protested. "Don't you guys go world-jumping all the time?"

Hearth signed, *Too much.*

"Kid," Blitz said, "the more frequently you travel between the worlds, the harder it gets. It's kind of like overheating an engine. At some point, you have to stop and let the engine cool down. Besides, jumping randomly from one world to another is one thing. Traveling on a quest—that's different. We can't be sure where exactly we need to go."

I turned to Sam. "What about you?"

"When I was a Valkyrie, it would've been no problem. But now?" She shook her head. "You're a child of Frey. Your father is the god of growth and fertility. You should be able to coax Yggdrasil's branches close enough to let us jump on. Besides, it's your quest. You have the best chance of navigating. Just use the sculpture as a point of focus. Find us the quickest path."

She would've had better luck explaining calculus to me.

I felt stupid, but I knelt next to the sculpture. I touched the duckling at the end of the line. Cold crept up my arm. I sensed ice, fog, and darkness—somewhere harsh and unwelcoming.

"This," I decided, "is the quickest way to Niflheim."

"Excellent," Blitz said. "Let's not go there."

I was just reaching for the next duck when someone yelled, "MAGNUS CHASE!"

Two hundred yards away, on the opposite side of Charles Street, Captain Gunilla stood flanked by two other Valkyries. Behind them was a line of einherjar. I couldn't make out their expressions, but the gray looming mass of X the half-troll was unmistakable. Gunilla had drafted my own hallmates to fight against me.

My fingers twitched with anger. I wanted to get a meat hook and go fishing with Gunilla as bait. I reached for my pendant.

"Magnus, no," Sam said. "Concentrate on the ducks. We have to change worlds *now*."

On either side of Gunilla, the Valkyries slung glowing

spears from their backs. They yelled at the einherjar to ready their weapons. Gunilla pulled two of her hammers and threw them in our direction.

Sam deflected one with her shield. She knocked the other aside with her ax, spinning the hammer into the nearest willow tree, where it embedded itself up to the handle. Across the street, all three Valkyries rose into the air.

"I can't fight them all," Sam warned. "It's leave now or be captured."

My anger turned to panic. I looked at the row of bronze ducks, but my concentration was shattered. "I—I need more time."

"We don't *have* time!" Sam deflected another hammer. The force of the blow cracked her shield down the middle.

"Hearth." Blitzen nudged the elf's arm. "Now would be good."

A frown tugged at the corners of Hearthstone's mouth. He reached into his pouch and pulled out a runestone. He cupped it in his hands and muttered to it silently, as if speaking to a captured bird. He threw the stone into the air.

It exploded above us, creating a rune of burning golden light:

Between Gunilla's hunting party and us, distance seemed to elongate. The Valkyries flew toward us at top speed; my einherjar comrades drew their weapons and charged; but they made no progress.

It reminded me of those cheap 1970s cartoons where a character runs but the scenery behind him just keeps repeating itself. Charles Street spiraled around our pursuers like a giant hamster wheel. For the first time, I got what Sam had told me about runes being able to change reality.

"*Raidho,*" Blitzen said appreciatively. "It stands for the wheel, the journey. Hearthstone has bought you some time."

Only seconds, Hearth signed. *Hurry.*

He promptly collapsed into Sam's arms.

I ran my hands quickly across the bronze ducks. At the fourth one, I stopped. I felt warmth, safety . . . a sense of rightness.

"This one," I said.

"Well, open it!" Blitzen shouted.

I rose to my feet. Not sure what I was doing, I pulled my pendant from its chain. The Sword of Summer appeared in my hands. Its blade purred like a demented cat. I tapped it against the bronze duck and sliced upward.

The air parted like a curtain. Stretching in front of me, instead of a sidewalk, was an expanse of tree branches. The nearest one, as wide as Beacon Street, ran directly under us, maybe three feet down, suspended over a gray void. Unfortunately, the cut I'd made in the fabric of Midgard was already closing.

"Hurry!" I said. "Jump!"

Blitzen didn't hesitate. He leaped through the rift.

Over on Charles Street, Gunilla screamed in outrage. She and her Valkyries were still flying full-tilt on their cartoon hamster wheel, the einherjar stumbling along behind them.

"You are doomed, Magnus Chase!" Gunilla shouted. "We will pursue you to the ends of—"

With a loud *POP,* Hearth's spell broke. The einherjar fell

face first in the street. The three Valkyries shot over our heads. Judging from the sound of breaking glass, they must have hit a building over on Arlington Street.

I didn't wait for my old hallmates to recover their senses.

I grabbed Hearth's left arm while Sam took his right. Together, we leaped into the World Tree.

THIRTY-SEVEN

I Am Trash-Talked by a Squirrel

I ALWAYS LIKED CLIMBING TREES.

My mom had been pretty understanding about that. She'd only get nervous if I got above twenty feet. Then a little tension crept into her voice. "Pumpkin, that branch may not hold you. Could you come down a little?"

On the World Tree, *every* branch would hold me. The biggest ones were wider than Interstate 93. The smallest were as large as your average redwood. As for Yggdrasil's trunk, it was so immense it just didn't compute. Each crevice in its surface seemed to lead to a different world, as if someone had wrapped tree bark around a column of television monitors glowing with a million different movies.

The wind roared, ripping at my new denim jacket. Beyond the tree's canopy I saw nothing but a hazy white glow. Below was no ground—just more branches crisscrossing the void. The tree had to be rooted somewhere, but I felt woozy and unbalanced—as if Yggdrasil and everything it contained, including my world, was free-floating in primordial mist—the Ginnungagap.

If I fell here, in the best-case scenario I'd hit another branch and break my neck. Worst-case scenario, I'd keep falling forever into the Great White Nothingness.

I must've been leaning forward, because Blitzen grabbed my arm. "Careful kid. First time in the tree will make you dizzy."

"Yeah, I noticed."

Hearthstone still sagged between Sam and me. He tried to find his footing, but his ankles kept bending in odd directions.

Sam stumbled. Her broken shield slipped from her grip and somersaulted into the abyss.

She crouched, a look of barely controlled panic in her eyes. "I liked Yggdrasil a lot better when I could fly."

"What about Gunilla and the others?" I asked. "Will they be able to follow us?"

"Not easily," Sam said. "They can open another portal, but it won't necessarily lead to the same branch of the tree. Still, we should keep moving. Being on Yggdrasil is not good for your sanity."

Hearthstone managed to stand on his own. He signed: *I'm okay. Let's go.* Though his hands were so shaky it looked more like: *You are a rabbit tunnel.*

We moved farther along the branch.

The Sword of Summer hummed in my hand, tugging me along like it knew where we were going. I hoped it did, anyway.

Hostile winds buffeted us from side to side. Branches swayed, throwing deep pools of shadow and brilliant patches of light across our path. A leaf the size of a canoe fluttered by.

"Stay focused," Blitzen told me. "That feeling you had when you opened the portal? Look for it again. Find us an exit."

After walking about a quarter of a mile, we found a smaller branch crossing directly under ours. My sword hummed louder, tugging to the right.

I looked at my friends. "I think we need to take this exit."

Changing branches might sound easy, but it involved sliding down ten feet from one curved surface to another, with the wind howling and the branches swaying apart. Amazingly, we managed it without anyone getting crushed or falling into oblivion.

Navigating the narrower branch was worse. It bobbed more violently under our feet. At one point I got flattened by a leaf—like a green tarp dropping on top of me out of nowhere. At another point I looked down and realized I was standing over a crack in the bark. Half a mile down, *inside* the branch, I could see a snow-capped mountain range, as if I were standing in a glass-bottom airplane.

We picked our way through a maze of lichen patches that looked like hills of burned marshmallows. I made the mistake of touching one. My hand sunk up to my wrist and I almost couldn't pull it free.

Finally the lichen dispersed into smaller clumps like burned marshmallow sofas. We followed our branch until it split into half a dozen unclimbable twigs. The Sword of Summer seemed to go to sleep in my hand.

"Well?" Sam asked.

I peered over the side. About thirty feet below us, a larger branch swayed. In the middle of that branch, a hot-tub-size knothole glowed with soft warm light.

"That's it," I said. "That's our way out."

Blitzen scowled. "You sure? Nidavellir isn't warm and glowy."

"I'm just telling you—the sword seems to think that's our destination."

•

Sam whistled silently. "Quite a jump. If we miss the hole . . ."

Hearthstone spelled out, *S-P-L-A-T.*

A gust of wind hit us, and Hearth stumbled. Before I could catch him, he fell backward into a clump of lichen. His legs were promptly swallowed in the marshmallow gunk.

"Hearth!" Blitzen scrambled to his side. He pulled at Hearth's arms, but the mucky lichen held on to his legs like a needy toddler.

"We can cut him out," said Sam. "Your sword, my ax. It'll take time. We'll have to be careful of his legs. But it could be worse."

Naturally, things got worse. From somewhere above us came an explosive *YARK!*

Blitzen crouched under his pith helmet. "Ratatosk! That damnable squirrel *always* appears at the worst time. Hurry with those blades!"

Sam cut into the lichen with her ax, but her blade stuck. "This is like cutting through melting tires! It's not going to be quick."

GO! Hearth signed. *Leave me.*

"Not an option," I said.

YAAAAARRRRK! The sound was much louder this time. A dozen branches above us, a large shadow passed across the leaves.

I hefted my sword. "We'll fight the squirrel. We can do that, right?"

Sam looked at me like I was mad. "Ratatosk is invulnerable. There is no fighting him. Our options are running, hiding, or dying."

"We can't run," I said. "And I've already died twice this week."

"So we hide." Sam unwrapped her hijab. "At least, Hearth and I do. I can cover two people, no more. You and Blitz run—find the dwarves. We'll meet up with you later."

"What?" I wondered if Utgard-Loki was messing with her brain somehow. "Sam, you can't hide under a green piece of silk! The squirrel can't be that stupid . . ."

She shook out the fabric. It grew to the size of a twin sheet, the colors rippling until the hijab was exactly the same brown and yellow and white of the lichen patch.

She's right, Hearth signed. *GO.*

Sam crouched next to him and pulled the hijab over them both, and they vanished, blending perfectly against the lichen.

"Magnus." Blitz tugged at my arm. "It's now or never." He pointed to the branch below. The knothole was closing.

At that moment, Ratatosk broke through foliage above. If you can imagine a Sherman tank covered in red fur, barreling down the side of a tree . . . well, the squirrel was *way* scarier than that. His front teeth were twin wedges of white enamel terror. His claws were scimitars. His eyes were sulfur yellow, burning with fury.

YARK! The squirrel's battle cry pierced my eardrums. A thousand insults were packed into that one sound, all of them invading my brain, drowning out any rational thought.

You have failed.

No one likes you.

You are dead.

Your dwarf's pith helmet is stupid.

You could not save your mother.

I fell to my knees. A sob built in my chest. I probably would have died then and there if Blitz hadn't hauled me up with all his dwarven strength and slapped me across the face.

I couldn't hear him, but I read his lips well enough: "NOW, KID!"

Gripping my hand in rough calloused fingers, he jumped off the branch, dragging me with him into the wind.

THIRTY-EIGHT

I Break Down in a Volkswagen

I STOOD IN A SUNLIT meadow with no memory of how I got there.

In the distance, wildflowers dusted rolling green hills. The breeze smelled of lavender. The light was warm and rich as if the air had turned to butter.

My thoughts moved sluggishly. Light . . . sunlight was bad for dwarves. I was pretty sure I'd been traveling with a dwarf—someone who had slapped me and saved my life.

"Blitz?"

He stood to my left, holding his pith helmet at his side.

"Blitz, your hat!"

I was afraid he'd already become stone.

Then he turned. His eyes were stormy and distant. "It's okay, kid. This isn't regular sunlight. We're not on Midgard anymore."

He sounded like he was talking through wax paper. The squirrel's yap had left a crackling in my ears and some corrosive thoughts rattling around in my brain.

"Ratatosk . . ." I couldn't finish the sentence. Just saying his name made me want to curl up in the fetal position.

"Yeah," Blitz said. "His bark is literally worse than his bite. He . . ." Blitz looked down, blinking rapidly. "He's the most destructive creature in the World Tree. He spends his time running up and down the trunk, carrying insults from the eagle who lives at the top to Nidhogg, the dragon who lives at the roots."

I gazed toward the hills. Faint sounds of music seemed to be coming from that direction, or maybe it was the static in my ears. "Why would a squirrel do that?"

"To damage the tree," Blitz said. "Ratatosk keeps the eagle and the dragon whipped into a frenzy. He tells them lies, rumors, nasty gossip about each other. His words can . . . well, you know what his words can do. The dragon Nidhogg is always chewing on the roots of the World Tree, trying to kill it. The eagle flaps his wings and creates windstorms that rip the branches and cause devastation throughout the Nine Worlds. Ratatosk makes sure the two monsters stay angry and in competition with each other, to see which one can destroy their end of Yggdrasil faster."

"But that's . . . crazy. The squirrel *lives* in the tree."

Blitz grimaced. "We all do, kid. People have destructive impulses. Some of us want to see the world in ruins just for the fun of it . . . even if we're ruined along with it."

Ratatosk's chatter echoed in my head: *You have failed. You could not save your mother.* The squirrel had driven me to despair, but I could see how his bark might stir up other emotions—hatred, bitterness, self-loathing.

"How did you keep your wits?" I asked Blitz. "When the squirrel barked, what did you hear?"

Blitz ran his fingers across the brim of his pith helmet, pinching the edge of the black veil. "Nothing I don't tell myself all the time, kid. We should get going."

He trudged off toward the hills. Despite his short stride, I had to power walk to keep up.

We crossed a stream where a picturesque little frog sat on a lily pad. Doves and falcons spiraled through the air like they were playing tag. I half expected a chorus line of fuzzy animals to pop out of the wildflowers and launch into a Disney musical number.

"I'm guessing this is not Nidavellir," I said as we climbed the hill.

Blitzen snorted. "No. Much worse."

"Alfheim?"

"Worse." Blitzen stopped just short of the crest and took a deep breath. "Come on. Let's get this over with."

At the top of the hill I froze. "Whoa."

Down the other side, green fields stretched to the horizon. Meadows were strewn with picnic blankets. Crowds of people were hanging out—eating, laughing, chatting, playing music, flying kites, tossing beach balls. It was the world's largest, most laid-back outdoor concert, minus the concert. Some folks were dressed in various bits of armor. Most had weapons, but they didn't seem very interested in using them.

In the shade of an oak tree, a couple of young ladies were sword fighting, but after crossing blades a few times, they got bored, dropped their weapons, and started chatting. Another guy lounged in a lawn chair, flirting with the girl on his left while he casually parried attacks from the guy standing on his right.

Blitz pointed to the crest of the next hill about half a mile away, where a strange palace gleamed. It looked like an upside-down Noah's Ark made of gold and silver.

"Sessrumnir," said Blitzen. "The Hall of Many Seats. If we're lucky, maybe she won't be home."

"Who?"

Instead of answering, he waded into the crowd.

We hadn't gone twenty feet before a guy on a nearby picnic blanket called, "Hey, Blitzen! What's up, dude?"

Blitzen ground his teeth so hard I could hear them popping. "Hello, Miles."

"Yeah, I'm good!" Miles raised his sword absently as another guy in beach trunks and a muscle shirt charged toward him with a battle-ax.

The attacker screamed, "DIE! Ha, ha, just kidding." Then he walked away eating a chocolate bar.

"So, Blitz," Miles said, "what brings you to Casa de Awesome?"

"Nice seeing you, Miles." Blitzen grabbed my arm and led me onward.

"Okay, cool!" Miles called after us. "Keep in touch!"

"Who was that?" I asked.

"Nobody."

"How do you know him?"

"I don't."

As we made our way toward the upside-down ark mansion, more people stopped and said hello to Blitzen. A few greeted me and complimented me on my sword, or my hair, or my shoes. One girl said, "Oh, nice ears!" Which didn't even make sense.

"Everybody is so—"

"Stupid?" Blitzen offered.

"I was going to say *mellow*."

He grunted. "This is Folkvanger, the Field of the Army . . . or you could translate it as the People's Battlefield."

"So this is Volkswagen." I scanned the crowds, wondering if I would spot my mother, but I couldn't imagine her in a place like this. There was too much lounging around, not enough action. My mom would've rousted these warriors to their feet, led them on a ten-mile hike, then insisted they set up their own campsites if they wanted any dinner. "They don't seem like much of an army."

"Yeah, well," Blitz said, "these fallen are just as powerful as the einherjar, but they have a different attitude. This realm is one little subsection of Vanaheim—sort of the Vanir gods' flipside version of Valhalla."

I tried to picture myself spending eternity here. Valhalla had its good points, but as far as I'd seen it didn't have picnics or beach balls, and I definitely wouldn't describe it as mellow. Still . . . I wasn't sure I liked Folkvanger any better.

"So half the worthy dead go here," I remembered, "half go to Valhalla. How do they pick who goes where? Is it a coin toss?"

"That would make more sense, actually."

"But I was trying to get us to Nidavellir. Why did we come here?"

Blitzen stared at the mansion atop the hill. "You were looking for the path we needed for our quest. That path led us through Folkvanger. Unfortunately, I think I know why. Let's go pay our respects before I lose my nerve."

As we approached the gates, I realized Sessrumnir wasn't just built to look like an upside-down ship. It actually *was* an upside-down ship. The rows of tall windows were oar slots. The sloping walls of the hull were made from clinkered gold planks riveted with silver nails. The main entrance had a long awning that would've served as a gangplank.

"Why is it a boat?" I asked.

"What?" Blitzen fiddled nervously with his carnation. "Not so unusual. Your Norse ancestors made lots of buildings by turning their ships upside down. In the case of Sessrumnir, when the Day of Doom comes around, they'll just flip the palace over and *voilà*, it's a vessel big enough for all the warriors of Folkvanger to sail nobly to their deaths. Sort of like we're doing now."

He led me inside.

I'd been expecting a gloomy interior like the hold of a ship, but the Hall of Many Seats was more like a cathedral. The ceiling rose all the way to the keel. The oar-hole windows crosshatched the air with bars of light. The entire space was open, no separate rooms or partitions—just clusters of sofas, comfy chairs, throw pillows, and freestanding hammocks, most of which were occupied by snoring warriors. I hoped the half million inhabitants of Folkvanger liked one another's company, because there was *no* privacy. Me being me, the main thing I wondered was where they all went to the bathroom.

Down the center of the hall ran an aisle of Persian carpets, flanked by braziers with glowing spheres of gold light. At the far end stood a throne on a raised dais.

Blitz marched in that direction, ignoring the warriors who greeted him with "Dude!" and "Sup, Dwarf Man!" and "Welcome home!"

Welcome home?

In front of the dais, a cozy fire crackled in the hearth. Piles of jewelry and precious gems glittered here and there as if somebody had swept them up just to get them off the floor. On either side of the steps lounged a calico house cat the size of a saber-toothed tiger.

The throne was carved from wood as soft and buttery as the light—linden wood, maybe. The back was draped with a cloak of downy feathers like on the underside of a falcon. In the throne itself sat the most beautiful woman I'd ever seen.

She looked maybe twenty years old, surrounded by an aura of golden radiance that made me realize what Blitzen meant earlier when he'd said the daylight here wasn't normal. The entire realm of Folkvanger was warm and bright, not because of the sun, but because it basked in this woman's power.

Her blond hair fell across her shoulder in a single long plait. Her white halter top showed off her tan shoulders and smooth midriff. Her knee-length skirt was belted with a gold braid holding a sheathed knife and a ring of keys. Around her neck was a dazzling piece of jewelry—a lacework collar of gold and gems, like Ran's net in miniature, except with rubies and diamonds instead of sailors' souls and hubcaps.

The woman fixed me with her sky-blue eyes. When she smiled, heat traveled from the tips of my ears right down to my toes. I would have done anything to make her keep smiling at me. If she'd told me to jump off the World Tree into oblivion, I would've done it in a second.

I remembered her picture from my old children's mythology book, and realized how ridiculously it undersold her beauty. *The goddess of love was very pretty! She had cats!*

I knelt before my aunt, the twin sister of my father. "Freya."

"My dear Magnus," she said, "how nice to meet you in person!" She turned to Blitzen, who was glowering at his boots.

"And how are you, Blitzen?" asked the goddess.

Blitzen sighed. "I'm fine, Mom."

THIRTY-NINE

Freya Is Pretty! She Has Cats!

"MOM?" I WAS SO STARTLED I wasn't sure I'd said it aloud. "Wait . . . You, Blitzen. *Mom?*"

Blitzen kicked me in the shin.

Freya continued smiling. "I suppose my son didn't tell you? He's quite modest. Blitzen dear, you look very nice, but could you straighten your collar?"

Blitzen did, muttering under his breath, "Been a little busy running for my life."

"And, dear," Freya said, "are you sure about the vest?"

"Yes, Mom," Blitz grumbled, "I'm sure about the vest. Vests are making a comeback."

"Well, I suppose you know best." Freya winked at me. "Blitzen is a *genius* with fabrics and fashion. The other dwarves don't appreciate his expertise, but I think it's marvelous. He wants to open his own—"

"Anyway," Blitzen said, a little too loudly, "we're on this quest. . . ."

Freya clapped. "I know! It's very exciting. You're trying to get to Nidavellir to find out more about the rope Gleipnir. And so, naturally, the World Tree directed you first to me."

One of her cats clawed at a Persian rug, ripping several

thousand dollars of weaving into fluff. I tried not to imagine what the cat could do to me.

"So, Lady Freya," I said, "can you help us?"

"Of course!" said the goddess. "More importantly, you can help *me*."

"Here we go," said Blitzen.

"Son, be polite. First, Magnus, how are you faring with your sword?"

I missed a beat.

I guess I still didn't think of the Sword of Summer as *mine*. I pulled off the pendant and the blade took shape in my hand. In Freya's presence, it was silent and still like it was playing dead. Maybe it was afraid of cats.

"I haven't had much time to use it," I said. "Just got it back from Ran."

"Yes, I know." Freya's nose wrinkled with the slightest hint of distaste. "And you delivered an apple to Utgard-Loki in exchange. Perhaps not the wisest move, but I won't criticize your choices."

"You just did," Blitzen said.

The goddess ignored his comment. "At least you didn't promise *me* to Utgard-Loki. Usually when giants make demands, they want apples *and* my hand in marriage." She flipped her braid over her shoulder. "It gets very tiresome."

I had a hard time looking at Freya without staring. There really wasn't anything safe to focus on—her eyes, her lips, her belly button. I silently scolded myself, *This is Blitzen's mom! This is my aunt!*

I decided to focus on her left eyebrow. There was nothing entrancing about a left eyebrow.

"So anyway," I said, "I haven't really killed anything yet with the eyebrow—I mean the sword."

Freya sat forward. "*Killed* anything with it? Oh, dear, that's the least of its powers. Your first task is to befriend the sword. Have you done this?"

I imagined the sword and me sitting side by side in a movie theater, a tub of popcorn between us. I imagined dragging the sword on a leash, taking it for a walk through the park. "How do I befriend a sword?"

"Ah . . . well, if you have to ask—"

"Look, Aunt Freya," I said, "couldn't I just give the sword to you for safekeeping? It's a Vanir weapon. You're Frey's sister. You've got a few hundred thousand well-armed, laid-back warriors to guard it from Surt—"

"Oh, no," she said sadly. "The sword is already in your hands, Magnus. You summoned it from the river. You have laid claim to it. The best we can hope for is that *Sumarbrander*, the Sword of Summer, will allow you to use it. Keeping it from Surt is *your* job now, as long as you manage to stay alive."

"I hate my job."

Blitz elbowed me. "Don't say that, kid. You'll offend the blade."

I looked down at the gleaming runes on the blade. "I'm sorry, long sharp piece of metal. Did that hurt your feelings? Also, if you *allow* people to wield you, why would you allow an evil fire giant to do so? Why wouldn't you want to go back to Frey, or at least his lovely sister here?"

The sword did not reply.

"Magnus," said the goddess, "this is no jesting matter. The sword is fated to belong to Surt, sooner or later. You know this. The sword cannot escape its destiny any more than you can escape yours."

I envisioned Loki chuckling as he lounged on the High Seat of Odin. *Our choices can alter the details.* That's *how we rebel against destiny.*

"Besides," Freya said, "the sword would never allow me to use it. Sumarbrander holds me partially responsible for its loss. . . . It resents me almost as much as it resents Frey."

Maybe it was my imagination, but the sword seemed to become colder and heavier.

"But it's Frey's sword," I protested.

Blitzen grunted. "It *was.* I told you, kid, he gave it away for love."

The calico cat on Freya's right rolled over and stretched. Its spotted tummy was pretty cute, except for the fact that I kept imagining how many warriors it could comfortably digest.

"When Frey sat on Odin's throne," continued the goddess, "he did so for *my* sake. It was a dark time for me. I was wandering the Nine Worlds, grieving and bereft. Frey hoped that by sitting in the throne, he might find me. Instead, the throne showed him his heart's desire—a frost giantess, Gerd. He fell madly in love with her."

I stared at Freya's eyebrow. Her story wasn't helping my opinion of my dad.

"He fell in love at first sight . . . with a frost giantess."

"Oh, she was beautiful," Freya said. "Silver to Frey's gold, cold to his warmth, winter to his summer. You've heard that opposites attract? She was his perfect match. But she was a giant. She would never agree to marry a Vanir. Her family would not allow it. Knowing this, Frey fell into despair. Crops stopped growing. Summer lost its warmth. Finally, Frey's servant and best friend came to ask him what was wrong."

"Skirnir," I said. "The dude who got the sword."

Freya frowned. "Yes. *Him.*"

Blitzen took a step back, like he was afraid his mom might explode. For the first time, I realized how scary the goddess could look—beautiful, yes, but also terrifying and powerful. I imagined her armed with a shield and spear, riding with the Valkyries. If I saw her on the battlefield, I would run the other direction.

"Skirnir promised he could deliver Gerd within nine days," said the goddess. "All he required was a small fee for his services—the Sword of Summer. Frey was so love-stricken that he asked no questions. The sword . . . I can only imagine how it felt when it was betrayed by its master. It allowed Skirnir to wield it, though not happily."

Freya sighed. "That is why the sword will never allow Frey to use it again. And that is why, at Ragnarok, Frey is fated to die because he does not have his weapon."

I wasn't sure what to say. *Bummer* didn't seem to cover it. I remembered Loki's warning about sitting on Odin's throne, looking for my heart's desire. What would I look for? My mother's whereabouts. Would I give up a sword to find her? Of course. Would I risk getting killed or even hastening Doomsday? Yes. So maybe I couldn't judge my father.

Blitz gripped my arm. "Don't look so glum, kid. I have faith in you."

Freya's expression softened. "Yes, Magnus. You *will* learn to use the sword—and I don't mean just swinging it like a brute. Once you discover its full abilities, you will be formidable indeed."

"I don't suppose it comes with a user's manual?"

Freya laughed gently. "I'm sorry I didn't get you in Folkvanger, Magnus. You would've been a good addition to my followers. But Valhalla called you first. It was meant to be."

I wanted to argue that the Norns, the einherjar, and the captain of the Valkyries didn't seem to think so.

Thinking about Gunilla made me remember our flight into the World Tree, and Sam and Hearthstone hiding under a veil from a murderous squirrel. "Our friends . . . we got separated from them on Yggdrasil. Freya, do you know if they made it here safely?"

Freya peered into the distance. "They are not in Folkvanger. I see them . . . Yes. Wait. Lost them again. Ah!" She winced. "That was a close call, but they're fine for the moment. A resourceful pair. I sense they will not come here. You must continue on and meet them in Nidavellir. Which brings us to your quest."

"And how we can help you," Blitz said.

"Exactly, darling. Your need brought you here. *Need* speaks strongly when you travel the World Tree. After all, that's how my poor son found himself being a bondservant to Mimir."

"We're not having this discussion again," Blitz said.

Freya turned over her lovely hands. "Fine. Moving along. As you well know, the dwarves created the rope Gleipnir, which bound Fenris Wolf. . . ."

"Yes, Mom," Blitz said, rolling his eyes. "Everyone learns that nursery rhyme in kindergarten."

I squinted at him. "Nursery rhyme?"

" '*Gleipnir, Gleipnir, strong and stout, wrapped the Wolf around the snout.*' Humans don't learn that one?"

"Um . . . I don't think so."

"At any rate," said the goddess, "the dwarves will be able to tell you more about how the rope was made, and how it might be replaced."

"Replaced?" I willed the sword back into pendant form. Even so, hanging around my neck, it seemed to weigh a hundred pounds. "I thought the idea was to keep the rope from getting cut in the first place."

"Ah . . ." Freya tapped her lips. "Magnus, I don't want to discourage you, but I'd say there is a good chance, perhaps a seventy-five percent chance, that even if you keep the sword from Surt, the fire giant will still find a way to free Fenris Wolf. In such a case, you must be prepared with a replacement rope."

My tongue felt almost as heavy as my sword pendant. "Yeah, that's not at all discouraging. The last time the Wolf was free, didn't it take all the gods working together to bind him?"

Freya nodded. "It took three tries and much trickery. Poor Tyr lost his hand. But don't worry. The Wolf will never fall for the hand-in-the-mouth trick again. If it comes to that, you will have to find another way to bind him."

I bet Miles out in the People's Battlefield didn't have these sorts of problems. I wondered if he'd be interested in trading places for a while, going after Fenris Wolf while I played volleyball. "Freya, can you at least tell us where the Wolf *is*?"

"On Lyngvi—the Isle of Heather." The goddess tapped her chin. "Let's see, today is Thor's Day the sixteenth."

"You mean Thursday?"

"That's what I said. The island will rise on the full moon six days from now, on the twenty-second, which is Woden's Day."

"Wednesday?" I asked.

"That's what I said. So you should have plenty of time to get my earrings before you seek out the Wolf. Unfortunately, the island's location shifts every year as the branches of Yggdrasil sway in the winds of the void. The dwarves should be able to help you locate it. Blitzen's father knew the way. Others might as well."

At the mention of his father, Blitz's face clouded over. Very carefully, he took the carnation from his vest and tossed it into the hearth fire. "And what do you want, Mother? What's your part in this?"

"Oh, my needs are simple." Her fingers fluttered over her golden lace collar. "I want you to commission some earrings to match my necklace Brisingamen. Something nice. Not too flashy, but noticeable. Blitzen, you have excellent taste. I trust you."

Blitzen glared at the nearest pile of riches, which contained dozens, maybe hundreds of earrings. "You know who I have to talk to in Nidavellir. Only one dwarf has the skill to replace the rope Gleipnir."

"Yes," Freya agreed. "Fortunately, he's also an excellent jeweler, so he will be able to accommodate both our requests."

"Unfortunately," said Blitzen, "this particular dwarf wants me dead."

Freya waved aside his objection. "Oh, he can't possibly. Not after all this time."

"Dwarves have very long memories, Mother."

"Well, generous payment will soften his attitude. I can help with that." She called across the hall, "Dmitri? I need you!"

From one of the sofa clusters, three guys scrambled to their feet, grabbed their musical instruments, and hustled over. They wore matching Hawaiian shirts, Bermuda shorts, and sandals. Their hair was greased back in pompadours. The first guy had a guitar. The second had bongos. The third had a triangle.

The guy with the guitar bowed to Freya. "At your service, my lady!"

Freya gave me a conspiratorial smile, as if she had some wonderful secret to share. "Magnus, meet Dmitri and the Do-Runs, the best band you've never heard of. They died in 1963, just as they were about to get their big break. So sad! They valiantly swerved their car off Route One to spare a busload of schoolchildren from a terrible collision. In honor of their selfless deaths, I brought them here to Folkvanger."

"And we're very grateful, my lady," said Dmitri. "Being your house band has been a sweet gig!"

"Dmitri, I need to cry," she said. "Could you please play the one about my lost husband? I love that song."

"I hate that song," Blitzen mumbled under his breath.

The trio hummed. Dmitri strummed a chord.

I whispered to Blitzen, "Why does your mom need to cry?"

He turned toward me and made a finger-down-the-throat gesture. "Just watch. You'll see."

Dmitri began to sing:

> *"Oh, Odur! Od, Od, Odur,*
> *Where is that Odur; where is my love?"*

The other two musicians harmonized on the chorus:

> *"Od wanders far, my Odur is missing,*
> *How odd it is, not to be kissing*
> *My Odur! My sweet Od Odur!"*

Triangle.

Bongo solo.

Blitzen whispered, "Her godly husband was an Aesir named Odur, Od for short."

I wasn't sure which name was worse.

"He disappeared?" I guessed.

"Two thousand years ago," Blitzen said. "Freya went looking for him, disappeared herself for almost a century while she searched. She never found him, but that's why Frey sat in Odin's chair in the first place—to look for his sister."

The goddess leaned forward and cupped her face in her hands. She drew a shaky breath. When she looked up again, she was weeping—but her tears were small pellets of red gold. She wept until her hands were full of glittering droplets.

"Oh, Odur!" she sobbed. "Why did you leave me? I miss you still!"

She sniffled and nodded to the musicians. "Thank you, Dmitri. That's enough."

Dmitri and his friends bowed. Then the best band I wished I'd never heard of shuffled away.

Freya raised her cupped hands. Out of nowhere, a leather pouch appeared, hovering above her lap. Freya spilled her tears into the bag.

"Here, my son." Freya passed the pouch to Blitzen. "That

should be enough payment if Eitri Junior is at all reasonable."

Blitzen stared glumly at the pouch of tears. "The only problem is, he's *not*."

"You will succeed!" Freya said. "The fate of my earrings is in your hands!"

I scratched the back of my neck. "Uh, Lady Freya . . . thanks for the tears and all, but couldn't you just go to Nidavellir and pick out your own earrings? I mean, isn't shopping half the fun?"

Blitzen shot me a warning look.

Freya's blue eyes turned a few degrees colder. Her fingertips traced the filigree of her necklace. "No, Magnus, I *can't* just go shopping in Nidavellir. You *know* what happened when I bought Brisingamen from the dwarves. Do you want that to happen again?"

Actually, I had no idea what she was talking about, but she didn't wait for an answer.

"Every time I go to Nidavellir, I get myself in trouble," she said. "It's not my fault! The dwarves *know* my weakness for beautiful jewelry. Believe me, it's *much* better that I send you. Now, if you'll excuse me, it's time for our evening luau with optional combat. Good-bye, Magnus. Good-bye, my darling Blitzen!"

The floor opened beneath us, and we fell into darkness.

FORTY

My Friend Evolved from a— Nope. I Can't Say It

I DON'T REMEMBER LANDING.

I found myself on a dark street on a cold, cloudy night. Three-story clapboard row houses edged the sidewalk. At the end of the block, a tavern's grimy windows glowed with neon drink signs.

"This is Southie," I said. "Around D Street."

Blitzen shook his head. "This is Nidavellir, kid. It looks like South Boston . . . or rather, South Boston looks like *it*. I told you, Boston is the nexus. The Nine Worlds blend together there and affect one another. Southie has a definite dwarvish feeling to it."

"I thought Nidavellir would be underground. With claustrophobic tunnels and—"

"Kid, that's a cavern ceiling above your head. It's just a long way up and hidden by air pollution. We don't have daytime here. It's this dark all the time."

I stared into the murky clouds. After being in Freya's realm, the world of the dwarves seemed oppressive, but it also seemed more familiar, more . . . genuine. I guess no true Bostonian would trust a place that was sunny and pleasant all the time. But a gritty, perpetually cold and gloomy neighborhood? Throw in a couple of Dunkin' Donuts locations, and I'm right at home.

Blitz wrapped his pith helmet in its dark netting. The

whole thing collapsed into a small black handkerchief, which he tucked into his coat pocket. "We should get going."

"We're not going to talk about what happened up there in Volkswagen?"

"What's there to say?"

"For one thing, we're cousins."

Blitz shrugged. "I'm happy to be your cousin, kid, but children of the gods don't put much stock in that sort of connection. Godly family lines are so tangled—thinking about it will drive you crazy. Everybody's related to everybody."

"But you're a demigod," I said. "That's a good thing, right?"

"I hate the word *demigod*. I prefer *born with a target on my back*."

"Come on, Blitz. Freya is your mom. That's important information you kinda forgot to mention."

"Freya is my mother," he agreed. "A lot of svartalfs are descended from Freya. Down here, it's not such a big deal. She mentioned how she got Brisingamen? A few millennia ago she was strolling through Nidavellir—who knows why—and she came across these four dwarves who were crafting the necklace. She was obsessed. She had to have it. The dwarves said sure, for the right price. Freya had to marry each of them, one after the other, for one day each."

"She . . ." I wanted to say, *Gross, she married four dwarves?* Then I remembered who was telling the story. "Oh."

"Yeah." Blitz sounded miserable. "She had four dwarvish children, one for each marriage."

I frowned. "Wait. If she was married for one day to each dwarf and a pregnancy lasts . . . the math doesn't work out on that."

"Don't ask me. Goddesses live by their own rules. Anyway, she got the necklace. She was ashamed of herself for marrying dwarves. Tried to keep it a secret. But the thing is, she *loved* dwarven jewelry. She kept coming back to Nidavellir to pick out new pieces, and every time . . ."

"Wow."

Blitzen's shoulders slumped. "That's the main difference between dark elves and regular dwarves. The svartalfs are taller and generally more handsome because we have Vanir blood. We're descended from Freya. You say I'm a demigod. I say I'm a receipt. My dad crafted a pair of earrings for Freya. She married him for a day. She couldn't resist his craftsmanship. He couldn't resist her beauty. Now she sends me to purchase a new pair of earrings because she's tired of the old ones and Asgard forbid she find herself saddled with another little Blitzen."

The bitterness in his voice could've melted iron plating. I wanted to tell him I understood how he felt, but I wasn't sure I did. Even if I never knew my dad, I'd had my mom. That had always been enough for me. For Blitzen . . . not so much. I wasn't sure what had happened to his father, but I remembered what he'd told me at the Esplanade lagoon: *You're not the only one who's lost family to the wolves, kid.*

"Come on," he told me. "If we stand in the street any longer, we'll get mugged for this bag of tears. Dwarves can smell red gold a mile away." He pointed to the bar on the corner. "I'll buy you a drink at Nabbi's Tavern."

Nabbi's restored my faith in dwarves, because it was in fact a claustrophobic tunnel. The ceiling was a low-clearance hazard. The walls were papered with old fight posters like DONNER

THE DESTROYER VS. MINI-MURDER, ONE NIGHT ONLY! featuring pictures of muscular snarling dwarves in wrestling masks.

Mismatched tables and chairs were occupied by a dozen mismatched dwarves—some svartalfs like Blitzen who could easily have passed for human, some much shorter guys who could have easily passed for garden gnomes. A few of the patrons glanced at us, but nobody seemed shocked that I was a human . . . if they even realized. The idea that I could pass for a dwarf was pretty disturbing.

The most unreal thing about the bar was Taylor Swift's "Blank Space" blasting from the speakers.

"Dwarves like human music?" I asked Blitzen.

"You mean humans like *our* music."

"But . . ." I had a sudden image of Taylor Swift's mom and Freya having a girls' night out in Nidavellir. "Never mind."

As we made our way toward the bar, I realized that the furniture wasn't just mismatched. Every single table and chair was unique—apparently handcrafted from various metals, with different designs and upholstery. One table was shaped like a bronze wagon wheel with a glass top. Another had a tin and brass chessboard hammered into the surface. Some chairs had wheels. Others had adjustable booster seats. Some had massage controls or propellers on the back.

Over by the left wall, three dwarves were playing darts. The board's rings rotated and blew steam. One dwarf tossed his dart, which buzzed toward the target like a tiny drone. While it was still in flight, another dwarf took a shot. His dart rocketed toward the drone dart and exploded, knocking it out of the air.

The first dwarf just grunted. "Nice shot."

Finally we reached the polished oak bar, where Nabbi himself was waiting. I could tell who he was because of my highly trained deductive mind, and also because his stained yellow apron read HI! I'M NABBI.

I thought he was the tallest dwarf I'd met so far until I realized he was standing on a catwalk behind the counter. Nabbi was actually only two feet tall, including the shock of black hair that stuck up from his scalp like a sea urchin. His clean-shaven face made me appreciate why dwarves wear beards. Without one, Nabbi was gods-awful ugly. He had no chin to speak of. His mouth puckered sourly.

He scowled at us like we'd tracked in mud.

"Greetings, Blitzen, son of Freya," he said. "No explosions in my bar this time, I hope?"

Blitzen bowed. "Greetings, Nabbi, son of Loretta. To be fair, I wasn't the one who brought the grenades. Also, this is my friend Magnus, son of—"

"Um. Son of Natalie."

Nabbi nodded to me. His busy eyebrows were fascinating. They seemed to move like live caterpillars.

I reached for a bar stool, but Blitzen stopped me.

"Nabbi," he said formally, "may my friend use this stool? What is its name and history?"

"That stool is Rear-Rester," said Nabbi. "Crafted by Gonda. Once it held the tush of the master smith Alviss. Use it in comfort, Magnus, son of Natalie. And Blitzen, you may sit on Keister-Home, famed among stools, made by yours truly. It survived the Great Bar Fight of 4109 A.M.!"

"My thanks." Blitzen climbed on his stool, which was polished oak with a velvet-padded seat. "A fine Keister-Home it is!"

Nabbi looked me expectantly. I tried my stool, which was hard steel with no cushion. It wasn't much of a Rear-Rester. It was more of a Magnus Mangler, but I tried for a smile. "Yep, that's a nice stool all right!"

Blitzen rapped his knuckles on the bar. "Mead for me, Nabbi. And for my friend—"

"Uh, soda or something?" I wasn't sure I wanted to be walking around Dwarven Southie with a mead buzz.

Nabbi filled two mugs and set them in front of us. Blitzen's goblet was gold on the inside, silver on the outside, decorated with images of dancing dwarf women.

"That cup is Golden Bowl," said Nabbi. "Made by my father, Darbi. And this one"—he nudged my pewter tankard—"is Boom Daddy, made by yours truly. Always ask for a refill before you reach the bottom of the cup. Otherwise"—he splayed his fingers—"boom, Daddy!"

I really hoped he was kidding, but I decided to take small sips.

Blitz drank his mead. "Mmm. A fine cup for quaffing! And now that we are past the formalities, Nabbi . . . we need to speak with Junior."

A vein throbbed in Nabbi's left temple. "Do you have a death wish?"

Blitz reached into his pouch. He slid a single gold tear across the counter. "This one is for you," he said in a low voice. "Just for making the call. Tell Junior we have more. All we want is a chance to barter."

After my experience with Ran, the word *barter* made me

even more uncomfortable than Rear-Rester. Nabbi looked back and forth between Blitzen and the tear, his expression vacillating between apprehension and greed. Finally the greed won. The barkeep snatched the drop of gold.

"I'll make the call. Enjoy your drinks." He climbed off his catwalk and disappeared into the kitchen.

I turned to Blitz. "A few questions."

He chuckled. "Only a few?"

"What does 4109 A.M. mean? Is it the time, or—"

"Dwarves count years from the creation of our species," Blitz said. "A.M. is *After Maggots*."

I decided my ears must still be defective from Ratatosk's barking. "Say what?"

"The creation of the world . . . Come on, you know the story. The gods killed the largest of the giants, Ymir, and used his flesh to create Midgard. Nidavellir developed *under* Midgard, where maggots ate into the giant's dead flesh and created tunnels. Some of those maggots evolved, with a little help from the gods, into dwarves."

Blitzen looked proud of this historical tidbit. I decided to do my best to erase it from my long-term memory.

"Different question," I said. "Why does my goblet have a name?"

"Dwarves are craftsmen," said Blitzen. "We're serious about the things we make. You humans—you make a thousand crappy chairs that all look alike and all break within a year. When *we* make a chair, we make one chair to last a lifetime, a chair unlike any other in the world. Cups, furniture, weapons . . . every crafted item has a soul and a name. You can't appreciate something unless it's good enough for a name."

I studied my tankard, which was painstakingly engraved with runes and wave designs. I wished it had a different name—like *No Way Will I Explode*—but I had to admit it was a nice cup.

"And calling Nabbi son of Loretta?" I asked. "Or me the son of Natalie?"

"Dwarves are matriarchal. We trace our lineage through our mothers. Again, it makes much more sense than your patrilineal way. After all, one can only be born from a single biological mother. Unless you are the god Heimdall. He had nine biological mothers. But that's another story."

Synapses melted in my brain. "Let's move along. Freya's tears . . . red gold? Sam told me that's the currency of Asgard."

"Yes. But Freya's tears are one hundred percent pure. The finest red gold in creation. For the pouch of tears we're carrying, most dwarves would give their right eyeballs."

"So this guy Junior—he'll bargain with us?"

"Either that," Blitz said, "or he'll chop us into small pieces. You want some nachos while we wait?"

Blitz Makes a Bad Deal

I HAD TO HAND IT TO NABBI. He served good near-death nachos.

I was halfway through my plate of guacamole-enhanced tastiness when Junior showed up. On first sight, I wondered if it would be faster just to drain Boom Daddy and go boom, because I didn't like our chances of bartering with the old dwarf.

Junior looked about two hundred years old. Scraps of gray hair clung to his liver-spotted head. His beard gave *scraggly* a bad name. His malicious brown eyes flitted around the bar as if he were thinking, *I hate that. I hate that. And I* really *hate that.* He wasn't physically intimidating, shuffling along with his gold-plated walker, but he was flanked by a pair of dwarven bodyguards, each so burly that they could've been used as NFL tackle dummies.

The other customers got up and quietly left, like in a scene from an old Western. Blitzen and I both stood.

"Junior." Blitz bowed. "Thank you for meeting with us."

"Some nerve," Junior snarled.

"Would you like my seat?" Blitzen offered. "It is Keister-Home, made by—"

"No, thanks," Junior said. "I'll stand, compliments of my

walker, Granny Shuffler, famous among geriatric products, made by Nurse Bambi, my private assistant."

I bit the inside of my cheek. I doubted that laughing would be good diplomacy.

"This is Magnus, son of Natalie," Blitzen said.

The old dwarf glared at me. "I know who he is. Found the Sword of Summer. You couldn't wait until after I died? I'm too old for this Ragnarok nonsense."

"My bad," I said. "I should have checked with you before I got attacked by Surt and sent to Valhalla."

Blitzen coughed. The bodyguards appraised me like I might have just made their day more interesting.

Junior cackled. "I like you. You're rude. Let's see this blade, then."

I showed him my magic pendant trick. In the dim neon lights of the barroom, the blade's runes glowed orange and green.

The old dwarf sucked his teeth. "That's Frey's blade, all right. Bad news."

"Then, perhaps," Blitzen said, "you'll be willing to help us?"

"*Help you?*" Junior wheezed. "Your father was my nemesis! *You* besmirched my reputation. And you want my help. You've got iron guts, Blitzen, I'll give you that."

The tendons in Blitz's neck looked like they might bust his well-starched collar. "This isn't about our family feud, Junior. This is about the rope. It's about securing Fenris Wolf."

"Oh, of course it is." Junior sneered at his bodyguards. "The fact that *my father*, Eitri Senior, was the only dwarf talented enough to *make* Gleipnir, and your father, Bilì, spent his life questioning the quality of the rope—that has nothing to do with it!"

Blitzen clenched his pouch of red gold tears. I was afraid he might smack Junior upside the head with it. "The Sword of Summer is right here. In just six Midgardian nights, Surt is planning to free the Wolf. We're going to do our best to stop him, but you *know* the rope Gleipnir is beyond its expiration date. We need information about the Wolf's bindings. More importantly, we need a replacement rope just in case. Only you have the talent to make one."

Junior cupped his ear. "Say that last part again."

"You're talented, you crusty old—" Blitzen stopped. "Only you have the skill to make a new rope."

"True." Junior smirked. "It so happens I *have* a replacement rope already made. Not because of any problems with Gleipnir, mind you, or because of any of your family's scandalous accusations about its quality—just because I like to be prepared. Unlike *your* father, I might add, going off alone to check on Fenris Wolf like an idiot and getting himself killed."

I had to step in front of Blitzen to keep him from attacking the old dwarf.

"Okay, then!" I said. "Guys, this isn't the time. Junior, if you've got a new rope, that's great. Let's talk price. And, um, we'll also need a nice set of earrings."

"Heh." Junior wiped his mouth. "Of *course* you will. For Blitzen's mother, no doubt. What are you offering in payment?"

"Blitzen," I said, "show him."

Blitz's eyes still danced with rage, but he opened the pouch and spilled some red gold tears into his palm.

"Huh," said Junior. "An acceptable price . . . or it *would* be, if it wasn't from Blitzen. I'll sell you what you want for that pouch of tears, but first my family's honor must be satisfied.

It's high time we settled this feud. What do you say, son of Freya? A contest—you and me. The traditional rules, the traditional wager."

Blitzen backed into the bar. He squirmed so badly I could almost believe he had evolved from maggots. (ERASE. *Bad*, long-term memory. ERASE!)

"Junior," he said, "you know I don't—I couldn't possibly—"

"Shall we say tomorrow at mossglow?" Junior asked. "The panel of judges can be headed by a neutral party—perhaps Nabbi, who I'm sure is not eavesdropping behind the bar right now."

Something banged against the catwalk. From below the counter, Nabbi's muffled voice said, "I would be honored."

"There you are, then!" Junior smiled. "Well, Blitzen? I have challenged you according to our ancient customs. Will you defend the honor of your family?"

"I . . ." Blitzen hung his head. "Where should we meet?"

"The forges in Kenning Square," Junior said. "Oh, this will be amusing. Come on, boys. I have to tell Nurse Bambi about it!"

The old dwarf shuffled out with his bodyguards in tow. As soon as they were gone, Blitzen collapsed on Keister-Home and drained Golden Bowl.

Nabbi emerged from behind the counter. His caterpillar eyebrows wriggled with concern as he refilled Blitz's goblet. "This one's on the house, Blitzen. It's been nice knowing you."

He went back to the kitchen, leaving Blitz and me alone with Taylor Swift singing "I Know Places." The lyrics took on a whole new meaning in a subterranean dwarf world.

"Are you going to explain what just happened?" I asked Blitz. "What is this contest at mossglow? Also, what is mossglow?"

"Mossglow . . ." Blitzen stared into his cup. "Dwarf version of dawn, when the moss begins to glow. As for the contest . . ." He swallowed back a sob. "It's nothing. I'm sure you'll be able to continue the quest without me."

Just then the barroom doors burst open. Sam and Hearthstone tumbled inside like they'd been pushed from a moving car.

"They're alive!" I jumped up. "Blitz, look!"

Hearthstone was so excited he couldn't even sign. He rushed over and almost tackled Blitzen off his stool.

"Hey, buddy." Blitz patted his back absently. "Yeah, I'm glad to see you, too."

Sam didn't hug me, but she managed a smile. She was scratched up and covered with leaves and twigs, but she didn't look badly hurt. "Magnus, glad you haven't died yet. I want to be there for that."

"Thanks, al-Abbas. What happened to you guys?"

She shrugged. "We hid under the hijab as long as we could."

With all the other stuff going on, I'd forgotten about the scarf. "Yeah, what was that about? You've got an invisibility hijab?"

"It doesn't make me invisible. It's just camouflage. All Valkyries are given swan cloaks to help us hide when necessary. I just made mine a hijab."

"But you weren't a swan. You were tree moss."

"It can do different things. Anyway, we waited until the squirrel left. The barking left me in bad shape, but, thankfully, Hearth wasn't affected. We climbed Yggdrasil for a while—"

A moose tried to eat us, Hearth signed.

"Excuse me?" I asked. "A moose?"

Hearth grunted in exasperation. He spelled out: *D-E-E-R.* *Same sign for both animals.*

"Oh, that's much better," I said. "A deer tried to eat you."

"Yes," Sam agreed. "Dvalinn or maybe Duneyrr—one of the stags that roam the World Tree. We got away, took a wrong turn into Alfheim . . ."

Hearthstone shuddered, then simply signed, *Hate.*

"And here we are." Sam eyed Blitzen, whose expression was still blank with shock. "So . . . what's going on?"

I told them about our visit with Freya, then our conversation with Junior. Hearthstone steadied himself on the bar. He spelled with one hand: *M-a-k-i-n-g?* Then he shook his head vehemently.

"What do you mean, *making?*" I asked.

"A making," Blitz muttered into his goblet, "is the dwarven contest. It tests our crafting skills."

Sam tapped her fingers on her ax. "Judging from your expression, I'm guessing you don't trust your skills."

"I am rubbish at crafting," Blitzen said.

Not true, Hearth protested.

"Hearthstone," Blitzen said, "even if I was *excellent* at crafting, Junior is the most skilled dwarf alive. He'll destroy me."

"Come on," I said. "You'll do fine. And if you lose, we'll find another way to get that rope."

Blitzen looked at me mournfully. "It's worse than that, kid. If I lose, I pay the traditional price: my head."

FORTY-TWO

We Have a Pre-decapitation Party, with Egg Rolls

CRASHING AT BLITZEN'S apartment was the high point of our trip. Not that that was saying much.

Blitz rented the third floor of a row house across the street from Svartalf Mart (yes, that's a real thing). Considering the fact that he was due to be decapitated the next day, he was a good host. He apologized for not cleaning up (though the place looked spotless to me), microwaved some egg rolls, and brought out a liter of Diet Sergeant Pepper and a six-pack of Fjalar's Foaming Mead, each bottle uniquely handcrafted in a different color of glass.

His furniture was spare but stylish: an L-shaped sofa and two space-age armchairs. They probably had names and were famous among living-room furniture, but Blitzen didn't introduce them. Neatly arranged on the coffee table was a spread of dwarf men's fashion and interior design magazines.

While Sam and Hearth sat with Blitz, trying to console him, I paced the room. I felt angry and guilty that I'd put Blitzen in such a tight spot. He'd already risked enough for me. He'd spent two years on the streets watching out for me when he could've been here, kicking back with egg rolls and foaming mead. He'd tried to protect me by attacking the lord of the fire giants with a toy sign. Now he was going to lose his head in a craft-off with an evil senior citizen.

Also . . . the dwarven philosophy of crafting had unsettled me. In Midgard, most things were breakable, replaceable junk. I'd *lived* off that junk for the last two years—picking through what people discarded, finding bits I could use or sell or at least make a fire with.

I wondered what it would be like living in Nidavellir, where every item was crafted to be a lifetime work of art—right down to your cup or your chair. It might get annoying to have to recite the deeds of your shoes before you put them on in the morning, but at least you'd know they were amazing shoes.

I wondered about the Sword of Summer. Freya had told me to befriend it. She'd implied that the weapon had thoughts and feelings.

Every crafted item has a soul, Blitz had told me.

Maybe I hadn't properly introduced myself. Maybe I needed to treat the sword like another companion. . . .

"Blitz, you must have a specialty," Samirah was saying. "What did you study in trade school?"

"Fashion." Blitzen sniffled. "I designed my own degree program. But clothing isn't a recognized craft. They'll expect me to hammer molten ingots or tinker with machinery! I'm no good at that!"

You are, Hearth signed.

"Not under pressure," Blitz said.

"I don't get it," I said. "Why does the loser have to die? How do they decide the winner?"

Blitzen stared at the cover of *Dwarf Quarterly–New Looks for Spring! 100 Uses for Warg Leather!* "Each contestant makes three items. They can be anything. At the end of the day, the judges rate each item according to its usefulness, beauty, quality, whatever. They can assign points any way they wish. The contestant with the most overall points wins. The other guy dies."

"You must not have a lot of competitions," I said, "if the loser always gets decapitated."

"That's the traditional wager," Blitz said. "Most people don't insist on it anymore. Junior is old-fashioned. Also, he hates me."

"Something about Fenris Wolf and your dad?"

Hearth shook his head to shut me up, but Blitzen patted his knee. "It's okay, buddy. They deserve to know."

Blitz leaned back on the sofa. He seemed suddenly calmer about his impending doom, which I found unsettling. I kind of wanted him to be punching walls.

"I told you dwarven items are made for life?" he said. "Well . . . *lifetime* for a dwarf can mean hundreds of years."

I studied Blitz's beard, wondering if he dyed out the gray whiskers. "How old are you?"

"Twenty," Blitz said. "But Junior . . . he's going on five hundred. His dad, Eitri, was one of the most famous craftsmen in dwarven history. He lived over a thousand years, made some of the gods' most important items."

Samirah nibbled on an egg roll. "Even *I've* heard of him. He's in the old stories. He made Thor's hammer."

Blitz nodded. "Anyway, the rope Gleipnir . . . you could argue it was his most important work, even more than Thor's hammer. The rope keeps Fenris Wolf from getting free and starting Doomsday."

"I'm with you so far," I said.

"The thing is—the rope was a rush job. The gods were clamoring for help. They'd already tried to bind Fenris with two massive chains. They knew their window of opportunity was closing. The Wolf was getting stronger and wilder by the day. Pretty soon he'd be uncontrollable. So Eitri . . . well, he did his best. Obviously, the rope has held together this long. But a thousand years is a long time, even for a dwarven rope, especially when the strongest wolf in the universe is straining against it day and night. My dad, Bili, was a great rope maker. He spent years trying to convince Junior that Gleipnir needed to be replaced. Junior wouldn't hear of it. Junior said he went to the Wolf's island from time to time to inspect the rope, and he swore that Gleipnir was fine. He thought my dad was just insulting his family's reputation. Finally my dad . . ."

Blitz's voice cracked.

Hearthstone signed, *You don't have to tell.*

"I'm okay." Blitzen cleared his throat. "Junior used all his influence to turn people against my dad. Our family lost business. Nobody would buy Bili's crafts. Finally Dad went to the island of Lyngvi himself. He wanted to check the rope, prove that it needed replacing. He never came back. A few months later a dwarven patrol found . . ." He looked down and shook his head.

Hearthstone signed: *Clothes. Ripped. Washed up on shore.*

Either Samirah was catching on to sign language or she got the general idea. She put her fingertips to her mouth. "Blitz, I'm so sorry."

"Well"—he shrugged listlessly—"now you know. Junior

is still holding a grudge. My dad's death wasn't enough. He wants to shame and kill *me*, too."

I set my drink on the coffee table. "Blitz, I think I speak for all of us when I say that Junior can shove his Granny Shuffler—"

"Magnus . . ." Sam warned.

"What? That old dwarf needs to be decapitated in the worst way. What can we do to help Blitz win the contest?"

"I appreciate it, kid." Blitz struggled to his feet. "But there's nothing. I . . . if you'll excuse me . . ."

He staggered to his bedroom and shut the door behind him.

Samirah pursed her lips. She still had a twig of Yggdrasil sticking out of her coat pocket. "Is there any chance Junior isn't *that* good? He's very old now, isn't he?"

Hearthstone unwrapped his scarf and threw it on the couch. He wasn't doing well in the darkness of Nidavellir. The green veins on his neck stood out more than usual. His hair floated with static, like plant tendrils searching for sunlight.

Junior is very good. He made a sign like ripping a piece of paper in half and throwing away the pieces: *Hopeless.*

I felt like throwing bottles of Fjalar's Foaming Mead out the window. "But Blitz *can* craft, right? Or were you just being encouraging?"

Hearth rose. He walked to a sideboard along the dining room wall. I hadn't paid the table much attention, but Hearth pressed something on its surface—a hidden switch, I guess— and the tabletop opened like a clamshell. The underside of the top section was one big light panel. It flickered to life, glowing warm and golden.

"A tanning bed." As soon as I said that, the truth sank in. "When you first came to Nidavellir, Blitzen saved your life. That's how. He made a way for you to get sunlight."

Hearth nodded. *First time I used runes for magic. Mistake. I dropped into Nidavellir. Almost died. Blitzen–he can craft. Kind and smart. But no good under pressure. Contests . . . no.*

Sam hugged her knees. "So what do we do? Do you have any magic that will help?"

Hearth hesitated. *Some. Will use before contest. Not enough.*

I translated for Sam and then asked, "What can I do?"

Protect him, Hearth signed. *Junior will try to s-a-b-o-t-a-g-e.*

"Sabotage?" I frowned. "Isn't that cheating?"

"I've heard about this," Sam said. "In dwarven contests, you can mess with your competitor as long as you aren't caught. The interference has to look like an accident, or at least something the judges can't trace back to you. But it sounds like Junior doesn't need to cheat to win."

He will cheat. Hearth made a sign like a hook swinging into a latch. *Spite.*

"Okay," I said. "I'll keep Blitz safe."

Still not enough. Hearth peered at Sam. *Only way to win– mess with Junior.*

When I told Sam what he'd signed, she turned as gray as a dwarf in sunlight. "No." She wagged her finger at Hearth. "No, absolutely not. I *told* you."

Blitz will die, Hearth signed. *You did it before.*

"What's he talking about?" I asked. "What did you do before?"

She got to her feet. The tension in the room was suddenly at DEFCON Five. "Hearthstone, you said you wouldn't mention it. You promised." She faced me, her expression shutting down any further questions. "Excuse me. I need some air."

She stormed out of the apartment.

I stared at Hearthstone. "What was that?"

His shoulders slumped. His face was empty, drained of hope. He signed, *A mistake.* Then he climbed onto his sun bed and turned toward the light, his body casting a wolf-shaped shadow across the floor.

FORTY-THREE

Let the Crafting of Decorative Metal Waterfowl Begin

KENNING SQUARE looked like a basketball court without the baskets. A chain-link fence bordered a stretch of cracked asphalt. Along one side stood a row of stone pillars carved like totem poles with dragon heads, centipedes, and troll faces. Along the other side, bleachers were packed with dwarf spectators. On the court, where the free-throw lines would've been, two open-air blacksmith shops were ready for action. Each had a forge with bellows to stoke the fire, an assortment of anvils, a few sturdy tables, and racks of tools that looked like torture equipment.

The crowd seemed prepared for a long day. They'd brought coolers, blankets, and picnic baskets. A few enterprising dwarves had parked their food trucks nearby. The sign for ÌRI'S HANDCRAFTED CONFECTIONS showed a waffle cone topped with a three-story ice-cream palace. BUMBURR'S BREAKFAST BURRITOS had a line twenty dwarves long, which made me sorry I'd eaten stale doughnuts at Blitz's place.

As we approached the court, the crowd gave Blitzen a smattering of applause. Sam was nowhere to be seen. She'd never come back to the apartment the previous night. I wasn't sure whether to be worried or angry.

Junior was waiting, leaning on his gold-plated walker. His

two bodyguards stood behind him, dressed like their boss in overalls and leather gauntlets.

"Well, well, Blitzen." The old dwarf sneered. "Mossglow started ten minutes ago. Were you getting your beauty sleep?"

Blitzen looked like he hadn't slept at all. His eyes were sunken and bloodshot. He'd spent the past hour worrying about what to wear, finally deciding on gray slacks, a white dress shirt with black suspenders, pointy black shoes, and a porkpie hat. He might not win for his crafting, but he would definitely get the vote for best-dressed blacksmith.

He glanced around distractedly. "Get started?"

The crowd cheered. Hearthstone accompanied Blitzen to the forge. After a night on Blitzen's tanning bed, the elf's face had a rosy sheen as if he'd been infused with paprika. Before we left the apartment, he'd cast a rune on Blitz to help him feel rested and focused, which had left Hearth exhausted and unfocused. Nevertheless, Hearth stoked the forge while Blitzen puttered around his workstation, staring in confusion at the racks of tools and baskets of metal ore.

Meanwhile Junior scooted around on his walker, barking at one of his bodyguards to fetch him a lump of iron and a sack of bone chips. The other bodyguard stood watch, scanning for anything that might disrupt his boss's work.

I tried to do the same for Blitz, but I doubted I looked as intimidating as a muscular dwarf in overalls. (And, yes, that was depressing.)

After about an hour, my initial adrenaline rush wore off. I began to realize why the spectators had brought picnic lunches. Crafting was not a fast-moving sport. Every once in a while the crowd would clap or murmur approvingly when

Junior struck a good hit with his hammer, or plunged a piece of metal into the cooling vat with a satisfying hiss. Nabbi and two other judges paced back and forth between the work-stations, scribbling notes on their clipboards. But for me, most the morning was standing around with the Sword of Summer in my hand, trying not to look like a fool.

A couple of times I had to do my job. Once a dart shot out of nowhere, heading for Blitzen. The Sword of Summer leaped into action. Before I even knew what was happening, the blade sliced the dart out of the air. The crowd applauded, which would have been gratifying if I'd actually done anything.

A little later, a random dwarf charged me from the side-lines, swinging an ax and screaming, "BLOOD!" I hit him in the head with the hilt of my sword. He collapsed. More polite applause. A couple of bystanders hauled the dwarf away by his ankles.

Junior was busy hammering out a red-hot iron cylinder the size of a shotgun barrel. He'd already crafted a dozen smaller mechanisms that I guessed would fit together with the cylin-der, but I couldn't tell what the final product was supposed to be. The old dwarf's walker didn't slow him down at all. He had some trouble shuffling around, but he could stand in one place just fine. Despite his age, his arm muscles were ripped from a lifetime swinging hammers at anvils.

Meanwhile, Blitzen hunched over his worktable with a pair of needle-nose pliers, connecting thin sheets of curved metal into some kind of figurine. Hearthstone stood nearby, drenched with sweat from working the bellows.

I tried not to worry about how exhausted Hearth looked,

or where Sam was, or how many times Blitzen dropped his tools and wept over his project.

Finally Nabbi yelled, "Ten minutes until mid-morning break!"

Blitzen sobbed. He attached another sheet of metal to his project, which was starting to resemble a duck.

Most of the crowd focused on the other workstation, where Junior was attaching various mechanisms to the cylinder. He hobbled to the forge and reheated the whole contraption until it was glowing red.

Carefully, he set the cylinder against the anvil, holding it steady with his tongs. He raised his hammer.

Just as he struck, something went wrong. Junior screamed. The hammer went askew, flattening the cylinder and sending attachments flying everywhere. Junior staggered backward, his hands cupped over his face.

His bodyguards rushed to his aid, crying, "What? What it is?"

I couldn't hear the whole conversation, but apparently some kind of insect had bitten Junior between the eyes.

"Did you get it?" asked one of the guards.

"No! The little pest flew off! Quick, before the cylinder cools—"

"Time!" shouted Nabbi.

Junior stomped his foot and cursed. He glared at his ruined project and yelled at his bodyguards.

I went to check on Blitzen, who sat slumped on his anvil. His porkpie hat was pushed back on his head. His left suspender had snapped.

"How you doing, champ?" I asked.

"Horrible." He gestured at his project. "I made a duck."

"Yeah . . ." I searched for a compliment. "It's a really nice duck. That's the bill, right? And those are the wings?"

Hearthstone sat next to us on the asphalt. *Ducks,* he signed. *Always ducks.*

"I'm sorry," Blitz moaned. "When I'm stressed, I default to waterfowl. I don't know why."

"No worries," I said. "Junior had a setback. His first project is pretty much ruined."

Blitz tried to brush the cinders off his white shirt. "It doesn't matter. Junior's first item is always his warm-up. He's got two more chances to destroy me."

"Hey, none of that." I rummaged through our supply bag and handed out canteens of water and some peanut butter crackers.

Hearthstone ate like a starving elf. Then he sat back and shone a flashlight on his face, trying to absorb the rays. Blitzen barely sipped his water.

"I never wanted this," Blitz murmured. "Crafting contests, magic items. All I ever wanted was to design quality clothing and sell it at reasonable prices in my own store."

I stared at his sweat-stained collar and thought about what Freya had said: *Blitzen is a genius at fabrics and fashion. The other dwarves don't appreciate his expertise, but I think it's marvelous.*

"That's your dream," I realized. "That's why you drank from Mimir's Well—to find out how to open a clothing shop?"

Blitzen scowled. "It was more than that. I wanted to follow my dream. I wanted other dwarves to stop laughing at me. I wanted to avenge my father's death and restore the family's honor! But those things didn't go together. I went to Mimir for advice."

"And . . . what did he say?"

Blitzen shrugged helplessly. "Four years of service—that was the price for drinking from his well. He said the cost of knowledge was also the answer. By serving him, I would get what I wanted. Except I didn't. Now I'm going to die."

No, Hearth signed. *Someday you will get your dream.*

"How, exactly?" Blitzen asked. "It's a little hard to cut and sew fabric when you're decapitated."

"That's not going to happen," I said.

In my chest, several ideas started to smelt together into a usable molten ingot—unless that sensation was just the peanut butter crackers. I thought about my sword that could turn into a pendant, and Sam's hijab that was magical high-tech camouflage. "Blitz, your next two items are going to be awesome."

"How do you know? I might panic and make more ducks!"

"You want to make clothing, right? So make clothing."

"Kid, this is a *forge*, not a haberdashery. Besides, fashion is not a recognized craft."

"What about armor?"

Blitz hesitated. "Well, yeah, but—"

"What about fashionable clothing that doubles as armor?"

Blitz's mouth fell open. "Balder's Bling . . . Kid, you may be on to something!" He shot to his feet and began hurrying around the workspace, gathering tools.

Hearth beamed at me—literally, since he still had the flashlight aimed at his face. He tapped his free hand to his head—the sign for *genius.*

When Nabbi called time, I took over at the bellows to give

Hearth a rest. He stood guard. Stoking the fire was about as fun as riding a stationary bike inside a baking oven.

After a while, Blitzen took me off the bellows and had me assist with the crafting. I was hopeless at it, but being forced to give me directions seemed to increase Blitz's confidence. "No, put that here. No, the big tongs! Hold it steady, kid! That's not steady!"

I lost track of time. I didn't pay much attention to what Blitz was making—something small, woven from chain. Instead I kept thinking about the Sword of Summer, now back in pendant form around my neck.

I remembered walking from the docks to Copley Square, half delirious with hunger and exhaustion, and the imaginary conversation I'd had with the blade. I considered how the sword either hummed or stayed silent, either guided my hand or lay heavy and inert. If it had a soul and emotions—then I hadn't given it enough credit. I'd been treating it like a dangerous object. I should be treating it like a person.

"Thanks," I said under my breath, trying not to feel ridiculous. "When you cut that dart out of the air earlier, you saved my friend. I should've thanked you sooner."

The pendant seemed to grow warmer, though standing next to the forge, it was hard to be sure.

"Sumarbrander," I said. "Is that what you like to be called? Sorry I've been ignoring you."

Hmmm, the pendant hummed skeptically.

"You're much more than a sword," I said. "You're not just for slashing at things. You—"

From across the courtyard, Nabbi yelled, "Ten minutes until lunch break!"

"Oh, gods," Blitzen muttered. "I can't— Kid, quick! Hand me that texturing hammer."

His hands flew, snatching up various tools, making minor adjustments to his creation. It didn't look like much—just a flat narrow length of chain mail—but Blitz worked as if his life depended on it, which it did.

He folded and crimped the chain mail into its final shape, then soldered the seam.

"It's a necktie!" I realized. "Blitzen, I actually recognize what you made!"

"Thank you. Shut up." He raised his soldering gun and announced, "Done!" just as a crash reverberated from Junior's workstation.

"GAAHHH!" screamed the old dwarf.

The entire crowd surged to their feet.

Junior was on his butt, cradling his face in his hands. On his worktable sat a flattened, misshapen lump of cooling iron.

His bodyguards rushed to help him.

"Damnable insect!" Junior howled. He was bleeding from the bridge of his nose. He looked at his palms but apparently found no squashed bug. "I hit it this time, I'm sure! Where is it?"

Nabbi and the other judges frowned in our direction, as if we somehow might have orchestrated a kamikaze insect attack. I guess we looked clueless enough to convince them otherwise.

"Time for lunch," Nabbi announced. "One more item shall be made this afternoon!"

We ate quickly, because Blitz was raring to get back to work.

"I've got the hang of it now," he said. "I've *got* it. Kid, I owe you big-time."

I glanced over at Junior's workstation. His bodyguards were glaring at me, cracking their knuckles.

"Let's just get through the contest," I said. "I wish Sam was here. We may need to fight our way out."

Hearth gave me a curious look when I mentioned Sam.

"What?" I asked.

He shook his head and went back to eating his watercress sandwich.

The afternoon session went quickly. I was so busy on guard duty I barely had time to think. Junior must have hired some extra saboteurs, because every half hour or so I had to deal with a new threat: a spear thrown from the audience, a rotten apple aimed at Blitzen's head, a steam-powered predator drone, and a pair of dwarves in green Spandex jumpsuits, wielding baseball bats. (The less said about that, the better.) Each time, the Sword of Summer guided my hand and neutralized the threat. Each time, I remembered to thank the sword.

I could almost discern its voice now: *Yeah, okay. Mmm-hmm. I suppose.* Like it was slowly warming up to me, getting over its resentment at being ignored.

Hearthstone rushed around the workstation, bringing Blitz extra materials and tools. Blitz was weaving a larger, more complicated piece of metal fabric. Whatever it was, he seemed pleased.

Finally, he set down his bezel roller and shouted, "Success!"

At the same moment, Junior suffered his most spectacular fail. His bodyguards had been standing close, ready for another kamikaze insect attack, but it made no difference. As Junior brought down his hammer for a masterstroke, a dark speck zipped out of the sky. The horsefly bit Junior on the face so hard he spun sideways under the momentum of his hammer. Wailing and staggering, he knocked both his guards unconscious, destroyed the contents of two worktables, and swept his third invention into the forge before he collapsed on the asphalt.

It shouldn't have been funny—an old dwarf getting humiliated like that. Except that it was, kind of. Probably because that old dwarf was a spiteful, nasty piece of work.

In the midst of the commotion, Nabbi rang a hand bell. "The contest has ended!" he announced. "Time for judging the items . . . and killing the loser!"

FORTY-FOUR

Junior Wins a Bag of Tears

SAM PICKED THAT MOMENT TO SHOW UP.

She shouldered through the crowd, her headscarf pulled low over her face. Her jacket was dusted with ash, as if she'd spent the night in a chimney.

I wanted to yell at her for being gone so long, but my anger evaporated when I noticed her black eye and swollen lip.

"What happened?" I asked. "Are you okay?"

"Little scuffle," she said. "No worries. Let's watch the judging."

Spectators gathered around two tables on the sideline, where Junior's and Blitzen's crafts were on display. Blitzen stood with his hands clasped behind his back, looking confident despite his snapped suspenders, his grease-strained shirt, and his sweat-soaked porkpie hat.

Junior's face was a bloody mess. He could barely hold himself up on his walker. The murderous gleam in his eyes made him look like a serial killer exhausted after a hard day's work.

Nabbi and the other judges circled the tables, inspecting the crafted items and jotting notes on their clipboards.

At last Nabbi faced the audience. He arched his wriggly eyebrows and tried for a smile.

"Well, then!" he said. "Thank you all for attending this

contest, sponsored by Nabbi's Tavern, famous among taverns, built by Nabbi and home to Nabbi's Stout, the only mead you'll ever need. Now our contestants will tell us about their first items. Blitzen, son of Freya!"

Blitz gestured to his metal sculpture. "It's a duck."

Nabbi blinked. "And . . . what does it do?"

"When I press its back . . ." Blitzen did so. The duck swelled to three times its size, like a frightened pufferfish. "It turns into a larger duck."

The second judge scratched his beard. "That's it?"

"Well, yes," Blitz said. "I call it the Expando-Duck. It's perfect if you need a small metal duck. Or a larger metal duck."

The third judge turned to his colleagues. "Garden knick-knack, perhaps? Conversation piece? Decoy?"

Nabbi coughed. "Yes, thank you, Blitzen. And now you, Eitri Junior, son of Edna. What is your first creation?"

Junior wiped the blood out of his eyes. He held up his flattened iron cylinder, with several springs and latches dangling from it. "This is a self-guiding troll-seeking missile! If it were undamaged, it could destroy any troll at a distance of half a mile. And it's reusable!"

The crowd murmured appreciatively.

"Um, but does it work?" asked the second judge.

"No!" Junior said. "It was ruined on the final hammer stroke. But if it *did* work—"

"But it doesn't," observed the third judge. "So what is it at the moment?"

"It's a useless metal cylinder!" Junior snarled. "Which isn't my fault!"

The judges conferred and scribbled some notes.

"So, in the first round," Nabbi summed up, "we have an expandable duck versus a useless metal cylinder. Our contestants are running very close indeed. Blitzen, what is your second item?"

Blitzen proudly held up his chain mail neckware. "The bulletproof tie!"

The judges lowered their clipboards in perfect synchronicity.

"What?" asked Nabbi.

"Oh, come now!" Blitz turned to the audience. "How many of you have been in the embarrassing situation of wearing a bulletproof vest without a matching bulletproof tie?"

In the back of the crowd, one dwarf raised his hand.

"Exactly!" Blitzen said. "Not only is this accessory fashionable, but it will stop anything up to a 30-06 round. It can also be worn as a cravat."

The judges frowned and took notes, but a few audience members seemed impressed. They examined their shirts, maybe thinking how underdressed they felt without a chain mail neckpiece.

"Junior?" asked Nabbi. "What is your second work of craftsmanship?"

"The Goblet of Infinity!" Junior gestured to a misshapen hunk of iron. "It holds a limitless amount of any liquid—great for road trips through waterless wastelands."

"Uh . . ." Nabbi pointed with his pen. "It looks a bit crushed."

"Stupid horsefly again!" Junior protested. "It bit me right between the eyes! Not *my* fault if an insect turned my brilliant invention into a slag heap."

"Slag heap," Nabbi repeated, jotting on his clipboard. "And Blitzen, your final item?"

Blitzen held up a glittering length of woven metal fabric. "The chain mail vest! For use with a three-piece suit of chain mail. Or, if you want to dress it down, you can wear it with jeans and a nice shirt."

And a shield, Hearthstone offered.

"Yes, and a shield," Blitzen said.

The third judge leaned forward, squinting. "I suppose it would offer some minor protection. If you were stabbed in the back at a disco, for instance."

The second judge jotted something down. "Does it have any magic abilities?"

"Well, no," Blitz said. "But it's reversible: silver on the outside, gold on the inside. Depending on what jewelry you're wearing, or what color armor—"

"I see." Nabbi made a note on his clipboard and turned to Junior. "And your final item, sir?"

Junior's fists trembled with rage. "This is unfair! I have never lost a contest. All of you know my skills. This meddler, this *poseur* Blitzen has somehow managed to ruin my—"

"Eitri Junior, son of Edna," interrupted Nabbi, "what is your third item?"

He waved impatiently at the furnace. "My third item is in there! It doesn't *matter* what it was, because it's now boiling sludge!"

The judges circled up and conferred. The crowd shifted restlessly.

Nabbi faced the audience. "Judging has been difficult. We have weighed the merits of Junior's boiling sludge, slag heap, and useless metal cylinder against the chain mail vest, bullet-proof tie, and Expando-Duck. It was a close call. However, we judge the winner of this contest to be Blitzen, son of Freya!"

Spectators applauded. Some gasped in disbelief. A female dwarf in a nurse's outfit, possibly Bambi, famous among dwarf nurses, passed out cold.

Hearthstone jumped up and down and made the ends of his scarf do the wave. I looked for Sam, but she was hanging back at the edges of the crowd.

Junior scowled at his fists as if deciding whether to hit himself. "Fine," he growled. "Take my head! I don't want to live in a world where Blitzen wins crafting contests!"

"Junior, I don't want to kill you," Blitzen said. Despite his win, he didn't sound proud or gloating. He looked tired, maybe even sad.

Junior blinked. "You—you don't?"

"No. Just give me the earrings and the rope as you promised. Oh, and a public admission that my father was right about Gleipnir all along. You should have replaced it centuries ago."

"Never!" Junior shrieked. "You impugn my father's reputation! I cannot—"

"Okay, I'll get my ax," Blitzen said in a resigned tone. "I'm afraid the blade is a little dull. . . ."

Junior gulped. He looked longingly at the bulletproof necktie. "Very well. Perhaps . . . perhaps Bilì had a point. The rope needed replacement."

"And you were wrong to tarnish his reputation."

The old dwarf's facial muscles convulsed, but he managed to get out the words. "And I was . . . wrong. Yes."

Blitzen gazed up into the gloom, whispering something

under his breath. I wasn't a good lip-reader, but I was pretty sure he said, *I love you, Dad. Good-bye.*

He refocused on Junior. "Now, about the items you promised . . ."

Junior snapped his fingers. One of his bodyguards wobbled over, his head newly bandaged from his recent encounter with a hammer. He handed Blitzen a small velvet box.

"Earrings for your mother," Junior said.

Blitz opened the box. Inside were two tiny cats made from gold filigree like Brisingamen. As I watched, the cats stretched, blinking their emerald eyes and flicking their diamond tails.

Blitz snapped the box shut. "Adequate. And the rope?"

The bodyguard tossed him a ball of silk kite string.

"You're joking," I said. "That's supposed to bind Fenris Wolf?"

Junior glowered at me. "Boy, your ignorance is breathtaking. Gleipnir was just as thin and light, but its paradox ingredients gave it great strength. This rope is the same, only better!"

"Paradox ingredients?"

Blitz held up the end of the rope and whistled appreciatively. "He means things that aren't supposed to exist. Paradox ingredients are very difficult to craft with, very dangerous. Gleipnir contained the footfall of a cat, the spittle of a bird, the breath of a fish, the beard of a woman."

"Dunno if that last one is a paradox," I said. "Crazy Alice in Chinatown has a pretty good beard."

Junior huffed. "The point is, this rope is even better! I call it Andskoti, the Adversary. It is woven with the most powerful paradoxes in the Nine Worlds—Wi-Fi with no lag, a politician's sincerity, a printer that prints, healthy deep-fried food, and an interesting grammar lecture!"

"Okay, yeah," I admitted. "Those things don't exist."

Blitz stuffed the rope in his backpack. He took out his pouch of tears and handed it to the old dwarf. "Thank you, Junior. I consider our bargain complete, but I would ask one more thing. Where is the island of Fenris Wolf?"

Junior hefted his payment. "If I could tell you, Blitzen, I would. I'd be happy to see you ripped apart by the Wolf like your father was! Alas, I don't know."

"But—"

"Yes, I said I checked on the rope from time to time. I lied! The truth is, very few gods or dwarves know where the Wolf's island appears. Most of them are sworn to secrecy. How your father found the place, I really don't know, but if you want to find it, the best person to ask is Thor. He knows, and he has a big mouth."

"Thor," I said. "Where do we find Thor?"

"I have no idea," Junior admitted.

Hearthstone signed, *Sam might. She knows a lot about the gods.*

"Yeah." I turned. "Sam, get over here! Why are you lurking?"

The crowd parted around her.

As soon as Junior saw her, he made a strangled squawk. "You! It was you!"

Sam tried to cover her busted lip. "Sorry? Have we met?"

"Oh, don't play innocent with me." Junior scooted forward on his walker, his flushed scalp turning his gray hair pink. "I've seen shape-shifters before. That scarf is the same color as the horsefly's wings. And that black eye is from when I swatted you! You're in league with Blitzen! Friends, colleagues, honest dwarves—kill these cheaters!"

I was proud that the four of us responded as a team. In perfect unison, like a well-oiled combat machine, we turned and ran for our lives.

FORTY-FIVE

I Get to Know Jack

I'M PRETTY GOOD at multitasking, so I figured I could flee in terror and argue at the same time.

"A horsefly?" I yelled at Sam. "You can turn into a horsefly?"

She ducked as a steam-powered dart buzzed over her head. "Now is not the time!"

"Oh, excuse me. I should wait for the designated talk-about-turning-into-horseflies time."

Hearthstone and Blitzen led the way. Behind us, a mob of thirty dwarves was closing fast. I didn't like their murderous expressions or their fine assortment of handcrafted weapons.

"This way!" Blitzen ducked down an alley.

Unfortunately, Hearthstone wasn't watching. The elf barreled straight ahead.

"Mother!" Blitz cursed—at least, I thought it was a curse until Sam and I reached the corner and faltered.

A few steps down the alley, Blitz was trapped in a net of light. He squirmed and cussed as the glowing web lifted him into the air. "It's my mother!" he yelped. "She wants her damnable earrings. Go! Catch up with Hearthstone! I'll meet you—"

POP! Our dwarf disappeared in a flash.

I glanced at Sam. "Did that just happen?"

"We've got other problems." She pulled out her ax.

The mob had caught up with us. They fanned out in an angry semicircle of beards, scowls, baseball bats, and broadswords. I wasn't sure what they were waiting for. Then I heard Junior's voice somewhere behind them. "Hold on!" he wheezed. "I—" *Wheeze.* "Kill—" *Wheeze.* "First!"

The mob parted. Flanked by his bodyguards, the old dwarf pushed his walker toward us.

He eyed me, then Sam.

"Where are Blitzen and the elf?" Junior muttered. "Well, no matter. We'll find them. You, boy, I don't care about so much. Run now and I might let you live. The girl is obviously a daughter of Loki. She bit me and ruined my crafting! She dies."

I pulled off my pendant. The Sword of Summer grew to full length. The crowd of dwarves edged backward. I guess they knew a dangerous blade when they saw one.

"I'm not going anywhere," I said. "You'll have to take on both of us."

The sword hummed for attention.

"Correction," I said. "You'll have to take on all *three* of us. This is Sumarbrander, the Sword of Summer, crafted by . . . actually I'm not sure, but it is definitely famous among swords, and it is about to kick your collective butts."

"Thank you," said the sword.

Sam made a squeaking noise. The dwarves' shocked expressions told me I hadn't imagined hearing the sword's voice.

I held up the blade. "You can talk? I mean . . . of course you can talk. You have many, uh, incredible abilities."

"That's what I've been saying." The sword's voice was definitely male. It emanated from the runes along the blade, which vibrated and glowed with every word like the lights on a stereo equalizer.

I gave the dwarves an arrogant look, like, *Yeah, that's right. I've got a talking disco sword and you don't.*

"Sumarbrander," I said, "how do you feel about taking on this mob?"

"Sure," said the sword. "You want them dead or . . . ?"

The mob shuffled backward in alarm.

"Nah," I decided. "Just make them go away."

"You're no fun," the sword said. "Okay, then, let go."

I hesitated. I didn't particularly want to hold a flashing talking humming sword, but dropping my weapon didn't seem like the natural first step toward victory.

Junior must've sensed my reluctance.

"We can take him!" he yelled. "He's one boy with a sword he doesn't know how to use!"

Sam snarled. "And a former Valkyrie with an ax she very much *does* know how to use."

"Bah!" Junior said. "Let's get 'em, boys! Granny Shuffler, activate!"

Rows of dagger blades extended from the front of his walker. Two miniature rocket engines fired in the back, propelling Junior toward us at a mind-boggling one mile an hour. His comrades roared and charged.

I let go of my sword. It hovered in the air for a split second. Then it flew into action. Faster than you could say *son of Edna*, every dwarf was disarmed. Their weapons were cut in half, split down the middle, knocked to the ground, or diced into hors d'oeuvre-size cubes. The daggers and rockets were sheared off Junior's walker. The severed ends of thirty beards fluttered to the pavement, leaving thirty shocked dwarves with fifty percent less facial hair.

The Sword of Summer hovered between the mob and me.

"Anybody want more?" the sword asked.

The dwarves turned and fled.

Junior yelled over his shoulder as he hobbled away, following his bodyguards, who were already a block ahead of him. "This isn't over, boy! I'll be back with reinforcements!"

Sam lowered her ax. "That was . . . Wow."

"Yeah," I agreed. "Thank you, Sumarbrander."

"De nada," said the sword. "But you know, Sumarbrander is a really long name, and I've never liked it much."

"Okay." I wasn't sure where to look when addressing the sword—the glowing runes? The tip of the blade? "What would you like us to call you?"

The sword hummed thoughtfully. "What is your name?"

"Magnus."

"That's a good name. Call me Magnus."

"You can't be Magnus. *I'm* Magnus."

"Then what is her name?"

"Sam. You can't be Sam, either. It would be too confusing."

The blade swished from side to side. "Well, what *is* a good name? Something that fits my personality and my many talents."

"But I don't really know you as well as I'd like to." I looked at Samirah, who just shook her head like, *Hey, it's your disco sword.*

"Honestly," I said. "I don't know jack—"

"Jack!" the sword cried. "Perfect!"

The thing about talking swords . . . it's hard to tell when they're kidding. They have no facial expressions. Or faces.

"So . . . you want me to call you Jack."

"It is a noble name," said the sword. "Fit for kings and sharp carving implements!"

"Okay," I said. "Well, then, Jack, thanks for the save. You mind if . . . ?" I reached for the hilt, but Jack floated away from me.

"I wouldn't do that yet," he warned. "The price of my amazing abilities: as soon as you sheathe me, or turn me into a pendant, or whatever, you will feel just as exhausted as if you had performed all my actions yourself."

My shoulder muscles tightened. I considered how tired I would feel if I had just destroyed all those weapons and cut all those beards. "Oh. I didn't notice that earlier."

"Because you hadn't used me for anything amazing yet."

"Right."

In the distance, an air raid horn howled. I doubted they got many air raids in an underground world, so I figured the alarm had to do with us.

"We need to go," Sam urged. "We have to find Hearthstone. I doubt Junior was joking about reinforcements."

Finding Hearthstone was the easy part. Two blocks away, we ran into him as he was coming back to find us.

What the H-e-l-h-e-i-m? he signed. *Where is Blitzen?*

I told him about Freya's gold net. "We'll find him. Right now, Junior is calling up the Dwarven National Guard."

Your sword is floating, Hearth noted.

"Your elf is deaf," Jack noted.

I turned to the sword. "I know that. Sorry, introductions. Jack, Hearth. Hearth, Jack."

Hearth signed, *Is it talking? I don't read sword lips.*

"What is he saying?" Jack asked. "I don't read elf hands."

"Guys." Sam pointed behind us. A few blocks away, an iron-plated vehicle with caterpillar treads and a mounted turret was turning slowly onto our street.

"That's a tank," I said. "Junior has a *tank*?"

"We should leave," Jack said. "I am awesome, but if I try to destroy a tank, the strain might kill you."

"Yeah," I agreed. "How do we get out of Nidavellir?"

Hearthstone clapped for my attention. *This way.*

We sprinted after him, zigzagging through alleys, knocking over carefully handcrafted garbage cans that probably had names and souls.

From somewhere behind us, a deep *BOOM!* rattled windows and made pebbles rain from above.

"Is the tank shaking the *sky*?" I yelled. "That *can't* be good."

Hearthstone led us down another street of clapboard row houses. Dwarves sat on stoops, clapping and cheering as we ran by. A few of them recorded videos of us on uniquely crafted smartphones. I figured our attempted getaway would go viral on the Dwarven Internet, famous among Internets.

Finally we reached what would've been the southern edge of South Boston. On the far side of the avenue, instead of the M Street Beach, the ground dropped off into a chasm.

"Oh, this is very helpful," Sam said.

Behind us in the gloom, Junior's voice shouted, "Bazookas, take the right flank!"

Hearthstone led us to the rim of the canyon. Far below, a river roared.

He signed: *We jump in.*

"Are you serious?" I asked.

Blitzen and I did this before. River washes out of Nidavellir.

"To where?"

Depends, Hearthstone signed.

"That's not reassuring," said Sam.

Hearthstone pointed back toward the avenue. The dwarven mob was gathering, tanks and jeeps and RPGs and a whole bunch of really angry geriatric dwarves in armor-plated walkers.

"We jump," I decided.

Jack the Sword hovered next to me. "Better hold me now, boss. Otherwise I might get lost again."

"But you said the exhaustion—"

"Might make you pass out," the sword agreed. "On the bright side, it looks like you're going to die anyway."

He had a point. (Oh, sorry. That was bad.) I took the sword and willed it back into pendant form. I just had time to attach it to the chain before my legs buckled.

Sam caught me. "Hearthstone! Take his other arm!"

As my vision went dark, Sam and Hearth helped me leap off the cliff. Because, you know, what are friends for?

FORTY-SIX

Aboard the Good Ship *Toenail*

I KNEW I WAS IN TROUBLE when I woke up dreaming.

I found myself standing next to Loki on the deck of a massive ship.

"There you are!" said Loki. "I was starting to wonder."

"How . . . ?" I noticed his outfit. "What are you wearing?"

"You like it?" His scarred lips twisted into a grin. His white admiral's jacket gleamed with medals, but Loki wasn't exactly wearing it regulation-style. It was open over a black T-shirt featuring Jack Nicholson's face from *The Shining*. The caption read: HEEEERE'S LOKI!

"Where are we?" I asked.

Loki polished his medals with his coat sleeve. "Well, neither of us is *here*, of course. I'm still tied up on a stone slab with snake poison dripping in my face. You're dying on the banks of a river in Jotunheim."

"I'm what?"

"Whether you live or not, this may be our last chance to talk. I wanted you to see this—*Naglfar*, the Ship of Nails! It's almost complete."

The ship came into clearer focus—a Viking longship larger than an aircraft carrier. The main deck could've accommodated the Boston Marathon. Giant shields lined the railings.

Fore and aft rose thirty-foot-tall figureheads shaped like snarling wolves. Naturally, they had to be wolves.

I peered over the side between two shields. A hundred feet down, braided iron cables moored the ship to a dock. The gray sea churned with ice.

I ran my hand along the railing. The surface was bumpy and prickly—enameled with white and gray ridges like fish scales or pearl shavings. At first glance, I'd assumed the deck was made of steel, but now I realized the whole ship was constructed of this weird translucent material—not metal, not wood, but something strangely familiar.

"What is this?" I asked Loki. "I don't see any wood or nails. Why is it called the Ship of Nails?"

Loki chuckled. "Not *carpentry* nails, Magnus. *Naglfar* is made from the fingernails and toenails of dead men."

The deck seemed to pitch beneath me. I wasn't sure if it was possible to puke in a dream, but I was tempted. It wasn't just the obvious grossness of standing on a ship made of nail clippings that made me nauseated—it was the sheer *volume* of the material. How many corpses had had to contribute their nails to make a ship this size?

Once I managed to steady my breathing, I faced Loki. "Why?"

Even with the ruined lips and scarred face, Loki's grin was so infectious, I almost smiled back—*almost*.

"Amazingly disgusting, isn't it?" he said. "Back in the old days, your ancestors knew that nail clippings carried part of your spirit, your essence . . . your DNA, you'd call it now. Throughout their lives, mortals were careful to burn any clippings they made. When they died, their nails would be trimmed and the clippings destroyed so the material wouldn't contribute to this great ship. But sometimes"—Loki shrugged—"as you can see, the proper precautions weren't taken."

"You've built yourself a battleship out of toenails."

"Well, the ship is building *itself*. And, technically, *Naglfar* belongs to Surt and the fire giants, but when Ragnarok comes, I will guide this ship out of the harbor. We'll have an army of giants led by Captain Hrym, plus hundreds of thousands of dishonored dead from Helheim—all those who were careless or unlucky enough to die without a sword in their hand, a proper burial, and a decent post-mortem mani-pedi. We'll sail to Asgard and destroy the gods. It'll be awesome."

I looked aft, expecting to see an army gathering on the shore, but the mist was so thick I couldn't see the end of the dock. Despite my usual resistance to cold, the damp air soaked into my bones and made my teeth chatter.

"Why are you showing me this?" I asked.

"Because I like you, Magnus. You've got a sense of humor. You've got *zing*. So rare in a demigod! Even rarer among the einherjar. I'm glad my daughter found you."

"Samirah . . . that's how she can turn into a horsefly. She's a shape-shifter like you."

"Oh, she's Daddy's girl, all right. She doesn't like to admit it, but she's inherited a lot of things from me: my abilities, my dashing good looks, my keen intellect. She can spot talent too. After all, she chose you, my friend."

I clutched my stomach. "I don't feel so good."

"Duh! You're on the verge of death. Personally, I hope you wake up, because if you kick the bucket now, your death will be meaningless and nothing you've done will matter."

"Thanks for the pep talk."

"Listen—I brought you here for some perspective. When Ragnarok comes, *all* bonds will break, not just the ropes binding Fenris. The moorings of this ship—*snap*. The bindings that hold me captive—*snap*. Whether or not you keep that sword out of Surt's hands, it's only a matter of time. One bond will snap and they'll all start going—unraveling like one huge tapestry."

"You're trying to discourage me? I thought you wanted Ragnarok delayed."

"Oh, I do!" He put up his hands. His wrists were raw and bleeding, as if he'd been handcuffed too tightly. "I'm totally on your side, Magnus! Look at the figureheads. The wolves' snouts aren't finished yet. Is there anything more embarrassing than sailing into battle with half-finished figureheads?"

"So what do you want?"

"The same thing I've always wanted," Loki said. "To help you fight your fate. Which of the gods besides me has bothered to speak to you as a friend and an equal?"

His eyes were like Sam's—bright and intense, the color of burning—but there was something harder and more calculating about Loki's gaze—something that didn't jibe with his friendly smile. I remembered how Sam had described him: *a liar, a thief, a murderer.*

"We're friends now?" I asked. "Equals?"

"We could be," he said. "In fact, I have an idea. Forget going to Fenris's island. Forget facing Surt. I know a place where the sword will be safe."

"With you?"

Loki laughed. "Don't tempt me, kid. No, no. I was thinking about your Uncle Randolph. He understands the value of the sword. He's spent his life looking for it, preparing to study it. You might not know it, but his house is *heavily* fortified with magic. If you took the sword to him . . . well, the old man can't use it himself. But he would store it away. It would be out of Surt's hands. And that's what matters, eh? It would buy us all some time."

I wanted to laugh in Loki's face and tell him no. I figured he was trying to trick me. Yet I couldn't see his angle.

"You think it's a trap," Loki said. "I get that. But you must have wondered why Mimir told you to take the blade to the Wolf's island—the very place where Surt *wants* to use it. What's the sense in that? What if Mimir is playing you? I mean, come on. That old severed head runs a pachinko racket! If you don't bring the sword to the island, Surt won't be able get his hands on it. Why take the risk?"

I struggled to clear my thoughts. "You're—you're a smooth talker. You'd make a good used car salesman."

Loki winked. "I think the term is *pre-owned*. You've got to make a choice soon, Magnus. We may not be able to speak again. If you want a gesture of good faith, however, I can sweeten the deal. My daughter Hel and I . . . we've been talking."

My heart jackknifed. "Talking about . . ."

"I'll let her tell you. But now . . ." He tilted his head, listening. "Yes, we don't have much time. You might be waking up."

"Why were you bound?" The question forced itself out before I realized I was thinking it. "I remember you killed somebody. . . ."

His smile hardened. The angry lines around his eyes made him look ten years older.

"You know how to ruin a conversation," Loki said. "I killed Balder, the god of light—the handsome, perfect, *incredibly* annoying son of Odin and Frigg." He stepped toward me and poked my chest, emphasizing each word. "And—I'd—do—it—again."

In the back of my brain, my common sense yelled, *DROP IT!* But as you have probably figured out by now, I don't listen to my common sense much.

"Why did you kill him?"

Loki barked a laugh. His breath smelled of almonds, like cyanide. "Did I mention he was annoying? Frigg was *so* worried about him. The poor baby had been having bad dreams about his own doom. Welcome to *reality*, Balder! We *all* have bad dreams. But Frigg couldn't stand the idea that her precious angel might bruise his little foot. She exacted promises from everything in creation that nothing would hurt her beautiful son—people, gods, trees, rocks. . . . Can you imagine exacting a promise from a rock? Frigg managed it. Afterward, the gods had a party to celebrate. They started throwing things at Balder just for laughs. Arrows, swords, boulders, each other . . . nothing would hurt him. It was as if the idiot was surrounded by a force field. Well . . . *I'm sorry*. The thought of Mr. Perfect also being Mr. Invulnerable made me sick."

I blinked, trying to get the sting out of my eyes. Loki's voice was so full of hatred it seemed to make the air burn. "You found a way to kill him."

"Mistletoe!" Loki's smile brightened. "Can you imagine? Frigg forgot one tiny little plant. I fashioned a dart from the stuff, gave it to Balder's blind brother, a god named Hod. I didn't want him to miss the fun of chucking deadly objects at

Balder, so I guided Hod's hand and . . . well, Frigg's worst fears came true. Balder *deserved* it."

"For being too handsome and popular."

"Yes!"

"For being loved."

"Exactly!" Loki leaned forward until we were almost nose-to-nose. "Don't tell me *you* haven't done the same kinds of things. Those cars you broke into, those people you stole from . . . you picked people you didn't like, eh? You picked the rich handsome stuck-up snobs who *annoyed* you."

My teeth chattered harder. "I never *killed* anyone."

"Oh, please." Loki stepped back, examining me with a look of disappointment. "It's only a matter of degree. So I killed a god. Big deal! He went to Niflheim and became an honored guest in my daughter's palace. And *my* punishment? You want to know *my* punishment?"

"You were tied on a stone slab," I said. "With poison from a snake dripping on your face. I know."

"*Do* you?" Loki pulled back his cuffs, showing me the raw scars on his wrists. "The gods were not content to punish me with eternal torture. They took out their wrath upon my two favorite sons—Vali and Narvi. They turned Vali into a wolf and watched with amusement while he disemboweled his brother Narvi. Then they shot and gutted the wolf. The gods took my innocent sons' own entrails . . ." Loki's voice cracked with grief. "Well, Magnus Chase, let's just say I was not bound with *ropes*."

Something in my chest curled up and died—possibly my hope that there was any kind of justice in the universe. "Gods."

Loki nodded. "Yes, Magnus. The *gods*. Think about that when you meet Thor."

"I'm meeting Thor?"

"I'm afraid so. The gods don't even *pretend* to deal in good and evil, Magnus. It's not the Aesir way. Might makes right. So tell me . . . do you really want to charge into battle on their behalf?"

The ship trembled under my feet. Fog rolled across the deck.

"Time for you to go," Loki said. "Remember what I said. Oh, and have fun getting mouth-to-mouth from a goat."

"Wait . . . what?"

Loki wiggled his fingers, his eyes full of malicious glee. Then the ship dissolved into gray nothingness.

FORTY-SEVEN

I Psychoanalyze a Goat

AS LOKI HAD PROMISED, I woke up with a goat in my face.

Confession time: My only previous experience with kissing had been with Jackie Molotov in seventh grade, behind the bleachers at a school dance. Yes, I know that's lame, seeing as how I was now sixteen. But during the past few years I'd been a little busy, living on the street and whatnot. Anyway, with apologies to Jackie, getting mouth-to-mouth from a goat reminded me of her.

I rolled over and puked into the river conveniently located right next to me. My bones felt as if they'd been broken and mended with duct tape. My mouth tasted like chewed grass and old nickels.

"Oh, you're alive," said the goat. He sounded mildly disappointed.

I sat up and groaned. The goat's horns curved outward like the top half of an hourglass. Sticker burrs matted his shaggy brown fur.

A lot of questions crowded into my head: *Where am I? Why are you a talking goat? Why does your breath smell so bad? Have you been eating spare change?*

The first question that came out was: "Where are my friends?"

"The elf and girl?" asked the goat. "Oh, they're dead."

My heart threatened to exit via my throat. "What? No!"

The goat gestured with his horns. A few yards to my right, Hearthstone and Sam lay crumpled on the rocky beach.

I scrambled over. I placed my hands on their throats and almost passed out again, from relief this time.

"They're not dead," I told the goat. "They both have pulses."

"Oh." The goat sighed. "Well, give them a few more hours and they'll probably be dead."

"What is *wrong* with you?"

"Everything," said the goat. "My whole life is one big—"

"Never mind," I said. "Just be quiet."

The goat brayed. "Sure, I understand. You don't want to know my problems. No one does. I'll be over here, weeping or whatever. Just ignore me."

Keeping my hands against Sam's and Hearthstone's carotid arteries, I sent warmth through my fingertips into their circulatory systems.

Sam was easy to heal. Her heart was strong. She responded almost immediately, her eyes fluttering open, her lungs gasping for air. She curled sideways and began vomiting, which I took as a good sign.

Hearthstone, though . . . something was wrong beyond the water in his lungs and the cold in his limbs. Right at his core, a dense knot of dark emotion sapped his will to live. The pain was so intense it threw me back to the night of my mother's death. I remembered my hands slipping from the fire escape, the windows of our apartment exploding above me.

Hearthstone's grief was even worse than that. I didn't

know exactly what he had suffered, but his despair almost overwhelmed me. I grasped for a happy memory—my mom and me picking wild blueberries on Hancock Hill, the air so clear I could see Quincy Bay glittering on the horizon. I sent a flood of warmth into Hearthstone's chest.

His eyes flew open.

He stared at me, uncomprehending. Then he pointed at my face and gestured weakly—the sign for light.

"What do you mean?" I asked.

Sam groaned. She rose on one arm and squinted at me. "Magnus . . . why are you glowing?"

I looked at my hands. Sure enough, I seemed to have been dipped in Folkvanger light. The warm buttery aura was starting to fade, but I could feel residual power tingling along my arm hairs.

"Apparently," I said, "if I heal too much at once, I glow."

Sam winced. "Well, thanks for healing us. But try not to self-combust. How is Hearth?"

I helped him sit up. "How you feeling, buddy?"

He made a circle with his thumb and middle finger, then flicked it upward, the sign for *terrible*.

No surprise. Given the depth of pain I'd felt within him, I was surprised he wasn't constantly screaming.

"Hearth . . ." I started to say, "when I healed you, I—"

He put his hands over mine—a sign language version of *hush*.

Maybe we had some residual connection from the healing magic, but when I met Hearthstone's eyes, I could tell what he was thinking. His message was an almost audible voice in my head—like when Jack the sword had started to speak.

Later, Hearth told me. *Thank you . . . brother.*

I was too startled to reply.

The goat plodded over. "You really should take better care of your elf. They need lots of sunshine—not this weak Jotunheim light. And you can't overwater them by drowning them in rivers."

Hearthstone frowned. He signed, *The goat is speaking?*

I tried to clear my head. "Uh, yeah, he is."

"I also read sign language," said the goat. "My name is Tanngnjóstr, which means Teeth Grinder, because . . . well, it's a nervous habit of mine. But nobody calls me Tanngnjóstr. It's a horrible name. Just call me Otis."

Sam struggled to her feet. Her hijab had come undone and now hung around her neck like a gunslinger's bandanna. "So, Otis, what brings you here to this place that is . . . wherever we are?"

Otis sighed. "I got lost. Which is typical. I was trying to find my way back to camp when I found you all instead. I suppose you'll kill me and eat me for dinner now."

I frowned at Sam. "Were you planning to kill the goat?"

"No. Were you?"

I looked at Otis. "We weren't planning to kill you."

"It's okay if you want to," Otis said. "I'm used to it. My master kills me all the time."

"He . . . does?" I asked.

"Oh, sure. I'm basically a talking meal on four hooves. My therapist says that's why I'm so down all the time, but I don't know. I think it goes way back to when I was a kid—"

"Sorry. Wait. Who is your master?"

Hearthstone spelled out, *T-H-O-R. D-U-H.*

"That's right," said the goat. "Although his last name is not *Duh.* You haven't seen him, have you?"

"No . . ." I thought about my dream. I could still smell the bitter almonds on Loki's breath. *The gods don't even pretend to deal in good and evil, Magnus. Think about that when you meet Thor.*

Junior had told us to seek out Thor. The river had somehow brought us to where we needed to be. Only now, I wasn't sure I wanted to be here.

Sam readjusted her headscarf. "I'm not a big fan of Thor, but if he can give us directions to Lyngvi, we need to talk to him."

"Except the goat is lost," I said. "So how do we find Thor?"

Hearthstone pointed to my pendant. *Ask Jack.*

Instead of spelling the name, he made the sign for *jack-in-the-box,* which looked like a finger rabbit popping up from behind his hand. Sometimes sign language can be a little too literal.

I pulled off the pendant. The sword grew to full length and began to hum.

"Hey," said Jack, the runes glowing along his blade, "glad you survived! Oh, is that Otis? Cool! Thor must be around here somewhere."

Otis bleated. "You have a talking sword? I've never been killed by a talking sword before. That's fine. If you could just make a clean cut right across the throat—"

"Otis!" Jack said. "Don't you know me? I'm Frey's Sword, Sumarbrander. We met at that party at Bilskirnir—the one where you were playing tug-of-war with Loki?"

"Oh . . ." Otis shook his horns. "Yes. That was embarrassing."

"Jack," I said, "we're looking for Thor. Any chance you can point us in the right direction?"

"Easy McSqueezy." The sword tugged at my arm. "I'm reading a big concentration of hot air and thunder that way!"

Sam and I helped Hearthstone to his feet. He wasn't looking too good. His lips were pale green. He wobbled like he'd just gotten off a Tilt-a-Whirl.

"Otis," Sam said, "can our friend ride you? It might be quicker."

"Sure," the goat said. "Ride me, kill me, whatever. But I should warn you, this is Jotunheim. If we go the wrong way, we'll run across giants. Then we'll all be butchered and put in a stew pot."

"We won't go the wrong way," I promised. "Will we, Jack?"

"Hmm?" said the sword. "Oh, no. Probably not. Like, a sixty percent chance we'll live."

"Jack. . . ."

"Kidding," he said. "Jeez, so uptight."

He pointed upstream and led us through the foggy morning, with spotty snow flurries and a forty percent chance of death.

FORTY-EIGHT

Hearthstone Passes Out
Even More than Jason Grace
(Though I Have No Idea
Who That Is)

JOTUNHEIM LOOKED a lot like Vermont, just with fewer signs offering maple syrup products. Snow dusted the dark mountains. Waist-high drifts choked the valleys. Pine trees bristled with icicles. Jack hovered in front, guiding us along the river as it zigzagged through canyons blanketed in subzero shadows. We climbed trails next to half-frozen waterfalls, my sweat chilling instantly against my skin.

In other words, it was a huge amount of fun.

Sam and I stayed close to Hearthstone. I hoped my residual aura of Frey-glow might do him some good, but he still looked pretty weak. The best we could do was keep him from sliding off the goat.

"Hang in there," I told him.

He signed something—maybe *sorry*—but his gesture was so listless I wasn't sure.

"Just rest," I said.

He grunted in frustration. He groped through his bag of runes, pulled one out, and placed it in my hands. He pointed to the stone, then to himself, as if to say *This is me*.

The rune was one I didn't know:

Sam frowned when she saw it. "That's *perthro*."

"What does it mean?" I asked.

She glanced cautiously at Hearth. "Are you trying to explain what happened to you? You want Magnus to know?"

Hearthstone took a deep breath, like he was preparing for a sprint. He signed: *Magnus–felt–pain.*

I closed my fingers around the stone. "Yeah. . . . When I healed you, there was something dark—"

Hearth pointed again at the stone. He looked at Sam.

"You want me to tell him?" she asked. "You sure?"

He nodded, then rested his head against the goat's back and closed his eyes.

We walked for about twenty yards before Sam said anything.

"When Hearth and I were in Alfheim," she started, "he told me part of his story. I don't know all the details, but . . . his parents . . ." She struggled to find words.

Otis the goat bleated. "Go on. I love depressing stories."

"Be quiet," Sam ordered.

"I'll just be quiet, then," the goat agreed.

I studied Hearthstone's face. He looked so peaceful asleep. "Blitzen told me a little bit," I said. "Hearth's parents never accepted him, because he was deaf."

"It was worse than that," Sam said. "They were . . . not good people."

Some of Loki's acidic tone crept into her voice, as if she were imagining Hearth's parents on the receiving end of mistletoe darts. "Hearth had a brother—Andiron—who died very young. It wasn't Hearthstone's fault, but his parents took out their bitterness on him. They always told him the wrong brother had died. To them, Hearth was a disappointment, a disabled elf, a punishment from the gods. He could do no right."

I clenched the runestone. "He still carries all that pain inside. Gods . . ."

Sam laid her hand on Hearth's ankle. "He couldn't tell me the details of how he grew up, but I—I got the feeling it was worse than you can imagine."

I looked at the rune. "No wonder he daydreamed about working magic. But this symbol . . . ?"

"Perthro symbolizes an empty cup lying sideways," Sam said. "It could be spilled drink, or a cup waiting to be filled, or a cup for throwing dice, like fate."

"I don't understand."

Sam brushed some goat hair from Hearthstone's pants cuff. "I think . . . I think perthro is the rune Hearthstone personally relates to. When he went to Mimir and drank from the well, Hearthstone was offered a choice between two futures. If he took the first path, Mimir would grant him speech and hearing and send him back to Alfheim to live a normal life, but he would have to give up his dream of magic. If he chose the second path—"

"He'd learn magic," I guessed, "but he would stay the way he is—deaf and dumb, hated by his own parents. What kind of messed-up choice is that? I should've stepped on Mimir's face when I had the chance."

Sam shook her head. "Mimir just presented the choices. Magic and normal life are mutually exclusive. Only people who have known great pain have the capacity to learn magic. They have to be like hollow cups. Even Odin . . . he gave up an eye to drink from Mimir's well, but that was just the beginning. In order to learn the runes, Odin fashioned a noose and hanged himself from a branch of the World Tree for nine days."

My stomach checked to see if it had anything left to retch. It settled for dry spasms. "That's . . . not right."

"But it was necessary," Sam said. "Odin pierced his side with his own spear and hung there in pain, without food or water, until the runes revealed themselves. The pain made him hollow . . . a receptacle for magic."

I looked at Hearthstone. I wasn't sure whether to hug him or wake him up and scold him. How could anyone willingly choose to hold on to that much pain? What kind of magic could possibly be worth the cost?

"I've done magic," I said. "Healing, walking into flames, blasting weapons out of people's hands. But I've never suffered like Hearth has."

Samirah pursed her lips. "That's different, Magnus. You were born with your magic—an inheritance from your father. You can't choose your abilities or change them. Alf seidr is innate. It's also lesser magic compared to what the runes can do."

"Lesser?" I didn't want to argue about whose magic was more impressive, but most of the things I'd seen Hearthstone do had been pretty . . . subtle.

"I told you back in Valhalla," Sam said, "the runes are

the secret language of the universe. Learning them, you can recode reality. The only limits on your magic are your strength and your imagination."

"So why don't more people learn runes?"

"That's what I've been telling you. It requires incredible sacrifice. Most people would die before they got as far as Hearthstone has."

I tucked Hearthstone's scarf around his neck. I understood now why he'd been willing to risk rune magic. To a guy with his troubled past, recoding reality must have sounded pretty good. I also thought about the message he'd whispered into my mind. He'd called me *brother*. After everything Hearthstone had been through with his own brother's death . . . that could not have been easy.

"So Hearth made himself an empty cup," I said. "Like perthro."

"Trying to fill himself with the power of magic," Sam agreed. "I don't know all the meanings of perthro, Magnus. But I do know one thing—Hearthstone cast it when we were falling from the cliff into the river."

I tried to remember, but I'd been overwhelmed with exhaustion as soon as I gripped the sword. "What did it do?"

"It got us *here*," Sam said. "And it left Hearthstone like that." She nodded to his snoring form. "I can't be sure, but I think perthro is his . . . what do Christians call it? A 'Hail Mary pass.' He was throwing that rune like you'd throw dice from a cup, turning our fate over to the gods."

My palm was now bruised from clenching the stone. I still wasn't sure why Hearthstone had given it to me, but I felt a strong instinct to keep it for him—if only temporarily. No one should carry that kind of fate alone. I slipped the rune into my pocket.

We trekked through the wilderness in silence for a while. At one point, Jack led us over the river on a fallen tree trunk. I couldn't help looking both ways for giant squirrels before crossing.

In places the snow was so deep we had to hop from boulder to boulder while Otis the goat speculated about which one of us would slip, fall, and die first.

"I wish you'd be quiet," I muttered. "I also wish we had snowshoes."

"You'd need Uller for that," said the goat.

"Who?"

"The god of snowshoes," said Otis. "He invented them. Also archery and . . . I don't know, other stuff."

I'd never heard of a snowshoe god. But I would've paid real money if the god of snowmobiles had come roaring out of the woods right then to give us a lift.

We kept trudging along.

Once, we spotted a stone house on the summit of a hill. The gray light and the mountains played tricks with my perception. I couldn't tell if the house was small and nearby, or massive and far away. I remembered what my friends had told me about giants—that they lived and breathed illusions.

"See that house?" Jack said. "Let's not go there."

I didn't argue.

Judging time was difficult, but by late afternoon the river had turned into a raging current. Cliffs rose along the opposite bank. In the distance, through the trees, I heard the roar of a waterfall.

"Oh, that's right," said Otis. "I remember now."

"You remember what?" I asked.

"Why I left. I was supposed to get help for my master."

Sam brushed a clump of snow off her shoulder. "Why would Thor need help?"

"The rapids," said Otis. "I guess we'd better hurry. I was supposed be quick, but I stood watching you guys for almost a day."

I flinched. "Wait . . . we were unconscious for *a whole day?*"

"At least," said Otis.

"He's right," Jack said. "According to my internal clock, it's Sunday the nineteenth. I warned you, once you took hold of me . . . well, we fought those dwarves on Friday. You slept all the way through Saturday."

Sam grimaced. "We've lost valuable time. The Wolf's island will appear in three more days, and we don't even know where Blitzen is."

"Probably my fault," Otis offered. "I should've saved you earlier, but giving a human mouth-to-mouth—I had to work up my nerve. My therapist gave me some breathing exercises—"

"Guys," Jack the sword interrupted, "we're close now. For real this time." He hovered off through the woods.

We followed the floating sword until the trees parted. In front of us stretched a beach of jagged black rocks and chunks of ice. On the opposite bank, sheer cliffs rose into the sky. The river had turned into full-on class five rapids—a combat zone of whitewater and half-submerged boulders. Upstream, the river was compressed between two skyscraper-size stone columns—man-made or natural, I couldn't tell. Their tops were lost in the clouds. From the fissure between them, the river blasted out in a vertical sheet—less like a waterfall and more like a dam splitting down the middle.

Suddenly Jotunheim did not seem like Vermont. It seemed more like the Himalayas—someplace not meant for mortals.

It was hard to focus on anything except the raging falls, but eventually I noticed a small campsite on the beach—a tent, a fire pit, and a second goat with dark fur pacing nervously on the shore. When the goat saw us, he came galloping over.

Otis turned to us and shouted over the roar of the river, "This is Marvin! He's my brother! His proper name is Tanngrisnr—Snarler—but—"

"Otis!" Marvin yelled. "Where have you been?"

"I forgot what I was doing," said Otis.

Marvin bleated in exasperation. His lips were curled in a permanent snarl, which—gee, I dunno—might have been how he got the name Snarler.

"This is the help you found?" Marvin fixed his yellow eyes on me. "Two scrawny humans and a dead elf?"

"He's not dead!" I yelled. "Where is Thor?"

"In the river!" Marvin pointed with his horns. "The god of thunder is about to drown, and if you don't figure out a way to help him, I'll kill you. By the way, nice to meet you."

FORTY-NINE

Well, There's Your Problem.
You've Got a Sword Up Your Nose

I COULDN'T HELP IT.

When I heard the name Thor, I thought about the guy from the movies and comics—a big superhero from outer space, with bright Spandex tights, a red cape, goldilocks hair, and maybe a helmet with fluffy little dove wings.

In real life, Thor was scarier. And redder. And grungier.

Also, he could cuss like a drunken, creative sailor.

"Mother-grubbing scum bucket!" he yelled. (Or something along those lines. My brain may have filtered the actual language, as it would've made my ears bleed.) "Where is my backup?"

He stood chest-deep in the flood near the opposite side, clinging to a scrubby bush that grew from the cliff. The rock was so smooth and slick there were no other handholds. The bush looked like it was about to pull free of its roots. Any minute, Thor was going to get flushed downstream, where rows of jagged rocks shredded the current in a series of cataracts, perfect for making a Thor smoothie.

From this distance, through the spray of water and mist, I couldn't see much of the god himself: shoulder-length red hair, a curly red beard, and bodybuilder arms protruding from a sleeveless leather jerkin. He wore dark iron gauntlets that reminded me of robot hands, and a chain mail vest Blitzen would've found very trendy.

"Beard-burning son of a mud-lover!" roared the god. "Otis, is that you? Where's my artillery? My air support? Where the Helheim is my cavalry?"

"I'm here, boss!" Otis called. "I brought . . . two kids and a dead elf!"

"He's not dead," I said again.

"A half-dead elf," Otis corrected.

"What good is that?" Thor bellowed. "I need that giantess killed, and I need her killed NOW!"

"Giantess?" I asked.

Marvin head-butted me. "That one, stupid."

He nodded toward the waterfall. For a moment, the fog cleared from the tops of the cliffs, and I saw the problem.

Next to me, Sam made a sound like she was being garroted. "Holy Heimdall."

Those skyscraper-size pillars of rock were actually legs—*immense* legs so gray and rough they blended in with the surrounding cliffs. The rest of the woman was so tall she made Godzilla look like a toy poodle. She made the Sears Tower look like a traffic cone. Her thigh-length dress was stitched together from so many animal hides it probably represented the extinction of several dozen species. Her face, somewhere up there in the stratosphere, was as stony and grim as a Mount Rushmore president's, surrounded by a hurricane of long dark hair. She gripped the cliff tops on either side of the river as if straddling the torrent was hard even for her.

She looked down, smiling cruelly at the little speck of thunder god caught in the current, then squeezed her legs closer together. The waterfall sprayed out between her shins in a highly pressurized curtain of liquid force.

Thor tried to shout but got a mouthful of river. His head went under. The bush he was clinging to bent sideways, its roots snapping one after the other.

"She's going to wash him into oblivion!" Marvin said. "Do something, humans!"

Like what? I thought.

"He's a god," I said. "Can't he fly? Can't he zap her with lightning or—what about his hammer? Doesn't he have a hammer?"

Marvin snarled. He was very good at snarling. "Gee, why did *we* think of that? If Thor could do any of those things without losing his grip and getting instantly killed, don't you think he would've done it by now?"

I wanted to ask how a god could get killed, since they were supposed to be immortal. Then I thought about Mimir existing forever as a severed head, and Balder getting cut down by a mistletoe dart and spending eternity down in Hel World.

I looked at Sam.

She shrugged helplessly. "Against a giant that big, I have nothing."

Hearthstone mumbled in his sleep. His eyelids were starting to flutter, but he wasn't going to be casting magic anytime soon.

That left me only one friend to call on.

"Jack."

The sword hovered next to me. "Yeah?"

"You see that massive giantess blocking the river?"

"Technically speaking," Jack said, "I can't see anything, because I don't have eyes. But yes, I see the giant."

"You think you could fly up there and, I dunno, kill her?"

Jack hummed indignantly. "You want me to kill a two-thousand-foot-tall giantess?"

"Yeah."

"Well, here's the thing. You'd need to grab me and throw me like you've never thrown anything before. You'd need to *really* believe that killing this giantess is a worthy deed. And you'd need to be prepared for what will happen when you take hold of me again. How much energy would it take you, personally, to climb that two-thousand-foot-tall giant and kill her?"

The effort would probably destroy me, I thought. But I didn't see much choice.

We needed information from Thor. Sam and Hearthstone and two antisocial talking goats were depending on me.

"Let's do it." I grabbed the sword.

I tried to focus. I didn't care so much about saving Thor. I didn't even know the guy. Nor did I particularly care why a half-mile-tall giantess thought it was funny to stand in a river and spray a waterfall between her shins.

But I *did* care about Sam, Blitzen, and Hearthstone. They'd risked their lives to get me this far. No matter what Loki promised, I had to find a way to stop Surt and keep Fenris Wolf chained. The Wolf had caused my mother's death. Mimir had said that Fenris sent his two children. . . . They were supposed to kill *me.* My mom had sacrificed her life to keep me alive. I had to make her sacrifice *mean* something.

The huge gray giantess represented everything that was in my way. She had to go.

With every bit of my strength, I threw the sword.

Jack sliced skyward like a rocket-powered boomerang.

What happened next . . . well, I wasn't sure I saw correctly. It was a long way up. But it looked like Jack flew into the giantess's left nostril.

The giantess arched her back. She made a face like she was going to sneeze. Her hands slipped from the cliff tops. Jack flew out of her right nostril as the giantess's knees buckled and she fell toward us.

"Timber!" Jack yelled, spiraling back to me.

"RUN!" I screamed.

Too late. The giantess face-planted in the river with a mighty *FLOOM!*

I have no memory of the wall of water that washed me into a tree, along with Sam, a half-asleep Hearthstone, and the two startled goats. Nevertheless, that's what must have happened. By sheer luck, none of us died.

The giantess's body had completely changed the topography. Where there had been a river, there was now a wide icy marsh, with water gurgling and spluttering around Dead Lady Island as it tried to find new ways to get downstream. The beach was six inches underwater. Thor's campsite had vanished. The god himself was nowhere to be seen.

"You killed Thor!" Otis bleated. "You dropped a giantess on him!"

The giantess's right arm twitched. I almost fell out of the tree. I was afraid Jack had only stunned her, but then Thor wriggled his way out of the giantess's armpit with much cursing and grunting.

Sam and I helped Hearthstone out of the tree as the god of thunder trudged across the giantess's back, jumped into the marsh, and waded toward us. His eyes were blue, rimmed with angry red. His expression was so fierce it would've sent wild boars running for their mommies.

Jack the sword appeared at my side, glistening with various types of goo typically found in a giant's nostril.

"So what do you think, *señor*?" His runes glowed. "You proud of me?"

"I'll answer that if I survive the next two minutes."

The angry god stopped in front of me. Water dripped from his red beard onto his extremely large chain-mail-clad chest. His pot-roast-size fists were clenched in their iron gauntlets.

"That"—he cracked a grin—"was amazing!"

He clapped me on the shoulder so hard he dislocated several joints. "Join me for dinner! We can kill Otis and Marvin!"

FIFTY

No Spoilers. Thor Is *Way* Behind on His Shows

YEP. WE KILLED THE GOATS.

Thor promised they would be resurrected good as new the next morning, so long as we didn't break any bones. Otis assured me frequent death was good for his exposure therapy. Marvin growled at me to get on with it and not be a weak-kneed wimp.

It was a lot easier killing Marvin.

After two years of homelessness, I thought I knew how tough it could be to keep myself fed, but let me tell you: killing and butchering an animal for my own supper was a new experience. You think it's gross to pull a half-eaten sandwich out of a trash bin? Try skinning a goat, cutting it into chunks, building a fire, then cooking the meat on a spit while attempting to ignore the goat heads staring at you from the scrap pile.

You might assume that kind of experience would turn me into a vegetarian. But nope. As soon as I smelled the cooking meat, my hunger took over. I forgot all about the horrors of goat slaughter. Those Otis-kebabs were the best things I ever tasted.

As we ate, Thor chatted about giants, Jotunheim, and his opinions of Midgard television shows, which, for some reason, he followed religiously. (Can I say a god did something religiously?)

"Giants!" He shook his head in disgust. "After all these centuries, you'd think they would learn to stop invading Midgard. But no! They're like the . . . what is it? The League of Assassins in *Arrow*! They just keep coming back! As if I would let anything happen to humans! You guys are my favorite species!"

He patted my cheek. Fortunately, he had taken off his iron gloves, or he would've broken my jaw. Unfortunately, he hadn't washed his hands after gutting the goats.

Hearthstone sat at the fire, nibbling on a piece of Marvin haunch. He was getting some of his strength back, though every time I looked at him I had to force myself not to sob. I wanted to hug the poor guy, bake him a batch of cookies, and tell him how sorry I was about his crappy childhood, but I knew he wouldn't want pity. He wouldn't want me to start treating him differently.

Still . . . the empty cup runestone weighed heavily in my coat pocket.

Sam stayed at the edge of the fire, as far from Thor as she could get. She said as little as possible and made no sudden movements, which meant that most of Thor's attention was on me.

Everything the thunder god did, he did with gusto. He loved cooking his goats. He loved eating and drinking mead. He loved telling stories. And he loved farting. Boy, did he love farting. When he got excited, sparks of electricity flew from his hands, his ears, and . . . well, I'll leave the rest to your imagination.

Unlike his movie version, there was nothing polished about

Thor. His face was handsome in a beat-up way, like he'd spent years in the boxing ring. His chain mail was filthy. His leather jerkin and trousers had worn to the color of dirty snow. Tattoos covered his muscular arms. On his left biceps, SIF was inscribed inside a heart. Around his right forearm coiled a stylized World Serpent. Across his knuckles on either hand, in block letters, were the names MAGNI and MODI. At first I was nervous about the name *Magni*, because it was so close to *Magnus*—the last thing I wanted was my name printed across the thunder god's fist—but Sam assured me, quietly, that it was a totally different name.

Thor regaled me with his theories about a hypothetical death match between Daryl from *The Walking Dead* and Mike from *Breaking Bad*. Back when I was hanging out on the sidewalks of Boston, I would've been happy to talk TV for hours just to pass the time, but now I had a quest looming. We'd lost a whole day to unconsciousness. Speculating on the new fall lineup wasn't going to mean much if the world was consumed in flames three days from now.

Still, Thor was having so much fun it was hard to change the subject.

"So what do think?" he asked. "Best villain in an ongoing series?"

"Uh . . . wow, tough one." I pointed at his knuckles. "Who are Magni and Modi?"

"My sons!" Thor beamed. With the goat grease in his beard and the random electrical sparks flying from his fingers, I was worried he might set himself on fire. "I've got a lot of sons, of course, but they're my favorites."

"Yeah?" I asked. "How old are they?"

He frowned. "Ah, this is embarrassing, but I'm not sure. They might not even be born yet."

"How—?"

"Magnus," Sam interrupted, "Lord Thor's two sons Magni and Modi are fated to survive Ragnarok. Their names are spoken in the prophecies of the Norns."

"That's right!" Thor leaned toward Sam. "Who are you again?"

"Uh . . . Sam, my lord."

"You have a familiar aura, girl." The god furrowed his red eyebrows. "Why is that?"

"I was a Valkyrie . . . ?" Sam inched backward.

"Oh. Maybe that's it." Thor shrugged. "You'll have to excuse me. I've been on three thousand five hundred and six consecutive deployments to the eastern front, keeping the giants at bay. I get a little jumpy sometimes."

Hearthstone signed, *And gassy.*

Thor belched. "What did the elf say? I do not speak Gesticulation."

"Um, he was wondering how you keep current on television," I said, "seeing as you're out in the field so much."

Thor laughed. "I have to do *some*thing to keep myself sane!"

Hearthstone signed: *How's that working out for you?*

"The elf agrees!" Thor guessed. "I can watch my shows anywhere, or at least I *could*. Among its many other powers, my hammer Mjolnir got full bars of service and HD resolution in any of the Nine Worlds!"

"*Got*, past tense?" Sam asked.

Thor cleared his throat loudly. "But enough about

television! How's that goat meat? You didn't break any bones, did you?"

Sam and I exchanged looks. When we'd first introduced ourselves to the god, I'd found it strange that Thor didn't have his hammer. It was sort of his signature weapon. I'd figured maybe it was just in disguise, like my sword. Now I was starting to wonder. His piercing bloodshot gaze made me think it might be dangerous to ask, though.

"Uh, no, sir," I said. "We didn't break any bones. Just theoretically, what would happen if we did?"

"The goats would be resurrected with that damage," he said. "Which would take a long time to heal and be very annoying. Then I'd either have to kill you or make you my slave forever."

Hearthstone signed, *This god is a freak.*

"You're right, Mr. Elf," Thor said. "It is a fair and just punishment! That's how I got my regular manservant, Thjalfi." Thor shook his head. "Poor kid. These deployments were starting to get to him. I had to grant him a furlough. I really *could* use another slave . . ." He studied me appraisingly.

"So . . ." I set aside my goat meat. "How did you end up in the river, and why was that giantess trying to drown you?"

"Oh, her." Thor glowered at the neighborhood-size corpse in the middle of the icy swamp. "She's a daughter of Geirrod, one of my old enemies. I hate that guy. He's always sending his daughters to kill me." He gestured toward the cliffs. "I was heading to his fortress to see if— Well, no matter. Thank you for the assist. That was Frey's sword, wasn't it?"

"Yes. Jack's around here somewhere." I whistled. Jack came hovering over.

"Hello, Thor," said the sword. "Long time no see."

"Ha!" The god clapped his hands in delight. "I thought I recognized you. But isn't your name Sumarbrander? Why did the human call you Jorvik?"

"Jack," the sword corrected.

"Yak."

"No," the sword said patiently. "Jack, with the English *jay* sound."

"Okay, fine. Well, nice job with the giantess."

"You know what they say." Jack sounded smug. "The bigger they are, the easier it is to fly up their nasal cavity."

"True," Thor said. "But I thought you were lost. How did you come to be with these strange folk?"

He calls us *strange?* Hearthstone signed.

"Lord Thor," Sam said, "we actually came here looking for you. We need your help, as Magnus will now explain." She stared at me like, *If he knows what's good for him.*

I told Thor about the Norns' prophecy—nine days hence, sun going east, Surt explodes everything, Fenris Wolf, nasty teeth, eats world, et cetera.

Thor became agitated. Sparks flew from his elbows. He rose and paced around the fire, occasionally punching nearby trees.

"You want me to tell you where the island is," he deduced.

"That would be great," I said.

"But I can't," Thor muttered to himself. "I can't be sending random mortals on wolf-watching tours. Too dangerous. But Ragnarok. Not ready. No. Not unless—" He froze, then turned toward us with an eager gleam in his eyes. "Perhaps *that's* why you're here."

I do not like this, Hearthstone signed.

Thor nodded. "The elf agrees! You have come to assist me!"

"Exactly!" said Jack, humming with excitement. "Let's do it, whatever it is!"

I had a sudden desire to hide behind the goat carcasses. Anything the god of thunder and the Sword of Summer agreed on, I didn't want to be part of.

Sam placed her ax at her side, as if she anticipated needing it soon. "Let me guess, Lord Thor: you've lost your hammer again."

"Now, I did *not* say that!" Thor wagged a finger at her. "You did *not* hear that from me. Because if that were true, hypothetically speaking, and if word got out, the giants would invade Midgard immediately! You mortals don't realize how often I keep you safe. My reputation alone makes most giants too afraid to attack your world."

"Back up," I said. "What did Sam mean by *again*? You've lost your hammer before?"

"Once," Thor said. "Okay, twice. Three times if you count this time, which you shouldn't, because I am not admitting that the hammer is missing."

"Right . . ." I said. "So how did you lose it?"

"I don't know!" Thor started to pace again, his long red hair sparking and popping. "It was just like . . . *Poof!* I tried retracing my steps. I tried the Find My Hammer app, but it doesn't work!"

"Isn't your hammer the most powerful weapon in the universe?" I asked.

"Yes!"

"And I thought it was so heavy nobody except you could pick it up."

"True. Even *I* need my iron gloves of strength to lift it! But giants are tricky. They're big and strong and they have magic. With them, many impossible things are possible."

I thought about the eagle Big Boy and how easily he'd suckered me. "Yeah, I get it. Is that why you were going to A-Rod's?"

"Geirrod's," Thor corrected. "And, yes. He's a likely suspect. Even if he doesn't have it, he might know who does. Besides, without my hammer I can't watch my shows. I'm a season behind on *Sherlock* and it's killing me! I was ready to go to Geirrod's fortress myself, but I'm very glad you volunteered to go for me!"

We did? Hearthstone asked.

"That's the spirit, Mr. Elf! I'm glad you are ready to die for my cause!"

Really not, Hearth signed.

"Just go to Geirrod's fortress and check for my hammer. Of course it's important you don't let on that it is missing. If Geirrod *doesn't* have it, we don't want him to know that *I* don't have it. But, you know, if he doesn't have it, obviously ask him if he knows who does, without actually admitting that it's missing."

Samirah pressed her fingers to her temples. "I'm getting a headache. Lord Thor, how are we supposed to find your hammer if we can't mention—"

"You'll figure it out!" he said. "You humans are a clever bunch. Then, once you've determined the truth, I will know you are worthy of facing Fenris Wolf. I'll give you the location of his island and you can stop Ragnarok. You help me, I help you."

It sounded more like *You help me, then you help me some more,* but I doubted there was a polite way to decline without getting an iron gauntlet in my teeth.

Sam must have been thinking the same thing. Her face turned roughly the same shade of green as her hijab. "Lord Thor," she said, "invading a giant's fortress with only three people would be . . ."

Suicidal, Hearthstone suggested. *Stupid.*

"Difficult," Sam said.

Just then, a nearby pine tree shuddered. Blitzen dropped from the branches and landed waist-deep in a pile of slush.

Hearthstone scrambled over and helped him to his feet.

"Thanks, buddy," Blitz said. "Stupid tree travel. Where—?"

"Is this a friend of yours?" Thor raised one ironclad fist. "Or should I—"

"No! I mean, yes, he's a friend. Blitzen, Thor. Thor, Blitzen."

"*The* Thor?" Blitzen bowed so low it looked like he was trying to avoid an air strike. "Honored. Seriously. Hi. Wow."

"Well, then!" The thunder god grinned. "You have *four* people to storm the giant's citadel! Friend dwarf, help yourself to my goat meat and my fire. As for me, after being stuck in that river so long, I'm going to turn in early. In the morning, you all can set off to find my hammer, which of course is not officially missing!"

Thor tromped over to his bed of furs, threw himself down, and began snoring with as much gusto as he'd been farting.

Blitzen frowned at me. "What have you gotten us into?"

"Long story," I said. "Here, have some Marvin."

FIFTY-ONE

We Have the Talk-About-Turning-Into-Horseflies Chat

HEARTHSTONE WENT to sleep first, mostly because he was the only one who *could* sleep with Thor's snoring. Since the god had crashed outside, Hearthstone commandeered the two-man tent. He crawled inside and promptly collapsed.

The rest of us stayed up and talked around the campfire. At first I was worried we might wake Thor, but I soon realized we could've tap-danced around his head, banged gongs, shouted his name, and set off large explosions, and he would've slept right through it.

I wondered if that was how he had lost his hammer. The giants could've waited until he was asleep, backed up a couple of industrial cranes, and done the job easy.

As night fell, I was grateful for the fire. The darkness was more complete than in the wildest places my mom and I had ever camped. Wolves howled in the forest, which gave me a bad case of the shivers. Wind moaned through the canyons like a chorus of zombies.

I mentioned this to Blitzen, but he set me straight.

"No, kid," he said. "Norse zombies are called *draugr*. They move silently. You'd never hear them coming."

"Thanks," I said. "That's a huge relief."

Blitzen stirred his cup of goat stew, though he didn't seem

interested in tasting it. He'd changed into a blue wool suit with a cream-colored trench coat, perhaps so he could blend in with the Jotunheim snow in the most stylish way possible. He'd also brought each of us a new supply pack filled with fresh winter clothes, which of course he'd sized perfectly just by guessing. Sometimes it pays to have a friend who's a thoughtful clotheshorse.

Blitz explained how he'd delivered the earrings to his mother, then gotten detained in Folkvanger for various duties as Freya's representative: judging an oyster bake, refereeing a volleyball game, serving as guest of honor at the 678th annual ukulele festival.

"It was murder," he said. "Mom liked the earrings. Didn't ask how I got them. Didn't want to hear about the contest with Junior. She just said, 'Oh, don't you wish you could do work like this, Blitzen?'" From his coat pocket, he pulled the rope Andskoti. The ball of silk glowed silver like a miniature moon. "I hope this was worth it."

"Hey," I told him, "what you did in that contest? I've never seen *anybody* work that hard. You poured your heart and soul into that Expando-Duck. And the bulletproof tie? The chain mail vest? Just wait. We'll get you an endorsement deal with Thor, and you'll start a fashion trend."

"Magnus is right," Sam said. "Well, maybe not about the endorsement deal with Thor—but you have real talent, Blitzen. If Freya and the other dwarves don't see it, that's their problem. Without you, we never would've gotten this far."

"You mean you wouldn't have gotten kicked out of the Valkyries; Magnus wouldn't have died; we wouldn't have half the gods mad at us; fire giants and einherjar wouldn't be out to kill us; and we wouldn't be sitting in the wilderness of Jotunheim with a snoring god?"

"Exactly," Sam said. "Life is good."

Blitzen snorted, but I was happy to see a little spark of humor in his eyes. "Yeah, okay. I'm going to sleep. I'll need it if we're going to storm a giant's castle in the morning."

He crawled into the tent and muttered to Hearthstone, "Make some room, you tent hog!" Then he draped his overcoat across the elf, which I thought was kind of sweet.

Sam sat cross-legged in her jeans and new snow jacket, her hood pulled over her headscarf. Snow had started to fall—big fluffy flakes that dissolved and hissed in the flames.

"Speaking of the contest in Dwarfland," I said, "we never got to talk about the horsefly—"

"Hush." Sam glanced apprehensively at Thor. "Certain people aren't keen on my father, or my father's children."

"Certain people are snoring like a chain saw."

"Still . . ." She studied her hand as if making sure it hadn't changed. "I promised myself I wouldn't shape-shift, and in the last week I've done it twice. The first time . . . well, the stag was after us on the World Tree. I turned into a deer to distract it so Hearthstone could get away. I didn't think I had a choice."

I nodded. "And the second time, you turned into the horsefly to help Blitzen. Those are both great reasons. Besides, shape-shifting is an awesome power. Why wouldn't you want to use it?"

The firelight made her irises almost as red as Surt's. "Magnus, true shape-shifting isn't like my hijab's camouflage. Shape-shifting doesn't just change your appearance. It changes *you.* Every time I do it, I feel . . . I feel more of my father's nature trying to take hold of me. He's fluid, unpredictable, untrustworthy—I don't want to be like that."

I gestured at Thor. "You could have *him* for a dad—a farting giant with goat grease in his beard and tattoos on his knuckles. Then everybody in Valhalla would love you."

I could tell she was trying not to smile. "You are *very* bad. Thor is an important god."

"No doubt. So is Frey, supposedly, but I've never met him. At least your dad is kind of charming, and he has a sense of humor. He may be a sociopath, but—"

"Wait." Sam's voice tightened. "You talk as if you've met him."

"I . . . I kind of walked right into that, didn't I? Truth is, he's been in a few of my near-death experiences."

I told Sam about the dreams: Loki's warnings, his promises, his suggestion that I take the sword to my Uncle Randolph and forget about the quest.

Sam listened. I couldn't tell if she was angry or shocked or both.

"So," she said, "you didn't tell me this earlier because you didn't trust me?"

"Maybe at first. Later, I just—I wasn't sure what to do. Your dad is kind of unsettling."

She tossed a twig into the flames and watched it burn. "You can't do what my dad suggests, no matter what he promises. We have to face Surt. We'll need the sword."

I remembered my dream of the burning throne—the dark face floating in the smoke, the voice with the heat of a flamethrower. *YOU AND YOUR FRIENDS WILL BE MY TINDER. YOU WILL START THE FIRE THAT BURNS THE NINE WORLDS.*

I looked around for Jack, but I didn't see him. The sword had volunteered to hover the perimeter "on patrol," as he put it. He suggested I wait until the last possible minute to reclaim him, since once I did, I would pass out instantly from the strain of murdering a giantess by nostrilcide.

Snow continued to fall, steaming against the stones around the fire pit. I thought about our near-lunch in the food court of the Transportation Building, how nervous Sam had acted around Amir. That seemed like a thousand years ago.

"When we were on Harald's boat," I recalled, "you said your family had a long history with all the Norse god stuff. How? You said your grandparents came from Iraq . . . ?"

She threw another stick into the flames. "Vikings were traders, Magnus. They traveled everywhere. They got all the way to America. It shouldn't be a surprise they got to the Middle East, too. Arabic coins have been found in Norway. The best Viking swords were modeled after Damascus steel."

"But *your* family . . . You've got a more personal connection?"

She nodded. "Back in medieval times, some of the Vikings settled in Russia. They called themselves the Rus. That's where the word *Russian* comes from. Anyway, the Caliph—the big king down in Baghdad—he sent an ambassador north to find out more about the Vikings, set up trade routes with them, that kind of stuff. The ambassador's name was Ahmed ibn-Fadlan ibn-al-Abbas."

"Fadlan like Fadlan's Falafel. Al-Abbas like—"

"Right. Like me. Al-Abbas means *of the lion*. That's my branch of the clan. Anyway"—she pulled a sleeping bag out of her backpack—"this guy Ibn Fadlan kept a journal about his time with the Vikings. It's one of the only written sources about what the Norse were like back then. Ever since, my family and the Vikings have been intertwined. Over the centuries, my relatives have racked up a lot of weird encounters with . . . supernatural beings. Maybe that's why my mother wasn't too surprised when she found out who my dad really was." She spread out her sleeping bag next to the fire. "And that's why Samirah al-Abbas is fated never to have a normal life. The end."

"Normal life," I mused. "I don't even know what that means anymore."

She looked like she wanted to say something, then changed her mind. "I'm going to sleep."

I had a weird vision of our ancestors, medieval Chase and medieval al-Abbas, sitting around a campfire in Russia twelve hundred years ago, comparing notes on how the Norse gods had messed up their lives, maybe with Thor snoring on a bed of furs nearby. Sam's family might be intertwined with the gods, but as my Valkyrie she was also intertwined with *my* family now.

"We'll figure things out," I promised. "I don't know about *normal*, but I'll do everything I can to help you get what you want—a place in the Valkyries again, your marriage with Amir, a pilot's license. Whatever it takes."

She stared at me as if processing the words from another language.

"What?" I asked. "Do I have goat blood on my face?"

"No. Well, yes, you do have goat blood on your face. But that's not . . . I was just trying to remember the last time anybody said something that nice to me."

"If you want, I'll go back to insulting you tomorrow," I said. "For now, get some sleep. Sweet dreams."

Sam curled up by the fire. Snow settled lightly on the sleeve of her coat. "Thank you, Magnus. But no dreams, please. I don't want to dream in Jotunheim."

FIFTY-TWO

I Got the Horse Right Here.
His Name Is Stanley

THOR WAS STILL SNORING like a defective wood chipper when we were ready to leave the next morning. That's really saying something, since I had slept forever. Jack the sword had not been kidding about the effect of killing the giantess. As soon as I'd reclaimed the sword after Sam fell asleep, I had passed out instantly.

At least I hadn't lost a full twenty-four hours this time. With Fenris Wolf appearing in only two more days, I couldn't afford any more long naps. I wondered if maybe, just maybe, I was growing more resilient as I became bonded to the sword. I hoped so, but I still felt like I'd been flattened under a rolling pin all night.

We packed up our gear and ate a cold breakfast of MORNING, MAGGOT! energy bars from Blitz's supply bags (yum). Then Hearthstone nestled the severed heads of the two still-dead goats in Thor's arms like teddy bears. Never let it be said that elves don't have a sense of humor.

I looked down at the drool turning to ice in Thor's beard. "And to think that the defense of Nine Worlds rests on this god."

"Let's get going," Blitzen muttered. "I don't want to be around when he wakes up with Otis and Marvin."

The dead giantess proved helpful. We climbed over her to cross the icy swamp. Then we discovered that we could scale her left foot to reach the first ledge in the side of the cliff.

Once we got that far, I stared up at the remaining five hundred meters of sheer icy rock. "Awesome. Now the real fun begins."

"Wish I could still fly," Sam murmured.

I imagined she *could* fly, with a little shape-shifting, but after our conversation last night, I decided against mentioning that.

Blitz handed his pack to Hearthstone, then wriggled his stubby fingers. "Don't worry, kids. You're climbing with a dwarf today."

I frowned. "You're a mountaineer now as well as a master of fashion?"

"I told you, kid, dwarves were formed from maggots that burrowed through Ymir's flesh."

"And you seem strangely proud of it."

"Rock to us is like . . . well, not rock." He punched the side of the cliff. Rather than breaking his fist, he left an indentation just the right size for a handhold. "I'm not saying it'll be fast or easy. It takes me a lot of effort to shape rock. But we can do it."

I glanced at Sam. "Did you know dwarves could punch through stone?"

"Nope. That's new to me."

Hearthstone signed, *Use the magic rope? Rather not fall to death.*

I shuddered. I couldn't think about the rope Andskoti without thinking about the Wolf, and I didn't like thinking about the Wolf. "We need that rope to bind Fenris, right? I don't want to do anything that might weaken it."

"Don't worry, kid." Blitz brought out the silken cord. "This rope can't be weakened. And Hearthstone's right. We might as well tie it to one another for safety."

"That way if we fall," Sam said, "we'll fall together."

"Sold," I said, trying to tamp down my anxiety. "I love dying with friends."

We got hitched (so to speak) and followed our intrepid rock-shaping, fashion-conscious guide up the side of Mount You-Gotta-Be-Kidding-Me.

I'd heard homeless military vets describe war as ninety-five percent boredom and five percent terror. Climbing the cliff was more like five percent terror and ninety-five percent excruciating pain. My arms shook. My legs wobbled. Every time I looked down I wanted to cry or throw up.

Despite the handholds and footholds Blitzen made, the wind almost knocked me off several times. There was nothing I could do except keep going.

I knew for certain that my Valhalla-enhanced strength was the only thing keeping me alive. Magnus 1.0 would have fallen to his death. I didn't understand how Hearthstone could manage, bringing up the end of the rope, but he did. And Sam . . . demigod or not, she didn't have the advantage of being an einherji. Yet she didn't complain, didn't waver, didn't slip—which was good, since she was climbing right above me.

Finally, as the sky began to darken, we reached the top. Down in the canyon we'd come from, the body of the giantess was so small it looked like a normal-sized body. The river glittered in the gloom. If Thor's camp was still there, I saw no sign of it.

In the other direction, Jotunheim spread out like an electron microscope landscape—impossibly jagged peaks, crystalline cliffs, ravines filled with ovoid clouds like floating bacteria.

The good news: I could see the giant's fortress. Across a mile-wide chasm, windows glowed red in the side of a mountain. Towers rose from the summit as if they'd been shaped from the rock dwarven-style rather than built.

The bad news: did I mention the mile-wide chasm? The cliff top where we were standing was no more than a narrow plateau. The drop on the other side was just as precipitous as the one we'd climbed.

Considering it had taken us all day to get this far, I figured we'd reach the castle in another six months, easy. Unfortunately, it was Monday evening and the Wolf's island was supposed to rise on Wednesday.

"Let's camp here tonight," Blitzen said. "Maybe in the morning we'll see a better way across."

Despite our time crunch, nobody argued. We were all so tired we collapsed.

As is so often the case, in the fresh light of morning our situation looked much worse.

There were no stairs, no convenient zip lines, no direct commuter flights to Geirrod's fortress. I was about to risk an ax in the face by suggesting that Sam shape-shift—maybe change into a giant sugar glider and carry us across—when Hearthstone signed: *Have an idea.*

He pulled out a runestone:

M

"M," I said.

He shook his head then spelled out the name: *E-H-W-A-Z*.

"Right," I said. "Because calling it *M* would be too easy."

Sam plucked the stone from Hearth's palm. "I know this one. It symbolizes a horse, right? The shape is like a saddle."

I squinted at the rune. The wind was so cold and harsh that I had a hard time thinking imaginatively, but the symbol still looked like an M to me. "How does this help us?"

Hearthstone signed: *Means horse, transportation. Maybe a way to go*—he pointed to the castle.

Blitzen tugged his beard. "Sounds like powerful magic. Have you tried it before?"

Hearthstone shook his head. *Don't worry. I can do it.*

"I know you can," said Blitz. "But you've already taxed yourself to the limit several times."

Be fine, Hearth insisted.

"I don't see that we have much choice," I said, "since we don't have anyone who can grow wings."

"I will push you off this mountain," Sam warned.

"All right," Blitzen decided, "let's try it. I mean the rune, not pushing Magnus off the mountain. Maybe Hearth can summon a helicopter."

"Geirrod would hear a helicopter," I said. "And probably throw rocks at us. And kill us."

"Well, then," Blitzen said, "perhaps a stealth helicopter. Hearthstone, do your stuff!"

Sam returned the stone. Hearth passed his hand over it, moving his lips as if imagining how the syllables might sound.

The runestone burst into dust. Hearthstone stared at the white powder trickling through his fingers.

"I'm guessing it wasn't supposed to do that?" I asked.

"Guys." Sam's voice was so small it was almost lost in the wind.

She pointed up, where a gray shape was hurtling out of the clouds. It moved so fast and blended with the sky so well, I didn't realize what the creature was until it was almost on top of us—a stallion twice the size of a normal horse, his coat rippling like liquid steel, his white mane billowing, his eyes glittering black.

The stallion had no wings, but he galloped through the air as easily as if he were running down a gentle slope. Only when he landed next to us did I notice he had four, five, six . . . *eight* legs—a pair in each place where a normal horse would have one, kind of like dual wheels on a pickup truck.

I turned to Hearthstone. "Dude, when you summon a horse, you don't mess around."

Hearthstone grinned. Then his eyes rolled up in his head and he fell forward. I managed to catch him and ease him to the ground while Blitzen and Sam moved warily around the stallion.

"It—it c-can't be," Blitzen stammered.

"One of Sleipnir's offspring?" Sam wondered. "Gods, what a magnificent animal."

The horse nuzzled her hand, clearly pleased with the compliment.

I moved toward him, fascinated by his intelligent eyes and

his regal stance. The stallion gave the word *horsepower* a new meaning. He radiated strength.

"Is somebody going to introduce me?" I asked.

Sam shook herself out of her reverie. "I . . . I don't know who he is. He looks like Sleipnir, Odin's steed, but this can't be him. Only Odin can summon him. I'm guessing this is one of Sleipnir's sons."

"Well, he's amazing." I extended my hand. The horse brushed his lips against my fingers. "He's friendly. And he's definitely big enough to carry us all across the chasm. Would you be okay with that, buddy?"

The horse nickered, like, *Uh, duh, that's why I'm here.*

"The eight legs are . . ." I was about to say *weird* but changed my mind. "Awesome. How did that happen?"

Blitzen glanced at Sam. "Sleipnir was one of Loki's children. They tend to come out . . . interesting."

I smiled. "So this horse is your nephew, Sam?"

She glared at me. "Let's not go there."

"How did your dad father a horse?"

Blitzen coughed. "Actually, Loki was Sleipnir's mother."

"What—?"

"Let's *definitely* not go there," Sam warned.

I filed that away for later research. "Okay, Mr. Horse, since we don't know your name, I'm going to call you Stanley, because you look like a Stanley. That okay with you?"

The horse seemed to shrug, which was good enough for me.

We draped Hearthstone over Stanley's extra-long back like a sack of elfish potatoes. The rest of us climbed on.

"We're going to that castle over there, Stanley," I told the stallion. "Looking for a quiet entrance. That work for you?"

The horse whinnied. I was pretty sure he was warning me to hold on.

I wondered what exactly I should hold on *to*, since there were no reins and no saddle. Then the stallion pawed the rocks with his front four hooves, leaped off the side of the cliff, and plummeted straight down.

And we all died.

FIFTY-THREE

How to Kill Giants Politely

JUST KIDDING THIS TIME.

It only *felt* like we were going to die.

The horse must have enjoyed the feeling of free fall. I didn't. I grabbed his neck and screamed in terror (which was not very stealthy). Meanwhile, Blitzen grabbed my waist, and behind him Sam somehow stayed on board while managing to keep Hearthstone from slipping into oblivion.

The fall felt like hours, though it probably lasted only a second or two. During that time I thought of several more colorful names for Stanley. Finally he churned his eight legs like locomotive wheels. We leveled out and began to climb.

Stanley punched through a cloud, zigzagged along the face of the mountain, and landed on a window ledge near the top of the fortress. I dismounted, my legs shaking, then helped the others with Hearthstone.

The ledge was so wide, the four of us plus the horse could stand in one corner and seem no bigger than mice. The window had no glass (probably because there wasn't that much glass in the world), but Stanley had landed us behind a panel of gathered curtain, so nobody inside could've seen us, even if they were randomly scanning the window for mice.

"Thanks, buddy," I told Stanley. "That was horrifying. I mean, great."

Stanley nickered. He gave me an affectionate nip, then disappeared in a burst of dust. On the windowsill where he'd been standing was the ehwaz runestone.

"He seemed to like me," I noted.

Blitzen slid down next to Hearthstone and said, "Eep."

Only Sam didn't seem ruffled. In fact, she seemed exhilarated. Her eyes sparkled and she couldn't stop smiling. I guess she really *did* love flying, even if it was a near-death free fall on an eight-legged horse.

"Of course Stanley liked you." She picked up the runestone. "Horses are one of Frey's sacred animals."

"Huh." I thought about my experiences with the Boston mounted police that patrolled the Public Garden. The horses always seemed friendly, even if their riders weren't. One time, when a mounted officer had started to question me, his horse had suddenly taken off, galloping toward the nearest low-hanging tree branch.

"I've always liked horses," I said.

"Frey's temples kept their own herds," Sam told me. "No mortal was allowed to ride them without the god's permission."

"Well, I wish Stanley had asked my permission before leaving," I said. "We have no exit strategy, and Hearthstone doesn't look like he's going to be casting more spells anytime soon."

The elf had regained consciousness . . . sort of. He leaned against Blitz, giggling silently and making random signs like, *Butterfly. Pop. Yippee.* Blitzen clutched his stomach and stared into space as if he were thinking of interesting ways to die.

Sam and I crept to the edge of the curtain. We peeked around it and found we were at ceiling level of a stadium-size room. In the hearth burned a fire as big as an urban riot. The only exit was a closed wooden door on the far wall. In the center of the room, seated at a stone table, two giantesses were having dinner, ripping into a carcass that reminded me of the roast beast in Valhalla's dining hall.

The giantesses didn't look as tall as the dead one back in the river, though it was hard to be sure. In Jotunheim, proportions made no sense. My eyes felt like they were constantly adjusting to different funhouse mirrors.

Sam nudged my arm. "Look."

She pointed to a birdcage suspended from the ceiling, hanging just about eye-level to us. Inside the cage, waddling around on a bed of straw and looking miserable, was a white swan.

"That's a Valkyrie," Sam said.

"How can you be sure?"

"I just am. Not only that . . . I'm pretty sure it's Gunilla."

I shuddered. "What would she be doing here?"

"Looking for us. Valkyries are excellent trackers. I imagine she got here before we did and . . ." Sam mimed a hand snatching something out of the air.

"So . . . do we leave her?"

"For the giants to eat? Of course not."

"She set you up. She got you kicked out of the Valkyries."

"She's still my captain," Sam said. "She . . . well, she has her reasons for mistrusting me. A few centuries ago, there was a son of Loki who made it into Valhalla."

"He and Gunilla fell in love," I guessed. "I kind of got that impression when she was taking me on a tour of the hotel."

Sam nodded. "The son of Loki betrayed her. Turned out he *was* a spy for my dad. Broke her heart. Well . . . you get the picture. Anyway, I'm not going to leave her to die."

I sighed. "Okay."

I pulled off my pendant.

Jack the sword hummed to life.

"About time," he said. "What did I miss yesterday?"

"Bunch of climbing," I told him. "Now we're looking at two more giantesses. How do you feel about flying up their nostrils?"

The sword tugged at my hand, his blade peeking around the corner of the curtain. "Dude, we're on their windowsill. We've technically crossed the threshold of the giants' home."

"So?"

"So you have to follow the rules! Killing them in their home without provocation would be rude!"

"Right," I said. "We wouldn't want to kill them rudely."

"Hey, *señor*, guest rights and host rights are important magic protocols. They keep situations from escalating."

Blitzen groaned in the corner. "The sword has a point, kid. And, no, that wasn't a joke. We should go in, claim guest rights, and barter for what we need. If the giants try to kill us, *then* we can attack."

Hearthstone hiccupped, grinned, and signed: *Washing machine.*

Sam shook her head. "You two are in no condition to go anywhere. Blitz, stay here and watch Hearthstone. Magnus and

I will go in, find Thor's hammer, and free Gunilla. If things go wrong, it'll be up to you two to figure out how to rescue us."

"But—" Blitzen put his fist over his mouth and stifled an *urp*. "Yeah . . . okay. How are you guys going to get down there?"

Sam peered over the ledge. "We'll use your magic rope to reach the floor. Then we'll walk up to the giants and introduce ourselves."

"I hate this plan," I said. "Let's do it."

FIFTY-FOUR

Why You Should Not Use a Steak Knife as a Diving Board

RAPPELLING DOWN THE WALL was the easy part.

When we reached the bottom, I started having serious doubts. The giantesses were definitely smaller than their dead sister—maybe fifty feet tall. If I'd been asked to wrestle one of their big toes, I could've won no problem. Other than that, I didn't like my chances.

"I feel like Jack up the beanstalk," I muttered.

Sam laughed under her breath. "Where do you think that story comes from? It's a cultural memory—a watered-down account of what happens when humans blunder into Jotunheim."

"Super."

The sword buzzed in my hand. "Besides, you can't be Jack. I'm Jack."

I couldn't argue with that logic.

We navigated across the stone floor, through a wasteland of dust bunnies, food scraps, and grease puddles.

The fireplace was so hot my clothes steamed. My hair crackled. The smell of the giants' body odor—a combination of wet clay and sour meat—was almost as deadly as a sword flying up my nose.

We got within shouting distance of the dining table, but the two giantesses still hadn't noticed us. They both wore sandals, size 120 leather dresses, and Flintstones-style necklaces made from polished boulders. Their stringy black hair was woven into pigtails. Their gray faces were hideously painted with rouge and lipstick. I didn't have my fashion advisor Blitzen with me, but I guessed the giant sisters were dolled up for a girls' night out, even though it was barely lunchtime.

"Ready?" Sam asked me.

The answer was no, but I took a deep breath and yelled, "Hello!"

The giantesses kept chatting, banging their cups, and chomping their meat.

I tried again. "YO!"

The big ladies froze. They scanned the room. Finally the one on the left spotted us. She burst out laughing, spraying bits of mead and meat. "More humans! I don't believe it!"

The other giantess leaned over. "Is that another Valkyrie? And . . ." She sniffed the air. "The boy is an einherji. Perfect! I was just wondering what we'd have for dessert."

"We claim guest rights!" I yelled.

The giantess on the left made a sour face. "Now, why did you have to go and do that?"

"We want to barter." I pointed to the birdcage, now so far above us I could only see its rusted base hovering like a moon. "For that swan's freedom. And also . . . possibly, you know, if you have any stolen weapons lying around. Like, I don't know, a hammer or something."

"Smooth," Sam muttered.

The giantesses looked at each other like they were trying not to giggle. They'd obviously been hitting the mead pretty hard.

"Very well," said the giantess on the left. "I am Gjalp. This is my sister Greip. We agree to host you while we barter. What are your names?"

"I am Magnus, son of Natalie," I said. "And this is—"

"Samirah, daughter of Ayesha," said Sam.

"You are welcome in the house of our father, Geirrod," said Gjalp. "But I can barely hear you down there. Do you mind if I put you in a chair?"

"Uh, okay," I said.

The other sister, Griep, snatched us up like toys. She set us on an empty chair, its seat the size of a living room. The tabletop was still a good five feet above my head.

"Oh, dear," Griep said. "That's still too low. May I raise your chair for you?"

Sam started to say, "Magnus—"

I blurted out, "Sure."

With a shriek of glee, Griep picked up our chair and thrust it over her head. If not for the backrest, Sam and I would've been smashed flat against the ceiling. As it was, we got knocked off our feet and showered in plaster.

Griep put down the chair. It took a moment for my eyeballs to stop rattling. Then I saw the giantesses' scowling faces looming over us.

"It didn't work," Griep said, with obvious disappointment.

"Of course it didn't work," Gjalp growled. "You *never* do that trick right. I told you, it has to be something without a back, like a stool. And we should have installed those spikes in the ceiling."

"You were trying to kill us!" I said. "That can't be in the rules for good hosts."

"Kill you?" Gjalp looked offended. "That's an absolutely baseless accusation. My sister only did as you requested. She asked your permission to raise the chair."

"You just said it was a trick."

"Did I?" Gjalp blinked. Up close, her heavily mascaraed lashes looked like the obstacle course for a mud run. "Pretty sure I didn't."

I looked at the Sword of Summer, which was still in my hand. "Jack, have they broken the host rules yet? Because trying to kill us seems kinda borderline."

"Not unless they admit their intent," Jack said. "And they're saying it was an accident."

The giantesses both straightened.

"A talking sword?" Gjalp said. "Well now, that's interesting."

"You sure I can't raise your chair for you again?" Griep offered. "I could run to the kitchen and get a stool. It's no trouble."

"Honored hosts," Sam said, her voice shaky, "please put us gently and safely on the top of your table, so we may barter with you."

Griep muttered unhappily, but she did as Sam asked. The giantess deposited us next to her fork and knife, which were roughly the same size as me. Her mug would've made a fine water tower for a rural town. I just hoped it wasn't named Boom Daddy.

"So . . ." Griep plopped back in her chair. "You want freedom for the swan? You'll have to wait until our father gets home to negotiate terms. She is his prisoner, not ours."

"She's a Valkyrie, of course," Gjalp added. "Flew in our window last night. She refuses to show her true form. Thinks she can fool us by staying in that silly swan costume, but Dad is too clever for her."

"Bummer," I said. "Well, we tried."

"Magnus . . ." Sam chided. "Gracious hosts, will you at least consent not to kill the swan until we've had a chance to speak with Geirrod?"

Gjalp shrugged. "Like I said, her fate is up to Dad. He might let her go if you surrendered yourselves in exchange, but I don't know. We need *something* spicy for the stew tonight."

"Let's put a pin in that," I said.

"Which is only an expression," Sam added hastily. "By no means is my friend granting you permission to put a pin in anything, especially us."

"Nice save," I told her.

Sam gave me a *you're-such-an-idiot* look. I was getting used to that.

Gjalp crossed her arms, forming a new mesa against her chest. "You said you also wanted to barter for a stolen weapon?"

"Yeah," I said. "Something thunder-goddish, if you have it—not that any particular thunder god is missing any particular weapon."

Griep cackled. "Oh, we have something like that . . . something that belongs to Thor himself."

Since Thor wasn't there to creatively cuss, Sam did the honors, muttering a few comments that I doubted her grandparents would approve of.

"Those are just expressions," I added hastily. "In no way was my friend giving you permission to do . . . any of those rude and colorful things. Will you barter with us for the h—for the weapon you spoke of?"

"Of course!" Gjalp grinned. "In fact, I'd like to wrap up these negotiations quickly since my sister and I have an appointment—"

"With hot frost giant twins," Griep said.

"—so we'll make you a fair deal," Gjalp continued. "We'll give you Thor's weapon for that lovely talking sword. And we'll release the swan—I'm pretty sure Dad will be okay with that—as long as you give yourselves in exchange. You won't get a better deal than that."

"That's hardly a deal," Sam growled.

"Then you can refuse," Griep said, "and leave in peace. It's all the same to us."

Jack thrummed indignantly, his runes glowing. "Magnus, you'd never give me up, right? We're friends! You're not like your dad, gonna toss me aside as soon as you see something you like better?"

I thought about Loki's suggestion that I give the sword to my Uncle Randolph. At the time, I'd actually been tempted. Now, the idea seemed impossible—and only partly because the giantesses wanted to put us in a cage and have us for dinner. Jack had saved our lives at least twice now. I liked him, even if he did occasionally call me *señor*.

An alternative came to me. A bad idea, yes, but better than the giants' offer.

"Jack," I said, "hypothetically speaking, if I told these giantesses how we killed their sister, would that break the rules of guest etiquette?"

"*What?*" Gjalp cried.

Jack's runes glowed a more cheerful shade of red. "No etiquette problem there, my friend, because that happened before we were guests here."

"Okay." I smiled at the giantesses. "We killed your sister—big ugly lady, trying to block the river and drown Thor? Yeah. She's dead now."

"LIES!" Gjalp shot to her feet. "Puny humans! You could not possibly have killed our sister!"

"Actually, my sword flew up her nose and scrambled her brains."

Griep howled in outrage. "I should have crushed you like bugs! Curse my lack of a stool and strategically placed ceiling spikes!"

I'll admit, having two giantesses tower over me bellowing death threats was a wee bit unnerving.

But Sam kept her cool.

She pointed her ax accusingly at Griep. "So, you *were* trying to kill us just now!"

"Of course, you dolt!"

"Which violates the rules of hosts."

"Who cares?" Griep cried.

"Magnus's sword does," Sam said. "Jack, did you hear that?"

"I sure did. I'd like to point out, though, that the effort required to kill these two giantesses might be too much—"

"Do it!" I hurled the sword.

Jack spiraled upward, straight into Griep's right nostril and out her left. The giantess collapsed, shaking the room at 6.8 on the Richter scale.

Gjalp stifled a scream. She covered her nose and mouth and stumbled around as Jack tried in vain to stab his way through her fingers.

"Oh, this one is getting smart!" Jack yelled. "A little help over here?"

"Magnus!" Sam pushed the giantess's steak knife to the edge of the table until the blade extended like a diving board.

I got what she wanted me to do. It was stupid crazy, but I didn't give myself time to reflect. I ran full tilt at the knife and jumped toward the end of the blade.

Sam yelled, "Wait!"

By then I was already in midair. I landed on the knife, which catapulted upward as I dropped. The plan worked, sort of. I landed on the empty seat of the chair, which was not far enough down to kill me, but was enough to break my leg. Hooray! The pain drove a hot nail up the base of my spine.

Gjalp got it worse. The spinning steak knife hit her in the chest. It didn't impale her. It didn't even go through her dress, but the poke was enough to make her yell. She lowered her hands, grabbing instinctively for her chest, which allowed Jack full access to her nose.

A second later, Gjalp was lying dead on the floor next to her sister.

"Magnus!" Sam lowered herself off the table and dropped next to me on the chair. "You fool! I wanted you to help me throw a saltshaker on the blade! I didn't expect you to jump on it yourself!"

"You're welcome." I grimaced. "Also, *ow*."

"Is it broken?"

"Yeah. Don't worry, I'm a fast healer. Give me an hour—"

"I don't think we have—" Sam started to say.

From the next room, a deep voice boomed, "Girls, I'm home!"

FIFTY-FIVE

I'm Carried into Battle by the First Dwarven Airborne Division

THERE'S NEVER A GREAT TIME for Daddy Giant to come home.

But when you're sitting in his dining room with your leg broken, the corpses of two of his daughters sprawled nearby . . . that's an *especially* bad time. Sam and I stared at each other as the giant's footsteps echoed louder and louder in the next chamber.

Sam's expression said: *I got nothing.*

I, also, had nothing.

Which is exactly the sort of moment when you might welcome a dwarf, an elf, and a swan parachuting onto your chair. Blitzen and Hearth were lashed side-by-side in the harness, with Gunilla the waterfowl cradled in Hearthstone's arms. Blitzen pulled the steering toggles and executed a perfect landing. Behind him pooled the parachute—a swath of turquoise silk that exactly matched Blitz's suit. That was the only fact about his entrance that did *not* surprise me.

"How?" I asked.

Blitzen scoffed. "Why do you look so amazed? You distracted those giantesses long enough. I'd be a poor dwarf indeed if I couldn't rig a grappling hook, shoot a line from the window to the birdcage, shimmy across, free the swan, and use my emergency parachute to get down here."

Sam pinched her nose. "You've had an emergency parachute this entire time?"

"Don't be silly," Blitzen said. "Dwarves always carry emergency parachutes. Don't you?"

"We'll talk about this later," I said. "Right now—"

"Girls?" called the giant from the next room. His speech sounded a little slurred. "Wh-where are you?"

I snapped my fingers. "Come on, guys, options. Sam, can you and Gunilla camouflage us?"

"My hijab can only cover two people," Sam said. "And Gunilla . . . the fact that she's still a swan might indicate she's too weak to change back to normal."

The swan honked.

"I'll take that as a yes," Sam said. "It could be a few hours."

"Which we don't have." I looked at Hearth. "Runestones?"

No strength, he signed, though he hardly needed to tell me that. He was upright and conscious but still looked like he'd been run over by an eight-legged horse.

"Jack!" I called to the sword. "Where is Jack?"

From the table above us, the sword yelled, "Dude, what? I'm washing off in this goblet. Give a guy some privacy, huh?"

"Magnus," Sam said, "you can't ask him to kill three giants in a row. That much effort really *will* kill you."

In the next room, the footsteps got louder. The giant sounded like he was stumbling. "Gjalp? Griep? I swear—*HIC!*— if you're texting those frost giant boys again, I will wring your necks!"

"The floor," I decided. "Get me to the floor!"

Blitzen scooped me up, which almost made me black out from pain. He yelled, "Hang on!" and leaped from the chair, somehow managing to paraglide me down safely. By the time I regained my senses, Sam, Hearth, and his new pet swan were standing next to us, apparently having used the chair leg as a fire pole.

I shivered with nausea. My face was slick with sweat, and my broken leg felt like one enormous open blister, but we had no time for minor concerns like my unbearable pain. Across the threshold of the dining room door, the shadows of the giant's feet got closer and darker, though they did seem to be weaving back and forth.

"Blitzen, carry me under that door!" I said. "We have to intercept Geirrod."

"Excuse me?" asked the dwarf.

"You're strong! You're already holding me. Hurry!"

Grumbling, he jogged toward the door, every bounce sending a stab of pain into the base of my skull. The parachute slithered behind us. Sam and Hearth followed, the swan honking unhappily in Hearthstone's arms.

The doorknob started to turn. We ducked under the sill and charged out the other side, right between the giant's feet.

I yelled, "HI, HOW YA DOING!"

Geirrod stumbled back. I guess he hadn't been expecting to see a paratrooper dwarf carrying a human, followed by another human and an elf holding a swan.

I wasn't prepared for what I saw either.

For one thing, the room we entered was about half the size of the one we'd just left. By most standards, the hall would've been considered grand. The black marble floor gleamed. Rows of stone columns were interspersed with iron braziers filled with burning coals like dozens of barbecue grills. But the ceilings were only about twenty-five feet tall. Even the door we'd come through was smaller on this side, though that made no sense.

Squeezing back under the sill would be impossible. In fact, I didn't see how Gjalp or Griep could have fit through the doorway, unless they changed size as they moved from room to room.

Maybe that's what they did. Giants were shape-shifters. Magic and illusion were second nature to them. If I spent much more time here, I'd have to bring a large supply of motion sickness medicine and some 3-D glasses.

In front of us, Geirrod was still staggering around, sloshing mead from his drinking horn.

"Whoeryou?" he slurred.

"Guests!" I called. "We have claimed guest rights!"

I doubted those applied anymore, since we'd killed our hosts, but since my etiquette-minded sword was still in the next room, washing the nostril goo off his blade, nobody challenged me.

Geirrod frowned. He looked like he'd just come from a wild party at the Jotunheim Marquee, which was weird, since the day was young. Giants apparently partied 24/7.

He wore a rumpled mauve jacket, an untucked black dress shirt, striped slacks, and dress shoes that many patent leather animals had died to create. His dark hair was greased back but springing up in unruly cowlicks. His face had a three-day stubble. He reeked of fermented honey. The overall impression was less "fashionable nightclub dude" and more "well-dressed wino."

The weirdest thing about him was his size. I'm not going to say he was short. Twenty feet tall is still good if you're looking for somebody to play point in the NBA or change those hard-to-reach lightbulbs. But the guy was minuscule compared to his daughters, who were, of course, now dead.

Geirrod belched. Judging from his expression, he was making a mighty effort to form rational thoughts. "If you're guests . . . why have you got my swan? And where are my daughters?"

Sam forced a laugh. "Oh, those crazy girls? We were bartering with them for your swan."

"Yeah," I said. "Right now they're on the floor in the other room. They don't look so good." I mimed drinking from a bottle, which probably confused Hearthstone, as it looked like the sign for *I love you*.

Geirrod seemed to get my meaning. His shoulders relaxed, as if the idea of his daughters passing out drunk on the floor was nothing to be concerned about.

"Well, then," he said, "as long as they weren't—*HIC!*—entertaining those frost giant boys again."

"Nope, just us," I assured him.

Blitzen grunted as he shifted me in his arms. "Heavy."

Hearthstone, trying to keep up with the conversation, signed *I love you* at the giant.

"Oh, Great Geirrod!" Sam said. "We actually came here to bargain for Thor's weapon. Your daughters told us you have it."

Geirrod glanced to his right. Against the far wall, almost hidden behind a column, was a human-sized iron door.

"And the weapon is behind that door," I guessed.

Geirrod's eyes widened. "What sorcery is this? How did you know that?"

"We want to barter for the weapon," I repeated.

In Hearthstone's arms, Gunilla honked irritably.

"And also for the freedom of this swan," Sam added.

"Ha!" Geirrod sloshed more mead from his drinking horn. "I don't—*HIC!*—need anything you could offer. But perhaps you could—*BELCH*—earn the weapon and the golden goose."

"The swan," I corrected.

"Whatever," said the giant.

Blitzen whimpered, "Heavy. Very heavy."

The pain in my leg made it hard to think. Every time Blitzen moved I wanted to scream, but I tried to keep a clear head.

"What did you have in mind?" I asked the giant.

"Entertain me! Join me in a game!"

"Like . . . Words with Friends?"

"What? No! Like catch!" He gestured disdainfully toward the dining room. "I have only daughters. They never want to play catch with me. I like playing catch! Play catch with me."

I glanced at Sam. "I think he wants to play catch."

"Bad idea," she murmured.

"Survive ten minutes!" Geirrod said. "That's all I ask! Then I'll be—*HIC!*—happy."

"Survive?" I asked. "A game of catch?"

"Good, so you agree!" He stumbled to the nearest brazier and scooped up a red-hot coal the size of an easy chair. "Go long!"

FIFTY-SIX

Never Ask a Dwarf to "Go Long"

"RUN!" I TOLD BLITZEN. "Run, run, run!"

Blitzen, who was still trailing the parachute, only managed a dazed stumble. "Heavy, very heavy," he wheezed again.

We made it about twenty feet before Geirrod yelled, "CATCH!"

The four of us ducked behind the nearest column as a coal cannonball slammed against it, burning a hole straight through the stone and spraying ash and sparks over our heads. The column groaned. Cracks spread all the way up to the ceiling.

"Run more!" Sam yelped.

We shambled across the hall as Geirrod scooped coals and threw them with appalling accuracy. If he hadn't been drunk, we would've been in serious trouble.

The next salvo set Blitzen's parachute on fire. Sam was able to cut it off with her ax, but we lost valuable time. Another chunk of flaming apocalypse blasted a crater in the floor next to us, singeing Gunilla's wings and Hearthstone's scarf. Sparks flew into Blitzen's eyes.

"I'm blind!" he yelped.

"I'll direct you!" I shouted. "Left! Left! Your other left!"

Meanwhile, across the hall, Geirrod was having a grand

old time singing in Jotunese, staggering from brazier to brazier, occasionally dousing himself in mead. "Come on now, little guests! This is not how you play. You're supposed to catch the coals and throw them back!"

I looked around desperately for exits. There was one other door, on the wall directly across from the dining room, but it was too small to crawl under and too big to force open, not to mention barred with a tree-trunk beam across iron brackets.

For the first time since becoming an einherji, I was annoyed that my super-quick healing wasn't super quick enough. If we were going to die, I at least wanted to be standing on my own two feet.

I glanced at the ceiling. Above the last column Geirrod had hit, cracks spread across the roof. The column bowed, ready to snap. I remembered the first time my mom had made me set up our camping tent by myself. The poles had been a nightmare. Getting them to hold the roof required just the right balance of tension. But making them collapse . . . that was easy.

"I've got an idea," I said. "Blitzen, you're going to have to carry me a while longer, unless Sam—"

"Um, no," said Sam.

"I'm fine," Blitzen whimpered. "I'm just great. I can almost see again."

"Okay, everybody," I said. "We're going to run toward the giant."

I didn't need sign language to read Hearth's expression: *Are you crazy?* The swan gave me the same look.

"Just follow my lead," I said. "It'll be fun."

"Please," Sam begged, "don't let those words be carved on my tombstone."

I yelled at the giant, "Hey, Geirrod, you throw like a Folkvanger person!"

"What? BAH!" Geirrod turned to scoop up another coal.

"Straight at him," I told my friends. "Go!"

As the giant prepared to throw, I told Blitzen, "Right, go right!"

We all ducked behind the nearest pillar. Geirrod's coal bored straight through it, spewing cinders and sending more cracks up the ceiling.

"Now left," I told my friends. "Toward him and up another row."

"What are you—" Sam's eyes widened with understanding. "Oh, gods, you really *are* crazy."

"Got a better idea?"

"Sadly, no."

We ran across Geirrod's line of sight.

"Your daughters aren't drunk!" I shouted. "They're dead!"

"*WHAT? NO!*"

Another coal cannonball hurtled toward us, hitting the nearest column with such force, it collapsed into a pile of colossal stone Lifesavers.

The ceiling groaned. The cracks spread. We ran into the central aisle and I yelled, "MISSED AGAIN!"

Geirrod howled in fury. He tossed aside his drinking horn so he could scoop coals with both hands. Fortunately for us, his anger and his double-handed throwing made his aim terrible. We jogged around him, weaving from column to column as he splattered coal everywhere, tipping over braziers, breaking pillars.

I insulted Geirrod's suit, his haircut, his patent leather

shoes. Finally the giant tossed an entire brazier at us, taking out the last support pillar on his side of the room.

"Retreat!" I told Blitzen. "Go! NOW!"

Poor Blitzen huffed and wheezed. We ran for the far wall as Geirrod shouted, "Cowards! I will kill you!"

He easily could have run after us and caught us, but the giant's drunken mind was still thinking in terms of projectile weapons. He searched around him for more coals as the ceiling above him crumbled.

Too late, he realized what was happening. He looked up and screamed as half the room collapsed on top of him, burying Geirrod under a thousand tons of rock.

The next thing I knew, I was on the floor in a whiteout of dust and debris, trying my best to cough up my lungs.

Slowly the air cleared. A few feet away, Sam sat cross-legged, also hacking and gasping, looking like she'd been rolled in flour.

"Blitzen?" I called. "Hearth?"

I was so worried about them I forgot about my broken leg. I tried to stand and was surprised to find that I could. The leg still throbbed with agony, but it held my weight.

Blitzen came stumbling out of a dust cloud. "Present." he squeaked. His suit was ruined. His hair and beard had gone prematurely gray with plaster.

I tackled him in a hug. "You," I said, "are the strongest, most amazing dwarf ever."

"Okay, kid, okay." He patted my arm. "Where's Hearthstone? Hearth!"

In moments like that, we forgot that yelling Hearthstone's name wasn't really helpful.

"Here he is," Sam called, brushing some rubble off the fallen elf. "I think he's okay."

"Thank Odin!" Blitz started forward but almost fell.

"Whoa, there." I propped him against one of the remaining columns. "Just rest for a sec. I'll be right back."

I jogged over to Sam and helped her extract Hearthstone from the wreckage.

His hair was smoldering, but otherwise he looked all right. We pulled him to his feet. Immediately he started scolding me in sign language: *Stupid? Trying to kill us?*

It took me a second to realize he wasn't holding the swan.

"Wait," I said. "Where's Gunilla?"

Behind me, Blitzen yelped. I turned and discovered a hostage situation in progress.

"I'm right here," Gunilla snarled. She was back in human form, standing behind Blitzen, the point of her blazing spear pressed to his throat. "And the four of you are coming back to Valhalla as my prisoners."

Sam Hits the EJECT Button

GUNILLA JABBED HER spear tip against Blitz's jugular.

"No closer," she warned. "Rogues and liars, all of you. You've endangered Midgard and Asgard, roused the giants, caused chaos across the realms—"

"We also rescued you from a birdcage," I added.

"After luring me here in the first place!"

"Nobody lured you," I said. "Nobody asked you to hunt us."

"Gunilla." Samirah placed her ax on the floor. "Let the dwarf go, please."

"Urgh," Blitzen agreed.

The Valkyrie captain glanced at Hearthstone. "You, elf— don't even *think* about it. Put that bag of runestones on the floor or I will burn you to ashes."

I hadn't realized Hearthstone was about to make a move. He complied with Gunilla's order, though his eyes blazed. He looked like he wanted to do something much worse to Gunilla than put her in a magic hamster wheel.

Sam raised her palms. "We're not going to fight you. Please, release the dwarf. We all know what a Valkyrie spear can do."

I didn't, actually, but I tried to look as meek and harmless as possible. As exhausted as I felt, it wasn't hard.

Gunilla eyed me. "Where is your sword, Magnus?"

I gestured to the ruined end of the hall. "Last I checked, he was taking a bath in a goblet."

Gunilla considered that. It was the sort of statement that only made sense in the loony world of the Vikings. "Very well." She shoved Blitzen toward me.

She swept her spear forward, keeping us all within striking distance. The weapon's light was so intense I felt like it was baking my skin.

"We will return to Asgard as soon as my full strength returns," said Gunilla. "In the meantime, explain why you were asking the giants about Thor's weapon."

"Oh . . ." I remembered Thor being pretty specific about not telling anyone of his missing hammer. "Well—"

"A trick," Sam interrupted. "To confuse the giants."

Gunilla narrowed her eyes. "A dangerous trick. If the giants believed Thor had lost his hammer . . . the consequences would be unthinkable."

"Speaking of unthinkable," I said, "Surt is going to release Fenris Wolf tomorrow night."

"Tonight," Sam corrected.

My stomach dropped. "Isn't it Tuesday? Freya said the full moon was Wednesday—"

"Which technically starts at sundown on Tuesday," Sam said. "The full moon rises tonight."

"Well that's just wonderful," I said. "Why didn't you say so?"

"I thought you understood."

"Silence, both of you!" Gunilla ordered. "Magnus Chase, you've fallen for the lies of this daughter of Loki."

"You mean the full moon isn't tonight?"

"No, it's tonight. I meant—" Gunilla scowled. "Stop confusing me!"

Blitzen whimpered as she throttled him with her light spear. Hearthstone edged next to me, his fists clenched.

I raised my hands. "Gunilla, all I'm saying is, if you don't let us go so we can stop Surt—"

"I warned you," Gunilla said. "Listening to Samirah will only hasten Ragnarok. Feel fortunate *I* found you rather than the other Valkyries who are hunting you, or your former einherjar hallmates. They are anxious to prove their loyalty to Valhalla by killing you. I, at least, will make sure you get a proper trial before the thanes cast your soul into Ginnungagap!"

Samirah and I exchanged glances. We didn't have time to be captured and sent back to Asgard. I definitely didn't have time to get my soul cast into a place I couldn't even pronounce.

Hearthstone saved us. His face became transfixed with horror. He pointed behind Gunilla as if Geirrod was rising from the rubble. It was the oldest trick in the Nine Worlds, and it worked.

Gunilla glanced behind her. Sam lunged with blinding speed. Instead of trying to tackle the Valkyrie captain, she simply touched the golden bracer on Gunilla's arm.

The air hummed as if someone had turned on an industrial vacuum cleaner.

Gunilla shrieked. She stared at Sam in dismay. "What have you—"

The Valkyrie imploded. She collapsed into a pinpoint of light and was gone.

"Sam?" I couldn't believe what had happened. "You—you killed her?"

"Of course not!" Sam swatted my arm. (Thankfully, I did not implode.) "I just recalled her to Valhalla."

"The armband?" asked Blitzen.

Sam smiled modestly. "I didn't know if it would work. I guess my fingerprints haven't been de-registered from the Valkyrie database yet."

Hearthstone rolled his hand. *Explain.*

"Valkyrie armbands have an emergency evacuation feature," Sam said. "If a Valkyrie is wounded in battle and needs immediate attention, another Valkyrie can send her back to the Halls of Healing simply by touching her armband. She'll be instantly extracted, but it's powerful magic. One use and the armband melts."

I blinked. "So Gunilla got yanked to Valhalla."

"Yep. But I haven't bought us much time. She'll be back as soon as she gathers her strength. I imagine she'll bring reinforcements, too."

"Thor's hammer," I said. "The storage room."

We ran for the small iron door. I'd like to say I had carefully planned the ceiling's collapse to make sure the door didn't get buried in wreckage. In truth, I just got lucky.

Sam's ax cut through the lock in one swipe. Hearthstone yanked open the door. Inside was a closet, empty except for an iron pole the size of a broom handle leaning against the corner.

"Well," I said. "That's kind of anticlimactic."

Blitzen studied the iron pole. "I dunno, kid. See this runework? It isn't Mjolnir, but this staff was forged with powerful magic."

Sam's face fell. "Oh . . . Thor's weapon. Just not the *right* weapon."

"Mmm." Blitzen nodded sagely.

"Mmm," I agreed. "Would one of you tell me what you're talking about?"

"Kid, this is Thor's backup weapon," Blitz explained. "The staff was a gift from a friend of his—the giantess Grid."

"Three questions," I said. "First: Thor has a giantess friend?"

"Yes," Blitz said. "Not all giants are bad."

"Second: Do all giantess names begin with G?"

"No."

"Last question: Thor is a martial artist? Does he have, like, backup nunchuks, too?"

"Hey, kid, don't dis the staff. It may not be dwarven work like the hammer, but giant-forged iron is still powerful stuff. I hope we're able to pick it up and carry it back to Thor. I'm sure it's heavy and protected by enchantments."

"You needn't worry about that!" bellowed a voice above.

From one of the high windows, the god of thunder soared into the room on a chariot pulled by Otis and Marvin. My sword Jack floated along next to them.

Thor landed in front of us in all his grungy glory. "Good work, mortals!" He grinned. "You found the staff. That's better than nothing!"

"And, dude," said Jack, "I take one quick bath. I turn around and not only have you left the room, but you've collapsed the exit. What's a sword supposed to think?"

I bit back a comment. "Yeah. Sorry, Jack."

Thor reached out toward the supply closet. The iron rod flew into his hand. Thor executed a few thrusts, swipes, and baton twirls. "Yes, this will do nicely until I find that—ah, *other* weapon which is not officially missing. Thanks!"

I tried to resist the urge to smack him. "You have a flying chariot?"

"Of course!" He laughed. "Thor without his flying chariot would be like a dwarf without an emergency parachute!"

"*Thank* you," Blitz said.

"You could have flown us straight here," I noted. "You could have saved us a day and a half and several close calls with death. But you let us climb that cliff, navigate a chasm—"

"I would never deprive you of the chance to prove your heroism!" the thunder god said.

Blitzen whimpered.

Hearthstone signed, *I hate this god.*

"Exactly, Mr. Elf!" Thor said. "I gave you the opportunity to prove your mettle. You're quite welcome!"

Otis bleated and clopped his hooves. "Besides, the boss couldn't show up here without his hammer, especially since his daughter was stuck in that birdcage."

Sam flinched. "You *knew* about that?"

Thor scowled at his goat. "Otis, we need to have another talk about you keeping your snout shut."

"Sorry." Otis hung his horns. "Go ahead and kill me. It's fine."

Marvin nipped him. "Will you shut up? Every time you get killed, I get killed!"

Thor rolled his eyes at the ceiling. " 'What kind of animals would you like pulling your chariot, Thor?' my dad asked me. 'Goats,' I said. 'Flying re-consumable goats would be great.' I could've chosen dragons or lions, but noooo." He faced Sam.

"To answer your question, yes, I sensed Gunilla was here. I can usually tell when one of my children is nearby. I figured, if you could save her, that would be a nice bonus. But I also didn't want her learning about my missing hammer. That information is a bit sensitive. You should feel honored I told *you* about it, daughter of Loki."

Sam inched away. "You know about that? Listen, Lord Thor—"

"Girl, stop calling me *lord*. I'm a god of the common people, not a lord! And don't worry, I won't kill you. Not all of Loki's brood is evil. Even Loki himself . . ." He heaved a sigh. "I kind of miss the guy."

Sam looked at him sideways. "You do?"

"Oh, sure." Thor scratched his red beard. "Most of the time I wanted to kill him, like when he cut off all my wife's hair, or convinced me to wear a bridal gown."

"Do what now?" I asked.

"But Loki made life interesting," Thor continued. "People got the idea we were brothers, which isn't true. He was *Odin's* blood brother. Still, I understand how the rumor got started. I hate to admit it, but Loki and I made a good team."

"Like Marvin and me," Otis suggested. "My therapist says—"

"Shut up, you dolt!" said Marvin.

Thor twirled his iron staff. "At any rate, thanks for this. It will help until I can find that *other* item. And please, *DO NOT* mention my loss to anyone. Not even my children. *Especially* not them. Otherwise I'd have to kill you, and I might even feel bad about that."

"But what will you do without Mjolnir?" Sam asked. "How will you—"

"Watch television?" Thor shrugged. "I know . . . the screen size and resolution on the end of this staff are pitiful, but I will have to make do. As for you, the island of Lyngvi rises from the waves tonight. You must hurry! Good-bye, mortals, and—"

"Hold up," I said. "We need the location of the island."

Thor frowned. "Oh, right. I was supposed to give that to you. Well, all you have to do is seek out the dwarf brothers at the Long Wharf in Boston. They will take you to the island. Their boat usually leaves at sunset."

"Ah, dwarves." Blitz nodded approvingly. "We can trust them, then?"

"Oh, no," Thor said. "They'll try to kill you at the first opportunity, but they *do* know the way to the island."

"Lord Th— I mean, Thor," said Sam, "Won't you come with us? This is an important battle—the fire lord Surt, Fenris Wolf. Surely that's worthy of your attention."

Thor's right eye twitched. "That's a fine offer. Really. I'd love to, but I have another pressing appointment—"

"Game of Thrones," Marvin explained.

"Shut up!" Thor raised his staff over our heads. "Use your time well, heroes. Prepare for battle, and be at the Long Wharf by sundown!"

The room started to spin. Jack the sword flew into my hand, flooding me with exhaustion.

I braced myself against the nearest column. "Thor, where are you sending us?"

The thunder god chuckled. "Wherever you each need to go."

Jotunheim collapsed around me like a tent falling on my head.

FIFTY-EIGHT

What the Hel?

I STOOD ALONE in a snowstorm on Bunker Hill.

My exhaustion was gone. Jack had returned to pendant form around my neck. None of that made sense, but I didn't seem to be dreaming.

I felt like I was really in Charlestown, just across the river from Boston, standing right where my fourth grade school bus had dropped us off for a class trip. Gauzy curtains of snow swept across the brownstones. The park itself wasn't much more than a white field dotted with bare trees. In the center, a gray obelisk rose into the winter sky. After my time in Geirrod's fortress, the monument looked small and sad.

Thor had said I'd be sent where I needed to go. Why did I need to be here, and where were my friends?

A voice at my shoulder said, "Tragic, isn't it?"

I hardly flinched. I supposed I was getting used to strange Norse entities popping up in my personal space.

Standing next to me, gazing at the monument, was a woman with elven-pale skin and long dark hair. In profile, she looked heart-achingly beautiful, about twenty-five years old. Her ermine cloak shimmered like a snowdrift rippling in the wind.

Then she turned toward me, and my lungs flattened against the back of my rib cage.

The right side of the woman's face was a nightmare—withered skin, patches of blue ice covering decayed flesh, membrane-thin lips over rotten teeth, a milky white eye, and tufts of desiccated hair like black spiderwebs.

I tried to tell myself, *Okay, this isn't so bad. She's just like that guy Two-Face from Batman.* But Two-Face had always struck me as kind of comical, like, come on, nobody with that much facial damage could be alive.

The woman in front of me was *very* real. She looked like someone who'd been stuck halfway through a door when a devastating blizzard struck. Or worse . . . some hideous ghoul who'd tried to transform into a human, only to get interrupted in the middle of the process.

"You're Hel." My voice sounded like I was five years old again.

She lifted her skeletal right hand, brushing a tuft of hair behind her ear . . . or the stub of frostbitten flesh that might once have been an ear.

"I am Hel," she agreed. "Sometimes called Hela, though most mortals dare not speak my name at all. No jokes, Magnus Chase? *Who the Hel are you? What the Hel do you want? You look Hela bad.* I was expecting more bravado."

I was fresh out of bravado. The best I could manage was not running away shrieking. Wind gusted around Hel, lifting a few flakes of blackened skin from her zombie forearm and swirling them into the snow.

"Wh-what do you want?" I asked. "I'm already dead. I'm an einherji."

"I know that, young hero. I don't want your soul. I have plenty of those already. I called you here to talk."

"*You* brought me? I thought Thor—"

"Thor." The goddess scoffed. "If you want someone who can navigate one hundred and seventy channels of HD content, go to Thor. If you want someone who can accurately send people through the Nine Worlds, he's not your guy."

"So—"

"So I thought it was high time we talked. My father did mention I'd be seeking you out, yes? He gave you an exit strategy, Magnus: Surrender the sword to your uncle. Remove it from play. This is your last opportunity. Perhaps you can take a lesson from this place."

"Bunker Hill?"

She turned toward the monument so only her mortal side was visible. "Sad and meaningless. Another hopeless battle, like the one you're about to engage in. . . ."

Granted, my American history was a little rusty, but I was pretty sure they didn't build monuments at the site of sad and meaningless events.

"Wasn't Bunker Hill a victory? Americans holding off the British at the top of the hill? Don't fire until you see . . ."

She fixed me with her milky zombie gaze, and I couldn't make myself say *the whites of their eyes.*

"For every hero, a thousand cowards," said Hel. "For every brave death, a thousand senseless ones. For every einherji . . . a thousand souls who enter *my* realm."

She pointed with her withered hand. "Right over there, a British boy of your age died behind a hay bale, crying for his mother. He was the youngest of his regiment. His own commander shot him for cowardice. Do you think he appreciates this lovely monument? And there, at the top of the hill, after their ammunition ran out, your ancestors threw rocks at the British, fighting like cavemen. Some fled. Some stayed and were butchered with bayonets. Which were smarter?"

She smiled. I wasn't sure which side of her mouth was more ghastly—the living zombie, or the beautiful woman who was amused by massacres.

"No one ever said *the whites of their eyes*," she continued. "That's a myth, made up years later. This isn't even Bunker Hill. It's Breed's Hill. And though the battle was costly to the British, it was an American defeat, not a victory. Such is human memory . . . you forget the truth and believe what makes you feel better."

Snow melted against my neck, dampening my collar. "What's your point? I shouldn't fight? I should just let Surt free your brother the Big Bad Wolf?"

"I merely point out options," Hel said. "Did Bunker Hill really affect the outcome of your Revolution? If you face Surt tonight, will you delay Ragnarok or hasten it? Charging into battle is what the hero would do—the sort of person who ends up in Valhalla. But what of the millions of souls who lived more careful lives and died peacefully in their beds at an old age? They ended up in my realm. Were they not wiser? Do you really belong in Valhalla, Magnus?"

The words of the Norns seemed to spiral around me in the cold. *Wrongly chosen, wrongly slain; a hero Valhalla cannot contain.*

I thought about my hallmate T.J., still carrying his rifle and wearing his Civil War coat, charging up hills day after day in a series of endless battles, waiting for his final death at Ragnarok. I thought about Halfborn Gunderson, trying to stay sane by earning PhDs in literature when he wasn't going berserk and smashing skulls. Did I belong with those guys?

"Take the sword to your uncle," Hel urged. "Let events unfold without you. This is the safer course. If you do so . . . my father Loki has asked me to reward you."

The skin on my face burned. I had an irrational fear that I might be decaying from frostbite, becoming like Hel. "Reward me?"

"Helheim is not such a terrible place," said the goddess. "My hall has many fine chambers for my favored guests. A reunion could be arranged."

"A reunion . . ." I could barely speak the words. "With my mother? You have her?"

The goddess seemed to consider the question, tilting her head from the living side to the dead. "I *could* have her. The status of her soul, of everything that she was, is still in flux."

"How . . . ? I don't—"

"The prayers and wishes of the living often affect the dead, Magnus. Mortals have always known that." She bared her teeth—rotten on one side, pristine white on the other. "I cannot return Natalie Chase to life, but I can unite you both in Helheim if you wish it. I can bind your souls there so that you will never be separated. You could be a family again."

I tried to imagine that. My tongue froze in my mouth.

"You need not speak," Hel said. "Only give me an indication. Cry for your mother. Let your tears fall, and I will know you agree. But you must decide now. If you reject my offer, if you insist on fighting your own Bunker Hill tonight, I promise you will never see your mother again in this life or any other."

I thought about my mother skipping stones with me at Houghton's Pond, her green eyes sparkling with humor. She spread her arms in the sunlight, trying to explain what my father was like. *That's why I bring you here, Magnus. Can't you feel it? He's all around us.*

Then I imagined my mother in a cold dark palace, her soul bound for eternity. I remember my own corpse in the funeral home—an embalmed relic, dressed up for display. I thought about the faces of the drowned souls swirling in Ran's net.

"You are crying," Hel noted with satisfaction. "Then we have a deal?"

"You don't understand." I looked at the goddess. "I'm crying because I know what my mother would want. She'd want me to remember her as she was. That's the only monument she needs. She wouldn't want to be trapped, preserved, forced to live as a ghost in some cold storage underworld."

Hel scowled, the right side of her face wrinkling and crackling. "You dare?"

"You want bravado?" I pulled my pendant from its chain. Jack the sword stretched to full length, his blade steaming in the cold. "Leave me alone. Tell Loki we have no deal. If I see you again, I'll cut you right down the dotted line."

I raised my blade.

The goddess dissolved into snow. My surroundings faded. Suddenly I found myself balanced at the edge of a rooftop, five stories above a stretch of asphalt.

FIFTY-NINE

The Terror That Is Middle School

BEFORE I COULD plummet to my death, someone grabbed me and pulled me back.

"Whoa, there, cowboy," Sam said.

She was dressed in a new peacoat—navy blue this time, with dark jeans and boots. Blue wasn't my favorite color, but it made her look dignified and serious, like an air force officer. Her headscarf was freckled with snow. Her ax wasn't at her side; I guessed it was tucked in the backpack over her shoulder.

She didn't look surprised to see me. Then again, her expression was preoccupied, her gaze stuck somewhere in the distance.

My senses started to adjust. Jack was still in my hand. For some reason, I didn't feel any exhaustion from his recent slaying of the giant sisters.

Below us, the patch of asphalt was not exactly a playground—more like a holding area between school buildings. Inside the chain-link fence, a few dozen students huddled in cliques, chatting in doorways or pushing each other around the icy pavement. They looked like seventh graders, though it was hard to be sure with everybody in their dark winter coats.

I willed my sword back into pendant form and returned it to its chain. I didn't figure I should be walking on the roof of a school with a broadsword.

"Where are we?" I asked Sam.

"My old stomping ground." Her voice had a bitter edge. "Malcolm X Middle School."

I tried to imagine Sam down in that courtyard, mingling with those cliques of girls, her headscarf the only splash of color in the crowd.

"Why did Thor send you back to middle school?" I asked. "That seems especially cruel."

She smirked. "He actually transported me home. I appeared in my bedroom, just in time for Jid and Bibi to barge in and demand to know where I'd been. That conversation was worse than middle school."

My heart sank. I'd been so focused on my own problems I'd forgotten that Sam was trying to balance a normal life on top of everything else. "What did you tell them?"

"That I'd been staying with friends. They'll assume I meant Marianne Shaw."

"Rather than three strange guys."

She hugged her arms. "I told Bibi I tried to text her, which is true. She'll assume it was her fault. Bibi is hopeless with phones. Actually, Jotunheim just has no reception. I—I try not to actually *lie*, but I hate misleading them. After everything they've done for me, they worry I'm going to get in trouble, turn out like my mom."

"You mean a successful doctor who liked to help people? Gee, that would be terrible."

She gave me an eye roll. "You know what I mean—a rebel,

an embarrassment. They locked me in my room, told me I was grounded until Doomsday. I didn't have the heart to tell them that might be tonight."

The wind picked up, spinning the old metal roof fans like pinwheels.

"How did you sneak out?" I asked.

"I didn't. I just appeared here." She gazed down into the courtyard. "Maybe I needed a reminder of how it all started."

My brain felt as rusty as the roof fans, but one thought gained traction and started to spin. "This is where you became a Valkyrie."

Sam nodded. "A frost giant . . . he'd gotten into the school somehow. Maybe looking for me, maybe hunting some other demigod. He wrecked a few classrooms, caused a panic. He didn't seem to care if there were mortal casualties. The school went on lockdown. They didn't know what they were dealing with. They thought some crazy human was making a scene. They called the police, but there was no time. . . ."

She slipped her hands into her coat pockets. "I taunted the giant—insulted his mom, that kind of thing. I lured him up here to the roof and . . ." She looked below us. "The giant couldn't fly. He landed right there on the asphalt and shattered into a million shards of ice."

She sounded strangely embarrassed.

"You took on a giant single-handedly," I said. "You saved your school."

"I suppose," she said. "The staff, the police . . . they never figured out what happened. They thought the guy must've fled the scene. In the confusion, nobody noticed what I'd done . . . except Odin. After the giant died, the All-Father appeared in front of me, right where you're standing. He offered me a job as a Valkyrie. I accepted."

After my conversation with Hel, I didn't think it was possible for me to feel worse. The loss of my mother still stung as painfully as the night she'd died. But Sam's story made me feel bad in a different way. Sam had brought me to Valhalla. She'd lost her place among the Valkyries because she believed I was a hero—a hero like *her*. And despite all that had happened since, she didn't seem to blame me.

"Do you regret it?" I asked. "Taking my soul when I fell?"

She laughed under her breath. "You don't get it, Magnus. I was *told* to bring you to Valhalla. And not by Loki. By Odin himself."

My pendant heated up against my collarbone. For an instant, I smelled warm roses and strawberries, as if I'd stepped through a pocket of summer.

"Odin," I said. "I thought he was missing . . . hadn't appeared since you became a Valkyrie."

"He told me to say nothing." Sam shivered. "I guess I failed in that, too. The night before your fight with Surt, Odin met me outside my grandparents' house. He was disguised as a homeless guy—a ratty beard, an old blue coat, a broad-brimmed hat. But I knew who he was. The eye patch, the voice. . . . He told me to watch for you, and if you fought well, to bring you to Valhalla."

Down in the courtyard, a period bell rang. The students headed inside, jostling and laughing. For them, it was a normal school day—the kind of day I could hardly remember.

"I was *wrongly chosen*," I said. "The Norns told me I wasn't supposed to be in Valhalla."

"Yet you were," Sam said. "Odin foresaw it. I don't know why the contradiction, but we have to finish this quest. We have to reach that island tonight."

I watched the snow erase footprints in the empty yard. Soon there'd be no more trace of the students than there was of the frost giant's impact from two years ago.

I wasn't sure what to think about Odin choosing me for Valhalla. I suppose I should've felt honored. The All-Father himself thought I was important. He had chosen me, no matter what the Norns said. But if that was true, why hadn't Odin bothered to meet me in person? Loki was bound on a slab for eternity. *He'd* found a way to talk to me. Mimir was a severed head. He'd made the trip. But the All-Father, the great sorcerer who could supposedly bend reality just by speaking a rune—he couldn't find the time for a quick check-in?

Hel's voice echoed in my head: *Do you really belong in Valhalla, Magnus?*

"I just came from Bunker Hill," I told Sam. "Hel offered me a reunion with my mother."

I managed to tell her the story.

Samirah reached out as if to touch my arm, then apparently changed her mind. "I'm so sorry, Magnus. But Hel lies. You can't trust her. She's just like my father, only colder. You made the right choice."

"Yeah . . . still. You ever do the right thing, and you *know* it's the right thing, but it leaves you feeling horrible?"

"You've just described most days of my life." Sam pulled up her hood. "When I became a Valkyrie . . . I'm still not sure why I fought that frost giant. The kids at Malcolm X were terrible to me. The usual garbage: they asked me if I was a terrorist.

They yanked off my hijab. They slipped disgusting notes and pictures into my locker. When that giant attacked . . . I could've pretended to be just another mortal and gotten myself to safety. But I didn't even think about running away. Why did I risk my life for those kids?"

I smiled.

"What?" she demanded.

"Somebody once told me that a hero's bravery has to be unplanned—a genuine response to a crisis. It has to come from the heart, without any thought of reward."

Sam huffed. "That somebody sounds pretty smug."

"Maybe you didn't need to come here," I decided. "Maybe *I* did. To understand why we're a good team."

"Oh?" She arched an eyebrow. "Are we a good team now?"

"We're about to find out." I gazed north into the snowstorm. Somewhere in that direction lay downtown Boston and Long Wharf. "Let's find Blitzen and Hearthstone. We've got a fire giant to extinguish."

SIXTY

A Lovely Homicidal
Sunset Cruise

BLITZ AND HEARTH were waiting for us outside the New England Aquarium.

Blitz had scored a new outfit, of course: olive-colored fatigues, a yellow ascot, and a matching yellow pith helmet with yellow sun-proof netting. "My wolf-hunting clothes!" he told us cheerfully.

He explained how Thor's magic had transported him where he most needed to be: the best department store in Nidavellir. He'd used his Svartalf Express Card to charge a number of expeditionary supplies, including several spare outfits and a retractable bone steel harpoon.

"Not only that," Blitz said, "but the contest scandal with Junior? It backfired on the old maggot! Word got around about how badly he failed. Nobody is blaming me anymore, or the horsefly, or anything! People started talking about my stylish armor designs, and now they're clamoring for product. If I live through tonight, I might get to start my own clothing line after all!"

Sam and I both congratulated him, though living through the night did seem like a pretty big *if*. Nevertheless, Blitz was so happy, I didn't want to bring him down. He started bouncing on his heels, singing "Sharp Dressed Dwarf" under his breath.

As for Hearth, he'd done a different kind of shopping. He was now carrying a polished staff of white oak. At the top, the staff split into a Y like a slingshot. I got the feeling—I don't know how—that a piece was missing between the two prongs.

With his staff in hand, Hearth looked like a proper sword-and-sorcery elf—except that he was still wearing black jeans, a leather jacket over a HOUSE OF BLUES T-shirt, and a candy-striped scarf.

Hearth rested the staff in the crook of his arm and explained in signs how he'd ended up at Mimir's Well. The Capo had pronounced him a full master of alf seidr, ready to use a sorcerer's staff.

"Isn't that awesome?" Blitzen clapped him on the back. "I knew he could do it!"

Hearthstone pursed his lips. *I don't feel like a master.*

"I've got something that might help." I reached in my pocket and pulled out the runestone perthro. "A couple of hours ago I had a conversation with Hel. She reminded me of everything I've lost."

I told them what the half-zombie goddess had offered me.

"Ah, kid . . ." Blitzen shook his head. "Here I've been going on about my new clothing line, and you had to deal with *that*."

"It's okay," I assured him. Strangely, it *did* feel okay. "The thing is, when I appeared on Bunker Hill, I'd just used my sword to kill two giantesses. I should've passed out or died from exhaustion. I didn't. I think I know why."

I turned the runestone between my fingers. "The longer I'm with you guys, the easier it gets to use my sword, or heal, or do anything, really. I'm no magic expert, but I think . . . somehow, we're sharing the cost."

I held out the rune for Hearthstone. "I know what it feels like to be an empty cup, to have everything taken away from you. But you're not alone. However much magic you need to use, it's okay. We've got you. We're your family."

Hearth's eyes rimmed with green water. He signed to us, and this time I think he actually meant *I love you* and not *the giantesses are drunk.*

He took the rune and set it between the prongs of his new staff. The stone snapped into place the same way my pendant did on its chain. The symbol perthro glowed with a gentle gold light.

My sign, he announced. *My family's sign.*

Blitzen sniffled. "I like that. A family of four empty cups!"

Sam wiped her eyes. "Suddenly I feel thirsty."

"Al-Abbas," I said, "I nominate you for the role of annoying sister."

"Shut up, Magnus." She straightened her coat, shouldered her backpack, and took a deep breath. "All right. If we're done with the family bonding, I don't suppose anyone knows where we can find two dwarves with a boat?"

"I do." Blitzen fluffed his ascot. "Hearth and I scouted it out before you got here. Come on!"

He led the way down the pier. I think he just wanted us to appreciate how well he swaggered in his new yellow pith helmet.

At the end of Long Wharf, across from the closed-for-the-season kiosk for whale watching tours, another kiosk had been cobbled together from plywood scraps and cardboard appliance boxes. Above the service window, a sloppily finger-painted sign read: WOLF-WATCHING CRUISE. TONIGHT ONLY! ONE RED GOLD PER PERSON! CHILDREN UNDER FIVE FREE!

Sitting in the booth was a dwarf who was definitely less svartalf and more maggot. About two feet tall, he had so much facial hair it was impossible to tell if he had eyes or a mouth. He was dressed in a yellow rain slicker and a captain's hat, which no doubt protected him from the dim daylight and also made him look like the mascot for a gnomish lobster restaurant franchise.

"Hello, there!" said the dwarf. "Fjalar, at your service. Care to take the cruise? Lovely wolf-spotting weather!"

"Fjalar?" Blitzen's face sagged. "You wouldn't happen to have a brother named Gjalar?"

"Right over there."

I wasn't sure how I'd missed it, but docked a few feet away was a Viking longship fitted with an outboard motor. At the stern, chewing on a piece of jerky, sat another dwarf who looked exactly like Fjalar except he wore grease-stained coveralls and a floppy-brimmed felt hat.

"I can see you've heard about our exceptional service," Fjalar continued. "So can I put you down for four tickets? Once-a-year opportunity!"

"Excuse us a moment." Blitzen steered us out of earshot. "Those are Fjalar and Gjalar," he whispered. "They're notorious."

"Thor warned us," Sam said. "We don't have much choice."

"I know, but"—Blitzen wrung his hands—"Fjalar and Gjalar? They've been robbing and murdering people for over a thousand years! They'll try to kill us if we give them any opportunity."

"So basically," I summed up, "they're like pretty much everyone else we've met."

"They'll stab us in the back," Blitz fretted, "or strand us on a desert island, or shove us overboard into the mouth of a shark."

Hearth pointed to himself then tapped a finger to his palm. *I'm sold.*

We marched back to the kiosk.

I smiled at the homicidal lobster mascot. "We'd love four tickets, please."

SIXTY-ONE

Heather Is My New Least Favorite Flower

I DIDN'T THINK anything could be worse than our fishing expedition with Harald. I was wrong.

As soon as we left the harbor, the sky darkened. The water turned as black as squid ink. Through the haze of snow, the shoreline of Boston morphed into something primeval—the way it might have looked when Skirnir's descendant first sailed his longship up the Charles.

Downtown was reduced to a few gray hills. The runways at Logan Airport turned to sheets of ice floating on open water. Islands sank and rose around us like a time-lapse video of the last two millennia.

It occurred to me that I might be looking at the future rather than the past—the way Boston would appear after Ragnarok. I decided to keep that thought to myself.

In the quiet of the bay, Gjalar's outboard motor made an obscene amount of noise—rattling, growling, and coughing smoke as our boat cut through the water. Any monsters within a five-mile radius would know where to find us.

At the prow, Fjalar kept watch, occasionally shouting warnings to his brother, "Rocks to port! Iceberg to starboard! Kraken at two o'clock!"

None of that helped calm my nerves. Surt had promised

we would meet tonight. He planned on burning my friends and me alive, and destroying the Nine Worlds. But in the back of my mind lurked an even deeper fear. I was about to meet the Wolf at last. That realization dredged up every nightmare I'd ever had about glowing blue eyes, white fangs, feral snarls in the darkness.

Sitting next to me, Sam kept her ax across her lap, where the dwarves could see it. Blitzen fussed with his yellow ascot, as if he could intimidate our hosts with his wardrobe. Hearthstone practiced making his new staff appear and disappear. If he did it right, the staff shot into his hand out of nowhere, like a bouquet of flowers spring-loaded in a magician's sleeve. If he did it wrong, he goosed Blitzen or whopped me upside the back of the head.

After a few hours and a dozen staff-induced concussions, the boat shuddered like we'd hit a crosscurrent. From the bow, Fjalar announced, "It won't be long now. We've entered Amsvartnir—Pitch-Black Bay."

"Gee"—I looked at the inky waves—"why do they call it that?"

The clouds broke. The full moon, pale and silver, peered down at us from a starless void. In front of us, fog and moonlight wove together, forming a coastline. I'd never hated the full moon so much.

"Lyngvi," Fjalar announced. "The Isle of Heather, prison of the Wolf."

The island looked like the caldera of an ancient volcano—a flattened cone maybe fifty feet above sea level. I'd always thought of heather as purple, but the rocky slopes were carpeted with ghostly white flowers.

"If that's heather," I said, "there sure is a lot of it."

Fjalar cackled. "It's a magical plant, my friend—used to ward off evil and keep ghosts at bay. What better prison for Fenris Wolf than an island entirely ringed with the stuff?"

Sam rose. "If Fenris is as big as I've heard, shouldn't we be able to see him by now?"

"Oh, no," Fjalar said. "You have to go ashore for that. Fenris lies bound in the center of the island like a runestone in a bowl."

I glanced at Hearthstone. I doubted he could read Fjalar's lips behind that bushy beard, but I didn't like the reference to a runestone in a bowl. I remembered the other meaning of perthro: a dice-rolling cup. I didn't want to run blindly into that caldera and hope for Yahtzee.

When we were about ten feet from the beach, the keel of the boat ground against a sandbar. The sound reminded me unpleasantly of the night my mother died—our apartment door creaking just before it burst open.

"Out you go!" Fjalar said cheerfully. "Enjoy your walking tour. Just head over the ridge there. I think you'll find the Wolf well worth the trip!"

Maybe it was my imagination, but my nostrils filled with the smell of smoke and wet animal fur. My new einherji heart was testing the limits of how fast it could beat.

If it hadn't been for my friends, I'm not sure I would've had the courage to disembark. Hearthstone leaped over the side first. Sam and Blitzen followed. Not wanting to be stuck on the boat with lobster dwarf and his jerky-eating brother, I swung my legs overboard. The waist-deep water was so cold I imagined I would be singing soprano for the rest of the week.

I slogged onto the beach, and a wolf's howl split my eardrums.

Now, sure . . . I'd been expecting a wolf. Ever since childhood, wolves had terrified me, so I'd tried my best to gather my courage. But Fenris's howl was unlike anything I'd ever heard—a note of pure rage so deep it seemed to shake me apart, breaking my molecules into random amino acids and icy Ginnungagap run-off.

Safe in their boat, the two dwarves cackled with glee.

"I should have mentioned," Fjalar called to us, "the ride back is a little more expensive. All your valuables, please. Gather them together in one of your bags. Toss them to me. Otherwise, we'll leave you here."

Blitzen cursed. "They'll leave us here anyway. That's what they do."

At the moment, heading inland to confront Fenris Wolf was very low on my wish list. At the top of my wish list was: *Cry and Plead for the Treacherous Dwarves to Take Me Back to Boston.*

My voice quavered, but I tried to act more courageous than I felt.

"Get lost," I told the dwarves. "We don't need you anymore."

Fjalar and Gjalar exchanged looks. Already their boat was drifting farther away.

"Didn't you hear the Wolf?" Fjalar spoke more slowly, as if he'd overestimated my intelligence. "You're stuck on that island. With Fenris. That's a bad thing."

"Yeah, we know," I said.

"The Wolf will eat you!" Fjalar cried. "Bound or not, he will *eat* you. At dawn the island will disappear and take you with it!"

"Thanks for the lift," I said. "Pleasant trip back."

Fjalar flung up his hands. "Idiots! Suit yourself. We'll collect your valuables from your skeletal remains next year! Come on, Gjalar, back to the docks. We might have time to pick up another load of tourists."

Gjalar revved the motor. The longship turned and disappeared into the darkness.

I faced my friends. I got the feeling they wouldn't mind another rousing speech like, *We're a family of empty cups and we will dominate!*

"Well," I said, "after running from an army of dwarves, facing a monster squirrel, killing three giant sisters, and butchering a pair of talking goats . . . how bad can Fenris Wolf be?"

"Very bad," Sam and Blitz said in unison.

Hearthstone made two *okay* signs, crossed them at the wrists, and flicked them apart—the sign for *awful.*

"Right." I pulled my sword from pendant form. The blade's glow made the heather look even paler and more ghostly. "Jack, you ready?"

"Dude," said the sword, "I was *forged* ready. Still, I get the feeling we're walking into a trap here."

"Show of hands," I asked my friends, "is anybody surprised by that?"

Nobody raised their hand.

"Okay, cool," said Jack. "As long as you realize you'll probably all die in agony and start Ragnarok, I'm down. Let's do this!"

SIXTY-TWO

The Small Bad Wolf

I REMEMBER THE FIRST TIME I saw Plymouth Rock.

My reaction was, "That's *it*?"

Same with the Liberty Bell in Philadelphia and the Empire State Building in New York—up close and personal, they seemed smaller than I'd imagined, not worth the hype.

That's how I felt when I saw Fenris Wolf.

I'd heard all these terrible stories about him: the gods were too scared to feed him; he could break the strongest chains; he'd eaten Tyr's hand; he was going to swallow the sun on Doomsday; he was going to devour Odin in a single bite. I expected a wolf bigger than King Kong with flame-thrower breath, death-ray eyes, and laser nostrils.

What I got instead was a Wolf the size of a wolf.

We stood at the top of the ledge, looking down into the valley where Fenris sat calmly on his haunches. He was larger than an average Labrador retriever, but definitely no bigger than me. His legs were long and muscular, built for running. His shaggy gray coat swirled with tufts of black. Nobody would've called him *cute*—not with those gleaming white fangs, or the bones littering the ground around his paws—but he was a handsome animal.

I'd been hoping to find the Wolf lying on his side, hog-tied and fastened to the ground with nails, staples, duct tape, and Krazy Glue. Instead, the golden rope Gleipnir restrained him more like the leg irons used to transport criminals. The glimmering cord was tied around all four of his ankle joints, allowing enough slack for the Wolf to shuffle around. Part of the rope had apparently once been tied around the Wolf's snout like a muzzle. That section now fell across his chest in a loose loop. The rope didn't even appear to be anchored to the ground. I wasn't sure what was keeping Fenris from leaving the island unless there was one of those doggy no-no invisible fences around the perimeter.

All in all, if I were the god Tyr, getting my hand bit off so the other gods would have time to bind the Wolf, I would've been pretty torqued off at this shoddy work. Didn't the Aesir have *one* decent god of knots?

I glanced at my friends. "Where's the real Fenris? That has to be a decoy, right?"

"No." Sam's knuckles whitened on the handle of her ax. "That's him. I can sense it."

The Wolf turned toward the sound of our voices. His eyes shone with a familiar blue light that sent a xylophone mallet down the back of my rib cage.

"Well." His voice was deep and rich. His black lips curled in a very human sneer. "Who do we have here? Have the gods sent me a snack?"

I revised my impression of the Wolf. Maybe his size was ordinary. Maybe he didn't sneeze laser beams. But his eyes were colder and more intelligent than any predator I'd ever encountered—animal or human. His snout quivered as if he could smell the fear on my breath. And his voice . . . his voice flowed over me like molasses, dangerously smooth and sweet. I remembered my first feast in Valhalla, when the thanes didn't want Sam to speak in her defense because they feared the silver tongue of Loki's children. Now I understood.

The last thing I wanted to do was approach the Wolf. Yet his tone said, *Come on down. We're all friends here.*

The entire caldera was maybe a hundred yards across, which meant the Wolf was much closer than I would've liked. The ground sloped gently, but the heather was slick under my feet. I was terrified I might slip and slide right between the Wolf's paws.

"I'm Magnus Chase." My voice was *not* as smooth as molasses. I forced myself to meet Fenris's gaze. "We have an appointment."

The Wolf bared his teeth. "We do indeed, son of Frey. Vanir-spawn have such an interesting scent. Normally I only get to devour the children of Thor, or Odin, or my old friend Tyr."

"Sorry to disappoint."

"Oh, not at all." The wolf paced, the rope gleaming between his feet, barely slowing his gait. "I'm quite pleased. I've been waiting a long time for this."

On my left, Hearthstone banged his white oak staff against the rocks. The heather plants glowed brighter, a fine silvery mist rising from them like a lawn sprinkler system. With his free hand, Hearth signed to me, *Flowers make the prison. Stay within.*

Fenris Wolf chuckled. "The elf is wise. Not powerful enough—not *nearly* powerful enough to face me—but he is right about the heather. I can't stand the stuff. Funny, though . . .

how many brave mortals choose to leave its safety and come within my reach. They want to test their skill against me, or perhaps they simply want to make sure I am still bound." The Wolf leered at Blitzen. "Your father was one of those. A noble dwarf with the best of intentions. He approached me. He died. His bones are around here somewhere."

Blitzen let loose a guttural scream. Sam and I had to restrain him to keep him from charging the Wolf with his new harpoon.

"Quite sad, really," the Wolf mused. "Bilì was his name? He was right, of course. This ridiculous rope has been loosening for ages. At one time, I was completely unable to walk. After a few centuries, I managed to hobble. I still can't cross the heather. The farther I move from the center of the island, the more the rope tightens and the more pain I endure. But it's progress! The real breakthrough came . . . oh, a little over two years ago, when I finally managed to shake that cursed muzzle off my snout!"

Sam faltered. "Two years ago . . ."

The Wolf tilted his head. "That's right, little sister. Surely you knew. I began whispering in the dreams of Odin—what a fine idea it would be to make you, the daughter of Loki, a Valkyrie! What a fine way to turn a potential enemy into a valuable friend."

"No," Sam said. "Odin would never listen to you."

"Would he not?" The Wolf snarled with pleasure. "That's the wonderful thing about you so-called *good* folk. You hear what you want to believe. You think your conscience is whispering to you when it is, perhaps, the Wolf instead. Oh, you have done very well, little sister, bringing Magnus to me—"

"I didn't *bring* him to you!" Sam shouted. "And I'm not your little sister!"

"No? I smell the changeling blood in your veins. You could be powerful. You could make our father proud. Why do you fight it?"

The Wolf's teeth were as sharp as ever, his leer just as vicious, but his voice filled with sympathy, disappointment, melancholy. His tone said *I could help you. I am your brother.*

Sam took a step forward. I grabbed her arm.

"Fenris," I said, "you sent those wolves . . . the night my mother died."

"Of course."

"You wanted to kill me—"

"Now, why would I want that?" His blue eyes were worse than mirrors. They seemed to reflect back at me all my failures— my cowardice, my weakness, my selfishness in running away when my mother needed me most. "You were valuable to me, Magnus. But you needed . . . seasoning. Hardship is wonderful for cultivating power. And look! You have succeeded—the first child of Frey strong enough to find the Sword of Summer. You have brought me the means to escape these bonds at last."

The world spun beneath me. I felt like I was back on Stanley the horse—plummeting with no reins, no saddle, no control. All this time, I'd assumed Fenris wanted me dead. That's why his wolves had attacked our apartment. But his real target had been my mother. He'd killed her to affect me. That idea was even worse than believing my mom had died to protect me. She'd died so this monster could forge me into his harbinger— a demigod capable of attaining the Sword of Summer.

I was filled with so much rage I couldn't focus.

In my hand, the sword began to hum. I realized how long Jack had been silent. He pulled at my arm, tugging me forward.

"Jack," I muttered. "Jack, what are you—?"

The Wolf laughed. "You see? The Sword of Summer is destined to cut these bonds. You cannot stop it. The children of Frey have never been fighters, Magnus Chase. You can't hope to control the blade, much less fight me with it. Your usefulness is at an end. Surt will arrive soon. The blade will fly to his hands."

"Mistake . . ." Jack murmured, tugging to escape my grip. "Mistake to bring me here."

"Yes," the Wolf purred. "Yes, it was, my fine blade. Surt thinks all of this was *his* idea, you understand. He's an imperfect tool. Like most fire giants, he's a lot of hot air, more bluster than brains, but he will serve his purpose. He'll be very happy to take possession of you."

"Jack, you're my sword now," I said, though I could barely hold on with both hands.

"Cut the cord . . ." Jack hummed insistently. "Cut the cord."

"Do it, Magnus Chase," said Fenris. "Why wait for Surt? Cut me loose of your own free will and I will be grateful. Perhaps I would even spare you and your friends."

Blitzen growled even better than the Wolf. From his pack, he pulled out the new string, Andskoti. "I was ready to bind this mutt. Now I think I might just strangle him."

"I agree," Samirah said. "He dies."

I wanted more than anything to join them. I wanted to charge the beast and run him through. The Sword of Summer was supposed to be the sharpest blade in the Nine Worlds. Surely it could cut wolf hide.

I think we would've done it, but Hearthstone swept his

staff in front of us. The runestone perthro flared with gold light.

Look. The command was more a tremor than a sound. I turned and stared in amazement at Hearthstone.

The bones. He didn't use sign language. He didn't speak. His thought was simply *there*, clearing my mind like wind through fog.

I looked again at the skeletons littering the ground. All of them had been heroes—the children of Odin, Thor, or Tyr. Dwarves, humans, elves. They'd all been tricked, enraged, enchanted by Fenris. They'd all died.

Hearthstone was the only one of us who couldn't hear the Wolf's voice. He was the only one thinking clearly.

Suddenly the sword was easier to control. It didn't stop fighting me, but I felt the balance shift slightly in my favor.

"I'm not freeing you," I told the Wolf. "And I don't need to fight you. We'll wait for Surt. We'll stop him."

The Wolf sniffed the air. "Oh . . . too late for that. You don't need to fight me? Poor mortal . . . I don't need to fight you, either. There are others to do that for me. As I said, good folk are so easy to manipulate, so ready to do my work for me. Here are some now!"

Across the island, a voice yelled, "STOP!"

At the opposite side of the ridge stood our old friend Gunilla with a Valkyrie on either side of her. Fanning out to her left and right were my old hallmates: T.J., Halfborn, Mallory, and X the half-troll.

"Caught in the act of aiding the enemy," Gunilla said. "You've signed your own death warrants!"

SIXTY-THREE

I Hate Signing My Own Death Warrant

"WELL, WELL," said the Wolf. "I haven't had this much company since my binding party."

Gunilla gripped her spear. She didn't look at the Wolf, as if ignoring him might make him go away.

"Thomas Jefferson, Jr.," she said, "you and your hallmates take the prisoners. Go around the edges, obviously. Slow and careful."

T.J. didn't look happy about it, but he nodded. His army jacket was buttoned up tight. His bayonet gleamed in the moonlight. Mallory Keen gave me the stink eye, but that could have been her version of a happy greeting. The two of them went left, picking their way across the rim of the crater while the three Valkyries kept their spears pointed at Fenris.

X lumbered to the right, followed by Halfborn, who was twirling his battle-axes and whistling under his breath, as if this was a pleasant stroll through a field of fallen enemies.

"Sam," I muttered, "if we're taken—"

"I know."

"No one will be here to stop Surt."

"I know."

"We can take them," Blitz said. "They're not wearing armor, much less fashionable armor."

"No," I said. "These are my shield bro—my shield siblings. Let me try talking to them."

Hearth signed, *Crazy. You?*

The beauty of sign language: He could've meant *Are you crazy?* Or *I'm crazy. Just like you!* I decided to interpret it as a show of support.

Fenris Wolf sat on his haunches and tried to scratch his ear, which wasn't possible with the cord binding his legs.

He sniffed the air and grinned at me. "Interesting company you keep, Magnus Chase. Someone is hiding, but I can smell him. Which one is he, eh? Perhaps I will get a feast today after all!"

I glanced at Sam. She looked just as mystified as I felt.

"Sorry, fuzzball," I said. "No idea what you're talking about."

Fenris laughed. "We shall see. I wonder if he will dare to show his true face."

"Chase!" Gunilla plucked a hammer from her bandolier. "Do not speak with the Wolf again or I will cave in your skull."

"Gunilla," I said, "great to see you again too. Surt is on his way right now. We don't have time for this."

"Oh? Have you made common cause with the fire lord who killed you? Or perhaps that was part of the plan from the beginning—to get you into Valhalla."

Sam sighed. "For a child of Thor, you think too much."

"And you, daughter of Loki, listen too little. Jefferson, hurry it up!"

My hallmates got to either side of us.

Mallory made a *tsk-tsk* sound. "You led us on quite a chase, Chase."

"Clever," I said. "How long have you been waiting to use that line?"

Mallory smirked.

Next to her, X wiped beads of green sweat from his forehead. "Wolf's rope is loose. This is not good."

From across the valley, Gunilla yelled, "No fraternizing! I want them in chains!"

T.J. dangled four sets of handcuffs from his finger. "Here's the thing, Magnus: Gunilla made it clear that if we don't prove our loyalty to Valhalla by apprehending you, we will spend the next hundred years in the boiler room shoveling coal. So consider yourself under arrest, blah, blah, blah."

Halfborn grinned. "But the *other* thing is: we're Vikings. We're pretty bad at following orders. So consider yourself free again."

T.J. let the handcuffs slip from his finger. "Oops."

My spirits lifted. "You mean—"

"He means, you idiot," Mallory said, "that we're here to help."

"I love you guys."

"What do you need us to do?" T.J. asked.

Sam nodded to Blitzen. "Our dwarf has a rope to rebind the Wolf. If we can—"

"Enough!" Gunilla shouted. On either side, her Valkyrie lieutenants readied their spears. "I will take you *all* back in chains if I must!"

Fenris howled with pleasure. "That would be delightful to watch. Unfortunately, Valkyrie, you are too slow. My other friends have arrived, and they won't be taking any prisoners."

X gazed toward the south, his neck muscles rippling like freshly poured cement. "There."

At the same moment, Hearthstone pointed with his staff, the whole length of white oak suddenly burning with gold fire.

On the ridge to the right, between the Valkyries and us, a dozen fire giants marched into view. Each stood about ten feet tall. They wore leather scale armor, carried swords the size of plow blades, and had various axes and knives hanging from their belts. Their complexions were an assortment of volcanic colors—ash, lava, pumice, obsidian. The fields of heather may have been noxious to the Wolf, but the stuff didn't seem to bother the fire giants. Wherever they stepped, the plants burned and smoked.

In the middle of their line stood Satan's fashion consultant himself, the fire lord Surt, wearing a trim-cut three-piece suit of chain mail, a tie, and a dress shirt that appeared to be woven from flame—elegantly accessorized with a burning scimitar in his hand. He looked pretty good, despite the fact that his nose was still cut off. That fact, at least, made me happy.

Blitzen clenched his teeth. "That's my design. He *stole* my design."

"Magnus Chase!" Surt's voice boomed. "I see you have brought my new sword. Excellent!"

Jack almost leaped out of my hands. I must have looked ridiculous trying to keep him under control, like a fireman wrestling a high-pressure hose.

"My master . . ." Jack said. "He shall be my master."

Surt laughed. "Surrender the sword and I will kill you quickly." He sneered at Gunilla and her two lieutenants. "As for Odin's wenches, I make no promises."

Fenris Wolf rose and stretched. "Lord Surt, as much as I love posturing and threats, can we move things along? Moonlight is a-wasting."

"T.J.," I said.

"Yeah?"

"You asked how you could help. My friends and I need to rebind Fenris Wolf. Can you keep those fire giants busy?"

T.J. smiled. "I charged uphill against seventeen hundred Confederates. I think I can handle a dozen fire giants."

He called across the valley, "Captain Gunilla, are you with us? Because I'd rather not fight another Civil War."

Gunilla scanned the army of fire giants. Her expression soured, as if she found them even more repugnant than she found me. She raised her spear. "Death to Surt! Death to the enemies of Asgard!"

She and her lieutenants charged at the giants.

"I guess we're in business," T.J. said. "Fix bayonets!"

SIXTY-FOUR

Whose Idea Was It to Make This Wolf Un-killable?

VALHALLA'S DAILY COMBAT training finally made sense to me. After the terror and chaos of war in the hotel courtyard, I was more prepared to face Fenris Wolf and the fire giants, even if they didn't have AK-47s or chests painted with COME AT ME, BRO!

I was still having trouble controlling the sword, though. The only thing that helped: Jack now seemed divided between wanting to fly to Surt's hand or flying toward the Wolf. Lucky for me, I needed to approach the Wolf.

Sam knocked a giant's thrown ax out of the air. "Rebinding Fenris—any idea how we're doing that?"

"Yes," I said. "Maybe. Not really."

A fire giant charged in our direction. Blitzen was so angry—between the Wolf gloating about his dad's death and Surt stealing his fashion ideas—that he howled like Crazy Alice in Chinatown and rammed his harpoon right through the giant's gut. The fire giant stumbled off, belching flames and taking the harpoon with him.

Hearthstone pointed to the Wolf. *Idea,* he signed. *Follow me.*

"I thought we needed to stay in the heather," I recalled.

Hearthstone raised his staff. Across the ground at his feet, a rune spread like a shadow:

Heather bloomed around it, sprouting new tendrils.

"Algiz," Sam marveled. "The rune of shielding. I've never seen it used."

I felt as if I were seeing Hearthstone for the first time. He didn't stumble. He didn't faint. He strode confidently forward, the flowers expanding before him like an unrolling carpet. Not only was Hearth immune to the wolf's voice, his rune magic was literally redrawing the boundaries of Fenris's prison.

We inched into the valley, following Hearthstone. On the right side of the island, my einherjar friends clashed with Surt's forces. Halfborn Gunderson buried his ax in the breastplate of a giant. X picked up another fire-breather and tossed him off the side of the ridge. Mallory and T.J. fought back-to-back—jabbing and slashing and dodging blasts of flame.

Gunilla and her two Valkyrie lieutenants were fighting Surt himself. Between the shining white spears and the flaming sword, their combat was almost too bright to watch.

My friends fought valiantly, but they were outnumbered two-to-one. The fire giants didn't want to die. Even the one Blitzen had harpooned was still staggering around, trying to blowtorch the einherjar with his bad breath.

"We have to hurry," I said.

"Open to suggestions, kid," Blitzen said.

Fenris paced expectantly. He didn't seem concerned to see us shuffling toward him on a carpet of heather, collectively armed with an ax, a glowing white staff, an uncooperative sword, and a ball of string.

"By all means, come down," he said. "Bring that blade closer."

Blitzen huffed. "I'll tie him up. Hearth can guard me. Magnus and Sam—you two keep him from biting off my head for a few minutes."

"Terrible idea," Sam said.

"Got a better one?" Blitz asked.

"I do!" Fenris lunged. He could've torn my throat out, but that wasn't his plan. His front paws passed on either side of my sword. Jack cheerfully cooperated, slicing the rope in half.

Sam brought down her ax between the Wolf's ears, but Fenris leaped out of the way. His back legs were still hobbled, but his front paws were free. The Wolf's coat steamed from contact with the heather. Blisters swelled all over his legs, but he sounded too delighted to care.

"Oh, that's wonderful," he crowed. "Just the back legs now, please. Then we can get Ragnarok underway!"

All the rage that had built inside me for two years boiled to the surface.

"Blitz," I said, "do what you need to do. I'm going to knock this mutt's teeth out."

I ran at the Wolf—possibly my worst idea ever. Sam charged in next to me.

Fenris might have been the size of a normal wolf, but even with his back legs hobbled, his speed and strength were impossible to match.

As soon as I stepped from the edge of the heather, he became a blur of claws and teeth. I stumbled and fell, a line of deep cuts across my chest. Fenris would've torn me open if Sam's ax hadn't slammed him aside.

The Wolf snarled. "You can't hurt me. The *gods* couldn't hurt me. Don't you think they would've slit my throat if they could have? My destiny is fixed. Until Ragnarok, I am un-killable!"

"Must be nice." I stumbled to my feet. "But it won't keep me from trying."

Unfortunately, Jack wasn't helping. Every time I tried to attack, the sword turned and swerved, doing its best to cut the rope around the Wolf's back legs. My fight with the Wolf was more like a game of keep-away.

Blitzen lunged forward, the end of Andskoti tied in a noose. He tried to snare the Wolf's hindquarters, but he might as well have been moving in slow motion. Fenris stepped aside, dodging another strike from Sam's ax. The Wolf slashed Blitzen across the throat and the dwarf fell facedown. The string rolled away.

"NO!" I yelled.

I moved toward Blitzen, but Hearthstone was faster.

He slammed his staff across Fenris's skull. Golden fire blazed. The Wolf clambered away, whining in pain. A rune mark now steamed on his forehead—a simple arrow seared into the gray fur:

"*Tiwaz?*" The Wolf snarled. "You *dare* attack me with the rune of Tyr?" The wolf lunged at Hearthstone but seemed to hit an invisible barrier. He stumbled and howled.

Sam appeared next to me. Her ax was gone. Her left eye was swollen shut and her hijab had been cut to shreds. "Hearth used the rune of sacrifice," she said, her voice quavering. "To save Blitz."

"What does that mean?" I asked.

Hearth collapsed to his knees, leaning against his staff. Still he managed to put himself between the dwarf and the Wolf.

"You sacrifice your strength to shield your friend?" The Wolf laughed. "Fine. Enjoy your spellwork. The dwarf is already dead. Your own rune magic has doomed you. You can watch while I deal with my other tasty prey."

He bared his fangs at us.

Across the field, the battle was not going well.

One of Gunilla's Valkyries sprawled lifeless on the rocks. The other one fell, her armor burning from Surt's sword. Gunilla faced the Fire Lord alone, swinging her spear like a whip of light, but she couldn't last. Her clothes smoldered. Her shield was charred and cracked.

The einherjar were surrounded. Halfborn had lost one of his axes. He was covered with so many burns and gashes I didn't understand how he could still be alive, but he just kept fighting, laughing as he charged the giants. Mallory was on one knee, cursing as she parried attacks from three giants at once. T.J. swung his rifle wildly. Even X looked tiny compared to the enemies now looming over him.

My head throbbed. I could feel my einherji powers at work, trying to close the cuts on my chest, but I knew Fenris could kill me faster than I could possibly heal.

The Wolf sniffed, no doubt smelling my weakness.

"Ah, well," he chuckled. "A good try, Magnus, but the sons of Frey never were fighters. All that's left for me to do now is devour my enemies. I love this part!"

SIXTY-FIVE

I Hate This Part

THE STRANGEST THINGS can save your life. Like lions. Or bulletproof ascots.

Fenris lunged at my face. I cleverly escaped by falling on my butt. A blurred shape launched itself at the Wolf and knocked him aside.

Two animals tumbled across the bone yard in a whirl of fangs and claws. When they separated, I realized Fenris was facing a she-lion with a swollen eye.

"Sam?" I yelped.

"Get the rope." She kept her gaze on her enemy. "I need to have a talk with my brother."

The fact that she could speak in lion form freaked me out even more than the fact that she had a lion form. Her lips moved in a very human way. Her eyes were the same color. Her voice was still Sam's voice.

Fenris's fur stood up on the back of his neck. "So you accept your birthright as you are about to die, little sister?"

"I accept who I am," Sam said. "But not the way you mean. I am Samirah al-Abbas. Samirah of the Lion." She leaped at the Wolf. They clawed, bit, kicked, and howled. I'd heard the term *fur flying*, but I'd never realized what a horrific thing it could be. The two beasts literally tried to tear each other apart. And one of those beasts was a friend of mine.

My first instinct was to charge into battle. But that wouldn't work.

Freya had told me that killing was the least of the sword's powers.

The sons of Frey have never been fighters, the Wolf had said.

So what *was* I?

Blitzen rolled over, groaning. Hearthstone frantically checked the dwarf's neck.

The ascot glittered. Somehow, it had turned from yellow silk to woven metal, saving Blitzen's throat in the process. It was honest-to-Frigg bulletproof neckwear.

I couldn't help grinning. Blitz was alive. He had played to his strength.

He wasn't a fighter. Neither was I. But there were other ways to win a battle.

I snatched up the ball of string. It felt like woven snow—impossibly soft and cold. In my other hand, the sword became still.

"What are we doing?" Jack asked.

"Figuring stuff out."

"Oh, cool." The blade quivered as if stretching after a nap. "How's that going?"

"Better." I stabbed the end of the blade into the ground. Jack did not try to fly away. "Surt may get you someday," I said, "but he doesn't understand your power. I do now. We're a team."

I looped the string's noose around Jack's hilt and pulled it tight. The battle seemed to fade around me. I stopped thinking about how to fight the Wolf. He couldn't be killed—at least not now, not by me.

Instead, I focused on the warmth I felt whenever I healed someone: the power of growth and life—the power of Frey. The Norns had told me nine days ago: *The sun must go east.*

This place was all about night, winter, and silver moonlight. I needed to be the summer sun.

Fenris Wolf noticed the change in the air. He swiped at Sam and sent her tumbling across the lawn of bones. His snout was shredded with claw marks. The rune of Tyr glistened ugly and black on his forehead.

"What are you up to, Magnus? None of that!" He lunged, but before he could reach me, he fell out of the air, twisting and howling in pain.

Light surrounded me—the same golden aura as when I'd healed Sam and Hearthstone in Jotunheim. It wasn't hot like the fires of Muspellheim. It wasn't particularly bright, but it obviously pained the Wolf. He snarled and paced, squinting at me like I'd become a spotlight.

"Stop that!" he howled. "Are you trying to *annoy* me to death?"

Sam the lion struggled to her feet. She had a nasty cut on her flank. Her face looked like she'd rear-ended a tractor-trailer. "Magnus, what are you doing?"

"Bringing the summer."

The cuts on my chest mended. My strength returned. My father was the god of light and warmth. Wolves were creatures of darkness. The power of Frey could constrain Fenris just as it constrained the extremes of fire and ice.

Sticking up from the ground, Jack hummed with satisfaction. "Summer. Yeah, I remember summer."

I rolled out Andskoti until it trailed Jack like a kite string.

I faced the Wolf. "An old dwarf once told me that the most powerful crafting materials are paradoxes. This rope is made of them. But I've got one more—the final paradox that will bind you: the Sword of Summer, a weapon that wasn't designed to be a weapon, a blade that is best used by letting go of it."

I willed Jack to fly, trusting he would do the rest.

He could have sliced the last of the Wolf's bonds. He could have flown across the battlefield straight into Surt's hands, but he didn't. He zipped under the Wolf's belly, threading the cord Andskoti around his legs faster than Fenris could react, binding him and toppling him.

Fenris's howl shook the island. "No! I will not—!"

The sword zipped around his snout. Jack tied off the rope in an aerial pirouette then floated back to me, his blade glowing with pride. "How'd I do, boss?"

"Jack," I said, "you are one awesome sword."

"Well, I *know* that," he said. "But how about that ropework, huh? That's a perfect stevedore's knot right there, and I don't even have hands."

Sam stumbled toward us. "You did it! You—ugh."

Her lion form melted into regular old Sam—badly injured, face battered, her side soaked with blood. Before she could fall, I grabbed her and dragged her away from the Wolf. Even fully bound, he thrashed and frothed at the mouth. I didn't want to be any closer to him than I had to be.

Hearthstone staggered after me, holding up Blitzen. The four of us fell together on a bed of heather.

"Alive," I said. "I wasn't expecting that."

Our moment of triumph lasted about . . . well, one moment. Then the sounds of battle became louder and clearer around us, as if a curtain had been ripped away. Hearthstone's shielding magic may have given us extra protection against the Wolf, but it had also sealed us off from the fight with the fire giants . . . and my einherjar friends weren't doing well.

"To the Valkyrie!" T.J. shouted. "Hurry!"

He stumbled across the ridge, bayoneting a fire giant and trying to reach Gunilla. All this time, while we'd been dealing with the Wolf, the Valkyrie captain had been holding off Surt. Now she was on the ground, her spear held weakly above her as Surt raised his scimitar.

Mallory staggered around weaponless, too far away and too bloodied to help. X was trying to dig his way out from beneath a pile of giant corpses. Halfborn Gunderson sat bloody and unmoving, his back propped against a rock.

I processed this in a split second. Just as quickly, I realized Hearth, Blitz, Sam, and I wouldn't be there in time to make a difference.

Nevertheless, I gripped my sword and rose. I staggered toward Gunilla. Our eyes met across the field, her last expression one of resignation and anger: *Make it count.*

The fire lord brought down his scimitar.

SIXTY-SIX

Sacrifices

I DON'T KNOW WHY IT BROKE ME SO BADLY.

I didn't even like Gunilla.

But when I saw Surt standing over her lifeless body, his eyes smoldering in triumph, I wanted to fall down in the pile of bones and stay there until Ragnarok.

Gunilla was dead. Her lieutenants were dead. I didn't even know their names, but they'd sacrificed their lives to buy me time. Halfborn was dead or dying. The other einherjar were not much better off. Sam and Blitz and Hearth were in no shape to fight.

And Surt was still on his feet, as strong as ever, his burning sword ready. Three of his fire giants were also still alive and armed.

After all we'd been through, the fire lord could kill me, take my sword, and cut the wolf free.

Judging from the smile on his face, Surt expected to do just that.

"I am impressed," he admitted. "The Wolf told me you had potential. I don't think even Fenris expected you to do this well."

The Wolf thrashed in his new magic bonds.

A few feet from the fire lord, T.J. crouched, his bayonet

ready. He glanced at me, waiting for a sign. I knew he was ready to charge one last time, distract the giants if it would help me, but I couldn't let another person die.

"Go now," I told Surt. "Go back to Muspellheim."

The fire lord threw back his head and laughed. "Brave to the end! I think not, Magnus Chase. I think you will burn."

He thrust out his hand. A column of fire shot toward me.

I stood my ground.

I imagined being with my mom in the Blue Hills on the first day of spring, the sunlight warming my skin, gently thawing three months of cold and darkness out of my system.

My mom turned to me, her smile luminous: *This is where I am, Magnus. In this moment. With you.*

A sense of serenity anchored me. I remembered my mom once telling me how the town houses in Back Bay, like our family's ancestral home, had been built on landfill. Every so often, engineers had to sink new pylons beneath the foundations to keep the buildings from collapsing. I felt like I'd had my pylons reinforced. I was solid.

Surt's flames rolled over me. They lost their intensity. They were nothing but ghostly flickers of warm orange, as harmless as butterflies.

At my feet, the heather began to bloom—white flowers spreading across the landscape, reclaiming the trampled and burned areas where Surt's warriors had walked, soaking up the blood, covering the corpses of the fallen giants.

"The battle is over," I announced. "I consecrate this ground in the name of Frey."

The words sent a shockwave in every direction. Swords, daggers, and axes flew from the fire giants' hands. T.J.'s rifle spun from his grasp. Even the weapons lying on the ground were expelled from the island, blasted into the darkness like shrapnel.

The only one left holding a weapon was me.

Without his flaming scimitar, Surt didn't look so confident. "Tricks and childish magic," he snarled. "You cannot defeat me, Magnus Chase. That sword will be mine!"

"Not today."

I threw the blade. It spiraled toward Surt, passing over the giant's head. Surt grabbed for it and missed.

"What was that?" The giant laughed. "An attack?"

"No," I said. "That was your exit."

Behind Surt, Jack slashed the air, ripping the fabric between the worlds. A zigzag of fire burned on the ridge. My ears popped. As if someone had shot out the window in an airplane's pressurized cabin, Surt and the other fire giants were sucked screaming into the rift, which closed behind them.

"Bye!" Jack called. "Catch you later!"

Except for the outraged snarling of the Wolf, the island was silent.

I stumbled across the field. I fell to my knees in front of Gunilla. I could tell immediately that the Valkyrie captain was gone. Her blue eyes stared into the dark. Her bandolier was empty of hammers. Her white spear lay broken across her chest.

My eyes stung. "I'm sorry."

For five hundred years she'd been in Valhalla, collecting the souls of the dead, preparing for the final battle. I remembered how she'd scolded me: *Even gazing upon Asgard, you have no sense of reverence.*

In death, her face seemed full of wonder and awe. I hoped she was gazing upon Asgard the way she wanted it to be—filled with Aesir, all the lights burning in her father's mansion.

"Magnus," called T.J., "we have to go."

He and Mallory were struggling to carry Halfborn Gunderson. X had managed to dig his way out from under the fire giant corpse pile and was now carrying the two other fallen Valkyries. Blitz and Hearthstone stumbled along together, Sam close behind.

I picked up the body of the Valkyrie captain. She was not light, and my strength was fading again.

"We have to hurry." T.J. spoke as gently as he could, but I heard the urgency in his tone.

The ground was shifting under my feet. I realized my glowing aura had done more than blind the wolf. The sunlight had affected the texture of the island. The island was supposed to disappear at dawn. My magic had hastened the process, causing the ground to dissolve into spongy mist.

"Only seconds," Sam gasped. "Go."

The last thing I felt capable of was a burst of speed, but somehow, carrying Gunilla, I followed T.J. as he led the way to the shore.

SIXTY-SEVEN

One More, for a Friend

"WE'VE GOT A FREY BOAT!" YELLED T.J.

I had no idea what a Frey boat was. I didn't see any boat on the beach, but I was too stunned and exhausted to ask questions. I felt like the extremes of heat and cold I'd tolerated my entire life were now taking revenge. My forehead burned with fever. My eyes felt close to boiling. My chest felt like a block of ice.

I plodded along. The ground became softer under my feet. The beach sank. The waves rushed in. My arm muscles screamed under the weight of the Valkyrie captain.

I started veering sideways. Sam grabbed my arm. "Just a little farther, Magnus. Stay with me."

We got to the beach. T.J. pulled out a piece of cloth like a handkerchief and tossed it into the surf. Immediately the cloth expanded, unfolding. By the count of ten, a full-size Viking warship bobbed in the surf with two oversize oars, a figurehead carved like a wild boar, and a green sail emblazoned with the Hotel Valhalla logo. Along the side of the prow, lettered in white, were the words: HOTEL VALHALLA COURTESY VEHICLE.

"In!" T.J. jumped aboard first and reached out to take Gunilla from me.

The wet sand pulled at my feet, but somehow I managed

to get over the rail. Sam made sure everyone else got in safely. Then she climbed aboard.

A deep hum reverberated across the island, like a bass amp turned to maximum. The Isle of Heather sank beneath the black waves. The ship's sail tacked by itself. The oars began to row, and the ship turned west.

Blitzen and Hearthstone collapsed at the bow. They started arguing with each other about which of them had taken the stupider risks, but they were so tired the debate deteriorated into a halfhearted poking contest, like a couple of second graders.

Sam knelt next to Gunilla. She folded the Valkyrie captain's arms across her chest and gently closed Gunilla's blue eyes.

"The others?" I asked.

X lowered his head.

He had set the two Valkyries in the stern, but it was clear they were gone. He folded their arms like Gunilla's. "Brave warriors." He touched their foreheads with tenderness.

"I didn't know them," I said.

"Margaret and Irene." Sam's voice was unsteady. "They— they never liked me much, but . . . good Valkyries."

"Magnus," T.J. called from amidships, "we need you."

He and Mallory were kneeling next to Halfborn Gunderson, whose berserker strength had finally failed him. His chest was a nightmarish patchwork of cuts and burns. His left arm hung at an unnatural angle. His beard and hair were sprinkled with blood and small bits of heather.

"Good—fight," he wheezed.

"Don't talk, you big idiot!" Mallory sobbed. "How *dare* you get yourself hurt like this?"

He grinned sleepily. "Sorry . . . Mother."

"Hang in there," T.J. said. "We can get you back to Vahalla. Then if—if anything happens, you can be reborn."

I put my hand on Halfborn's shoulder. I sensed damage so severe I almost pulled away. It was like forcing myself to explore a bowl of glass shards.

"There's no time," I said. "We're losing him."

Mallory choked on tears. "Not an option. No. Halfborn Gunderson, I hate you so much."

He coughed. Blood flecked his lips. "I hate you too, Mallory Keen."

"Hold him still," I said. "I'll do what I can."

"Kid, think about this," Blitz said. "You're already weak."

"I have to." I extended my senses, taking in Halfborn's broken bones, his internal bleeding, his bruised organs. Fear washed over me. It was too much, too close to death. I needed help.

"Jack," I called.

The sword hovered to my side. "Boss?"

"Halfborn is dying. I'll need your strength to help heal him. You can do that?"

The sword hummed nervously. "Yeah. But boss, the second you take hold of me—"

"I know. I'll be even more exhausted."

"It's not just binding the Wolf," Jack warned. "I also helped with the aura of golden light, which was pretty cool if I do say so myself. And then there was the Peace of Frey."

"The peace . . ." I realized he meant the shockwave that had disarmed everyone, but I didn't have time to worry about that. "Fine. Yes. We have to act now."

I grabbed the sword. My eyesight dimmed. If I hadn't been sitting already, I would've fallen down. I fought against the nausea and dizziness and placed the sword flat against Halfborn's chest.

Warmth flooded through me. Light turned Halfborn's beard to red gold. I sent the last of my strength coursing through his veins, repairing damage, closing ruptures.

The next thing I remember, I was lying faceup on the deck, staring at a green sail rippling in the wind as my friends shook me and shouted my name.

Then I was standing in a sunlit meadow at the edge of a lake with blue sky above me. A warm breeze ruffled my hair.

Somewhere behind me, a man's voice said, "Welcome."

SIXTY-EIGHT

Don't Be a No-bro, Bro

HE LOOKED LIKE a Hollywood Viking. He looked more like Thor from the movies than Thor did.

Blond hair fell to his shoulders. His tan face, blue eyes, hawkish nose, and stubbly beard would've worked equally well on the red carpet or the beaches of Malibu.

He reclined on a throne of living tree branches, the seat draped with deer hide. Across his lap lay a sort of scepter—a stag's antler fitted with a leather grip.

When he smiled, I saw my own self-conscious smirk, the same crooked chin. He even had the same cowlick I always got above my right ear.

I understood why my mom would've fallen in love with him. It wasn't just because he was handsome, or because his faded jeans, flannel shirt, and hiking boots were exactly her style. He radiated warmth and tranquility. Every time I'd healed someone, every time I'd called on the power of Frey, I'd captured a fragment of this guy's aura.

"Dad," I said.

"Magnus." Frey rose. His eyes twinkled, but he didn't seem sure what to do with his arms. "I'm so glad to see you at last. I'd—I'd give you a hug, but I imagine that would not be welcome. I understand you need more time—"

I charged in and gave him a bear hug.

That wasn't like me. I'm not a hugger, especially not with strangers.

But he wasn't a stranger. I knew him as well as I knew my mother. For the first time, I understood why my mom had been so insistent on taking me hiking and camping. Every time we were in the woods on a summer day, every time the sun came out from behind the clouds, Frey had been there.

Maybe I should have resented him, but I didn't. After losing my mother, I didn't have patience for grudges. My years on the street had taught me that it was pointless to whine and moan about what you could've had—what you deserved, what was fair. I was just happy to have this moment.

He cupped his hand gently on the back of my head. He smelled of campfire smoke, pine needles, and toasted s'mores. Did they have s'mores in Vanaheim?

It occurred to me why I must be here. I was dead. Or at least dying again.

I pulled away. "My friends—"

"Are safe," Frey assured me. "You pushed yourself to the verge of death healing the berserker, but he will live. So will you. You have done well, Magnus."

His praise made me uncomfortable. "Three Valkyries died. I almost lost every friend I had. All I did was bind the wolf with a new rope and send Surt back to Muspellheim—and Jack did all that work. It doesn't really change anything."

Frey laughed. "Magnus, you have changed *everything*. You, the wielder of the sword, are shaping the destiny of the Nine Worlds. As for the deaths of the Valkyries—that was a sacrifice they willingly made. Do not dishonor them by feeling guilt. You cannot prevent every death, any more than I can prevent each summer from becoming autumn . . . or any more than I can prevent my *own* fate at Ragnarok."

"Your fate . . ." I closed my fingers around the runestone, now back on its chain. "I have your sword. Couldn't you . . . ?"

Frey shook his head. "No, son. As your Aunt Freya told you, I can never wield the Sword of Summer again. Ask the sword, if you want to be sure."

I pulled off the pendant. Jack sprang to life, spewing a tirade of insults I can't really repeat.

"And another thing!" he yelled. "Giving me away so you could marry a giantess? Dude, what was *that*? Blades before babes, you know what I'm saying?"

Frey smiled sadly. "Hello, old friend."

"Oh, we're friends again?" the sword demanded. "Nah. Nuh-uh. We're done." Jack paused. "Your son's okay, though. I like him. As long as he's not planning to trade me for a giantess's hand in marriage."

"That's not on my to-do list," I promised.

"Then we're cool. But as for this sorry father of yours, this traitorous no-bro—"

I willed the sword back to pendant form. "No-bro?"

Frey shrugged. "I made my choice long ago. I surrendered the blade for the sake of love."

"But on Ragnarok, you'll die because you don't have it."

He held up the deer antler. "I will fight with this."

"An animal horn?"

"Knowing your fate is one thing. Accepting it is another. I

will do my duty. With this antler I will slay many giants, even Beli, one of their great generals. But you're right. It won't be enough to bring down Surt. In the end, I will die."

"How can you be so calm about it?"

"Magnus . . . even gods can't last forever. I don't expend my energy trying to fight the change of seasons. I focus on making sure the days I have, and the season I oversee, are as joyful, rich, and plentiful as possible." He touched my face. "But you already understand this. No child of Thor or Odin or even noble Tyr could have withstood Hel's promises, Loki's silver words. You did. Only a son of Frey, with the Sword of Summer, could choose to let go as you did."

"Letting go . . . My mom . . ."

"Yes." Frey retrieved something from his throne—a sealed ceramic jar about the size of a heart. He placed it in my hands. "You know what she would want?"

I couldn't speak. I nodded, hoping my expression told Frey how grateful I was.

"You, my son, will bring hope to the Nine Worlds. You have heard the term Indian summer? You will be our last such season—a chance for warmth, light, and growth before the long winter of Ragnarok."

"But . . ." I cleared my throat. "But no pressure."

Frey flashed his brilliant white teeth. "Exactly. Much needs to be done. The Aesir and Vanir are scattered. Loki grows stronger. Even in his bonds, he has played us against each other, distracted us, made us lose focus. I am guilty of becoming distracted as well. For too long I have been removed from the world of men. Only your mother managed to . . ." He focused on the jar in my hands. "Well, after my big speech about not holding on to the past . . ." He smiled ruefully. "She was a vibrant soul. She would be proud of you."

"Dad . . ." I wasn't sure what else to say. Maybe I just wanted to try out the word again. I'd never had much experience using it. "I don't know if I'm up to this."

From the pocket of his flannel shirt, he pulled a tattered piece of paper—the MISSING flyer Annabeth and her dad had been distributing on the day I died. Frey handed it to me. "You will not be alone. For now, rest, my son. I promise it won't be another sixteen years before we meet again. In the meantime, you should call your cousin. You should talk. You will need her help before all is said and done."

That sounded ominous, but I didn't get the chance to ask about it. I blinked and Frey was gone. I was sitting in the longship again, holding the flyer and the ceramic jar. Next to me sat Halfborn Gunderson, sipping from a cup of mead.

"Well." He gave me a bloody grin. Most of his wounds had faded to scar tissue. "I owe you my life. How about I buy you dinner?"

I blinked and looked around us. Our ship had docked in Valhalla, on one of the rivers that ran through the lobby. How we'd gotten there, I had no idea. My other friends stood on the wharf, speaking with Helgi the hotel manager—grim faces all around as they regarded the off-loaded bodies of the three dead Valkyries.

"What's going on?" I asked.

Halfborn drained his cup. "We've been summoned to the feast hall to explain ourselves before the thanes and the host of einherjar. I hope they let us eat before they kill us again. I'm starving."

SIXTY-NINE

Oh . . . So *That's* Who Fenris Smelled in Chapter Sixty-Three

WE MUST HAVE LOST an entire day returning to Valhalla, because dinner was under way in the Feast Hall of the Slain. Valkyries flew around with mead pitchers. Einherjar threw bread and roasted Saehrimnir at each other. Clusters of musicians jammed out all over the room.

The fiesta slowly quieted as our procession made its way toward the thanes' table. An honor guard of Valkyries carried the bodies of Gunilla, Irene, and Margaret, covered with white linen, on stretchers. I had hoped the fallen might come back to life when they reached Valhalla. Couldn't Valkyries become einherjar? But it didn't happen.

Mallory, X, T.J., and Halfborn followed the litters. Sam, Blitzen, Hearth, and I brought up the caboose.

Warriors glared at us as we passed. The Valkyries' expressions were even worse. I was surprised we weren't killed before we reached the thanes. I suppose the crowd wanted to see us publicly humiliated. They didn't know what we'd done. They just knew we were escaped rogues brought back for judgment, following the bodies of three Valkyries. We weren't shackled, but I still shuffled along as if the rope Andskoti was wrapped around my ankles. I cradled the ceramic jar in the crook of my arm. Whatever else happened, I couldn't lose that.

We stopped in front of the thanes' table. Erik, Helgi, Leif, and all the other Eriks looked grim. Even my old buddy Hunding the bellhop stared at me with shock and disappointment, as if I'd taken away his chocolate.

Helgi finally spoke. "Explain."

I saw no reason to hold anything back. I didn't speak loudly, but my words echoed through the hall. When I got to the fight with Fenris, my voice failed me. Sam picked up the story.

When she was done, the thanes sat silently. I couldn't read their mood. Perhaps they were more unsure now than angry, but it didn't matter. Despite my talk with my father, I didn't feel proud of what we'd accomplished. I was only alive because the three Valkyries in front of me had kept the fire giants at bay while we chained the wolf. No punishment from the thanes could make me feel worse than that.

Finally Helgi rose. "This is the most serious matter to come before this table in many years. If you speak truly, you have done deeds worthy of warriors. You have stopped Fenris Wolf from breaking free. You have sent Surt back to Muspellheim. But you acted as rogues—without the leave of the thanes, and in . . . questionable company." He glanced distastefully at Hearth, Blitz, and Sam. "Loyalty, Magnus Chase . . . loyalty to Valhalla is everything. The thanes must discuss all this in private before passing judgment, unless Odin wishes to intercede."

He glanced at the vacant wooden throne, which of course stayed empty. Perched on the backrest, the ravens fixed me with their glittering black eyes.

"Very well," Helgi sighed. "We—"

To my left, a booming voice said, "Odin wishes to intercede."

Nervous murmurs rippled through the feast hall. X raised his stone-gray face toward the thanes.

"X," T.J. whispered, "this is no time for jokes."

"Odin wishes to intercede," said the half-troll stubbornly.

His appearance changed. His huge trollish shape dropped away like camouflage fabric. In X's place stood a man who looked like a retired drill sergeant. He was barrel-chested, with massive arms stuffed in a short-sleeve Hotel Valhalla polo shirt. His gray hair was close-cropped, his beard cut square to accentuate his hardened weathered face. A black patch covered his left eye. His right eye was dark blue, the color of vein blood. At his side hung a sword so massive it made Jack the pendant tremble on his chain.

The man's name tag read: ODIN, ALL-FATHER, OWNER AND FOUNDER.

"Odin." Sam dropped to one knee.

The god smiled down at her. Then he gave me what I thought was a conspiratorial wink, though it was hard to tell, since he had only one eye.

His name rippled through the feast hall. The einherjar got to their feet. The thanes rose and bowed deeply.

Odin, formerly the half-troll known as X, marched around the table and took his place on the throne. The two ravens landed on his shoulders and pecked affectionately at his ears.

"Well!" Odin's voice boomed. "What does a god have to do to get a cup of mead around here?"

SEVENTY

We Are Subjected to the PowerPoint of Doom

ODIN GOT HIS DRINK, offered some toasts, then began pacing in front of his throne, talking about where he'd been and what he'd been doing the past few decades. I was too shocked to register much of Odin's speech. I think most of the einherjar felt the same way.

The room only began to unfreeze when Odin summoned up the glowing Valkyrie-Vision screens. Einherjar blinked and stirred as if coming out of mass hypnosis.

"I am a seeker of knowledge!" Odin announced. "This has always been true. I hung from the World Tree for nine days and nights, racked with pain, in order to discover the secret of runes. I stood in line in a blizzard for six days to discover the sorcery of the smartphone."

"What?" I muttered.

Blitzen coughed. "Just roll with it."

"And more recently," Odin announced, "I endured seven weeks of motivational speaker training at a hotel in Peoria to discover . . . this!"

A clicker appeared in his hand. On all the magical screens, a PowerPoint title slide glowed, with a whirling emblem that read: ODIN'S PLAN: HOW TO HAVE A HIGHLY SUCCESSFUL AFTERLIFE!

"What is going on?" I whispered to Sam.

"Odin is always trying different things," she said. "Looking in new places for knowledge. He is very wise, but . . ."

Hearthstone signed as discreetly as possible: *This is why I work for Mimir.*

"So you see," Odin continued, pacing back and forth, his ravens flapping their wings for balance, "everything these heroes have done, they did with my knowledge and my permission. I have been with them the entire time—either in person or in spirit."

The screen changed. Odin started lecturing through some bullet points. My eyes kind of glazed over, but he talked about why he'd hidden in Valhalla as X the half-troll:

"To see how you would welcome such a warrior, and how you would carry out your duties when you didn't think I was around. You all need to work on your positive empowerment and self-actualization."

He explained why he'd chosen Samirah al-Abbas as a Valkyrie:

"If the daughter of Loki can show such bravery, why can't we all? Samirah demonstrates the seven heroic qualities I'll be highlighting in my upcoming book, *Seven Heroic Qualities*, which will be available in the Valhalla gift shop."

He explained why the Norns' prophecy didn't mean what we thought it did:

"*Wrongly chosen, wrongly slain,*" he recited. "Magnus Chase was wrongly chosen by *Loki*–who thought this boy could be easily influenced. Instead, Magnus Chase proved himself a true hero!"

Despite the compliment, I liked Odin better as a taciturn half-troll than as a motivational speaker. The dinner crowd didn't seem sure what to make of him either, though some of the thanes were dutifully taking notes.

"Which brings us to the *affirmations* portion of this presentation." Odin advanced his slide show. A photograph of Blitzen popped up. It had obviously been taken during the crafting contest with Junior. Sweat streamed down Blitzen's face. His expression was agonized, as if somebody had just dropped a hammer on his foot.

"Blitzen, son of Freya!" Odin said. "This noble dwarf won the rope Andskoti, which rebound Fenris Wolf. He followed his heart, mastered his fears, and served my old friend Mimir faithfully. For your heroism, Blitzen, you shall be released from Mimir's service and given funding to open the shop you have always wanted. Because I have to say . . ." Odin waved his hand over his hotel polo shirt. Suddenly he was wearing a chain mail vest. "I picked up your prototype after the contest, and it's a very fine fashion statement. Any warrior would be wise to acquire one!"

The einherjar murmured in approval. Some oohed and ahhed.

Blitzen bowed deeply. "Thank you, Lord Odin. I am— I can't begin to— Could I use that endorsement for my product line?"

Odin smiled benevolently. "Of course. And next we have Hearthstone the elf!"

Hearth's photo appeared on the screens. He was slumped in the window of Geirrod's palace. He had a silly grin on his face. His hands were making the sign for *washing machine*.

"This noble creature risked everything to rediscover rune magic. He is the first true sorcerer to appear from the mortal realms in centuries. Without him, the quest to restrain the Wolf would have failed many times over." Odin beamed down at the elf. "My friend, you also shall be released from Mimir's service. I will personally bring you to Asgard, where I will teach you the runes in a ninety-minute one-on-one free tutoring session, accompanied by a DVD and signed copy of my book *Rune Magic with the All-Father.*"

Polite clapping.

Hearthstone looked stunned. He managed to sign, *Thank you.*

The screen changed. In Sam's photo, she was standing nervously at the counter of Fadlan's Falafel, her face turned aside, blushing furiously as Amir leaned toward her, grinning.

"Ooooooo," said the crowd of einherjar, followed by a fair amount of snickering.

"Kill me now," Sam muttered. "Please."

"Samirah al-Abbas!" Odin said. "I personally chose you to be a Valkyrie because of your courage, your resilience, your potential greatness. Many here mistrusted you, but you rose to the challenge. You followed my orders. You did your duty even when you were reviled and exiled. To you, I give a choice."

Odin regarded the fallen Valkyries who lay before the thanes' table. He allowed a respectful silence to fall across the room.

"Gunilla, Margaret, Irene—all knew the risks of being a Valkyrie. All gave their lives to make today's victory possible. In the end, they saw your true worth, and they fought at your side. I believe they would agree you should be reinstated as a Valkyrie."

Sam's knees almost gave out. She had to lean on Mallory Keen for support.

"I offer you a choice of jobs," Odin continued. "I need a

captain for my Valkyries. I can think of no one better than you. This would allow you more time to spend in the mortal world, perhaps a chance to rest after your harrowing quest. *Or*"—his blue eye gleamed—"you could choose a much more dangerous assignment, working directly for me as the need arises on other, shall we say, high-risk, high-reward missions."

Sam bowed. "All-Father, you honor me. I could never replace Gunilla. All I ask for is the chance to prove myself, as many times as necessary, until no one here has any doubt of my loyalties to Valhalla. I will take the more dangerous assignment. Command me, and I will not fail."

This went down pretty well with the crowd. The einherjar applauded. Some shouted approval. Even the other Valkyries regarded Sam with less hostile expressions.

"Very well," Odin said. "Once again, Samirah, you prove your wisdom. We will speak later of your duties. And now . . . Magnus Chase."

The screens changed. There I was: frozen mid-scream as I fell from the Longfellow Bridge. "Son of Frey, you retrieved the Sword of Summer. You kept it from the grip of Surt. You have proven yourself . . . well, perhaps not a great warrior—"

"Thanks," I muttered.

"—but certainly a great einherji. I think we are in agreement—all of us here at the thanes' table—that you, too, deserve a reward."

Odin glanced to his left and right. The thanes stirred, hastily muttering, "Yes. Um. Absolutely."

"I do not offer this lightly," Odin said. "But if you still feel that Valhalla is not your place, I will send you to Folkvanger, where your aunt holds court. As a child of the Vanir, perhaps that would be more to your liking. Or"—his blue eye seemed to pierce right through me—"if you wish, I will even allow you to return to the mortal world, and be released from your duties as an einherji."

The room filled with murmuring and tension. From the faces of the crowd, I could tell this was an unusual offer. Odin was taking a risk. If he set a precedent of letting einherjar return to the world, wouldn't others want to go too?

I looked at Sam and Blitzen and Hearthstone. I looked at my hallmates from floor nineteen—T.J., Halfborn, Mallory. For the first time in years, I didn't feel homeless.

I bowed to Odin. "Thank you, All-Father. But wherever these friends of mine are—that's my home. I am one of the einherjar. I am one of your warriors. That is reward enough."

The whole dining hall erupted in cheering. Goblets banged on tables. Swords clattered against shields. My friends surrounded me, hugging me and clapping me on the shoulders. Mallory kissed my cheek and said, "You are a *huge* idiot." Then she whispered in my ear, "Thank you."

Halfborn ruffled my hair. "We'll make you a warrior yet, Frey-son."

When the cheering died down, Odin raised his hand. His clicker elongated into a glowing white spear.

"By Gungnir, the hallowed weapon of the All-Father, I declare that these seven heroes shall have full rights of passage through the Nine Worlds, including Valhalla. Wherever they go, they shall go in my name, serving the will of Asgard. Let no one interfere on pain of death!" He lowered his spear. "Tonight, we feast in their honor. Tomorrow, our fallen comrades shall be given to water and flame!"

SEVENTY-ONE

We Burn a Swan Boat, Which I'm Pretty Sure Is Illegal

THE FUNERAL was held on the pond in the Public Garden. Somehow, the einherjar had gotten possession of a swan boat—the kind that normally don't ply the waters during the winter. They'd modified the boat, turning it into floating funeral pyre for the three Valkyries. The bodies were wrapped in white and laid on a bed of wood, with weapons and armor and gold heaped around them.

The pond was frozen over. There shouldn't have been any way to launch the boat, but the einherjar had brought along a friend—a fifteen-foot-tall giantess named Hyrokkin.

Despite the weather, Hyrokkin was dressed in cut-off shorts and an XXXXL T-shirt from the Boston Rowing Club. Before the ceremony, she stomped barefoot all over the pond, breaking the ice and scaring the ducks. Then she came back and waited respectfully at the shore, her shins glazed with freezing water, while einherjar came forward to say their good-byes to the fallen. Many left weapons, coins, or other keepsakes on the funeral pyres. Some spoke about how Gunilla, Margaret, or Irene had been responsible for bringing them to Valhalla.

Finally Helgi lit the fire. Hyrokkin pushed the boat into the pond.

There were no pedestrians in the Public Garden. Maybe

magic kept them away. If any had been around, maybe some glamour would've kept them from seeing the crowd of undead warriors watching a ship burn.

My eyes drifted to the spot under the bridge where two weeks ago I'd been alive, homeless, and miserable. Only now could I admit how terrified I'd felt all the time.

The boat roared into a column of fire, obscuring the bodies of the Valkyries. Then the flames vanished as if somebody had turned off the gas, leaving no trace of the boat—just a steaming circle in the pond.

Mourners turned and drifted through the park, heading toward the Hotel Valhalla on Beacon Street.

T.J. gripped my shoulder. "You coming, Magnus?"

"In a bit."

As my hallmates headed back home, I was happy to see Halfborn Gunderson slip his arm around Mallory Keen's waist. She didn't even cut his hand off for doing so.

Blitzen, Hearth, Sam, and I stayed behind, watching steam curl off the pond.

Finally Hearth signed: *I am going to Asgard. Thank you, Magnus.*

I'd seen the envious looks some of the einherjar had given him. For decades, maybe centuries, no mortal had been allowed to visit the city of the gods. Now Odin had agreed to teach an elf.

"That's awesome, man," I said. "But listen, don't forget to come back and visit, huh? You've got a family now."

Hearthstone smiled. He signed: *I hear you.*

"Oh, he'll visit, all right," Blitzen said. "He's promised to help me move into my new store. I'm not lugging all those boxes without some magic assistance!"

I felt happy for Blitz, though it was hard to think about yet another one of my friends going away. "I'm sure you'll have the best shop in Nidavellir."

Blitzen snorted. "Nidavellir? Bah. Dwarves don't deserve my fashion brilliance. That red gold from Odin will buy me a nice storefront on Newbury Street. *Blitzen's Best* will be open in the spring, so you have absolutely no excuse not to come by and get fitted for one of these." He brushed aside his overcoat, revealing a glittering, stylish bulletproof vest.

I couldn't help it. I gave Blitzen a hug.

"All right, kid, all right." He patted me on the back. "Let's not wrinkle the fabric."

Sam grinned. "Maybe you can make a new hijab for me. The old one got kind of ripped to shreds."

"I'll make it for you at cost, with more magical properties!" Blitzen promised. "And I have some ideas for colors."

"You're the expert," Sam said. "As for me, I've got to get home. I'm grounded. I have a pile of make-up work from school."

"And you have a boyfriend to deal with," I said.

She blushed, which was kind of cute. "He's not . . . All right, fine. Yes, I should probably deal with that, whatever that means." She poked me in the chest. "Thanks to you, I can fly again. That's the main thing. Try not to die too often until I see you again."

"When will that be?"

"Soon," Sam promised. "Odin wasn't kidding about the

high-risk assignments. The good news is"—she put a finger to her lips—"I can pick my own strike force. So all of you . . . consider yourselves warned."

I wanted to hug her, to tell her how much I appreciated everything she'd done, but I knew Sam wouldn't be comfortable with that. I settled for a smile. "Any time, al-Abbas. Now that Odin has given us permission to travel the worlds, maybe I can come visit you in Dorchester."

"That," she said, "is a truly mortifying idea. My grandparents would kill me. Amir would—"

"Okay, jeez," I said. "Just remember: you're not in this alone."

"Noted." She bumped me with her elbow. "And what about you, Magnus—back to Valhalla for the feast? Your hallmates have been singing your praises. I even heard a few Valkyries speculating that you might be made a thane one of these centuries."

I smiled, but I wasn't ready to think about *one of these centuries*. I gazed across the Public Garden. A taxi was just pulling up in front of the Cheers bar on the corner of Beacon and Brimmer. The ceramic jar weighed heavily inside my winter coat.

"First I have an appointment," I said. "I have to keep a promise."

I said good-bye to my friends. Then I went to meet my cousin.

SEVENTY-TWO

I Lose a Bet

"THIS IS WAY BETTER than the last memorial I attended," Annabeth said. "Yours."

We stood on a ridge in the Blue Hills, watching my mother's ashes drift across the snowy trees. Far below, the sun glittered on Houghton's Pond. The day was cold, but I didn't feel uncomfortable. I felt warm and calm—more *right* than I'd felt in years.

I tucked the empty ceramic jar under my arm.

"Thanks for coming with me," I said.

Annabeth's gray eyes studied me, the same way she seemed to study everything—assessing not just my appearance, but my composition, my stress points, my potential for renovation. This was a girl, after all, who had made Parthenon models out of runestones when she was six years old.

"Glad to," she said. "Your mom . . . from what I remember, she was great."

"She would've liked the fact that you're here."

Annabeth gazed across the tree line. Her face looked sunburned from the wind. "They cremated you, too, you know. I mean that other body . . . whatever that was. Your ashes were placed in the family mausoleum. I didn't even know we *had* a family mausoleum."

I shuddered, imagining those ashes in a porcelain vase in a dank stone cubbyhole. Much better to be here, in the fresh air and the frigid sunlight.

"Pretending I was dead couldn't have been easy for you," I said.

She brushed a strand of hair from her face. "The service was harder on Randolph, I think. He seemed pretty shaken up, considering, you know . . ."

"That he never cared about me?"

"Or any of us. My dad, though . . . Magnus, that was difficult. He and I have had a rocky history, but I'm trying to be honest with him now. I don't like hiding things."

"Sorry." I spread my hands. "I thought it was better if I didn't drag you into my problems. For the last few days, I wasn't sure if I was going to make it. Some . . . some dangerous things were happening. It had to do with my father's, uh, side of the family."

"Magnus, I might understand more than you think I do."

I thought about that. Annabeth *did* seem more attuned, more grounded than most people I talked to—even most of the people in Valhalla. On the other hand, I didn't want to put her at risk, or threaten the tenuous relationship we were starting to reconstruct.

"I'm okay now," I assured her. "I'm staying with friends. It's a good place, but it's not the kind of arrangement most people would understand. Uncle Randolph can't know about it. I'd appreciate it if you didn't tell anyone, not even your dad."

"Hmm," she said. "I don't suppose I get details?"

I thought about what Frey had told me: *You should talk. You will need her help before all is said and done.* I remembered what Sam had said about her own family—how they'd attracted the attention of the gods for generations. Randolph had hinted that our family was the same way.

"I just don't want to put you in danger," I said. "I kind of hoped you could be my one connection to the regular world."

Annabeth stared at me. She snorted and began to laugh. "Wow. You have no idea how funny that is." She took a deep breath. "Magnus, if you had any clue about how weird my life is—"

"Okay, but being here with you?" I said. "This is the most *normal* I've felt in years. After all the crazy fighting between our parents, the stupid grudges and years of not speaking to each other, I was hoping we could make our generation of the family not so messed up."

Annabeth's expression turned serious. "*That* kind of normal I like." She extended her hand. "To us, the Chase cousins. Here's to being less messed up."

We shook on it.

"Now spill," she commanded. "Tell me what's been going on. I promise I won't tell. I might even be able to help. I also promise that whatever's been going on with you, my life is weirder. It'll make yours look downright suburban."

I considered everything I'd been through—death and resurrection, fishing for the World Serpent, fighting with giants, running from monster squirrels, binding a wolf on a disappearing island.

"How much you want to bet?" I said.

"Bring it on, cousin."

"Lunch?" I suggested. "I know a great falafel place."

"You've got a bet," she said. "Let's hear what you've been up to."

"Oh, no," I said. "Your story is so amazing? You go first."

EPILOGUE

RANDOLPH HADN'T SLEPT since his nephew's funeral service.

Every day he visited the mausoleum, hoping for some sign, some miracle. He cried real tears, but not for young Magnus. He wept for everything he'd lost—everything that might never be recovered now.

He came in the back door of the town house, his hands shaking so badly he could barely work the lock. He removed his snow boots and his heavy coat, then padded upstairs, going over what he'd said to Magnus on the bridge for the millionth time, wondering what he could have done differently.

He froze in the doorway of his office. A man in a priest's frock was sitting on his desk, dangling his feet.

"Visiting the gravesite again?" Loki grinned. "Honestly, I thought the service provided some excellent closure."

"You were the priest?" Randolph sighed. "Of course you were the priest."

Loki chuckled. *"A young life cut short, but let us celebrate his gifts and the impact he had upon us . . .* I was improvising, of course. But that's what I do best."

Randolph had seen the god of lies a dozen times before—when Loki had chosen to send his essence to Midgard—but it was always a shock—those brilliant eyes, the hair like flames, the ruined lips, and the scars across his nose. He was unnaturally handsome and unnaturally terrifying in equal measure.

"You've come to kill me, I expect." Randolph tried to remain calm, but his heartbeat still pulsed in his ears. "Why did you wait this long?"

Loki spread his hands magnanimously. "I didn't want to be hasty. I needed to see how things played out. It's true you failed. I could kill you, but you might still be useful. After all, I still have something you want."

The god rose from the desk and opened his hand. Above his palm, flames flickered, consolidating into the miniature shapes of a woman and two girls. They writhed in the fire, reaching out to Randolph, silently pleading.

Only Randolph's cane kept him from collapsing. "Please. I tried. I didn't—I didn't anticipate the dwarf and the elf. Or that cursed Valkyrie. You didn't tell me—"

"Randolph, my dear friend . . ." Loki closed his hand, extinguishing the fire. "I hope you're not making excuses?"

"No, but—"

"I'm the *master* of excuses. You'd have to try really hard to impress me. Just tell me, do you still want your family returned?"

"Of—of course."

"Oh, good. How nice. Because I'm not done with you. Nor am I done with that little boy, Magnus."

"But he has the sword. He stopped your plan."

"He stopped *one facet* of my plan. Yes, it was very educational." Loki stepped forward. He cupped his hand on

Randolph's cheek—an almost tender gesture. "I must say, your nephew is impressive. I don't see the family resemblance at all."

Randolph smelled the poison before he felt it. Acrid steam curled into his nostrils. The side of his face erupted in white-hot pain. He fell to his knees, his throat seizing up in shock. He tried to pull away, but Loki's hand stayed stuck in place.

"There, there," Loki said soothingly. "It's just a little taste of my life—the snake venom that is splashed in *my* face every day. Perhaps you can understand why it makes me a tad grumpy."

Randolph screamed until his throat was raw.

"I won't kill you, old friend," Loki said. "But I do punish failure. Absolutely!"

He took the hand away. Randolph crumpled, weeping, the smell of burned flesh in his nose.

"Why . . ." he croaked. "Why . . . ?"

Loki raised his eyebrows in mock surprise. "Why what—torture you? Continue to use you? Fight against the gods? It is my nature, Randolph! Now, don't fuss. I'm sure you'll find a way to explain the horrible hand-shaped scar on your face. I think it lends you a certain . . . *gravitas*. The Vikings will be most impressed."

Loki strolled to Randolph's display cases. He ran his fingers along Randolph's collection of trinkets and talismans. "Ragnarok has many triggers, my friend. The Sword of Summer is not the only weapon in play."

He plucked a necklace from the display. His eyes gleamed as the small silver hammer pendant swung between his fingers.

"Oh, yes, Randolph." Loki grinned. "You and I are going to have lots of fun."

RD—god of ships, sailors, and fishermen; father of Frey
Freya

RNS—three sisters who control the destinies of both gods
humans.

RUMBEGA—a lost Norse settlement in their farthest point
xploration

N—the "All-Father" and king of the gods; the god of war
death, but also poetry and wisdom. By trading one eye for
ink from the Well of Wisdom, Odin gained unparalleled
wledge. He has the ability to observe all the Nine Worlds
his throne in Asgard; in addition to his great hall, he also
les in Valhalla with the bravest of those slain in battle.

NAROK—the Day of Doom or Judgment, when the bravest
ie einherjar will join Odin against Loki and the giants in
battle at the end of the world

l—goddess of the sea; wife of Aegir

ATOSK—an invulnerable squirrel that constantly runs up
down the World Tree carrying insults between the eagle
lives at the top and Nidhogg, the dragon that lives at the
s

GOLD—the currency of Asgard and Valhalla

IRIMNIR—the magical beast of Valhalla; every day it is
d and cooked for dinner and every morning it is resur-
d; it tastes like whatever the diner wants

RUMNIR—the Hall of Many Seats, Freya's mansion in
vanger

NIR—a god; Frey's servant and messenger

NIR—Odin's eight-legged steed; only Odin can summon
one of Loki's children

GLOSSARY

AEGIR—lord of the waves

AESIR—gods of war, close to humans

ALF SEIDR—elf magic

ANDSKOTI—the Adversary, the new, magic-infused rope binding Fenris Wolf

BALDER—god of light; the second son of Odin and Frigg, and
twin brother of Hod. Frigg made all earthly things swear
to never harm her son, but she forgot about mistletoe. Loki
tricked Hod into killing Balder with a dart made of mistletoe.

BIFROST—the rainbow bridge leading from Asgard to Midgard

DRAUGR—Norse zombies

EIKTHRYMIR—a stag in the Tree of Laeradr whose horns spray
water nonstop that feeds every river in every world

EINHERJAR (EINHERJI, sing.)—great heroes who have died
with bravery on Earth; soldiers in Odin's eternal army; they
train in Valhalla for Ragnarok, when the bravest of them will
join Odin against Loki and the giants in the battle at the end
of the world

FENRIS WOLF—an invulnerable wolf born of Loki's affair with
a giantess; his mighty strength strikes fear even in the gods,
who keep him tied to a rock on an island. He is destined to
break free on the day of Ragnarok.

FOLKVANGER—the Vanir afterlife for slain heroes, ruled by the goddess Freya

FREY—the god of spring and summer; the sun, the rain, and the harvest; abundance and fertility, growth and vitality. Frey is the twin brother of Freya and, like his sister, is associated with great beauty. He is lord of Alfheim.

FREYA—the goddess of love; twin sister of Frey; ruler of Folkvanger

FRIGG—goddess of marriage and motherhood; Odin's wife and the queen of Asgard; mother of Balder and Hod

GINNUNGAGAP—the primordial void; a mist that obscures appearances

GLEIPNIR—a rope made by dwarves to keep Fenris Wolf in bondage

HEIDRUN—the goat in the Tree of Laeradr whose milk is brewed for the magical mead of Valhalla

HEIMDALL—god of vigilance and the guardian of Bifrost, the gateway to Asgard

HEL—goddess of the dishonorable dead; born of Loki's affair with a giantess

HELHEIM—the underworld, ruled by Hel and inhabited by those who died in wickness, old age, or illness

HLIDSKJALF—the High Seat of Odin

HOD—Balder's blind brother

HONIR—an Aesir god who, along with Mimir, traded places with Vanir gods Frey and Njord at the end of the war between the Aesir and the Vanir

IDUN—she distributes the apples of immortality that keep the gods young and spry

JORMUNGAND—the World Serpent, born a giantess; his body is so long it wraps aro

JOTUN—giant

LOKI—god of mischief, magic, and artif giants; adept at magic and shape-shiftin malicious and heroic to the Asgardian god Because of his role in the death of Balder, Odin to three giant boulders with a poiso over his head. The venom of the snake c Loki's face, and his writhing is the cause

LYNGVI—the Isle of Heather, where Fenri island's location shifts every year as the b sway in the winds of the void. It only surf full moon of each year.

MAGNI AND MODI—Thor's favorite son Ragnarok

MIMIR—an Aesir god who, along with F with Vanir gods Frey and Njord at the end the Aesir and the Vanir. When the Vanir sel, they cut off his head and sent it to O head in a magical well, where the water b and Mimir soaked up all the knowledge o

MJOLNIR—Thor's hammer

MUSPELL—fire

NAGLFAR—the Ship of Nails

NARVI—one of Loki's sons, disemboweled who was turned into a wolf after Loki kill

NIDHOGG—the dragon that lives at the b Tree and chews on its roots

GLOSSARY

AEGIR—lord of the waves

AESIR—gods of war, close to humans

ALF SEIDR—elf magic

ANDSKOTI—the Adversary, the new, magic-infused rope binding Fenris Wolf

BALDER—god of light; the second son of Odin and Frigg, and twin brother of Hod. Frigg made all earthly things swear to never harm her son, but she forgot about mistletoe. Loki tricked Hod into killing Balder with a dart made of mistletoe.

BIFROST—the rainbow bridge leading from Asgard to Midgard

DRAUGR—Norse zombies

EIKTHRYMIR—a stag in the Tree of Laeradr whose horns spray water nonstop that feeds every river in every world

EINHERJAR (EINHERJI, sing.)—great heroes who have died with bravery on Earth; soldiers in Odin's eternal army; they train in Valhalla for Ragnarok, when the bravest of them will join Odin against Loki and the giants in the battle at the end of the world

FENRIS WOLF—an invulnerable wolf born of Loki's affair with a giantess; his mighty strength strikes fear even in the gods, who keep him tied to a rock on an island. He is destined to break free on the day of Ragnarok.

FOLKVANGER—the Vanir afterlife for slain heroes, ruled by the goddess Freya

FREY—the god of spring and summer; the sun, the rain, and the harvest; abundance and fertility, growth and vitality. Frey is the twin brother of Freya and, like his sister, is associated with great beauty. He is lord of Alfheim.

FREYA—the goddess of love; twin sister of Frey; ruler of Folkvanger

FRIGG—goddess of marriage and motherhood; Odin's wife and the queen of Asgard; mother of Balder and Hod

GINNUNGAGAP—the primordial void; a mist that obscures appearances

GLEIPNIR—a rope made by dwarves to keep Fenris Wolf in bondage

HEIDRUN—the goat in the Tree of Laeradr whose milk is brewed for the magical mead of Valhalla

HEIMDALL—god of vigilance and the guardian of Bifrost, the gateway to Asgard

HEL—goddess of the dishonorable dead; born of Loki's affair with a giantess

HELHEIM—the underworld, ruled by Hel and inhabited by those who died in wickness, old age, or illness

HLIDSKJALF—the High Seat of Odin

HOD—Balder's blind brother

HONIR—an Aesir god who, along with Mimir, traded places with Vanir gods Frey and Njord at the end of the war between the Aesir and the Vanir

IDUN—she distributes the apples of immortality that keep the gods young and spry

JORMUNGAND—the World Serpent, born of Loki's affair with
a giantess; his body is so long it wraps around the earth

JOTUN—giant

LOKI—god of mischief, magic, and artifice; the son of two
giants; adept at magic and shape-shifting. He is alternately
malicious and heroic to the Asgardian gods and to humankind.
Because of his role in the death of Balder, Loki was chained by
Odin to three giant boulders with a poisonous serpent coiled
over his head. The venom of the snake occasionally irritates
Loki's face, and his writhing is the cause of earthquakes.

LYNGVI—the Isle of Heather, where Fenris Wolf is bound; the
island's location shifts every year as the branches of Yggdrasil
sway in the winds of the void. It only surfaces during the first
full moon of each year.

MAGNI AND MODI—Thor's favorite sons, fated to survive
Ragnarok

MIMIR—an Aesir god who, along with Honir, traded places
with Vanir gods Frey and Njord at the end of the war between
the Aesir and the Vanir. When the Vanir didn't like his counsel, they cut off his head and sent it to Odin. Odin placed the
head in a magical well, where the water brought it back to life,
and Mimir soaked up all the knowledge of the World Tree.

MJOLNIR—Thor's hammer

MUSPELL—fire

NAGLFAR—the Ship of Nails

NARVI—one of Loki's sons, disemboweled by his brother Vali,
who was turned into a wolf after Loki killed Balder

NIDHOGG—the dragon that lives at the bottom of the World
Tree and chews on its roots

NJORD—god of ships, sailors, and fishermen; father of Frey and Freya

NORNS—three sisters who control the destinies of both gods and humans.

NORUMBEGA—a lost Norse settlement in their farthest point of exploration

ODIN—the "All-Father" and king of the gods; the god of war and death, but also poetry and wisdom. By trading one eye for a drink from the Well of Wisdom, Odin gained unparalleled knowledge. He has the ability to observe all the Nine Worlds from his throne in Asgard; in addition to his great hall, he also resides in Valhalla with the bravest of those slain in battle.

RAGNAROK—the Day of Doom or Judgment, when the bravest of the einherjar will join Odin against Loki and the giants in the battle at the end of the world

RAN—goddess of the sea; wife of Aegir

RATATOSK—an invulnerable squirrel that constantly runs up and down the World Tree carrying insults between the eagle that lives at the top and Nidhogg, the dragon that lives at the roots

RED GOLD—the currency of Asgard and Valhalla

SAEHRIMNIR—the magical beast of Valhalla; every day it is killed and cooked for dinner and every morning it is resurrected; it tastes like whatever the diner wants

SESSRUMNIR—the Hall of Many Seats, Freya's mansion in Folkvanger

SKIRNIR—a god; Frey's servant and messenger

SLEIPNIR—Odin's eight-legged steed; only Odin can summon him; one of Loki's children

SUMARBRANDER—the Sword of Summer

SURT—lord of Muspellheim

SVARTALF—dark elf, a subset of dwarves

THANE—a lord of Valhalla

THOR—god of thunder; son of Odin. Thunderstorms are the earthly effects of Thor's mighty chariot rides across the sky, and lightning is caused by hurling his great hammer, Mjolnir.

TREE OF LAERADR—a tree in the center of the Feast Hall of the Slain in Valhalla containing immortal animals that have particular jobs

TYR—god of courage, law, and trial by combat; he lost a hand to Fenris's bite when the Wolf was restrained by the gods

ULLER—the god of snowshoes and archery

UTGARD-LOKI—the most powerful sorcerer of Jotunheim; king of the mountain giants

VALA—a seer

VALHALLA—paradise for warriors in the service of Odin

VALI—Loki's son, who was turned into a wolf after Loki killed Balder; as a wolf he disemboweled his brother Narvi before he was gutted himself

VALKYRIE—Odin's handmaidens, who choose slain heroes to bring to Valhalla

VANIR—gods of nature; close to elves

YGGDRASIL—the World Tree

YMIR—the largest of the giants; father to both the giants and the gods. He was killed by Odin and his brothers, who used his flesh to create Midgard. This act was the genesis of the cosmic hatred between the gods and the giants.

THE NINE WORLDS

ASGARD—the home of the Aesir

VANAHEIM—the home of the Vanir

ALFHEIM—the home of the light elves

MIDGARD—the home of humans

JOTUNHEIM—the home of the giants

NIDAVELLIR—the home of the dwarves

NIFLHEIM—the world of ice, fog, and mist

MUSPELLHEIM—the home of the fire giants and demons

HELHEIM—the home of Hel and the dishonorable dead

RUNES (IN ORDER OF APPEARANCE)

DAGAZ—new beginnings, transformations

THURISAZ—the rune of Thor

FEHU—the rune of Frey

RAIDHO—the wheel, the journey

PERTHRO—the empty cup

EHWAZ—horse, transportation

ALGIZ—shielding

TIWAZ—the rune of Tyr

COMING IN FALL 2016

RICK RIORDAN

and the GODS of ASGARD

THE HAMMER OF THOR